MW00698596

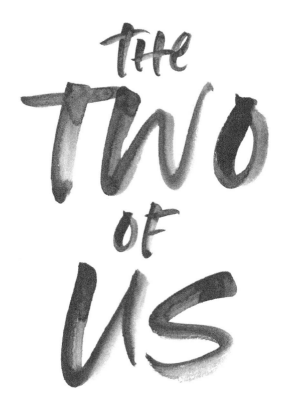

THE TWO OF US

TAYLOR TORRES

Copyright © 2023 Taylor Torres

All rights reserved. This book or any portion thereof may not be reproduced or used in any manner whatsoever without the express written permission of the publisher. This is a work of fiction. Names, characters, businesses, places, events, and incidents are either the products of the author's imagination or used in a fictitious manner. Any resemblance to actual persons, living or dead, or actual events is purely coincidental.

Cover Design by Books and Moods

Editing by My Brother's Editor

CONTENT WARNING:

Readers, please be advised that this book is intended for readers 18+ and deals with mature themes. There are mentions of addiction and the death of a loved one.

To all the girls who are told they are too sensitive in a world that desperately needs to be sensed.

Feeling deeply is not your curse.
It is your gift.

NOW

I don't know how I ended up behind the bar.

I mean, if we're talking *literally*, then yes, I'm very aware of how I got myself into this situation because I practically somersaulted over the cool marble in a matter of seconds. Perfect landing. Ten out of ten. Olympic-worthy.

Move over, Simone Biles.

But now that I'm here, I can't help but wonder about the series of events in my life that have gotten me to this point. The point where I'm seeking refuge beside a bottle of vodka on a Friday night, trying my best to ignore the sticky residue clinging to my back.

Don't get me wrong, the man in the bathroom was a great time. He was nice enough, and I liked the juxtaposition of his straight teeth and crooked nose. His lips were soft and his large hands swallowed the small of my back. Plus, I found him to be quite the gentleman for giving me one of his tequila shots even though it's Buy One, Get One night.

I'm a landing pad for men who do the bare minimum.

Everything was going *swimmingly* until he asked me out on a date. Which was comical, because everyone who hooks up in a bathroom knows the bathroom hook-up rule: thou shall not ever see each other again after this. So, I tugged my skirt back down, claimed I had an incoming call, and told him to hang tight.

And when I saw him exit the restroom before I could close out my tab, I did the first thing that came to mind and made eye contact with the barback.

"I'm *so* sorry."

Cue the Olympic-worthy somersault.

The woman with the full sleeve tattoo only sighed, like this happened to her a lot and I hated being added to her list of people who do weird shit at bars. She motioned for me to leave, but Crooked-Nose Guy must have come into view because she flashed her palm and I froze, watching her nose scrunch in disgust.

"Get down, get down!" Her hands flapped frantically. A phony smile broke out across her face as she greeted whom I assumed was my... acquaintance.

They exchanged a few words I couldn't hear and a moment later she stepped aside to mix his drink. She bent down to grab a lemon from the container near my head and I winced at the clear disappointment etched on her face.

"What were you *thinking*?"

"I know—"

"Was there a busted light in that bathroom?"

Groaning, I buried my face in my hands. "Trust me, *I know*."

She shook her head with a sigh. "Stay as long as you need."

I do, and for all I know, it's been hours because alcohol makes time an arbitrary concept. There's a good chance this is my home now.

It's not until I've responded to at least ten work emails—emails my coworkers won't even open until Monday morning—that the woman finally turns her attention back on me and says something I can't seem to make out.

Whoever's in charge of the music must have kicked the volume up a notch for the crowd making their way in because I have to cup my hand around my ear to hear.

"I said, *you can come out now*," she calls, louder this time.

"Oh." A breath of relief escapes me. "Great."

I slowly rise to my feet, a million needles poking at my half-asleep legs. Giving myself a running start, I attempt to jump back over the bar counter, but it's not nearly as impressive as the first time.

I take back what I said, Simone.

"Thanks," I mutter, flattening down my skirt before I give someone a show. Digging my credit card out of my bag, I slide it over to her. "I know this probably isn't what you signed up for when you came into work tonight."

"No worries." She passes me my receipt and a pen. "Happens all the time."

"People get behind the bar *all* the time?"

"Unfortunately."

"Well in that case..." I drop a crumpled twenty into her tip jar and she snorts like this also isn't the first time someone's done that.

So much for being original.

Squeezing my way through the horde of people growing larger by the minute, I head toward the exit before I get too overwhelmed, pulling up the only number I call as often as my dad.

It rings twice.

"Where are you this time?"

Tally's voice is leaden with exhaustion. When I double-check the time on my phone and see that it's almost two in the morning, guilt washes over me.

But it's not enough guilt to convince me to take the subway home alone in my current state. My last attempt at getting home while under the influence landed me on the R-line with a straight shot to Roosevelt Island. If you want to terrify a drunk person, have them end up in a location surrounded by water when they're supposed to be in the concrete jungle.

Not fun.

This is why I sigh and say, "Cross Tavern."

"Be there in a few."

Just like that. No questions, no admonishments. No reminders about how every time I go out in search of something that doesn't serve me, I come home feeling even more empty.

I don't deserve my best friend.

When Tally Walsh was assigned as my roommate during freshman orientation, I did my best to keep my distance. I had no desire to make friends.

But when someone sits at your bedside for three days hand feeding you chicken noodle soup while you battle strep throat, they kind of carve a space into your heart. Even if it's made of stone and requires a splitting hammer.

After fifteen minutes of fiddling with my necklace, her black Sentra pulls up to the curb. Through the window, all I can make out in the faint glow of the street lights are her auburn waves peeking out from her hoodie.

"Hey." I smile, slipping inside. The potent smell of leather seats assaults my nose, forcing me to breathe out of my mouth so I don't gag.

"Couldn't sleep again?" She graciously angles the air vents toward my disintegrating body. My response is a half-hearted grunt, which makes her laugh. "Why didn't you call earlier? You know you can always stay with me."

"If you brought me home like this, Jeremy would have a conniption."

Jeremy's a health nut. One of those people who refers to his body as a *temple*. The only thing that supersedes his tendency to casually drop words like "chard" and "clean eating" into every conversation is his knack for giving unsolicited advice on people's health choices.

But the joke's on him because his girlfriend dumps the smoothies he makes her down the toilet and hides Hershey Kisses in her underwear drawer.

"Besides, the problem isn't sleeping alone," I explain, "it's turning my mind off. Got any remedies for that?"

"Yeah, the first remedy is to stop answering work-related emails when it's officially the weekend. Give me that thing." Her hand strikes like a viper, but I quickly tuck my phone under my thigh, throwing my hands up in surrender. "I've never seen you in a more committed relationship than with that phone." She points an accusing finger.

There's no point in getting defensive because she's right.

Aside from the time I spend with Tally and going out on the occasional bar crawl by myself, I live and breathe my job.

You won't find me complaining, though. The web design agency pays time and a half, a rarity in the field, which allows me to pay for my glorified shoebox of an apartment and my dad's medical treatments.

It's also the distraction you crave.

She clicks on her blinker and makes a smooth turn onto my street. "Mitsu's accepting new clients, just say the word." Hopeful eyes glance my way. "We could go together. Share a box of tissues. Oh! My new embroidery machine came in—I could make *t-shirts*."

"What did we say about psychoanalyzing me?"

She sighs. "Only on Tues—"

"—only on Tuesdays, that's right. Keep hounding me and I'll make your website look like Craigslist."

Tally's small embroidery business kind of exploded last month when a popular social media influencer raved about her stuff online. Offering to revamp her website free of charge was a no-brainer considering how often she shows up for me, like tonight.

"All I'm saying is, Mitsu's like a laxative for emotionally constipated people. You, my friend, are red in the face constipated."

Mitsu this. Mitsu that.

You know who will change your life? Mitsu.

Blah blah Mitsu blah.

Soon enough, the car slows to a stop and I take in my dingy apartment building. A heaviness settles in the pit of my stomach.

I don't want to be alone.

In fact, being alone right now sounds more painful than the relentless throb in my temples, but verbalizing the thoughts racing through my mind doesn't feel like an option either. It's the worst catch-22 I've ever experienced.

Leaning over the console, I squeeze Tally. I'm not a hugger, but she is, so I suck it up. "Thanks for the ride," I whisper. "I swear this is the last time."

"Aw, sweetie." She gently pats my cheek. "You know, I actually think you believe that."

"Funny." I wave goodbye with my middle finger and I can hear her laughter even after shutting the door.

My ascent upstairs is a pitiful sight.

By the third floor, I'm on all fours and dry heaving, trying to drag myself the rest of the way.

New York City isn't for the fainthearted.

Once I'm inside, I flip the kitchen light on to find Cheddar perched on the sink—still as a statue—watching me like an axe murderer.

"Hey, big boy," I croon, dropping a kiss on the top of his head. "Enjoy the solitude while I was gone?"

He huffs at me and slinks away.

Okay.

Swinging open the freezer door, I plant myself in front of it and welcome the frigid air that dances over my heated skin. Once I've gotten my fill, I snatch a pair of earbuds off the counter, and head straight for my room, chucking off articles of clothing along the way.

Tally thinks I'm most committed to my phone, but she's wrong. I'm way more committed to my bed.

Cheddar curls into my side as I pull up my favorite playlist and raise the volume to a decibel that would probably concern most people. But it's the only way to push reality into the recesses of my mind, just the way I like. The way I *need*.

And when I'm met with the back of my eyelids, I'm grateful the darkness doesn't turn into the memories I desperately try to keep at bay.

Purring vibrations pound against my skull and I groan.

Why does it feel like a jackhammer?

I shove Cheddar off my face and sit up, immediately recoiling from the blinding light. I *knew* I'd regret getting sheer curtains.

As I reorient myself, flashes of last night come back to me: a brilliant smile, the curve of a nose, my skirt bunched up around my waist, and a man by the name of... of... whatever. A man.

I rub my bleary eyes and the tips of my fingertips come back coated in clumpy, day-old mascara. Forgetting to take my makeup off before bed? Now that's a new low, even for me.

The sound of piano scales fills my room thanks to the unit above me, and I mutter a curse under my breath.

Mrs. Kearny starts her lessons at nine, which means it won't be long before the hot water runs out. I rush into the bathroom and crank the shower nozzle as far left as it can go, whispering a silent plea.

To my surprise, the water begins to warm.

"Yes, yes, yes. You can do it," I chant, coaxing it along.

Steam billows out from the rusty shower head and I quickly yank the scrunchie from my hair, errant curls falling in a heap down the length of my back. I don't even need to look in the mirror to know how ridiculous I look right now.

The scalding spray of water comes down hard and I exhale a deep breath. Slowly but surely, the tension that takes up residence in my neck loosens and I relax, working the shampoo through my hair.

But the calm is short-lived because the negative thoughts that knock on the door of my brain like an old friend begin to trickle in.

What is it about showers that force us into downward spirals? Why is it that my brain decides that right now—the moment I'm sopping wet and naked and vulnerable—is the best time to drum up the past?

Shifting my attention to the fissures in the shower tile as a means of distraction, I count them one by one until I finish my routine. I rinse the soap from my hands and my eyes snag on the jagged two-inch scar trailing across my right palm.

Faded and painless, it's as much a part of me as any other physical attribute I have. My reminder that thirteen-year-olds make stupid decisions, especially with their best friends.

The sight of it still makes me squirm.

I step out as soon as the water begins to chill and cinch my robe tightly around my waist before I pad into the kitchen.

Eyes half closed, I toggle with the buttons on the coffee machine until I hear its familiar hum. "Make it a good one," I mumble.

I don't realize I've dozed off until my phone rattles against the peeling laminate countertop, followed by a banging at the front door.

I reach for the phone first.

Unknown.

That's... interesting. I click *Ignore.*

The last time I answered an unknown call, it was from student loan debt collectors, and I'm not in the mood this morning to mull over that five-digit number I owe.

The banging amplifies.

Skull-splitting migraine in full force now, I practically fly to the door because there's only one person who knocks like that and she'll break her way in if she needs to.

"I hear you!" I shout, answering it.

Tally taps her foot impatiently, hands propped firmly on her hips. Her bored stare penetrates the black shades swallowing her heart-shaped face and I snort. "You're earlier than usual."

I thought I looked bad this morning, but Tally looks like she's just returned from the Seventh Circle of Hell. And she's not even hungover, this is just what mornings look like for her.

"I need coffee," she grumbles, pushing past me.

It's the weekend, which means Jeremy's at the gym. Tally takes advantage of him being preoccupied and treks from Bushwick to my place in the Upper East Side so she can indulge in the foods he's put on the "no-no" list.

If anything should be on that list, it's men and not food.

I fill a large mug, adding a splash of the vanilla creamer she loves before extending it out to her. The side hug she gives me is hurried as she yanks it from my hands, causing a bit of the hot liquid to slosh onto her shirt.

She doesn't even *flinch*.

"The second I woke up this morning, Jeremy tried getting me to drink this massive glass of green shit. Said it was banana, spinach, and avocado, but he was lying, Mar. It was green shit." She shakes her head. "I saw my entire future flash before my eyes. Almost snapped like one of those killers from the true-crime doc—I'm sorry, is this *funny* to you?"

My phone buzzes again and I hold up a finger, biting back a laugh.

It's the unknown number again.

They're really trying to make their money today.

This time I put it on silent. "Sorry about that." I blow on my coffee. "Remind me—why are you with this guy again?"

"Because he has lickable abs, and he lets me lick those abs anytime I want."

"You weak, *weak* fool." I shake my head and feign disappointment. "Come on, let's watch some trash TV. I'll even let you pick." I trust fall onto the couch, burying myself beneath the throw pillows.

Tally stays rooted in place, tossing back the rest of her coffee in three large gulps.

"Dear God, woman."

"Can't stay." She drags her sleeve across her mouth. "Promised Jeremy I'd meet him after his workout for brunch."

"So what you're saying is, I'm nothing more than your goodies dealer? You're just gonna hit it and quit it?" I lay my palm over my heart. "I'm hurt."

She skips toward me with a smile that manages to be both annoying and endearing. "I'll come by tomorrow and we'll do a movie marathon. Everything with Julia Roberts in it, how's that sound?"

"You think you can just exploit my love for Julia Roberts and expect me to overlook the fact that you're ditching me right now? Because if so, you're correct, be here tomorrow by noon."

She claps in excitement. "Oh, and just so you know." Her tone grows serious. "You're my *favorite* dealer."

"Get out of here." I fling the nearest throw pillow at her face and she laughs.

As soon as I latch the deadbolt in place behind her, I can't help but think about those unknown calls.

It's not the first time I've gotten one, but two back-to-back is a little strange. Why wouldn't they just leave a message?

I grab my laptop off the coffee table and settle back onto the couch, stroking Cheddar's back as I pull up a client's website I've been working on for the past week. But after staring at my screen for five minutes, I realize it's no use. My concentration is kaput.

My eyes flit to the clock above the microwave. Ten in the morning, which means it's only two p.m. in Paris. After weighing the pros and cons, I decide to bite the bullet and call my mom. This can count as our weekly catch-up.

I hum to myself while I wait for her or my stepdad to pick up the landline. Why they still have one is beyond me.

When a deep, lilting voice answers, a smile comes to my face. "JP, it's Mara."

"Mara! *Bonjour*, my favorite girl."

"Favorite?" I snort. "What about Mom?"

"I love your mother, but you came from her, you see? That makes you equally my favorite."

That gets a laugh out of me. "Fair enough. Speaking of, is she around?"

"She's been at the studio since"—he takes a pause—"seven this morning."

Well, can't say I didn't try.

"Okay, just let her know I called." A beep comes through the line. "JP, I'm so sorry, I have a call coming in that I have to take."

"Not a worry, darling. We will talk soon. *Salut.*"

I quickly switch lines. "Hello?"

"Good morning, is this Mara Makinen?"

Pulling back, I frown at my phone. "Who's this?"

"This is Dr. Flemming from Seaview Hospital," the man says. "I need you to confirm your identity before I continue."

Seaview Hospital.

Bile rises in my throat. "Is he okay?"

"I need you to conf—"

"This is she. This is Mara Makinen. Is my dad *okay?*"

He clears his throat like he's preparing to read from a script. "As I'm sure you're aware, your father has been receiving treatment from us since his diagnosis last year."

"Go on," I urge.

"The progress he made during the onset of treatment was promising—truly. However, there's been..." I can tell this is uncomfortable for him, but I need him to get to the point. "There's been a shift."

My back straightens.

He lets out a sigh then. "We've seen this shift for a while, but we remained discreet out of respect for your father's wishes. He was hopeful he'd make a turnaround and didn't want to cause unnecessary duress on your end."

I flinch at the sharp ringing in my ears.

This isn't happening.

"Miss Makinen, that discretion is no longer necessary."

Everything he says after that becomes a jumbled mess in my mind. His words zoom through one side of my head and out the other before I can make sense of them.

By the time he finishes, I feel as though I've dissociated from my body and I'm watching all of this unfold from the outside.

"Miss Makinen?"

"Yes?" I croak.

"Did you understand anything I just said?"

I drag a trembling hand down my face. "I'll be honest with you, Doc. You've thrown a lot of complicated medical jargon at me in the last two minutes, so I'm going to need you to dumb it down for me. You say my father's condition has worsened but what *exactly* does that mean?" I hate how unsteady my voice sounds. How weak. "That he needs a new treatment plan? That we should try to get him into a clinical trial?"

Dr. Flemming's voice softens for the first time since he's called.

And I don't want it. I don't want the soft voice, the *sorry* voice, that promises to breathe life into my biggest fear.

But life isn't known for giving us what we want.

"Mara, it means it's time you come back to Speck Lake."

NOW

"Hold on. you're telling me you're at the airport *right now*? About to board a plane. This *very* second."

"As we speak." I shuffle forward a few steps. The man behind me steps on my heel and snickers like we aren't all going to the same place.

"I literally just saw you this morning."

"I know. It's a super last-minute thing."

"Who's going to take care of Cheese?"

I snort. "You know his name is Cheddar. And you are, my sweet friend."

Her laugh is obnoxious. "Why the hell would I do that?"

"Because," I say, handing the ticket agent my boarding pass with a smile, "I stocked the fridge with all your favorites before I left and have every streaming service you love."

A pause.

"How do I even get in? I don't have a key."

"Oh, please. We both know you made a copy of my key after watching that documentary on the dangers of women living alone."

"You tell no lies."

"Exactly. So just stop by once or twice a day to clean out his litter box and refill his food bowl. Other than that, he's as self-sufficient as it gets."

"Litter box?" She makes a sound of disgust. "You owe me." There's shuffling on her end. "Where did you say you were going again?"

And that's where she trips me up. "Um, I didn't. I'm headed to Maine to see my dad."

The shuffling stops.

"Didn't you say he was sick?"

I navigate my way through the narrow aisle, avoiding multiple elbows to the face. "...yes."

"Has he gotten worse?" Her voice gentles in a way that feels like an invitation to go deeper. "Mar, do you need me to come with you? Because I can, I—"

"Tally, I gotta go," I cut her off, voice tight. "We're getting ready to take off and the flight attendant is giving me the death glare."

"Mara—"

"I'll text you tomorrow. Love you."

I end the call.

Securing the seat belt around my waist, I lean back on the headrest and squeeze my eyes shut. I thought waking up this morning with a hangover would be the worst of my problems.

The plane pulls out onto the tarmac at a snail's pace and I decide to send one last text to Helen, my boss. When I filled her in on the situation, she gave me the green light to work remotely until further notice, but a small part of me hopes she'll give me a reason to stay so I can hide in my denial.

Me: Are you sure you'll be okay without me?

A text bubble with three little dots pops up immediately.

Helen: Aren't you on the plane by now?

Me: There's an emergency exit.

Helen: You millennials and your theatrics. I lived through a war and never shed a tear.

Me: That... that's concerning, Helen.

Helen: Look, you knocked the FlaxForm account out of the park with your web design. You haven't slowed down since you started at the agency three years ago. You're my best employee, but I'm afraid I've created a monster.

My fingers move to respond but she beats me to it with another message.

Helen: I promise you can keep your workaholic tendencies intact with the smaller projects I've added to your docket but try to do any more than that and I'll fire you.

Me: That seems a bit excessive.

Helen: I'm an excessive woman, dear. Excessively rich, excessively genius, and excessively tired of this conversation. I'm logging off now, goodbye!

Me: You can't log off text messaging, Helen.

Me: Helen?

Me: Helen!!!

"Miss, we need you to put your phone on airplane mode as we prepare for takeoff." The flight attendant's smile is warm, but I don't miss the purple-tinged bags under her eyes.

I nod, tossing my phone into my purse. The last thing I want to do is make her job harder.

The only other person in my row leans slightly over the middle seat between us and gestures toward the shade. "Do you want the window open so you can see out when we land?"

For the first time since I've sat down, I get a real look at the man. He resembles my *abuelo* with his checkered button-up and mini comb poking through his front breast pocket. A small patch of wispy white hair clings to his scalp for dear life.

His smile is so kind, it makes me want to crumble into a pile of tears. He has at least twenty years on my dad, but they have similar smiles.

"No," I say, offering one of my own. "I'm fine, thank you."

"Not interested in the view?"

I shrug, slipping on my headphones. "I'm from there. I couldn't forget the view if I tried."

An hour later, the pilot announces our initial descent.

Already?

I stretch the kink out of my neck. It's been seven years since I left and here I am, arriving in less time than it takes for me to reach the halfway point in my book. My nerves are shot, I'm sporting an airplane pimple, and I've started avoiding eye contact with the stewardess every time I order another Bloody Mary.

Just keep them coming, Carol. Nothing to see here.

Before the flight, I'd called my dad's nurse, Laura, for the fourth time to make sure I had all the information I needed to make his transition from the hospital seamless. She must have sensed the panic in my voice because she assured me all I'd have to do is head straight home and she'd take care of the rest.

Home.

Now there's a word that feels foreign. Can I call a place *home* if I've abandoned it without a second thought?

I should have come back sooner. I feel so incredibly *stupid*.

Of course my dad lied about how sick he truly is. The moment he told me of his diagnosis a year ago, I was ready. Bags were packed and even though it felt like I'd pass out from the fear, I was prepared to be on the next flight out.

But he said I was jumping the gun.

That it wasn't as bad as it sounded and the treatment plan was *promising*.

"Just give it a year. It's not as bad as you think. I'll be good as new in no time, you'll see."

So, I did what he allowed me to do, which wasn't much. I paid for the treatments and in-home nurses because I knew he'd need people hounding him to make his appointments. I happily endured late nights where my eyes burned from exhaustion, working while the rest of the world slept so I could pay for said treatments because our healthcare system is a joke with no punchline.

But I did all of that willingly because it provided me with some semblance of control. He let me believe it was all under control.

A shudder works its way through me. My dad always puts me first, that's not new. He's my protector through and through and I'd never complain about being so loved.

But how could he protect my feelings to this extent? How could he love me at the expense of himself? It's all wrong.

He's my *dad*. I would have come.

And now it's too late.

I'd be furious with him if the terror wasn't winning out.

"Are you visiting?"

A woman sitting in the aisle seat across mine watches me intently, a scuffed-up book on the history of the Latin Church resting on her lap.

With a gray-speckled braid draped over one shoulder, she's the picture of ease in a loose sweater and faded jeans.

For a moment, I envy her.

I crave that kind of comfort in my skin, but mine always feels itchy and unwelcome—like it's not the right fit.

"I'm from Speck Lake, actually. But I haven't been back in years, so maybe I am visiting." My laugh is hollow.

"How lovely! That's near Swanville, isn't it? I've driven through there before; it's the cutest little town. Don't take this the wrong way"—she chuckles—"but I wouldn't have pegged you for a local."

I glance down at the clothes I threw on in a rush this morning. A crisp white button-down paired with structured black trousers and low slingback heels. Not really an ensemble that reflects the laid-back nature of Speck Lake, but it's a style I've become accustomed to thanks to my job.

Suddenly, I feel overdressed.

"I guess I wasn't really thinking when I got ready this morning."

The plane dips and my stomach along with it.

I chug the rest of my drink.

"Not a fan of flying?" She grins.

I choke out a laugh. "Something like that."

"I'm Gladys, by the way."

"Mara."

The plane drops again and this time, the windows rattle. Someone once told me it helps to imagine that flying is like being suspended in Jello-O, but I can't remember the part of the analogy that makes it useful information, so now I'm terrified *and* hungry.

Breathe. We're almost there.

Desperate for a distraction, I dip my head toward Gladys's lap. "History of the Latin Church, huh? So you enjoy light reading."

She laughs and it settles my nerves by a fraction.

"I took a trip to Italy last summer and got caught up in a tour group learning everything there was to know about the saints." She shrugs. "Kind of turned into an obsession, I guess."

"Which ones are you learning about right now?"

The way her eyes light up makes me believe she's happy I asked. Like people don't do that very often.

She thumbs through the tattered pages and pushes her wiry glasses up the bridge of her nose before clearing her throat.

"Well, there's Saint Thomas Aquinas. Saint John Bosco, I enjoyed. Hmm, let me see…" she muses, tapping a finger against her chin. "Oh, the one I was just reading about was Saint Ambrose. I'm particularly interested in the chapter on Saint Vitus because I hear—" She stops, noticing my body has gone completely rigid. "Are you alright? Is it something I said?"

"No, no." I shake my head quickly. "It's not you."

It's just a coincidence, Mara. There's no reason to get worked up over a coincidence.

"I, uh, I just knew—*know*—somebody by that name, that's all."

The plane screeches its way into a landing and I take my first deep breath since we took off. I will never take the ground for granted again.

"Really?" She leans forward, curiosity infused in her hazel eyes. "What's their name?"

My tongue struggles to work itself around the name. The name I've refused to speak in seven years.

His name.

But once it does, a familiar spark rushes through me, resurrecting emotions I thought died long ago.

"Ambrose," I say. "Ambrose King."

THEN

AGE TEN

The boy stares back at us in silence.

Shifting from one foot to the other, I study him until someone decides to say something.

The first thing I notice is that he's taller than me, which doesn't impress me much. Dad always says boys grow faster because their bodies need more room to hold all their stupid.

Baby fat clings to his cheeks, making me think he's my age or very close to it, and the messy brown-black hair on his head is strikingly similar to an old mop we have in our garage.

Everything about him is average—unassuming—until you catch hold of his eyes. Sandwiched between thick lashes, their moss color pops against the rest of his appearance. They're sharp and intimidating, but I can't look away.

My dad clears his throat.

"Hey, there," he says with a warm smile. "I'm Solomon Makinen, and this is my daughter, Mara. We live just across the street." His thumb juts out toward the faded yellow house behind us. "Saw your family moving in last week and we wanted to introduce ourselves."

When the boy doesn't respond, he adds, "I'll bet you and Mara have a lot in common."

Why is he trying to push me on this kid like I'm a baby who needs help making friends?

The boy's eyes flicker between me and my dad, studying us like he can't comprehend how we're related. I'm used to those kinds of looks by now, especially from strangers. I got my mom's dark curly hair and warm brown skin thanks to her Caribbean roots while my dad's fine golden hair and pale freckled skin that requires multiple layers of sunscreen daily didn't stand a chance. Genetics are a funny thing.

Once he seems satisfied with his examination, he tilts his head, arms crossed like he's sizing me up. "Do you like animals?"

"Um..." I glance at my dad, who gives me a reassuring nod. "I like cats. I have one at home named Cheddar."

"Why would you name your cat Cheddar?"

"Because my cousin's name is Brie, so that was already taken."

When he doesn't laugh, I get all flustered and my face gets hot. I need to stop using that joke on people because I keep getting this reaction.

My dad clears his throat for the second time in three minutes. "Are your parents home, son?"

"Sure, just a second." He pokes his head into the house and calls out, "Mom!"

When a woman in scrubs takes up the space in the doorway with a smile plastered across her face, my anxiety immediately subsides.

She's beautiful with long waves and soft rounded cheeks. Her son takes after her for the most part in coloring from their dark hair to their slightly sun-kissed skin, but where his eyes are striking and intense, the brown in hers is warm and inviting.

My dad jumps back into introductions and I take the opportunity to tune everything out.

When my gaze flickers over to the boy again, I find that he's already watching me and it sends a shiver down my spine.

I wait, positive he'll break eye contact, but he never does.

Now, I've always been a competitive person. Even if the competition is only in my head, as my dad likes to remind me. So I can't help the fact that my eyes narrow and my hands find their way to my hips.

He mirrors my challenging stare, shifting his torso so it's more in line with mine and we stay like that—unblinking—until his mom directs her next words at me.

"Mara, I'm taking Ambrose and his sister to the zoo in half an hour. Would you and your father like to join us? We'd love to have you."

Ambrose.

The corner of his mouth twitches once he realizes I'll have to concede and face his mom. As soon as I do, I immediately search her eyes for signs of pity. The last thing I want is for her to feel some sort of obligation to me, but there's nothing in her expression except genuine excitement.

And just like that, we're on the road trailing behind the King family.

We keep the windows rolled down, relishing in the cool breeze that cuts through the summer heat. My face finds its way into the crook of my elbow as I take in the small lake town I've known all my life. We drive past the single-screen movie theater, past the school that holds grades one through twelve. My dad drums his calloused hands against the steering wheel like a bongo, humming Marc Anthony to himself, and I smile.

Those hands are the reason we live here.

Speck Lake used to be a retirement community—a sleepy little stop off the tracks where people would retreat once they'd lived enough life and wanted to slow down. But eventually, families looking for a safe, tight-knit community nudged their way in, including my own.

And when the town's local construction superintendent retired, opening up a job opportunity for my dad, my parents took it for what it was.

Kismet.

The recreational center comes into view then and I notice how my dad white-knuckles the wheel. My mom used to run the art classes there until it shut down this past spring and I think it still hurts him to see. It definitely hurts me.

But I think what hurts us more is the fact that she moved to Paris less than a month after it closed. The transition was so quick, I'm still reeling from the whiplash.

He often reminds me that their divorce has nothing to do with me, that the stress from both their layoffs is what pushed them apart, but I'm not so sure. It *feels* personal.

How could it not? She left me here.

"Come on, Mara, I'm going to miss my flight if I don't leave now. Don't cry, baby. I need you to be a big girl. Be a strong girl for Mommy."

As if reading my mind, my dad slides his gaze to me. "Heard from your mom lately?"

I respond with a half-hearted shrug. "For like, two seconds yesterday. She was busy."

His mouth starts to inch downward but he catches himself and twists it into a smile instead.

"Mrs. King seems nice, doesn't she? Ambrose too."

"I guess so."

"She was saying her husband, Robby, is starting the first soccer program at your school. I'm surprised they have enough interest to get one going, but I think it's great. We've never had anything for you kids to be active in." One heartbeat. Then another. "Maybe you should try out."

There it is.

He's been doing this since my mom stepped on that plane and chose croissants over her only daughter—attempting to get me involved in anything that will pull me out of my slump. He even got me Cheddar, which helped a lot but even my newfound love for my cat doesn't fill the gaping Mom-shaped hole in my chest. He must be running out of ideas though because we both know my coordination with a ball is a joke.

I should make more of an effort to ease his worry, though. The wrinkles around his eyes are deeper and he's sporting more gray hairs than ever before.

After a few more seconds of silence, I say, "Yeah, I guess I could give tryouts a chance."

He smacks the steering wheel, hooting with excitement and I giggle. "That's what I like to hear, *princesa*."

Gosh, I love it when he calls me that. It's the Spanish nickname he's had for me since I was a baby and he always uses it even though he has no cultural ties to the language.

My mom was born in Puerto Rico, but he's originally from Finland. His parents brought him to the states when he was still a baby, so English is his first language.

When my mom caught his eye at their small high school in Texas, he became determined to master her native tongue so he could impress her. And it must have worked because his Spanish is almost better than mine.

Almost.

"But you can't be disappointed when you realize I suck," I point out.

He runs his hand over my head, eyes filled with tenderness. "I'll be proud of you no matter what you accomplish in this life. You lock that away in that pretty little head of yours, okay?"

I smile. "Okay."

"Now, I don't know about you, but I think new friends across the street call for a celebration. How about we do Dellahs for dinner?"

My stomach rumbles at the mere mention of our local diner.

Dellahs is the one place where everyone stops by at least twice a week to eat with their family. They have the best blueberry flapjacks in the world and even though I haven't tried *all* the blueberry flapjacks in the world, I stand by this.

We've been going there more often, especially since my dad is slowly expanding on the meals he knows how to cook. I kind of like that we have this special thing that belongs to only us.

The man might not know everything there is to know about raising a young girl on his own—he ties my hair up with rubber bands from the post office and feeds me pancakes for dinner—but he's trying.

He's *here*. And I love him all the more for it.

The sound of gravel crushing under our wheels disrupts my thoughts and I glance out the window just as the Kings step out of their car. *This is going to be fun,* I tell myself. I just have to be open to it. Unbuckling my seatbelt, a thought hits me.

What does Ambrose King think about soccer?

The zoo's packed for a Saturday.

And by packed, I mean there are more than fifty people here. The colosseum-shaped building bordering the edge of town is newly renovated and inviting. Pride fills me knowing my dad had a hand in its construction.

Mrs. King, who insists I call her Alima, moves ahead of us to grab the tickets and when she returns, she hooks an arm around my shoulder, squeezing me like we didn't just meet half an hour ago.

The gesture pulls at my heartstrings. Maybe this won't be so bad after all.

Ambrose stalks off on his own, already scribbling into the pocket-sized notepad in his hand, while I find myself quietly trailing the younger sister, who I found out is the same age as me. She doesn't stay in one spot long and my legs work overtime to keep up.

Either she's too disinterested to care about the informational plaques on display or she's *so* interested, she's trying to see every animal as quickly as possible.

The moment I join her on the ledge in front of the capuchin monkeys, she sets her sights elsewhere and turns away. Breathing out a heavy sigh, I plant my feet and give up.

Delicate fingers wrap around my wrist.

"Aren't you coming?"

Big, round green eyes watch me expectantly. They resemble the pair that challenged me on the doorstep of her house, but more open and playful.

The girl smiles the kind of smile that makes you feel like you're already friends and you have been for years.

Not bothering to wait for my response, she drags me along to a giant tank overflowing with jellyfish. They swim back and forth, their heads jiggling across the glass like gelatin.

"I'm Cat," she says, pushing her nose up against the glass. It makes her look like Nadine Clark's pug, Roscoe, and I have to stifle my laugh with my hand.

"I'm Amará," I say tentatively. "But I just go by Mara."

"You should come over to my house to play sometime, Mara."

She peels her face from the glass and when I realize she isn't going to clean the cloudy streak marks she left behind, I use my sleeve to wipe it clean.

"Do you have a Pocket Princess?" she asks, tilting her head. "The one that just came out, not the old ones. You can always tell which ones are the old kind because their hair falls out when you brush it too much. Ambrose accidentally ran over one of my new Pocket Princesses with his skateboard, and my mom tried to replace it without me knowing, but I figured it out after I brushed her hair." She shrugs. "I have the entire village expansion pack if you want to bring yours over."

My eyes fall to my shoes.

Pocket Princesses recently spiked into popularity and while most girls my age have one, we've been a little tight on money lately while my dad tries to keep us afloat with the construction gigs he gets from nearby towns. I haven't even bothered to bring it up to him.

Cat clears her throat. "Actually, you should just use mine. You know, that way yours don't get lost at my house. My mom would *kill* me if someone lost something at our house."

I look up, surprised to find that there's no judgment on her face. She's offering me an out so I don't feel embarrassed and my chest expands with gratitude.

I manage a slight nod and she quickly changes the subject by pointing to her brother a few feet away.

Head tucked down, his entire face is hidden by that frayed notepad of his.

"He's only eleven, but he acts like he's *so* much older." Cat rolls her eyes. "I mean, look at him. We're supposed to be having fun and he's over there writing like he's taking a test or something."

She starts imitating him, stiffening her back and lifting her nose to the sky while her invisible pencil writes on her nonexistent notepad. I can't help but break out into a fit of laughter.

Wheat-colored strands fall around her animated face as she puts on her show, eyes glittering with pure mischief. She hardly resembles Alima or Ambrose, so I'm guessing she takes after her dad.

I've known her for five minutes and I can already tell we're nothing alike. But she seems like fun and I can't remember the last time I had some of that.

"Look! Penguins!" she squeals, dashing off.

I take a step to follow her but then decide against it. My heart rate has only just settled from chasing her around the first time.

Hanging back instead, I track Ambrose's movements until he plants himself in front of an aviary enclosure. Unable to smother my curiosity, I join his side to see what's captured his attention.

Behind the glass walls are hundreds of birds flying from one branch to the other, a chaotic blend of colors soaring across my vision. Some drink from the hanging water bowls while others build makeshift nests with the scattered twigs and branches that litter the enclosure's floor.

They all seem so different from each other and I can't help but wonder if any of them get targeted for not fitting in. My eyes hone in on a puffy yellow bird the size of my fist lingering in the corner all alone.

"I saw Cat got her hands on you." Ambrose chuckles under his breath. "She'll never let you go now."

I only nod slightly, preoccupied with the birds. "That's okay with me."

"Why do you look so sad?" he asks, studying me with a curious tilt of his head.

My eyes scan the area for Cat or our parents, but we're all alone.

"Who says I'm sad?"

His brow quirks.

My forehead wrinkles. "Well, I'm not."

"You are."

"Am not."

"You're frowning."

"*You* are making me frown." When he gives me a disbelieving look, I double down. "I'm *serious*."

He snorts. "Liar."

I scoff, crossing my arms, and when he does the same I realize he doesn't plan on backing down. I don't know why, but something about his persistence comforts me.

Sure, he might be a little brash, but at least he's not walking on eggshells around me like most people seem to be doing these days. Kind of feels nice to have someone push my buttons.

"I just wonder if any of these birds feel out of place, okay?" I finally admit. "If they ever get picked on by the other birds for being different. And if they do, then sure, maybe that makes me a little sad. Is that such a crime?"

The yellow puff remains alone in its corner, tweeting what I consider to be a ballad of woes.

You won't be lonely forever, little bird.

"Can I let you in on a secret?" Ambrose whispers, his warm shoulder pressing up against mine.

When did he get so close?

"There can be a lot of teamwork when it comes to different species. Look." I follow his pointed finger to a small group of birds. "Those little guys are building their nests near the larger ones because they think it'll protect them from predators. Even in the wild, different birds will sometimes search for food together."

He scratches his chin in thought before continuing.

"I don't know... I think they know you need friends who are good at the things you suck at. At least, that's what I'm guessing from all the books I've read."

"Wow." I ogle him, impressed. "So you *really* like animals."

He nods, the ghost of a smile playing on his lips. "What do you like?"

"Books. Movies. Books turned *into* movies."

"What about hanging out with your friends?"

That question makes me shift uncomfortably. I haven't played with anyone since my mom left. It's hard to pretend to be the same person I used to be—the person people loved—when I don't feel like her anymore.

"I'm not very good around people these days."

"You're better at it than you think."

Ambrose holds my gaze with that barely-there smile of his and it does something to my stupid ten-year-old heart.

What I don't realize is, Ambrose would have that kind of sway over my heart for many years to come.

The silence stretches between us and I figure now is as good a time as any to go find my dad. I open my mouth to say as much.

"Quiet," he interjects.

My face scrunches in confusion and he laughs for the first time, making my belly flop.

"It's a game." He nudges my shoulder playfully. "I say a word and then you say whatever word comes to your mind from that word. Give it a try. *Quiet.*"

"Uh... talking?" I whisper.

"Whisper."

"Secret."

"Best friends."

He notices I'm no longer smiling.

"What's wrong?"

"Um, it's just kind of hard to come up with a word from that, I guess. I don't have any best friends," I explain.

Ambrose turns back to the enclosure, smirking to himself like he's in on some secret. He tears a blank page from his notepad and pulls an extra pencil from his pocket before handing it to me.

"For now."

NOW

It takes a million phone calls to various car services before I finally find one willing to drive me from Bangor to Speck Lake.

I almost lost it when the fourth company I called said they'd never even heard of the town. The driver makes me shell out a hefty tip before we hit the road and I make sure to throw my luggage into his trunk with a heavy hand.

For the next hour, I work on a branding pitch I have for an up-and-coming fitness brand. When the *Welcome to Speck Lake* sign comes into view, I scoot closer to the window, shocked by how much the town's changed.

Changed is putting it lightly. It's hardly recognizable.

Main Street isn't bustling like it used to be. Back when I was a kid, there was always some sort of event happening on the historic brick-lined road, whether it was a bake sale or a block party. But now it's so empty, I half-expect a tumbleweed to roll past. The parking lot in front of Dellah's Diner is full, but they're an anomaly. Dellahs *is* Speck Lake.

"*No,*" I gasp as we pass The Plant Shack. The windows of the only plant nursery in town are boarded up. I used to work there when I was a teenager because they had *too much* business and needed an extra pair of hands.

"This is the place, right?"

"I'm not so sure anymore," I whisper in horror.

"You wanna speak up, sweetheart?"

I bristle at his snarky attitude. "Yes. This is it."

No wonder he made me tip upfront.

He turns onto Winsome Lane—the street I could find my way back to in my sleep. My pulse picks up at the sight of the empty cul-de-sac. It's quieter than I remember, but I guess that makes sense considering the three kids that gave it life are all gone now.

"Which house?" He taps his watch impatiently. "Come on, I got places to be."

I forgot how difficult it is to see the numbers on the houses in this area and his ancient GPS gave out on him ten minutes ago.

"That little yellow one, right there on the left."

For the first time during this entire car ride, he sounds semi-friendly when he says, "Cute. Looks like a lemon drop."

I tilt my head, seeing my childhood home through his eyes "Huh. You're right, it kind of does."

Whenever I conjured up the image of home over the years, it looked dull and muted. Nowhere near as inviting as it does now, but memories have a tendency of painting over the truth.

Brand-new shingles line the roof and the shutters are coated in a vibrant nautical blue. Dad must be paying someone to update the place to increase its market value.

My throat seizes.

He never offered me the house. He must not have thought I'd want it. And I don't, but it's still weird to think of someone else living here. I mean, proof of my literal growth as a human is carved into the kitchen's door frame.

"You gonna get out or what?"

So much for being friendly.

"Yeah. Sorry," I grumble, flipping him off with the hand hanging low at my side.

When I step out, I make sure to keep my eyes trained forward. I don't have to look across the street to remember what their house looks like because it's the last image I see every night before I fall asleep.

A tingling sensation sweeps across the nape of my neck like I'm being watched.

I'll bet anything it's Mr. and Mrs. King wondering what made the prodigal daughter decide to return home. There was a time when they loved me as their own, but those days are long gone.

The driver pops open his trunk and I lug my suitcases out, dragging them behind me. He doesn't even offer to help and once again, I'm bitter about the tip. I thrust the bundle of cash through his rolled-down window and watch him peel out of the driveway like he's afraid he'll get trapped in this ghost town the longer he lingers.

It's not until I've stumbled my way up to the front door, which smells of freshly coated varnish, that I realize I don't have a key. I don't have a key to my own house because I didn't think I'd ever need it again.

I knock, cursing under my breath. Having to be let into your own home is embarrassing. As a last-ditch effort, I quickly scour the deck for the garden gnome that usually hides a spare key, only to run back when the door starts to open.

A middle-aged woman in pale-pink scrubs with little hearts all over them beams at me, eyes sparkling like lapis lazuli. Her fair skin is slightly sunburnt, but that's normal for people who live here. Spending time outdoors is engrained in the culture.

"You must be Mara!" she exclaims, pulling me in for a bone-crushing hug. I swear my eyes bulge from their sockets.

"And I take it you're Laura." I wheeze. "Thanks for grabbing the door. I forgot I didn't have a key."

"No problem at all, hon." She gives me a hearty pat on the back as I gasp for air. "Come on in."

I slip by her and stop dead in my tracks.

It smells different in here. Off.

It smells like a hospital.

Flavorful aromas from foods like sancocho and alcapurrias, foods that marked my upbringing and embedded themselves into the walls—even after my mom left—are no longer existent.

The air is weighed down by the smell of antiseptics and an undercurrent of sweat. It cuts me like a knife edge because of what it means. The warning it carries.

Panic unfurls in my chest.

I didn't have much time before my flight to research hospice care. The only thing I have to go off of is what I've seen in movies, which isn't very helpful. I have so many questions I'm sure I'll be bombarding Laura with momentarily.

Moving out of the entryway, I'm caught off guard by the scraping of nails across the hardwood floors and before I know it, I'm flat on my back being licked by something that feels like a Brillo pad. I gasp, struggling to come up for oxygen.

Will I be able to breathe for more than five seconds at a time in this house?

"Otso, no! Down, boy!" Laura screeches, wrangling the dog away from my face.

I didn't go to Harvard, but this is not a dog.

This is a creature you'd avoid out in the woods. A yeti of sorts. I'm impressed that Laura's holding the beast back all by herself. She can't be more than five feet tall.

I scramble to my feet, pulling my soaked shirt away from my chest. "Is this your dog?"

"Otso? Absolutely not." She laughs. "No, this guy here is your dad's."

I take in the so-called "dog" again, shocked he hasn't turned one of my limbs into a chew toy yet. The Saint Bernard must be at least two hundred pounds. We make eye contact and his mouth opens, drool plopping onto the floor like I'm a snack.

Think again, beast.

Since when does my dad like dogs? I asked for one on my thirteenth birthday because I wanted Cheddar to have a friend, but he flat-out refused. Said they were too much of a handful.

On sheer principle alone, I decide not to like the dog in front of me even though he does look like he'd be a master at cuddling.

I smooth out my crumpled trousers as Laura drags him into another room and closes the door with him inside. "Otso, huh? That's an interesting name."

"It means *bear*."

My laugh is dry. "How fitting."

"Come, leave your suitcases for a second and I'll take you to your dad." She motions for me to follow her down the hall.

Suddenly, I remember why I'm here. My dad is somewhere in this house, dying, and I'm going to lay eyes on him for the first time since he last visited me in New York a year ago.

Inhale. Laura knocks gently before cracking open the door and beckons me forward with an encouraging smile. *Exhale.*

This room used to store all our holiday decorations and a treadmill machine my dad used for a total of two weeks. The image of him running is at odds with the man I see now. His bundled body lays motionless on an adjustable bed, positioned toward the window so sunlight shines over his face. The golden glow tries and fails to mask his pallid complexion.

He's skinnier than when I last saw him—his eyes like sunken weights on his face. My nerves scream to look away, but his protruding cheekbones are captivating in a morbid sort of way. I know he's asleep, but if Laura wasn't standing next to me with her calm demeanor, I'd think he'd passed away already.

A gentle hand squeezes my shoulder.

"Are you okay?"

"I don't know, honestly." My dad's fingers twitch by his side. "Is he... is he in pain?"

"No." Her head shakes, freeing the sandy blonde strands tucked behind her ear. "The painkillers help with that. He sleeps most of the time, but when he's awake, he's in pretty good spirits."

I smile, ignoring the burn in my eyes. "Of course he is."

"I didn't realize he would fall asleep this soon after his lunch. Would you like to sit with him? I need to run to the store and grab a couple of things for the house." She pulls out a scrap piece of paper with illegible markings all over it.

My eyes flit to the lone chair stationed near the head of his bed and for some reason, alarm bells sound off in my mind. The thought of sitting with him alone, wondering every few seconds if he's still breathing, makes me want to crawl out of my skin.

"You know what? Let me go to the store for you," I rush out.

"Oh sweetie, you don't have—"

"Honestly, I don't mind at all. It would be nice to stretch my legs after that flight and there are things I want to pick up anyway. I saw my dad's car keys on the kitchen counter, so I'll just run out quick."

I snatch the list from her hand and practically run from the room, tripping over my feet, before she can refuse my offer. I pull out onto the road in record time and it's in my haste that I miss the black Jeep Wrangler simultaneously backing out of 164 Winsome Lane.

I take my sweet time in the parking lot of Hensen's Super, picking up the discarded trash in my dad's car and organizing it all in a pile on the passenger seat until I realize how pathetic I'm being. I bang my head against the steering wheel, flinching when it honks. What am I *doing*?

If I can't face my dad while he's sleeping, how am I going to stand by his side as he inevitably gets worse?

Grow a pair, Mara.

I grab an abandoned shopping cart near the hood of the car and head inside. One of the cashiers does a double-take as I walk by and nudges his coworker bagging groceries. They watch me, whispering amongst themselves and I clench my jaw, pretending not to notice.

My movements down each aisle are painfully slow despite there only being five things on Laura's list.

A mother passes me, and I offer a friendly smile to the toddler seated in the front of the cart. The little girl thrashes her floaties-covered arms about, filling the aisle with uninhibited giggles. The world hasn't hurt her yet, and I want to beg her mother to shield her from what's to come.

When the woman crouches down to grab a bag of flour from the bottom shelf, her daughter seizes the opportunity to snatch a bag of cookies, chucking them into the cart behind her. She catches my eye, hiding a mischievous giggle in the palm of her hand and I use my fist to muffle my laugh. When her mother turns back around, she spots the sugar-filled addition.

She snorts, tickling her daughter's sides until she shrieks, and turns to me with a smile. "Do you have any?"

"Kids?" An uncomfortable laugh bubbles out of me. "Gosh, no. I don't make enough money to pay for the therapy they'd need."

She frowns.

I cringe.

"Well... happy shopping," I mutter, backing out of the aisle and fleeing to the next one over.

I bob my head to the music playing overhead, thankful for the distraction as I read and reread the ingredient list on a jar of pesto. Who knew pesto has pine nuts in it?

"Mouse?"

The air whooshes out of me as the hairs on my arms shoot straight up.

No. Please, no.

I don't recognize that voice, but there's only one person who calls me that. My heart rate quickens as I stand there, frozen, half-convinced that if I remain still, I'll become invisible and this interaction can be avoided altogether.

"*Mara.*"

He's closer now and my body hums to the deep timbre of his voice.

Garnering what little strength I have left in me after today's events, I clutch the jar of pesto to my chest and face the boy I left seven years ago.

Except he's not a boy anymore.

He's anything but.

I can feel Ambrose's heated stare burn into me as I appraise him from head to toe. The last time I saw him, he was attractive, but he was still young. Only nineteen. This Ambrose is no longer attractive.

He's *devastating.*

And while I'm all for self-punishment, this wasn't the cut I was expecting. He towers over all five-foot-four of me and I greedily devour the sight of him, branding him back into my memory.

He clenches the handle of his cart, waiting for me to speak.

My Ambrose.

My golden boy.

Not yours, Mara. Not anymore.

I finally allow myself to meet his gaze and his sharp green eyes strike me with immediate familiarity.

Another cut.

They're the same eyes I've always loved but they've aged. They carry a hint of sorrow, and if I'm not mistaken, a shade of regret.

My wave is pathetic. "Hi, Ambrose."

Someone reaches toward the shelf we're blocking and Ambrose moves closer to me, lowering his voice. "I just saw your dad last week. He never mentioned—" He runs a hand through his hair. "When did you get here, Mara?"

"Today." I force a swallow. "I got in today."

"I can't believe you actually came."

I inhale a sharp breath. That stings.

It more than stings, it feels like a knife to the chest.

Noticing the shift in my disposition, he scans my face with a tilt of his head. "He didn't tell you."

"Don't you think I'd have come back sooner if he did?"

"I don't know. I haven't seen or heard from you in seven years."

The way he's looking at me, the hurt in his eyes—I can't take it. My feet start to backtrack on their own accord.

"Listen, as much as I'd love to stay and talk, I'm in a rush and I—I need to get all these things back to my dad's. Laura, his nurse, she's swamped and needs my help right now." I swivel my cart, but Ambrose blocks my escape.

"That's it?" he bites out with a jaw so tight he could crack a molar or two. "You're just going to leave again?"

He's not angry. He's *furious*.

I can't speak. My mouth opens and nothing comes out despite how much I have bottled inside me. I'm drowning in all the words I wish I could say.

I'm sorry, forgive me, love me again.

The lump in my throat grows, and I look away quickly, blinking back tears.

Ambrose notices and concern quickly replaces any anger he carried just a few seconds ago.

"Hey, talk to me." His soft voice drapes over me like silk. "I have so many questions; things I need to know. Where have you been, how long are you here for—are you *okay*?" The back of his hand brushes against mine and just for a moment, I savor the feeling. Being touched by someone can feel meaningless until you're touched by the right person. "Let me take you home," he whispers. "I'll come back for your car. Please."

The very marrow in my bones calls out to him, so much so, I find myself leaning in.

No.

I jerk back, crashing my cart into a pyramid display. Rows of bagels begin toppling over and I scramble to catch them in my arms.

"No, I—uh. I don't think that's a good idea." For every bag I place back, two more fall. "Are you freaking *kidding* me right now?" I hiss.

The people gawking at us aren't even trying to be inconspicuous at this point.

Small towns live for gossip. Chisme, my mom calls it. They're vultures, circling for the chance to devour our private information like flesh on a carcass. This little reunion will be the subject of speculation by breakfast time tomorrow.

Calloused fingers curl firmly around my wrist and pull me close. "Forget the fucking bagels, Mara."

Ambrose's chest heaves against mine and I don't miss the way his eyes flicker to my mouth. The bags fall from my hands, landing on the ground with a soft *thud*.

"Is this about what happened with Cat?" he says, breathing hard. My blood runs cold at the mention of her name. "Mara... if you left because of what happened—"

"*Stop*," I command with more force than I intend. "There's no point in rehashing everything. It's in the past and it can stay there, okay? I don't think about any of that anymore."

Lie.

"I've moved on and I'm happy and I hope you're happy too, I do. But I'm not the same person I was seven years ago. We have nothing to talk about. *Nothing*. So please... please just leave me be."

Pain flashes across his face and I hate myself for it.

"Is that what you want?"

No. That's the last thing I want.

"Yes."

I can tell he wants to push back, but he doesn't. Instead, he bends down and picks up the wallet I didn't realize I'd dropped. My trembling fingers take it from his outstretched hand.

"Take care of yourself, Mara."

Cuts. Cuts everywhere and I'm bleeding out.

His retreating footsteps are drowned out by the music I danced to not five minutes ago and now I know what it feels like to have the person you love walk away from you.

I haul my heavy limbs toward the self-checkout lane and for someone who's a mouse, I despise the hell out of the silence that envelops me.

THEN

AGE ELEVEN

"What's it supposed to be?"

"Can't you tell?" he asks.

I tug the baseball cap further down my forehead, shielding my eyes from the piercing sun. I can't figure out what the heck I'm supposed to be looking at. It's only a week into summer vacation and Dad's already getting crafty.

Bless his heart.

I move under the shade of the looming Maple tree, forgetting for a moment that I'd sell any one of my organs to be swimming right now.

Dad always says the main reason he and Mom bought this house when I was born was because of this tree. Old Maple—that's what he named it.

Sure, other homes in Speck Lake boasted bigger backyards and docks nicer than ours, but they didn't have a tree like this. One with branches that spread out like arms reaching for the clouds and a trunk so wide, it feels like a shield, ready to protect you from harm's way.

Old Maple is perfect. So why would he ruin her like this?

"Mara." He lets out an exasperated breath. "It's a tree house."

My eyes swing from the tree to him and then back to the tree again. I squint. "*Where?*"

"*Where?* she asks," he mutters in disappointment.

Solomon Makinen is a big, burly construction man in his own right. He constructed half of this town for goodness' sake. But unless there is an intricate plan to follow, he can't build anything to save his life.

This became clear when I was five years old and made the mistake of entrusting him with the task of assembling my Barbie dream house after I accidentally threw away the manual. I can still recall the sight of Barbie's elevator crushed to bits in the palm of his hands as I screamed in horror.

Talk about traumatizing.

That's how I know this is a product of desperation in its purest form. He'll do anything to keep me from holing up in the house like I did when Mom left. It's not enough that I've been friends with Ambrose and Cat for an entire year, he wants me to play outside every day until I visit Paris in July.

And if this sad excuse for a tree house isn't enough proof of how deeply he loves me, the quarter-sized blisters on his hands sure are.

I tilt my head, forcing myself to see the tree house in a new light. The planks leading up the tree are jagged and uneven, but that could be a... fun challenge. And actually, it looks big enough to fit a couple of kids in there. If we all sit cross-legged. And don't mind the smell of each other's breath.

"It's perfect, Dad." I throw my arms around his midsection, squeezing tight. "I love it. And I know for a *fact* no other kid in Speck has something like this—it's too cool and unique." I cross two fingers behind my back, hoping it negates my lie.

Eyes narrowed, he lifts my chin. "Really?"

My head bobbles up and down. "*Oh, yeah.* Besides, who wants one of those big, over-the-top tree houses anyway? That's what real houses are for, and I'd much rather hang out with you than be in a tree house all day. Cat's going to love it. She'll want us to act out *Rapunzel*, I just know it."

I chuckle. "Ambrose will probably ask if there were any bird nests when you—what's wrong?" I stop rambling when I notice his glistening eyes.

He clears his throat. "Thank you, *princesa*," he whispers, planting a quick kiss on the top of my head. Gathering his toolbox in his arms at rapid speed, he retreats into the house.

Was it something I said?

Making my way to the front yard, I toss my water bottle high into the air to see if I can catch it. Soccer tryouts were a bust, but softball could be my calling for all we know.

The bottle comes flying back down and my hands miss.

I hear the loud smack against my face before I feel it. "*Ow.*"

So maybe softball is off the table too.

"Nicely done!" Cat shouts from across the street.

She and Ambrose are unloading groceries from the trunk of their mom's car. She sets the bags down and starts performing an impromptu cheer routine. It's surprisingly good.

I can't help but laugh. Usually, I'd be embarrassed, but Cat helps me not take things so seriously. Ambrose waves, a grin pulling at his mouth, and my cheeks go warm.

"Hurry up so you guys can come over!" I call out. "We can swim and then I'll give you a tour of my new castle!"

Okay, maybe "castle" is a little too generous.

"Boo!"

I snort, shaking my head at my best friend. "Cat, you can't scare someone if they see you walking up."

"But you'd never expect it, so it's even scarier. Trust me, I know what I'm talking about." She pulls me in for a hug, jumping in place. "Happy birthday!"

"Air." I laugh. "I need *air*."

Ambrose catches up to us and my hands immediately clam up. I wipe them on my jeans before smoothing down my hair. "Hey."

"Hey, Mouse. Happy Birthday." He smiles and what a smile it is. It makes every good thing louder, and every bad thing obsolete. I almost die right there on the spot.

I didn't know what to make of the nickname he gave me at first. Wasn't sure if it was a compliment or an insult. But one day he pulled me aside and assured me it was a good thing. It meant that I was quiet but observant. Small, but mighty.

I don't know how long we stare at each other before Cat clasps her hands together and announces, "Well, this is awkward."

Ambrose pulls her into a playful headlock and she giggles, which thankfully breaks the tension.

I motion toward Old Maple. "Let's go."

We climb up one by one, careful to avoid the weaker spots in the steps. Once we're inside, Cat bounces with excitement. "My mom's making her special lemon bars for your dinner tonight. And Ambrose made you those amazing..."—she turns to her brother— "what are they called again? Patel?"

"*Pastelles*," he corrects. His perfect Spanish pronunciation catches me off guard. "And Mom helped," he adds, shrugging off the praise.

We're keeping the birthday festivities light this year with dinner and a movie night since money is even tighter than usual. My dad says it has something to do with houses crashing. I don't know what that means, but I don't want my house to crash. I love my house.

"Has your mom called yet?" Cat asks hesitantly.

Ambrose shoves her shoulder. "Cat!"

"What?" She drops her head. "Sorry."

I discreetly loosen my shoelaces just so I can focus on retying them and avoid the overwhelming pity in their eyes.

"It's okay. She hasn't called yet, but I'm not worried. It's only like, nine o'clock her time right now. She usually stays up until at least ten-thirty." I gnaw at my bottom lip and Ambrose's frown deepens.

"Before I forget," I say, changing subjects, "my dad said he can take us to Lake Bonnie next weekend if you guys want."

Cat sighs. "We can't. We're leaving next week."

In only a matter of seconds, my body shifts into panic mode.

"Leaving?" I squeak. "B-but you just moved here. Where are you going? When?"

Ambrose places a gentle hand on my arm, his expression pinched with concern. "To Lake Tahoe. We're visiting family. It's not for good, we'll be back in two weeks."

"Oh."

My fear quickly morphs into an embarrassment for getting so worked up over nothing. I can't pinpoint exactly when it happened, but something has broken inside my brain. When people walk away from me, I have a hard time believing it's temporary. I watch their backs and pray with everything in me that the world won't snatch them up and deposit them elsewhere.

Sometimes I even hop on my bike and follow my dad's work truck for blocks when he heads off to a construction gig, sticking close to the bumper until my common sense tells me to hang back. It scares me how much I care about Ambrose and Cat, and how vulnerable it makes me. I feel like an exposed wound.

A voice calling out from below pulls me from my thoughts. I poke my head out of our makeshift window to find Dean Healey, a boy in Ambrose's grade already starting to climb his way up.

It's still hard to believe they're friends. Where Ambrose is straightforward and pensive, Dean is shifty and impulsive. He's like a woodpecker, but instead of pecking a thousand miles per hour, he talks.

Ambrose leans close to my ear. "I didn't invite him."

"Dean!" Cat squeals, waving so hard I'm surprised her arm stays attached to her shoulder. We scoot close together, making space as he hauls himself inside.

"Hey, Kitty Cat." His lopsided grin is flirty and Ambrose tenses beside me. Dean unleashes his boyish charm on everyone, but Ambrose doesn't seem too thrilled to see his little sister on the receiving end.

Dean clasps his hands behind his head and leans back against the wall. "So, what are we doing today?"

I inspect a fingernail, giving the floor to Ambrose and Cat. It's much easier to avoid conflict if you just go with the flow.

"We could play capture the flag," Cat suggests.

Ambrose is quick to respond. "We don't have a flag."

"Obviously. But we can use any piece of fabric—use your imagination, *Ambrose*." She shoots me a funny look and I make one right back.

"I think we should go on an animal exploration," he says. "I was reading a book the other day that said every American's backyard holds up to four thousand species. If we all split up, we can—"

"*Nope*. Next?" Cat clamps her small hand over his mouth and I bite back a laugh. Instead of getting annoyed like most older brothers would, Ambrose's chest shakes with laughter.

He shoves her off and shifts toward me. "What do you want to do, Mara?"

I open my mouth, but when nothing comes out, Dean seizes the opportunity.

"You guys are so boring. Let's play Truth or Dare!" He wags his eyebrows suggestively.

I've played Truth or Dare a few times before with Cat, but never with a boy who's said to have kissed most of the girls in his grade *and* mine. When no one answers right away, he says, "Come on, don't tell me you guys are *scared*."

Cat doesn't just take the bait; she swallows it whole. "I'm in."

Ambrose studies me like he's trying to read my mind and I offer him a small shrug. He sighs, running a hand through his hair. "Fine. We'll do it."

Dean whoops in place, repositioning his crisscrossed legs to get comfortable. He goes from playful to downright serious within seconds and sweat pools in my armpits. "I'll go first," he says. "Cat, truth or dare?"

"Truth."

"Is it true you held hands with Marco Sanchez *and* Ethan Graham on the bus ride back from the field trip last week?"

She arches a brow, unimpressed. "Yes."

"I respect that." They high-five and Ambrose rolls his eyes. Dean nods, signaling her turn.

A mischievous glint dances in her eyes as she faces me. "Mara. Truth or dare?"

I settle on the truth knowing she'd never abuse the opportunity. She has my complete trust.

"Who's your best friend in the entire world?"

I almost laugh. That's such a silly question; she has to know it's her. Well, Ambrose too, but mostly her. But there's an undercurrent of fear behind her playful eyes. Have I given her the impression she isn't my best friend?

I'm not very vocal about my emotions these days, but I just assumed she knew how much I loved her. Guilt pulls at me.

"You are, of course." I take her hand in mine and give it a gentle squeeze. "Always."

She grins ear to ear.

Realizing they're waiting on me to take my turn, I rack my brain, unsure who to choose. Ambrose comes to mind, but I can't think of a dare he won't do. On the other hand, I don't want him to know which truths I desire from him. I settle on my only other option. "Dean, truth or dare?"

"Hit me with the dare, baby."

His overexcitement alarms me.

"Um... I dare you to sing us your favorite lullaby... in an old lady's voice."

"Oh, Mara. That's cute." He clears his throat exaggeratively before belting an earsplitting rendition of "Rock-A-Bye Baby" in a voice one could only describe as ancient. I clamp my hands over my ears and we all burst into a raging fit of laughter. Dean may be unpredictable, but he's kind of fun.

It went on like that for a while.

I shocked everybody by licking the wall of the tree house for five seconds and Ambrose brought tears to our eyes when he admitted that the dumbest thing he'd ever believed was that stepping on a crack really would break his mother's back.

"It made sense at the time!" he yelled defensively.

We laughed and laughed and if the game ended there, I might have gone so far as to say that Truth or Dare was a new favorite for me. But it didn't end there and I should have known Dean wouldn't let us off so easily.

"Ambrose. Truth or dare?"

"Dare."

His smirk is downright wicked. "I dare you to kiss Mara."

The silence that ensues is enough to make me believe that the world has stopped. We are frozen in time and all signs of life outside have joined in at the standstill. No birds chirping in the trees. No dogs barking on the street. Nothing besides the sound of my heart clanging against the bones in my chest.

I'm terrified.

Terrified by the idea of Ambrose kissing me and how quickly my mind tells me that's something I *want*. But more than that, I'm terrified of the possibility that such a dare might disgust him.

Ambrose opens his mouth, then closes it just as quickly. "I-I don't think…"

"I knew you couldn't do it, dude, it's fine." Dean waves him off. "So, I dare you to dare *me* to kiss Mara."

My mouth falls open as Cat gasps. His intentions suddenly become crystal clear.

He never expected Ambrose to kiss me. He *knew* he wouldn't.

I wring my hands in my lap, ignoring the bile creeping up my throat.

"Mara, are you ready?" he asks, scooting closer to me.

The tree house feels ten times smaller.

It's just one kiss.

Cat's already kissed two boys in our grade. I swing my eyes in her direction, surprised to find her watching Ambrose with an expression I can't decipher.

I dig down deep for a kernel of courage. I have too much pride to let him think he's won. Angling my body to the side, we face each other head-on. I squeeze my eyes shut. The last thing I want to see is Dean's mouth coming at me.

I wait.

And then I wait some more.

I'm no expert in kissing, but I don't think it's supposed to take this long. There's a loud scrape against the floor and my eyes fly open just as Ambrose grips Dean by the collar of his shirt, holding him away from me.

"This game is over now," he grits.

None of us move.

I wait for Dean to put up a fight or make a sly joke, but he simply shrugs. "No worries." His smile is lazy and unaffected. "I should get home anyway. Gotta help my mom with dinner."

We scramble to our knees and make our way down from Old Maple. Dean waves goodbye and jumps onto his bike.

Cat tugs on Ambrose's sleeve. "I'll see you at home. I've been holding my pee for years." She starts jogging backward. "See you later tonight, Mar!"

I wave her off. "See you."

Ambrose doesn't move and I shift uncomfortably, twisting a curl around my finger. "I need to pick up my stuff from the dock, so..."

He slips his hands into his pockets and nods once. "I'll help."

We make our way over in silence.

The water glints like precious sapphires under direct sunlight. Small waves crash against the dock in a steady rhythm thanks to a nearby boat and the fading sound of children laughing brings a smile to my face.

Whenever the racing thoughts in my mind get to be too much, I come here. The water holds enough life to distract me from my own.

I pick up a wicker basket and Ambrose starts handing me things to toss inside. He picks up a bundle of jump-ropes, passing them to me.

"Hey." I gulp. "I'm sorry about what happened back there."

Light bounces off his eyes, making them look like honeydew. "Don't apologize. You didn't do anything wrong."

"Sor—" He quirks a brow and I chuckle. "Okay."

He grips the back of his neck. "It's not that I didn't want to kiss you." I stop moving. "I just didn't want to do it like that."

My heart trips up. "Like... that?"

"No, no," he blurts out. "What I mean is, um..." Fingers rake through his tousled hair as he struggles to express himself. "I guess I just, I don't expect you to—" He smacks his hand against his forehead.

I've never seen him like this. This contemplative boy who's always self-assured, always ready with an answer to every question, is at a loss for words. I think I broke Ambrose King.

I kind of like it.

"Here, just take this," he murmurs, shoving his hand into his pocket. "I wanted you to have it before your dinner tonight."

I step forward to get a better look.

"I don't know what the writing on the back means, but I figured you would. I could have asked my mom, but I didn't want her asking who it was for." He trades me for the basket in my hand and I bring the dainty gold chain up to my face. "It's from that antique festival we went to last weekend."

I brush my thumb over the face of the locket, tracing the grooves of its engraving—a tiny hummingbird mid-flight.

"Hummingbirds can beat their wings thousands of times per minute." His voice becomes steady. Confident, now that he's talking about something he loves. Setting the basket down, he takes the necklace from me and motions for me to turn around. "They're extremely strong—stronger than most people realize. And their wings beat so fast, it's near *invisible*. They're just there, doing this insanely incredible thing all day long and we can't even *see* it. But they still do it. It still matters even if it goes unobserved."

His words brush against my neck as he moves my hair aside and clasps the chain. "I don't know. It just reminded me of you." He exhales a sharp breath. "Sorry if I'm not making any sense."

I glance at him over my shoulder. Every part of me feels soft and fuzzy. Like a sugar high or a big hug after a good cry. "You always make sense to me."

I flip the locket over and have to blink multiple times to make sure I'm not hallucinating. The four words in delicate cursive tattoo themselves onto my brain.

Con amor para siempre.

"What does it mean?" he asks, leaning in.

"It means *always reach for new heights*," I lie. "It's perfect. Thank you." My lips curve upward.

"Mara!" My dad's head pokes out from the back sliding door. "Come inside and get cleaned up."

"Coming!" I call out. He waves at Ambrose before returning inside. "I gotta go. I'll see you later."

Ambrose hands me the basket and I turn to leave.

"Wait," he says, reaching for my hand. When he lingers, my face begins to warm. Then he leans in and brushes his soft lips against my cheek, just long enough for me to inhale a breath. "*That's* how I wanted to do it."

I stare at him blankly as he casually pivots, setting off in the direction of his house. I don't know how long I stay glued in place. In science class, we learned that our sense of smell holds strong ties to memories, but I'm positive it's my sense of touch that will remember this moment for the rest of my life.

My wooden legs start to move again and I lay my palm over my racing heartbeat, only sure of one thing. There's no way I'm washing my cheek clean tonight.

You couldn't even double-dog dare me.

NOW

I 'm an intruder in my own home.

I know these walls and I know these floors, but I'm an intruder all the same. The creaks in the walls at night are no longer familiar and my insomnia makes them hard to ignore. I guess I expected the comfort of my childhood home to lull me to sleep.

It doesn't.

Laura buzzes through the house, taking care of every little thing, while I remain a background player. I can picture her now, beckoning me with that gentle smile of hers, encouraging me to try adjusting my dad's oxygen mask or change him into a fresh set of pajamas, but the coward inside pulls me to the chair in the corner of his room every time.

Unlike that damn dog who elicits a smile every time he leaps onto my dad's bed, I resign myself to the silence I know I can't fill and spend my nights working on my laptop in my little corner when Laura heads home.

That's where I am tonight when I expand the tab on a project Helen listed as important, the blue glow from my screen serving as the only light in the room. The consistent pattern of my dad's faint wheezing keeps my concern at bay.

Otso lays claim to the corner of the bed, his shadow a monstrous shape in the dark. Must be nice being a dog. So oblivious to the heartache we'll soon endure. As if we aren't enduring it already. If I had the privilege of such ignorance, I'd run around licking people's faces too.

I click the mouse pad, enlarging my inbox. My fatal flaw is that I respond to emails faster than text messages. It's a pathetic sort of high, filing them away in the little categorized folders I've created. A *ping* notifies me of a new email from Helen.

FROM: HELEN REDFORD

SUBJECT: URGENT!

Health House wants more one-on-one attention than we previously discussed, so I'm having them sign an agreement for your billable rate. Please print and sign the attached form below.

Thanks,

Helen Redford

I drop my face into my hands and groan. Didn't we, as a society, graduate to e-signatures years ago? They're convenient and the cursive fonts provided always upstage my chicken scratch handwriting. How am I supposed to access a printer this late at night? The library's already closed, and it's not like the city where I can run to Staples until eleven p.m.

I sit up, remembering the printer in my old room upstairs. My dad is sure to have packed it away by now, but it wouldn't hurt to check. Helen would understand if I sent it tomorrow, but I want to make a good impression.

My attempt at tiptoeing my way out is squashed when the door I open creaks loudly.

"Mara?" The faint whisper fights against the hum of the machines. "That you?"

Blood rushes through my ears, but I drag myself to his bedside. I cup my hand around his cold cheek. "Hey."

"When did you get home?"

"A few days ago."

A smile stretches his cracked lips. "Thank you for coming."

He's *thanking* me?

I do not deserve this man.

"Don't thank me. I would have been here sooner if I'd known." My eyes burn as I plant a kiss on his forehead, dropping my voice to a whisper. "You lied to me, Dad."

He looks ahead, staring out the window. No one is out on the lake right now, so the water looks smooth and glass-like, reflecting the trees around it.

"I think in a way I was lying to myself too." Red-rimmed eyes flicker my way. "And some lies feel like promises. I'm sorry."

Holding his hand, I force a smile. "I'm here now. Let's just focus on that from here on out."

He offers me a small nod and I blow out a breath. "I need to take care of something real quick but when I come back, what do you say we cuddle up and watch a movie?"

He coughs out a chuckle. "You don't want to lay in this grimy old bed with me."

"Are you kidding?" I pat the mattress. "What is this, memory foam? I don't know, Dad... you get served every meal in bed. You have this call button right here to use at your disposal. If you ask me, I think you're getting a bit spoiled." He barks out a laugh, then wheezes like a bell whistle and I grimace. "Be right back."

I traipse up the stairs, the light sound of skittering paws following from behind. Otso closes the distance between us, letting out a low whine and I narrow my eyes at him. "Stalker."

His excessive drool plops onto the floor.

Classy.

I continue up a few more stairs, glancing over my shoulder when he doesn't follow.

"What are you waiting for, an invitation?"

He grunts and catches up to me. I don't want to see my room in its entirety, so I opt for the flashlight on my phone instead of the main light.

Boxes line every wall, stacked on top of each other like skyscrapers painting the New York City skyline. A part of me yearns for the other half of my double life. The easier half.

The only furniture left in the room is my old oak desk and I move closer to inspect it. My heart skips a beat when I catch sight of the clunky printer resting on top. I plug the dinosaur machine into the nearest outlet, shocked when the little green light sputters on. "*Yes.*"

When a red light starts blinking right next to it, I groan. "*No.*" Out of ink.

Morning field trip to the library it is.

Dust tickles my nose and the full-body sneezes that follow are enough to elicit a bark from Otso. I walk over to the window overlooking the cul-de-sac and crack it open an inch, letting the cool night air in. Every house on the street is swallowed in darkness and I envy everyone who's able to sleep right now.

Feeling somewhat bold, I sneak a glance across the street.

For a house that was once so pivotal in my life, it looks mundane. Unremarkable. Nothing's changed in seven years, including the picture-perfect landscaping.

When a black Jeep pulls into the driveway, I push my nose up against the glass for a better view. The thought of catching a glimpse of Mr. and Mrs. King makes my legs weaken, but I can't look away.

A tall figure slips out of the driver's seat. A man. Even amongst the shadows, I can make out the broad chest and thick arms. He rounds the hood of the car, stopping at the passenger side.

This isn't Mr. and Mrs. King.

A woman slips out and draws close to the man, seeking refuge in his arms. She buries her face into his neck and they stay rooted in place, even as her shoulders begin to shake. His grip remains firm on her waist. Steady.

My pulse quickens, but I ignore the voice urging me to turn around. The voice that I'm sure is my rationale. They chat for a minute, neither one making a move toward the house.

Then the garage light flickers on, casting them under a direct spotlight. Ambrose stands in clear view and my heart plummets.

The woman he's with is gorgeous—even from a distance—with glowing fair skin and pearl-blonde hair that stops at her shoulders. She resembles the fairy doll I used to play with when I was five and before I decide I don't like her, I remind myself that I have no right to be territorial over the man across the street cocooning her in his arms.

Ambrose is a catch, there's no question about that. He has an air of confidence about him that comes off as more magnetic than arrogant. He had no shortage of admirers when we were younger, so this makes complete sense.

But honestly, I've never allowed myself to imagine him with a partner over the years. I couldn't bear it, even though I'd never expected him to remain single. I know I didn't.

The dust must be compromising my remaining brain cells because I lift the window an inch higher, eager to eavesdrop on their intimate conversation.

I strain my ear toward their mumblings, but their volume stays low. The wind outside lets up and I can almost make out—

My phone rings.

Considering I always have it on vibrate, the sound nearly gives me a heart attack and it slips from my hand. Somehow, I manage to catch it before it cracks on the hardwood.

"Hello?" I whisper-hiss.

"Why are we aggressively whispering?"

My heart rate settles at the sound of Tally's voice. I've barely talked to her these last few days, so she's coming to collect. Besides the brief updates I sent about my dad, this is the first time we've spoken on the phone.

I keep my voice low. "Why are you calling me?"

"I can't begin to explain to you how special that question makes me feel."

"Shit." I flinch. "Sorry. I just meant, why are you calling me so *late*?"

I look up at Ambrose and his girlfriend or wife—whoever she is—still talking. The sight of her in his arms makes me feel ugly things so I tear my eyes away, seeking solace in the dark room.

Tally rattles on between the sound of chips crunching. "I knew you'd be awake. You're like a hamster."

"Thank you. How's Cheddar? Jeremy?"

"Who do you want to hear about first?"

"Surprise me."

Another crunch of a chip. "He's growing on me."

I snort. "Which one?"

"I'll never tell." She stops her munching. "Wait, you still haven't told me why you're whispering and why you sound so out of breath. Are you in the middle of sex or something?"

"I'm hanging up now."

"You saucy little minx! Pass him the phone. I want to say hi."

"You're out of your mind. I'm not having sex. I'm trying to be quiet because I don't want to wake my dad," I lie.

Her voice softens. "Oh, damn. Of course. I'm sorry, Mar."

I shouldn't fib, but if she thinks I'm with a guy, this call will never end.

"I just wanted to check in on you, but I'll let you go. Call me tomorrow so we can have a real conversation, okay? You can't keep avoiding me."

My mouth hangs open. "I'm not avoiding you."

She laughs. "Right."

"I'm sorry." I shift uncomfortably. "Want to play a game of online poker before you go to bed tonight?"

"You're on."

We say our goodbyes and I end the call, flipping the silent switch back in place. I shut the window and tug on the heavy curtain, permitting myself one last glance. The woman no longer stands in the driveway and the automatic light shut off, but I can make out Ambrose's body angled toward my house.

And he's staring right at me.

The questions that riddle my mind the next morning all center around one person.

Ambrose King.

Why is he still living in that house? Where are his parents? Who's that woman and am I going to have to watch them live happily ever after every day that I'm here?

As much as I try to convince myself I want nothing to do with the past, Ambrose remains at the forefront of my mind. It pains me that the limited time I have left with my dad is being consumed by thoughts of him.

Have some self-control, Mara.

After faxing over the form to Helen at the library, I drive around aimlessly for a while before turning onto Main Street. The families out and about abandon their cars in favor of walking on what would be considered a perfect summer's day.

I should get my body moving too. Living in New York means I could easily walk ten thousand steps a day—I need to act like it.

Ignoring the surprised glances I receive while I walk, I stop every so often to check out the shops. Some have adjusted their hours and are only open a few days out of the week, while others have closed permanently.

"*Seriously?*" I groan, coming up to my favorite ice cream shop. I run my fingers over the peeling sign on the window of Scoops, cupping my hands around my eyes to get a better look inside.

The red-striped booths are still there. So is the giant soft-serve machine, though it looks like it hasn't been touched in years. The candy displays are barren. Ambrose used to beg his mom to bring us here almost every weekend. His go-to was a Malt chocolate shake with two Maraschino cherries. I wonder what he thinks about this.

"Do you need a tissue, honey?" a woman calls from across the street and I flinch. "Oh, my." She chuckles. "New York's made you jumpy."

I shield the sun's glare away from my eyes and squint. "Nadine...?"

"If you tell me I don't look the same as I did almost ten years ago, you're going to break my heart." She pops her hip out. "Now get your butt over here. Stop making an old woman yell."

A grin breaks out across my face and I jog over.

I don't know how I didn't recognize her before. Same coily black hair cropped short to her chin—a bit grayer at the roots. Rich umber skin glowing under the summer sun. Warm, spirited eyes and a megawatt smile, sweet as sugar. Only a fool would forget Nadine Clark.

I step into her out-stretched arms. "Hi, Nadine."

Laughter vibrates through her chest, humming against my ear. "Hi, sweet girl."

Nadine owns The Plant Shack. Not only was she the best first boss a teenager could have, but she also made it a point to look out for me when I was younger. She taught me how to take care of my curly hair and how to hem my clothes. It was her I called when I first got my period in the middle of a school day.

"I drove past your shop when I got into town, but I didn't think you were still open," I say, tapping my knuckles against the sheet of wood.

"We aren't." She sighs. "At least, not really. We officially hand over the keys to the new landlord next month. Just trying to sell everything on the floor at this point."

"I'm so sorry to hear that."

"It is what it is." She shrugs. "I'm moving down to Florida to be closer to my daughter and my grandbabies." Her smile broadens. She always knew how to make the best out of a terrible situation.

"Wait!" I gasp. "Zoe's a mom now?"

"Mhm. Three boys. *Triplets* if you can believe it." She laughs and my smile widens.

I'm glad Nadine has something to look forward to once she moves out of Speck, but her situation leaves an unsettling feeling in the pit of my stomach.

What's happening to Speck Lake?

It's never been the most well-off place to live and many people struggled for a while after the recession, but it got better. I remember.

But this is different. It seems like everyone's jumping ship and for what?

"Is there anything I can do to help? I don't know how long I'll be around but..." I fidget with my keys. "My schedule is flexible."

"Don't worry about me, honey, I'll make do." Her eyes start to glisten. "You're going through enough as it is."

I clear my throat, unable to go there right now. "Well, at least let me take some of the stock off your hands. I'm sure you already know my dad's putting the house up for sale. I'd like to make the process as smooth as possible for him and your flowers alone could bump up the asking price—"

She yanks me in for another hug, this time giving it her full strength. And the woman is *strong*.

"I knew I always liked you," she murmurs. "Come inside. I know just the ones."

The flowers bundled in my arms sway across my vision as I transfer them to the backyard. Setting them down slowly, I push my sunglasses on top of my head, wiping away the sweat gathering between my brows. I'm already exhausted and I've only just started.

When Nadine offered to give me the rundown on how to transfer the flowers into the ground, I told her that was unnecessary. I mean, how hard can it be?

After digging a shallow hole with the small shovel I grabbed from the garage, I work the violas out of their container and drop them inside. Packing the dirt back into the space around it, I pat the ground. "You know what you gotta do."

I'm plopped down on my butt, admiring my quick work, when my peripheral catches movement. I scan the perimeter around Old Maple, but nothing seems out of the ordinary.

Shifting my body, I keep my eyes trained on the tree house in a way that isn't obvious, and while the second movement is barely discernible, I still catch it.

I jump to my feet. "Hello...?"

Nothing.

"I know someone's up there," I say, sharpening my tone. "Look, this isn't a spot for squatters. People live here. Come down now or I'll have to call the sheriff."

This stranger better not call my bluff. Sheriff Lang would be the one responding to that call and his being responsible for multiple towns makes him perpetually slow to the scene. My grip on the shovel tightens just in case I need it to double as a weapon.

"Please don't! I'm too young to go to jail!"

A kid?

I haven't seen any kids on this street since I've been back. Where did he come from? And what's he doing in my tree house? Unfortunately for him, I'm in no rush to get back to gardening, so I decide to have a little fun at his expense.

"If you can make it down in the next ten seconds, I'll make sure you don't wear an orange jumpsuit for the rest of your life." I struggle to muffle my laugh. This is the most entertained I've been all day.

A small body emerges from the tree house, flying down the steps at lightning speed. When the boy reaches the last few steps, he jumps the rest of the way, turning to face me full-on.

He can't be older than six years old. Trembling fingers tug at his ginger hair, eyes flickering back and forth between me and the street.

Realizing he might make a run for it, I ease up on the intimidation act. "What's your name? I'm—"

"Matty!" The booming voice comes from behind us.

The boy dramatically smacks his forehead and I think it might be the most adorable thing I've ever seen. "Crap."

I sigh. "Crap, indeed."

Ambrose strides across the yard with purpose. Once he makes it to my side, he zones in on the scrawny boy. "Matty, where have you been? I've been looking for you for over an hour!" The panic in his voice rocks me. It's the type of panic a parent feels when they can't find their child.

Unease fills me. I search for some sort of answer on his face, but he avoids my eyes. He doesn't look as good as the day I saw him in the grocery store.

He looks better.

An olive T-shirt stretches across his broad chest like a second skin. Then there are the jeans hanging viciously low on his hips. I quickly remove my gaze from his ass, ignoring the smell of fresh linen dancing off his skin.

"Sorry." Matty hangs his head and toes a couple of rocks with his shoe. "I was just playing in Old Maple."

I tilt my head. "How do you know—"

"It's my fault, Mara." Ambrose keeps his eyes trained on Matty. "Your dad's been letting him play in Old Maple for a while. I forgot to tell him it was off-limits now that you're back." It shouldn't, but the fact that Ambrose won't even look at me right now feels like a knife to the side. "You can't play here anymore, bud. Let's go," he says, extending his hand.

Matty looks back and forth between us. "But—"

"Let's go. *Now*."

Desperation fills Matty's eyes as he looks to me for a lifeline. I don't want to be on the receiving end of Ambrose's angry grown-up voice, but I also don't want to shatter this kid's fun. Old Maple was my safe place when I was his age. If it can offer him the same kind of solace, I don't want to be the reason it's taken away.

"It's fine," I say. "Old Maple deserves some action after all these years. You're welcome to play here whenever you want, Matty." I lower my voice. "Just know that I'll be collecting your rent starting next week."

His eyes fill with fear and I rush to assure him I'm joking.

I think I could be better with kids.

Ambrose finally looks at me, face full of uncertainty. "You sure?"

"Of course."

"Alright. If he gives you any trouble, let me know."

The brief interaction is stiff and formal and it's all my doing. But it's easier this way. I know that and he must know it too. Still, if we're going to see each other in passing, I'd like us to at least be cordial. Blame it on the small-town manners I was brought up on.

"He won't be any trouble." I attempt a half smile. "I barely heard him up there."

He checks the time on his phone before dipping his chin at me, his mouth pulled tautly. "Come on, Matty. You need to wash up before dinner. You stink."

They turn to leave and I catch a sliver of the smile he gives him. It's enough to knock the wind out of me.

Ambrose steers him in the direction of his house, and once again I wonder if the last seven years have gifted him a child. Matty's paler, with bright blue eyes and freckles splattered across his face—he couldn't look more different than Ambrose. But that still leaves stepfather on the table. Now that I think about it, I can't remember if I saw a ring on his finger.

Blowing out a frustrated breath that I even *care*, I drop to my knees and sink my hands back into the earth. It doesn't matter how dirty I get. The mess on the outside may as well mirror the mess on the inside.

Matty's voice drifts across the yard before they get out of earshot, asking something that gives me pause.

"Is that the girl you played Truth or Dare with?"

THEN

AGE TWELVE

"I 'm not doing it."

"Come on, Ambrose. Please?"

"Not a chance. I told you guys I'd be Harry Potter, but this is too weird."

"I told you a million times why we can't do those costumes. Right, Mara?"

I look up from the book in my lap, taking in my favorite brother-sister duo. I'm no stranger to their disagreements, so tuning them out has become second nature.

We're lounging on the floor in Cat's room on the night before Halloween. Tiny orange pumpkins lie haphazardly around the room while felt bats hang from her ceiling. Cat appreciates every holiday, but Halloween is her favorite. She says it's the one time of year you can pretend to be someone you aren't and get rewarded for it. And with *candy* of all things.

I like the hot apple cider and the pumpkin donuts and the jumping out of dark corners to make Cat pee her pants, but the candy doesn't hurt either. It's our second year doing group costumes and this time Cat begged Ambrose to join in.

Our costume plans were solid until she called an emergency meeting after school today. Cat heard from Sarah Winters, who heard from Caleb Santos, who heard from Macy Lang, that the Robertson triplets are also planning on being the iconic movie trio for Halloween. It's a popular series and Speck Lake's a small town, so it's not surprising that our costume ideas overlapped.

"I think we can still do it if we want to, but I get why you think the Robertsons will look better, them being triplets and all," I say, attempting a Switzerland approach.

"And this new costume idea is *perfect*," she presses. "It's different. No one will forget it."

Ambrose gapes at her. "Of course, no one will forget it! Who would forget seeing three people dressed as the human personification of *Rock, Paper, Scissors*?"

I fake a cough to cover the laugh bubbling in my throat. I don't mind an untraditional costume, but it *is* a bit odd.

"Besides," he continues, "I'm thirteen now. You both are too young to understand but my friends would tear me apart if they saw me in a costume like that."

Cat and I blink at him, taken aback. Ambrose has never given a second thought to what anyone thinks about him, much less about what people might think seeing him with *us*. It's the first time he's pointed out our age difference and it feels as though an invisible line has been drawn in the sand.

I hate it.

The air grows heavy with tension as he scratches his ear in discomfort. I watch the anxiety build within him, worried he'll need to grab his inhaler from his backpack. Getting anxious can trigger his asthma and when it happens, it's not a pretty sight.

"Fine," Cat huffs. "Mara and I will go as rock and scissors and you can dress up as a *teenager* or whatever it is you want to be these days."

She gathers the scraps of notebook paper off the floor where she'd doodled costume ideas and jotted down pros and cons in the margins. I don't move, torn and unsure of what to say to either of them. Ambrose's words hurt me too, but I don't voice it. Uncertainty mars his face as he watches Cat. Unlike a lot of siblings, they never fight.

Without a word, she grabs my hand and pulls me to my feet. I realize this is the part where we dramatically storm out, so I do my best to play the part.

"Wait!" Ambrose calls.

We pause at the doorframe.

"You both understand where I'm coming from, right?"

Cat's spine straightens with confidence and I follow suit.

"No. But maybe you can explain it to us when we're older."

We leave and don't look back, all the while contemplating why we've just excommunicated ourselves from Cat's bedroom.

We look ridiculous.

But at the end of the day, it only matters if we have fun. And no matter what I wear, if I'm with Cat, tonight will be just that. It's still kind of weird that I'm wearing cardboard taped to my body, though.

"You look perfect, *rock*." Cat smiles.

I do a spin in front of my full-length mirror. "You don't think I look like a potato?"

"Absolutely not."

"Why can't I be the scissors again?"

"Because you're not *cut* out for it," she drawls.

I snort and we put the finishing touches on our costumes. The plan is to start trick-or-treating in the neighborhood parallel to ours because it's where all the well-to-do retired folks live and they're notorious for passing out full-size candy bars instead of the chintzy mini ones.

There's a soft knock at my door and my dad pops his head in, one hand shielding his eyes.

"Are rock and scissors decent?"

"Yes, Dad." I laugh.

"Great. You girls better get going if you want a leg up on all the cute little toddlers out there. I wouldn't be surprised if they hog most of the inventory."

Valid point but I'm not sure if I should be proud or disappointed in him for basically encouraging us to steal candy from babies. *Ruthless man.* Cat and I snatch our white pillowcases off the bed.

"Is it okay if we stop by Macy Lang's house after we trick-or-treat? Her parents are letting her throw a party in their basement for the kids from school, but they'll be upstairs the whole time," I recite. Cat made me practice the script she wrote all day so I wouldn't choke up when asking permission.

"And what exactly will a bunch of middle schoolers be doing in a basement on Halloween night?"

"Um. Well. We'll probably play board games and trade candies... those kinds of things."

His nose scrunches up as if I reek of suspicion. But he must remember who his daughter is and how I've never so much as had a bad note from a teacher because his shoulders relax.

"Fine," he relents, leaving the room. "But no kissing."

"Ewww!" Cat and I respond exaggeratedly.

We're no longer at the age where we find kissing gross. In fact, we welcome it. But it doesn't hurt to perform for my dad if it sets his mind at ease.

∞

Macy Lang's house is the most well-known house in Speck Lake.

The pressure-washed, white colonial-style home sticks out like a sore thumb in our small lake town. Her dad is the part-time sheriff and her mom is the town's primary family physician.

They're basically our version of the Kennedys. Macy is the second-born child. The eldest, Brandon, is kind and laid back—the opposite of Macy—and her twin sisters, Kira and Kerrigan, are adorable seven-year-olds with a knack for biting.

I lift my hand to knock, but Cat stops me and points to a rocking chair holding the biggest goblet of candy I've ever seen. The thing is filled to the brim with king-size chocolate bars and *bags* of cookies. We scout the area and only once we're sure there's no one watching, rush forward to fill our pillowcases.

Cat rings the doorbell as we reel in our laughter. When Macy answers the door, she immediately races forward to hug Cat with a high-pitched squeal that pierces my ear. "Oh my gosh, I'm so glad you came. Everyone's here already. Are you supposed to be a pair of scissors? That's so cute!"

I don't understand how a pair of scissors could be considered cute, but I'm not surprised. Macy adores Cat as everyone does, and if she could find a way to get rid of me without anyone noticing, she probably would. It's not lost on me that my presence has yet to be acknowledged. I clear my throat.

"Oh!" She jerks back as if I've scared her. "Mara. Hi."

"Hey. Thanks for inviting us." I smile, hoping the gesture thaws her ice-cold heart.

"Yeah, sure—what are you supposed to be? A potato?"

"She's a *rock*." Cat straightens. "The rock to my scissors. Like Rock, Paper, Scissors, except my brother—oh never mind. Are you gonna invite us in or not?" Cat hooks her arm with mine.

Macy shoots one last disapproving look in my direction. "Follow me."

The basement is packed with every student in grades six through eight, which isn't as many kids as one would think.

Like fate, my eyes snag on the six-foot-long table in the corner, decked out with every junk food you can think of. Mummy cupcakes, chocolate fountains, even a red punch fountain spewing out of the mouth of a giant vampire head.

I've made it to the promised land.

Cat and I load our plates and settle into an empty corner, watching everyone laugh and chat with ease. It's fun for the first fifteen minutes, but then it hits me.

The desire to go home.

This always happens. I get myself pumped up to hang around a ton of kids, and then once I do, I crave nothing more than to be back home in my bed curled up with a book or watching a movie with my dad.

Socializing is fun in theory, but most of the time it just feels exhausting. Sometimes it even gives me a headache. And it's usually Ambrose who bails me out of situations like this once I've reached my limit.

Speaking of, I wonder if he's here yet. Alima said he went trick-or-treating with a few of his older friends, but ever since the fallout yesterday, we haven't seen him.

Girls flock around Cat like she's a siren luring them to her. She holds eye contact with me, telepathically sending me assurance that there's no chance she'll forget I'm here. I'm grateful I've never had to worry about that. Cat could easily catapult herself into a higher social status stratosphere if she ditched me, but she's never given any indication that I'm not enough. Besides, sharing her with the masses means I can disappear into the background for a little while.

"I'm going to find a bathroom," I shout over the music.

She instantly begins removing herself from the clutches of Leonna Stine. "I'll go with you!"

They fix their glares on me like I'm being an inconvenience.

"Stay, it's fine." I smile. "I'll be right back."

The rest of the house is cavernous and lonely—an exhibit on display. I drag my hand along the velvet-lined banister until I reach the second floor, passing paintings that most likely cost more than my house. Now that I think about it, I have yet to see Macy's parents tonight.

After popping my head into three different rooms, I find the guest bathroom at the far end of the hall. The toilet has an unacceptable number of buttons and instead of flushing it, I push something that causes water to spray onto my costume.

"Great," I groan.

I leave the bathroom, eyes downcast, hyperfocused on drying my shirt with a small towel. My face collides with a firm chest and it slips from my hand.

"*Oof.* I'm sor—Ambrose?" Ambrose's firm grip on my shoulders keeps me from tipping over. He looks down at me, eyes scanning the lines of my face.

When he realizes he's still holding me after a few seconds, he pulls away, blushing. It's then that I notice what he's wearing.

Ambrose King dons a black jumpsuit with cardboard attached to his chest resembling a piece of paper. Ambrose came as *paper.*

And he looks incredibly ridiculous.

Reading my mind, he smiles in earnest. I take a mental snapshot, storing the image away for safekeeping.

My mouth curves upward. "Nice costume."

"Yeah, yeah."

"What are you supposed to be?"

"*Very funny.*" His hand shoots out to tickle my side and I squeal with delight.

I flick the cardboard on his chest. "What will your friends think of you?"

"I don't know. But I realized I care what you and Cat think of me a lot more."

The fact that he includes me in on that—that my opinion matters so much to him—makes me think this may be the best Halloween of my life.

"Are you getting one of your headaches?" He frowns, taking a step closer to me. I didn't even realize I was rubbing my temples.

He gently strokes the side of my face with his thumb and I can sense he's about to go into protective mode.

"I think so." I shrug. "But it'll go away soon. I think I'm just a little overwhelmed. There are a lot of people here. For me, at least. And I feel like I'm supposed to talk to them all, you know? Which Cat would usually take care of, but I also don't want anyone to think I'm rude and—"

"Breathe." He laughs softly, but concern pinches his eyes. "Here, come with me. I know the perfect spot to get away for a minute." I cast a glance at the stairs. "Unless you'd rather go back?"

My heart races at the very thought of that basement right now.

"Lead the way."

I follow closely behind him as he weaves us through the back of the house where the voices from the party become muffled. After scanning the area to make sure the coast is clear, we slip through the sliding door and make a run for it. Our costumes bounce in the air and we laugh uncontrollably until we reach the end of the Lang's dock.

Ambrose motions to the two Adirondack chairs sitting side by side.

"We should probably take these off so we can sit," he says, tapping the cardboard on his chest. I nod in agreement.

I'm always amazed at how beautiful the lakes here are at night. Moonbeams reflect off the rippling water, giving it an iridescent shimmer. It's magical.

My eyes flutter closed and I inhale deeply, the worst of my headache subsiding. Water truly is healing in every sense of the word.

I turn to sit down but stop short. "Ah, shoot. This one's soaked." I poke at the seat cushion, reeling back at the squishy sound.

Ambrose scoots over, making room on his chair. "You can sit with me."

There's only a sliver of open space. "Um... I don't think there's enough room."

"Sure, there is." He pats the spot next to him. "Come here."

I chew on my lip, unsure. I don't want him to feel pressured to do this.

"Either you come and sit with me or I can come and get you." He quirks a brow. "Up to you."

Sure, I can keep pushing back but do I want to? Not really.

Closing the space between us, I lower myself into the small gap he's made. I wriggle around until my back meets the slats and we're shoulder to shoulder. His body's so warm against mine, it takes the edge off the chilly weather.

"Good?" he asks.

"Good."

Suddenly, out of nowhere, a dark blob swoops overhead and I jerk back in surprise. I don't even have time to register what's happening before it circles back and flies over our heads again. I shield my face, letting out a piercing shriek.

When I think it's finally gone, it descends once more and I punch at the sky.

Aliens are real. They're real and they're going to take us and my dad will spend the rest of his life searching for me.

Ambrose starts laughing so hard, he struggles to catch his breath.

"What the heck is that?" I cry.

"It was a bat," he says between laughs, attempting to pry my fingers from my eyes. "You can stop hiding now. It's gone."

As much as I love Speck Lake, the wildlife here has never been something I've warmed up to. Ambrose, on the other hand? It's his freaking dream come true.

"It almost *killed* us."

"They're harmless," he chuckles. "Kind of weird to see one, though. It's hibernation season."

"Of course you know that." I sigh. "I don't understand how you can remember all this stuff. I still don't know what breed Cheddar is and I've had him for two years."

"He's a Maine coon," he replies with a grin. "And animals are easy. It's people who are hard to figure out."

"Am I hard to figure out?"

"No." He shakes his head forcefully. "I know you like I know myself."

My entire face brightens at that.

"Tell me something," he says.

"What do you want to know?"

He shrugs and we're pressed together so tightly, my arm rises with his. "Tell me... tell me something you've never told anyone before." A contemplative look comes over his face before he adds, "Even Cat."

I take a moment to think about that. I've told Cat every secret I have, except for one. But that secret is one I struggle to admit, even to myself. Most of the time, it's something I'd rather forget. But the thought of sharing it with Ambrose doesn't make my heart race out of fear. I think a part of me has always known that if I were ever going to put something so vulnerable into the hands of another, it would be his. So I turn to him and say, "I miss my mom."

His brows furrow. "Isn't she flying in tomorrow?"

"You don't understand," I whisper with a slight shake of my head. "I mean, I *really* miss my mom. And I know I act like I don't care. Sometimes it's easier to pretend I don't. But most of the time, it feels like I can't breathe because of how much I miss her. Even when she's here. Even when she's only a few feet away from me. Want to know the worst part? I don't think she feels the same."

I don't realize I'm crying until Ambrose brushes a tear from my cheek with his thumb. "She'd be stupid not to."

My laugh is watery. "Thanks."

"And your secret is safe with me."

I exhale with relief.

Before now, I'd convinced myself that sharing my secret would bring nothing but embarrassment. But I don't feel embarrassed, I feel lighter. Like he's helping me carry the load of something I didn't realize was too heavy for my shoulders.

Our chests rise and fall in sync as we look out onto the water. I can't remember the last time I felt so calm, so at peace. I think some of the best friendships are ones like this, where you can sit in complete silence and never once feel lonely.

I replay the image of Ambrose in that silly costume again and a smile breaks out across my face. "Surprised."

"Oh, okay. Um…" He taps his chin in thought. "Birthdays."

"Party."

"Kids."

"Friends."

He hesitates but recovers quickly. "Us!"

I giggle. "You're losing your touch, slowpoke."

"That's more than one word."

"That wasn't my word!"

He smirks. "That's four words. You do know how this game works, right?"

I pinch his arm and he cackles, swatting me away. "Mara," I say.

"Pretty."

We both go still.

He looks at me in a way I don't think I've ever seen him look at me before.

Something blooms inside of me and I want to water it every day and let it grow because it's one of the most beautiful things I've ever felt.

The sliding door whips open and high-pitched shrieks fill the air as kids start chasing each other around the backyard with water balloons. Ambrose and I jump like we've been caught doing something we aren't supposed to and when we look at each other again, we start laughing.

"Come on." He stands to his feet. "Let's find Cat before she sends a search party for you."

Three nights later when my mom catches her flight back to Paris, I curl up in my bed, face buried deep into my pillow.

I don't want Dad to hear me crying.

He has to be up at the crack of dawn to fix someone's roof and he needs the rest.

Cheddar nips at my toes under the comforter, but I shoo him away, not in the mood to play.

There's a soft tapping noise at my window and my body tenses, all traces of oxygen leaving my lungs.

Fight-or-flight mode activated, I jump out of bed and grab the baseball bat leaning against my headboard. I'm about to scream for my dad when a muffled voice says, "Mara, open up. It's me."

"*Ambrose?*" The bat falls to the carpet.

I slip on a pair of sweatpants and rush to the window, lifting it halfway. Ambrose is casually hanging on to my trellis like there isn't a ten-foot drop below him. "What are you doing here?"

"I saw your mom leave." He shrugs. "Figured you could use a friend."

My eyes water again and this time I let the tears fall freely. I step aside and let him climb in before securing the window.

When he kicks off his shoes and sprawls out on the floor beside the bed, my eyes widen. "What are you doing?"

"I'm just gonna hang here until you fall asleep. Don't worry, I'll remember to leave."

My eyes flicker to the door. If my dad finds Ambrose in here, he'll kill me.

Although, it's not like he's spending the night. Ambrose said so himself. The last thing I want right now is to be alone.

Without a word, I grab him a throw blanket and an extra pillow from my closet. I crawl back under the covers and try my hardest to fall asleep.

But it's not long before the soft sobs begin working their way through my chest again. "S-sorry I keep c-c-crying so much."

Ambrose sits up and I turn on my side to face him.

"It's okay if you're sad, Mara," he whispers. "It doesn't scare me." I sniffle, running my hand down my face. "You aren't alone. You have your dad and Cat. You have me. I'll never leave you."

"You promise?"

"I swear."

He lies back down, resting his hand—palm up—on the side of my mattress.

Not allowing myself to overthink it, I weave my fingers through his.

It's the first time we've ever done something like this and I'm suddenly convinced that my hand was made to fit perfectly inside of his. I don't want to let him go. And I promise myself in that very moment that even after I fall asleep when he climbs out that window and breaks our physical connection, I never will.

I'll never let Ambrose King go.

NOW

"This isn't a good idea."

"Hon, I'll be back before you know it. It'll only take me forty-five minutes. An hour tops."

"But, Laura, what if he needs something? What if there's an emergency and I don't know what to do?"

I was enjoying a scalding mug of black coffee, getting ready to repaint the cabinets in the kitchen, when Laura strolled in and said seven words that threw me for a loop. *I need you to watch your father.*

Slipping her key band around her wrist, she hands me a piece of paper.

"These are all the numbers you'd ever need in case of an emergency, including mine. And I told you not to worry about fixing those." She points to the cabinets. "We have someone taking care of all that. Mara, you're going to be *fine.*" Her hands come up to my shoulders, squeezing gently. "I'm going to come back."

She sounds like she's talking me down from a ledge.

She might be.

Unfortunately for her, I refuse to go down without a fight. "Is it the store? Because I told you, I don't mind doing the grocery shopping."

"It's not the store. What I need to do isn't something you can help me with." Her face turns somber, and for the first time since meeting her, she looks uncomfortable. I don't want to push, so I remain silent.

To my surprise, she divulges anyway. "It's my sister. She's a bit... all over the place right now and she needs me." The frown she's sporting looks unnatural on her normally chipper face.

I realize how incessant I'm being. It's selfish of me not to consider that she has a family of her own to deal with on top of looking after my dad. She shouldn't overexert herself when the whole reason I'm here is to show up when I'm needed.

"I'm sorry," I say. "Take your time—I'm just being a baby."

She graces me with one of the warm smiles I'm starting to love and pushes a stray curl from my forehead. The gesture's gentle and motherly and I lean into the feeling of safety it offers.

Glancing at her watch, she quickly slips on her shoes. "Your father just ate, so no need to worry about that. He seems to be having a pretty good day. All bright-eyed and bushy-tailed when I left his room. Go in there and talk to him for a bit. I know he'd love that."

"I've spent a lot of time in his room." Even I can hear how defensive I sound.

An amused snort comes from Laura. "Maybe try spending time with him when he's *awake*," she suggests before closing the door behind her.

I purse my lips and close my laptop. With Laura gone, the house is eerily quiet. I now find a certain kind of comfort in the way she hums throughout the house, clinking pots and pans as she makes herself food.

The night is for silence. Stillness. But daytime deserves more movement, more sounds, more *life*. I crane my neck around the corner, spotting Otso passed out on his doggy bed.

My dad's door creaks as I open it. I slip off my shoes, careful not to wake him just in case he happened to doze off while Laura and I talked. We've had a few brief conversations here and there, but most of the time he falls back asleep after five minutes.

Something about being around him... terrifies me. And if there's one thing I know, it's that fear can bind you. Keep you away from the things that could very well fill your soul. The things that could heal you. We're well acquainted, fear and I.

Please be asleep.

"Laura?" a soft voice speaks.

I sigh in defeat as I enter, dragging my feet to his side. "Hey, Dad. It's Mara." Laura was right. Appearances alone, he seems to be having a good day. His eyes still look sunken but they're wide open instead of resting at their usual half-mast state. Familiar brown eyes land on me. "How are you feeling?"

He struggles to clear his throat, but when I turn to grab some water, he waves me off. "I don't want to talk about me right now. You can see for yourself what I look like." The breath he takes is labored. "How have you been since coming home?"

Only my dad would be more concerned with how I'm doing while he's on his deathbed.

"I'm fine, Dad. You don't have to worry about me."

"That's *why* I worry. Your old man is wasting away in hospice and you're *fine*."

My face wrinkles. "You're not wasting away, Dad, jeez. Don't be so morbid."

"You shouldn't be carrying all this on your own, *princesa*. It's too heavy a burden to bear, even for you. Your mom would come here if you asked."

"The last thing we need is that woman stomping around here, spitting on the American ways of life as if she didn't live here for over twenty years. She thinks she's Parisian now, you know."

He laughs, but it dissolves into a dry cough, wracking his fragile body. He knows I'm right. "Laura said you've been helping spruce up the place so it'll be ready for the realtor." There's a curious look on his face.

"Yeah. Nothing crazy, just a few fixes here and there. She mentioned you already have someone renovating the house, but I haven't seen anyone come by." I frown. "You didn't hire someone sketchy, did you?"

He opens his mouth, then closes it, measuring his next words. "Have you seen Ambrose yet?"

That's a weird shift in conversation.

"As a matter of fact, I have. Thank you for preparing me for that, by the way. It was *lovely* running into him without warning." I shake my head. "You could've told me he still lived here."

He sighs softly and I settle further into my chair. This man is about to use his precious energy to admonish me.

"I know you and *you* know you. If I'd told you Ambrose didn't move away with the rest of his family, you wouldn't have come."

My chest tightens. Is there a kernel of truth in that? Would I have avoided this time with my dad if I'd known Ambrose still lived across the street?

No.

I may not be the person I was seven years ago, but I still would have come. And even though it hurts knowing he has those kinds of doubts about me, I'm well aware that it's only because I've given him a reason to.

"You should catch up with him. Go grab a coffee or whatever it is young people do to reconnect these days. He's turned into a fine man over the years."

"Dad," I warn. "You're meddling."

"Me? Meddling?" He plasters on the fakest expression of innocence, and I shake my head. "Stubborn as ever," he mutters, his laugh mixing with another cough. "I don't know... I just think it says a lot about him that he stayed." Bony fingers interlock with mine. "Mara, after what happened between you two that night, he *stayed*."

His words suck up all the oxygen in the room. I start to pull away, determined to retreat from the discomfort but his grip tightens.

"Tell me about work," he whispers.

I jump on his offer and shift the conversation to a subject that doesn't make me squirm. We talk about my web designs, and our suspicions of Laura being a saint reincarnate. I grill him on the fact that he got a dog after denying me one my entire childhood, and I promise to spend more time with him during his limited wake windows.

It's not long before his eyes fall shut and when Laura comes to relieve me of my post, I tell her I'm fine right where I am.

"Teach me your ways, Master Laura," I hum around a bite of pasta.

"Honey, you already know how to cook noodles. You just need to get more creative with the rest of it."

The second Laura eyed me warming up ramen noodles on the stove, she took it as a personal affront and dumped it down the garbage disposal.

My shoulders bounce with excitement as she ladles a second helping of lemon ricotta pasta onto my plate.

"Have you always lived in Speck Lake?" I ask.

She shakes her head, bringing her napkin to her mouth. "Made the move after nursing school. My parents wanted to retire here eventually and they convinced me I wouldn't have a hard time finding a job with the demographics. I've always wanted to work in geriatrics."

Ambrose's mom used to be a geriatric nurse when we were kids. She could still be one, for all I know. It's a job that's in high demand here and

I was always inspired by how hard she worked. Taking the overnight shifts that no one wanted or going in on the holidays—all with a smile on her face. I think she and Laura would've been great friends.

"Are you married? Have any children?" She goes still and I smack my forehead. "Oh, wow. Please don't feel pressured to answer that. It's none of my business."

"No, that's okay," she says slowly. "I'm not married. Never really had the time to date, I guess." Then she sighs. "I planned on having children but life doesn't always consider our plans."

I understand that sentiment entirely.

"I have a younger sister, but she's always felt like my baby. My mother had a surprise pregnancy at forty while I was in nursing school and when I moved here, she needed more help with Anya than I'd realized." She pushes her food back and forth with her fork. "She passed away from a heart attack when Anya was five and my dad kind of checked out after that. He's in a retirement home over on Camden Road now."

"Laura, I—I'm so sorry."

Her smile is sad. "That's life for you. But losing a mother at such a young age... does a number on someone. I'm sure you can understand that. Anyway, let's just say I'm still taking care of that girl. I may not be a real mother, but I have more than enough people to take care of these days."

She stands, gathering our plates but I stop her. "Please, let me. Go kick up your feet or something." She smiles, seemingly thankful for the offer.

I drag the drying towel over the same dish for five minutes, contemplating everything she told me. I don't have siblings, but there was a time when the two kids across the street made me feel like I did. Even from where I stood, I could make out the markings of our varying heights over the years etched into the kitchen's door jam.

The doorbell rings and I set the dish towel down. I open the door to a little freckle-faced human staring up at me.

"Hey, Matty." I smile. "Everything okay with the tree house?"

"Do you like birds?"

I give him a quizzical look. "Pardon?"

"Birds. You know, the animals with wings that fly around in the sky?"

Smart-ass.

I raise an amused brow. "Yes, I know what *birds* are. And I'm impartial to them. Why?"

"Ambrose is taking me to the zoo today. Want to come?"

I peer across the street just as Ambrose tosses a cooler into the back seat of his Jeep. At the same moment, he turns toward us, a look of surprise coming over his face when he sees Matty talking to me. I can hear the deep sigh he releases from where I stand.

Damnit, he has no right to look that good walking this way.

"Matty..." His voice is laced with suspicion. "What are you doing?"

"I'm inviting her to the zoo!"

Ambrose clenches his jaw and I want to run my finger along the vein that appears.

Shit.

"Mara has better things to do today. Let's get going."

"What better things do you have to do today, Miss Mara?"

The sly look on Matty's face tells me he knows *exactly* what he's doing. If I weren't so impressed by the kid, I'd be afraid.

I do have things I need to get done today. Helen called me this morning on behalf of a client who was unsatisfied with the branding package a colleague put together and she begged me to take them on. I'm sure the begging was more so to stroke my ego because she already knows I'm a non-recovering workaholic.

But there is a small part of me that would like to go to the zoo with them, if only for nostalgia's sake. That place holds some of my most treasured memories.

I don't give myself the chance to overthink it before I say, "I'd be up for the zoo."

Ambrose pins me with a heavy glare. "Matty, go wait for me in the car."

"But—"

Ambrose only has to raise an eyebrow.

"*Fine*," Matty huffs, making his way to the Wrangler.

My smile's awkward, like a child who knows they're about to be reprimanded.

"What are you doing?"

"What do you mean?"

"I mean, what are you *doing*, Mara? You essentially told me to fuck off and now you want to spend the day with me and Matty? You're being confusing as hell."

I consider that, blowing out a breath. "You're right. I'm sorry—I'm not being fair."

Ambrose grunts in agreement but doesn't move.

Deep down, I know I shouldn't be spending time with him. I told him what I wanted and he respected my decision. But if I'm being honest with myself, I'm lonely. Work only consumes a fraction of my time right now, Tally is too far to keep me distracted and my dad requires uninterrupted rest most days.

If I could just have one day to escape the thoughts my solitude stirs up, I would gladly punish myself with isolation for the rest of my stay.

As if Ambrose senses my internal struggle, he turns away from the house without a word, his jaw tight, gesturing me to follow.

I thrust my feet forward before he can change his mind. In an ideal situation, I'd run upstairs and change but I think if I did, he'd leave me here. In my rush to keep up, I miss the rusted nail sticking straight up on one of the front porch stairs. My shoelace snags on it and I begin to stumble.

Ambrose is by my side in an instant, arm clutching my waist before my face eats concrete. Holding me firmly against his chest, his minty breath falls over my cheek and my stomach tightens. His face lowers an inch before he lets go abruptly and I stumble back a few steps. While I stand there like someone just threw ice water on me, Ambrose continues toward the car, flexing the hand that touched me.

Ears hot with embarrassment, I offer shotgun to Matty. He's all for it until Ambrose informs us that six-year-olds use booster seats. He drives in silence after that, granting every song request Matty has while gripping the wheel like he has a personal vendetta against it.

When we finally arrive at the zoo, I'm at least comforted to see it hasn't changed in the slightest. It's almost like it was thrown into a state of stagnancy and time danced around it. The parking lot shocks me the most. There are more cars than I thought existed in Speck Lake. How is it that the zoo became more popular while the rest of the town fell to shambles?

We join the line and before I have the chance to pull my wallet out, Ambrose hands me an all-exclusive wristband.

"Oh, you didn't have to cover for me," I say.

"I didn't."

Okay.

Matty tugs on the hem of my shirt. "Ambrose always gets us in for free because it's his zoo!"

I assume he's referring to an employee guest pass of sorts, but I don't dwell on it. We start with the amphibian exhibit before reaching the aviary enclosures. Matty runs to the birds and pulls a tiny journal from his pocket.

Déjà vu washes over me and my heart aches for a time when that little boy was Ambrose and I got to watch his eyes light up in that same way.

Ambrose points out a small picnic table off to the side and I follow.

"Coffee?" he asks, holding up a thermos.

"Yes, please."

He fills the cap to the brim and pushes it toward me, opting to drink straight from the thermos itself.

We watch Matty study the animals and while it's not the most comfortable silence I've ever experienced, it's not stifling either.

"He's lucky to have you," I say, taking a sip.

His eyes remain glued on Matty like the responsible adult he is. "You'd think that, but I'm the lucky one. I was just going through the motions before Matty. Eat, work, sleep, repeat. Kind of depressing. He reminded me that we need people." He steals a glance at me. "Relationships."

"Well, he couldn't have asked for a better father. I'm sure his mother feels the same."

Ambrose faces me and his expression is unreadable. "Matty isn't my son."

"I guess stepdad—"

"No." He shakes his head. "Matty isn't my son, period. I'm his big brother." My face crumples in confusion and he clarifies, "Big brother, as in the Big Brother's Club. I joined three years ago and got paired up with Matty. He doesn't have the best home life, so I take him a lot of the time when I'm not busy with work."

The longer I mull that over, the more it makes sense. Ambrose had always been the best big brother to Cat. If Matty needs someone protective and loyal to look out for him, Ambrose is his best bet.

"I saw the woman at your house. I guess I thought... I thought you were all... together."

His Adam's apple bobs around his coffee. "You saw his mom. We were together for a while, but it got complicated. The same thing kept getting in the way."

"What?"

Heated eyes bore into me. "Don't ask questions you already know the answer to."

My throat constricts. I shouldn't feel relief, but I do. A part of me wants to implore him to tell me more but I stop while I'm ahead.

"So, you work here, huh?" I ask, switching gears to lighter material. "I'd say I'm surprised, but that would be a lie. You would have lived here if you could when we were kids."

"I own the place."

"*What?*" I choke.

"The zoo. It's mine. I bought it."

"You bought... the zoo. When did you buy the fucking zoo?"

"*Language.* This is a family establishment," he says, but the corner of his mouth tips up just slightly. "When I graduated from college with my business degree, I didn't know what I wanted to do with it. You know my dad, always pushing us to do something practical. When I came back home, the zoo was on its last legs. It was going to end up like a lot of other businesses in town and I couldn't let that happen. Too many memories. So, I took a leap of faith and got a loan to purchase it."

"What's the deal with that anyway? Walking through Main Street is like walking through a cemetery. I have a hard time believing that business is so bad, all these places are having to close their doors for good."

His face is grim when he says, "There are not enough new people moving in to compensate for those who leave. A lot of folks need to be incentivized to move to a small town these days. It's just not as shiny and exciting as saying you live in a bustling city and in this age of social media and societal pressures, that shit matters to some people."

"So what's the solution?"

He tops off my coffee. "Pouring back into the community. Thinking up ways to increase cash flow. The zoo alone now brings in at least five thousand new visitors a year. We have a long way to go but... it's a start."

"Ambrose, that's incredible."

You're incredible.

He shrugs, humble as ever. "The place always had great bones; it just needed some modern-day marketing."

"Your family must be proud."

"Yeah, I'd like to think so."

I chuckle, jerking my chin toward Matty as he presses his face against the glass enclosure. "Does he know as much about animals as you used to when you were his age?"

"He knows more." He purses his lips, considering. "But I still try to teach him something new every once in a while so he doesn't think I'm completely useless," he adds with a grin.

"What are you teaching him about now?"

Ambrose looks at me, a flicker of something resembling affection there one second and gone the next.

"Hummingbirds."

The ride home is nothing short of bittersweet.

Leaning my head against the window, I watch as the setting sun paints the sky in varying shades of red and orange. Matty passes out within five minutes and even my eyelids fight to stay open.

The exhaustion of, well, *everything* is catching up with me and the fact that Ambrose allowed me to step away from reality for a few hours fills me with gratitude.

When we pull into his driveway, my heart rate picks up at the sight of Matty's mom standing up from the curb.

I don't know how long she's been waiting there, but she doesn't look happy.

Correction: she looks *pissed*.

Ambrose curses under his breath and shifts the car into *Park*. He slips out and rounds the hood of the car, gently pulling a sleeping Matty into his arms from the back seat.

Matty's mom rushes to his side, face scrunched with irritation. "I could have taken him today. That was shitty of you for not letting me come, Ambrose." I step out and her glare latches on to me. "But you had no problem inviting *her*."

Ambrose keeps his voice low, but stern. "You and I both know why you weren't there today. Don't play stupid, Anya."

Anya? Why does that name sound familiar?

"Oh, bite me, asshole. You can stop pretending like you're his father. Give him to me."

Her entire body trembles like a leaf in a thunderstorm and it doesn't seem like her anger is the sole reason.

Ambrose confirms my suspicions when he tilts his head to assess her. "Are you okay?" he asks. "You don't look so good."

"Give him to me!" She yanks on Matty's slack body, pulling him into her arms.

He looks like he wants to refuse, but even I know he doesn't have much ground to stand on here. He *isn't* Matty's father. There isn't anything he can do to stop her from taking him, no matter the circumstances.

Beads of sweat break out across Anya's forehead and as beautiful as she is, she looks off. *Sickly.*

She stomps off toward the house next door and we just stand there, watching them go.

The air thickens with tension.

I can practically feel the frustration coming off Ambrose in waves.

It must irk him, me witnessing something so personal after being gone so long. He slams the car door shut and brings a heavy fist down onto the hood.

"Ambrose—"

"Go home, Mara."

He disappears into the house, leaving me alone on the driveway.

And it's not until I'm twisting the key in my front door that I realize I just came face-to-face with Laura's little sister.

THEN

AGE THIRTEEN

The knock on my door is light.

"Mara? Can I come in?"

I figure if I don't respond, he might forget I exist.

"*Mara.*" The voice comes through the crack of my door, louder this time. "Can you hear me?" I press my hands over my ears. "Mara—"

"Oh my gosh, fine! Come in."

My dad slips inside and I can feel his triumphant smile radiating through my covers. He sits at the edge of my bed and it dips under his large frame. "Do you want to talk about it?"

"Do I have to?"

"No." There's a pause. "But do you *want* to?"

I try to swallow down the lump in my throat. A part of me wants to talk about it, but it's hard to find the words. Pulling the covers off my face, I look at my dad.

He folds his hands in his lap. "Take your time."

And I do.

We sit there for I don't know how long before I'm finally able to verbalize the isolating thought that has been occupying my mind for the last few days.

"I-I don't like how I look," I whisper.

My eyes flit up to his, expecting some big reaction, but he remains calm, cool, and collected. It's the encouragement I need to continue.

"Sometimes... sometimes I wish I looked like someone else." I swallow, feeling the pain rise in my chest. "I wish I had boobs like all the other girls at school." Quickly, I swipe the tears from my eyes. "And I'm tired of getting picked on for the hair on my arms—"

"Who's doing that?" He frowns.

My cheeks heat. "Amy Leeman."

For someone who rarely gets upset, I'm surprised to see his face reddening. "Yeah, well, Amy Leeman's dad doesn't pay taxes so she shouldn't be saying shit."

"*Dad!*" I choke out a laugh through my tears and he just shrugs unapologetically.

"I'll put a dollar in the swear jar. It was worth it."

I laugh again before a deep sigh rocks my body. "I just wish I was pretty, Dad."

He moves then, tucking me into his side. He brings the edge of his flannel up to my face and wipes away my snot and tears. It's gross but sweet.

"I can't begin to understand what you're feeling right now. I don't know what else to say other than I hear you. I promise I'll find someone you can talk to about this. Someone who will understand better than I can. Maybe your mom—"

"No!" I sit straight up. "Please don't tell Mom. She'll just say I'm overreacting."

"Mara..."

"*Please.*"

He seems unsure but gives a relenting nod anyway. "We'll circle back to that. But for now, get over here." He pulls me in for a long hug. "Let me just say this, and then I'll leave it be," he says, his tone serious. "I could sit here all day and try to convince you of how pretty you are, but I'm not going to because being pretty is not the accomplishment you think it is." His fingers lift my chin. "Be kind. Be funny. *Be interesting.* That is where you will find your power."

I let his words sink in.

After a few more minutes of holding me, he asks, "Are you alright?"

I settle for the truth.

"No," I whisper. "But I will be."

The smile he gives me lets me know everything's going to be okay.

Not wanting to waste the rest of my day moping, I scoop up my bike from the garage and set off toward Cat's house.

I usually walk, but these days we spend a lot of time riding over to Scoops with her on my pegs. Cat's bike is better than mine, but she says she feels safer when I lead the way.

Ambling up the driveway, I catch sight of Ambrose and his friends hanging around, fixing up an old four-wheeler. No idea when Ambrose got into four-wheelers, but that isn't much of a surprise. He's changed significantly in the last year.

These days you won't find him without the other three members of *The Lucky Four* glued to his side.

As I get closer, I see Dean Healey pass Ambrose a wrench, tossing his head back with a laugh at something he must have said. Shayla Marks is posted up beside them, sunbathing on an old beach chair while she flips through a magazine.

She moved to Speck this year, but her face bought her a one-way ticket into the most desirable social circle in school. She's tall and has long limbs like me, but where mine are gangly, hers are prepped and ready to strut down a runway. Intricate braids fall down her back like a waterfall and I feel a pinch of envy.

I quickly replay my dad's spiel about prettiness.

Sasha Baker stands to her left, clinging more to Ambrose than the very clothes on his back.

Out of all of them, I've had the least interactions with Sasha and yet, every time she looks at me, it's with disdain in her eyes.

I'm not sure what I did to her and she doesn't make it easy to figure out.

She has this way of insulting me without actually saying anything mean. It's impressive. It doesn't help that she looks like a saint either because it's usually the reason why people overlook her backhanded compliments.

Her chestnut-colored hair and soft hazel eyes deceive you into thinking she's sweet and approachable. Maybe she is to some people, but I wouldn't know.

When she spots me walking up the driveway, her smile doesn't reach her eyes.

"Your friend's here, Ambrose." She quickly brings her hand to her mouth. "Shoot, I'm sorry. I forgot you aren't friends anymore."

Ambrose turns, seemingly surprised to see me even though I'm here almost every day. His brows furrow for a split second and I look at the ground, not wanting him to notice my puffy eyes.

"Hey, Mara." Dean leans forward with a smirk. "What are you up to?"

"Just waiting for Cat," I mumble.

Shayla peeks at me from behind her magazine. She looks like she's about to say hi, but then she glances at Sasha and decides against it.

Dean leans against Alima's car and crosses his arms. "You should come to hang out with us today, Makinen."

Sasha glares his way.

"Um, I'm okay. Thank you, though."

"Oh, come on, beautiful. We don't bite—"

"Will you shut up, man?" Ambrose growls. "Stop messing around and give me a hand over here. This is *your* ATV, remember?"

"Alright, chill." Then I hear him say, "She's cute. Can you blame me?"

If the heat from my face could ignite a fire, we'd all be burning in the driveway.

The front door opens, and footsteps slap across the driveway.

Cat throws an arm around me, her smile almost making me forget the interaction I've just endured.

"Ready to go?" she asks, breathless.

I nod my head, not trusting myself to speak. I can usually smother my emotions, but if Cat hears my voice, all bets are off.

Sasha clears her throat. "Cat, you could hang out with us today if you want. Shayla and I are going to the movies in a bit and we happen to have an extra ticket."

It's so obvious what she's doing and while it hurts, Ambrose's silence hurts even more. Why is he being like this?

Tears threaten to overflow as I stare daggers into the back of his head. I know he senses it too because his back goes ramrod straight.

Cat takes a measured step forward, eyes narrowed in on Sasha. "You may have everyone in this town wrapped around your pretty little finger, but I see right through you." Sasha's face goes sheet white. "I would rather stab my eyes out with a hot poker than spend even ten minutes in your presence. You're a big bully, Sasha Baker. But you're an even bigger bitch."

Sasha and Shayla gasp in unison and Cat snatches my hand, pulling me toward my bike.

I think I hear Dean laughing, but then Sasha hisses, "You think this is funny? *You're supposed to be my boyfriend.*"

Cat passes me my helmet and pulls hers on.

"Cat!" Ambrose calls out. "Make sure you're back before dark. And watch for cars."

"Yeah, yeah," she drawls.

She hops on my pegs and we barely make it to the first stop sign before we burst into a fit of laughter.

"I can't believe you just did that," I wheeze.

"I know," she says between breaths. "Don't tell my mom."

"When I die, bury me with chocolate."

Cat and I sit on the curb outside of Scoops, indulging in the weekly treats we buy with our leftover lunch money. I've already finished my milkshake, but Cat's savoring every bite of her king-size Snickers bar.

"I can do that," I say.

"But only Snickers. If you try to pull a fast one on me and throw in Kit Kats or something, I'll come back from the grave and haunt you."

I chuckle. "I wouldn't dare try to deceive your ghost."

She inhales a chunk of her Snickers and crumbs fall onto her chin. "What do you want it to be like when you die?" she mumbles, mouth full.

My eyebrows furrow. "What do you mean? I don't think I have much say in the matter."

"Like, what do you want to wear? Where do you want to be buried? What song do you want us to dance to in your honor?"

I fiddle with my shoelaces as I think. "I don't know. I've never thought about it. Have you?"

Cat snorts in amusement. "Absolutely. I want to wear a lavender dress. Like the one from *Holly's Greatest Adventure*. I want to be buried under a huge tree. The biggest tree there is. So everyone can come and rest under me," she says, a soft smile lining her face. "Oh, and my song of choice is hands down 'Shake A Tail Feather.'"

I gape at her. "Why on earth would you want that song played at your funeral?"

"Because no one can stay sad listening to that song."

"But Cat... it's a funeral. It's supposed to be sad."

She contemplates that for a second. "No." She shakes her head. "When I die, I don't want people to be wrapped up in their sadness. I want them to remember the happy stuff. I want them to remember that I made them laugh. Made them dance."

Before I can disagree, Cat stuffs the Snickers wrapper into her pocket and jumps up in front of me. She yanks me off the curb and begins twisting her hips, bending at the knees.

I can't stop the giggles that escape my throat. "What are you *doing*?"

"I'm making you dance! This is how you're going to remember me!" She pulls on my arms, whipping her head back and forth to the nonexistent music.

If it were anyone else, I'd be mortified. But when you're around Cat, her confidence leaks onto you. It's like she shields you with her self-assurance and you become bold by association. We dance together, right there in the middle of the parking lot, uncoordinated and unabashed. People on their way out pin us with pointed stares, but we dance until our legs ache. And then we dance some more.

We take our time getting back to our neighborhood. I walk my bike alongside me, too exhausted to ride it with Cat on the back.

"Why do you think Ambrose hangs out with them?" I whisper.

I don't need to provide context. Where my thoughts end, hers begin.

"I don't know." She sighs. "He hasn't been himself lately. He's so angry all the time." He does seem different, but I'd just chalked it up to him being a moody teenager. "Don't get me wrong," she continues, "he's a douchebag. But I think there's more to it. He just won't tell me what it is. I kind of feel sorry for him."

I kick a rock out of my path. "I wish things could go back to how they were. Growing up sucks."

Cat hums in agreement and we walk for a while in silence.

"I think my parents are getting a divorce."

I stop in my tracks. "*What?*"

She's already sniffling back tears. "They've been arguing a lot. They think we don't hear, but the walls are thin. I want to ask my mom about it, but I'm not sure I want to know. At least right now I can pretend it's not happening." I understand all too well what she means and my heart breaks for her. I want to shield Cat from what divorce can do to a family. "I think that's why Ambrose has been so distant. He barely talks to me anymore."

Her sniffles break into a full-on sob and I let my bike crash to the ground, enveloping her in my arms. I stroke her back. "I'm so sorry, Cat. I don't even know what to say."

Fat tears streak her face. "Why do people give up on the ones they love?"

The question shakes me to my core. It's one I've asked myself more times than I'd like to admit. "I don't know. I wish there was an answer, but I'm not sure there is."

She gives a defeated nod. "Promise me something."

"Anything."

"Promise me we'll never leave each other. No matter what happens, no matter how many fights we have along the way... we'll never abandon each other."

I reach for her hand, wrapping her delicate pinkie around mine. "I promise."

That evening we curl up on the cloud sofa in Cat's den. The sofa is so deep, we can extend our bodies and still have enough room for a fort of pillows and blankets. Cat pops in our favorite movie, *Practical Magic*. We used to reserve it for Halloween, but at some point, it became our comfort movie. We resonate with the premise of two sisters who'd do anything for each other. And there's magic, so not a hard choice there. A bowl of popcorn bigger than our heads is firmly nestled between us.

"I can't believe I don't have Nicole Kidman's hair from this movie," Cat declares.

I chuckle. "Just from this movie?"

She nods vehemently. "Her hair is something else in this movie. It's iconic."

I don't disagree. It *is* iconic.

"Why do you get to be Nicole's character? Maybe I want to be her."

Cat pats my leg mockingly, squealing when I swat it away. "Come on, you know you're more like Sandra Bullock's character."

"Why, because I'm boring?"

"She is *not* boring." She gasps. "She's responsible and loyal. And give our girl some credit, she has incredible hair in this movie too."

I'm complaining for the heck of it because what Cat says holds some truth. She resembles the wild boy-crazy character, while I'm more like the sister who follows the rules, keeping her heart guarded with an iron gate.

"Cat, have you seen my tennis racket?" Ambrose asks, walking into the den. He pauses at the foot of the sofa, tensing when he notices me.

"It's in my room next to my closet."

His eyes narrow. "Why is my racket in your room?"

Cat, unfazed by the irritation in his voice, says, "I was having a concert. I used it as a microphone."

"I'm not even going to ask." He sighs heavily before bounding up the stairs.

My dad's sitting in the kitchen, engrossed in a pile of books. I walk over and squeeze his shoulder. "Hey, Dad."

He lowers his glasses down the bridge of his nose and embraces me in a side hug. Warm and steady. That's my dad. "Mara, what on earth happened to your hand?" he gasps.

I angle my body, pulling the hand wrapped in white gauze out of view. The lie comes easily. "Cat and I were dancing at Scoops earlier and we got a little too excited. I tripped and fell on some rocks, no biggie."

His eyes soften. "I'm sorry to say you have inherited my two left feet."

I slide into the chair next to him and bump his shoulder. "I sure did. What's for dinner?"

"Actually, there's something I want to talk to you about first."

I freeze at the uncertainty in his voice. "Okay..."

"I told your mother it would be better if she spoke with you about this, but she insisted that every time she calls you, the call drops. She thinks there's something wrong with our landline." He raises an eyebrow.

I bite my tongue. I'm content allowing her to believe it has something to do with our signal and not the irritation her voice causes me. "That's so weird. Maybe we should have the phone checked."

He looks skeptical. "As I said, your mother has some news she wants me to share with you."

"Let me guess, she's starting another business. Painting and bread baking this time. Or, let me see, she's moved into another flat because she wasn't feeling inspired enough by her old one. Or maybe she—"

"She's getting married, sweetheart."

We both go quiet.

The only sound is that of me and my dad breathing as I try to take stock of my emotions.

I'm not sad. I'm not angry. I'm not even surprised if I'm being honest with myself. I feel nothing at all.

My dad puts his hand over mine. "What are you feeling right now?"

I purse my lips. "I don't feel anything, Dad. If she wants to get married, she should do that." I squeeze his hand and smile, proving I'm okay. "I'm *fine*. Thank you for telling me. I'm going upstairs to change. Could you warm up some leftovers for me?"

"I was thinking we do Dellahs for dinner tonight. Would you like that?"

"Are you kidding?" I snort. "I'd love that. Can I get blueberry flapjacks?"

"Yep."

"With candied walnuts?"

"No other way to have them."

"Great." I smile. "I'll be down in ten."

His head bobs slightly. I think he expects me to cry, but like my mom said when I was seven years old, crying won't change anything. I make a clean escape before he pushes any further.

I've learned that disappointment is a by-product of expectation. I no longer expect things from my mother, so she no longer has the power to make me spiral. You can't change people; I know that now. And I will no longer concern myself with begging people to stay. Begging them to want me back. I'll take what I can get from those who will give it.

My mind drifts to Ambrose.

The Kings have their own mess to muddle through. I want to be understanding but a part of me resents him and his decision to ice me out amid his pain while Cat pulls me closer. His actions won't sway my emotions anymore. If he doesn't want to be friends, so be it.

I throw myself face-first into my bed, craving sleep until my twentieth birthday. I can't imagine life is this hard when you're an adult. One day, Cat and I will leave Speck Lake together. We've already talked about the places we dream of going. Cat's set on California because of the never-ending sunshine and surfer boys, but I always make my case for New York City. She said she'd consider it when I dangled the idea of going to Broadway shows every weekend.

I bring the picture frame on my nightstand to my face. Me, Cat, and Ambrose are huddled so close, you can't see where one body ends and the other begins. It's from last Halloween when Ambrose surprised us by participating in our group costume at the last minute. The flash from the camera washed out the background, but if I squint hard enough, I can make out Sasha Baker pouting off to the side. She may have Ambrose in her clutches now, but this picture... it's just for me. A moment in time immortalized. Something that can't change no matter what happens from here on out.

Cat's eyes twinkle as she beams at the camera, throwing up her signature peace sign. It's one of my favorite things about the photo, but something else convinced me to keep it at my bedside for the last year. I run a finger along the ridges of the frame. Ambrose and I hold up peace signs too, our way of mocking Cat at the time. We're just as happy, but we aren't smiling at the camera.

We're smiling at each other.

NOW

"I can't watch any longer. It's hurting my eyes."

I grunt as I tug on the nail buried deep within the dilapidated stair. How this deck isn't surrounded by caution tape is beyond me. I broke a sweat ten minutes ago when I managed to lift the nail maybe an inch. Laura watches me with the most pitiful look I've ever seen.

"Very funny." I breathe heavily, wiping the sweaty hairs from my face. "You on your way out?"

She's still wearing the top from her scrubs, but she's changed into a pair of jeans. "Yep. My sister was a no-show at my nephew's school today and they just called, asking me to go pick him up."

I rip off my work gloves, wiping my hands on my thighs. "Anya, right? Yeah, I think I met her."

Laura frowns. "Met her when?"

"The other day. I went to the zoo with Ambrose and Matty. We ran into Anya when we got back." What I don't tell her is that Anya looked strung out. She also looked like she wanted to feed me to a group of sharks. Which, thanks to Ambrose and his uncanny knowledge of animals, I know is called a *shiver*.

Laura digs for the keys in her purse. "And how was that?"

"She seemed like a nice girl," I say, my voice pitchy.

She snorts. "Now I know you're lying. Listen, Mara... I love my sister. Lord knows I do. I would walk through fire for that girl, but she has baggage. And not a carry-on either, I'm talking about the kind of baggage they make you pay extra for. Where she goes, trouble follows. That's just how it is with Anya. So, trust me when I tell you to keep your distance. No use in spending time around the things or *people* in her orbit."

Her subliminal warning is about as subtle as a freight train.

I return to working on the stubborn nails with a heightened level of aggression. "I have no idea what you're talking about."

"And I'm Beyoncé. Don't think I don't see you staring at that house all day long, pining like a teenage girl."

My mouth drops open. "I do not *pine*."

"Honey, you pine. She pines. Hell, even I pine. That man is someone worth pining for. All I'm saying is, be careful. You have enough to worry about."

Some might think Laura is overstepping her boundaries, but I no longer see her as an employee whose only job is to clock in and out. She's become a friend over the last few weeks and I'm thankful for her presence. If she has the advice to offer, I'll gladly take it.

"I hear you, Laura. Ambrose and I are just... well we aren't even friends. We've just known each other since childhood, that's all."

Laura cackles as she descends the stairs. Then she stops, turns to face me, and barks out another obnoxious laugh. "*That's all.*"

I roll my eyes as she peels out of the driveway then head inside to reward myself with a ten-minute break. After chugging my third glass of water, there's a knock at the door. Otso speeds passed me, barking like I'm a damsel in distress in need of protection. He jumps on his hind legs, scratching the door erratically.

"Down, boy! I just refinished this, you little shit."

I grab his collar, doing my best to pull him behind me before opening the door a crack. Ambrose stares back at me, a large duffel slung over his shoulder.

"Ambrose... what are you doing here?"

"I came to work on the house."

I tilt my head. "What do you mean?"

He looks down at Otso soaking my hand in drool. "I'm here to fix some stuff around the house. I do it all the time. Solomon already knows about it."

Why didn't my dad or Laura mention anything?

"That's nice of you but that won't be necessary. I've been fixing things myself."

Ambrose glances behind him with a look of amusement. "I can see that."

"As I said, the offer is appreciated but we're all good here."

Ambrose presses his lips into a straight line before turning on his heel. "I'll be working on the back patio if you have any questions about those stairs. Otso, come."

Otso rushes after him with my hand still clutched to his collar. I plunge forward, face-planting the doorframe.

"*Ow,*" I mutter, rubbing my face.

Not only has Ambrose disregarded everything I've said, but now he's stolen my damn dog too.

By a quarter past five, wooden planks surround me on the ground, leaving an exposed concrete structure behind.

I give myself a mental pat on the back. Ambrose underestimated me.

I've only seen him a handful of times in the last couple of hours when he'd walk into the house for a bathroom break or a glass of water. Each time he'd take stock of my progress, he'd laugh under his breath. Bastard.

He probably thinks my time in New York has stripped me of all my handiwork skills, which were minimal to begin with, but that's beside the point.

I brush the dirt from my hands on the coveralls I borrowed from my dad's closet, moving to sort the wood into discard piles. I'm debating whether I should treat myself to a milkshake or cookies or both when Ambrose rounds the corner. He stops and stares at the deck, hands propped on his hips.

My skills have stunned him into silence. *Go me.*

I plaster on a smug smile. "Took a while, but nothing a determined woman can't handle."

Ambrose scratches at the scruff on his chin. "When are you putting in the new ones?" he asks, looking around.

I pause. "Come again?"

He tilts his head in my direction, squinting his eyes away from the sun. "You gutted the wooden planks covering the steps, but when are you installing the *new* ones? You can't just leave the concrete exposed like that. One slip after some rain and someone could end up with a broken neck or worse."

I look back and forth between the deck and Ambrose's judging eyes.

I still need to install the new stairs.

How did that not cross my mind? I've been so focused on removing them, I forgot about replacing them entirely. The little pride I had left drains from my body, seeping into the ground beneath my toes. I inhale a few deep breaths, but the exhaustive hours spent in the heat make my blood boil.

I rarely let my emotions get the best of me, if ever, but I explode like a defective pressure cooker. "*Motherfuckingbitch!*" I stomp my foot, chucking my work gloves to the ground. Groaning, I throw my head back in frustration.

Succumbing to my anger, I rush over to one of the piles of discarded wood and begin stuffing pieces into a contractor bag. When a sliver of wood buries itself deep beneath the skin of my palm, I cry out in pain.

Ambrose charges to my side and grabs my hand, pulling me close. When I try to pull it away, he tugs me even closer. "Stop squirming and I can fix it," he grinds out.

He swallows the little space between us, my body practically flush with his. He prods the splinter with his thumb and I yelp.

"Ambrose!"

"Don't be such a baby," he whispers and I can smell the mint on his breath.

Heat pools in my core and I begin counting down from one hundred in an attempt to distract myself from what his touch is doing me.

"I can't get it," he grunts.

"Just leave it," I beg. "It's not that bad—*ow!*"

He angles my palm to get a better view before lowering his hot mouth onto my skin.

Then he starts sucking.

A small gasp escapes me and his shoulders go rigid but he doesn't stop.

He sucks at the meaty part of my palm and the sight of his full lips around my flesh...

Kill me now.

Ambrose raises his head and there between his teeth is the piece of wood.

"Thanks," I murmur, cradling my hand to my chest.

"Mhm." He watches me before looking back at my mess. "Don't be too hard on yourself. Not everyone's good with their hands." I jerk my eyes upward to find a playful glint in his eyes.

He's teasing me.

I give him a pointed look. "If you're such a pro, let's see what you've accomplished." I set off in the direction of the backyard, more than happy to walk off my sexual frustration. He follows me in silence. When I reach the back of the house, I can't help but gawk.

The improvements Ambrose made... they're *incredible*.

It looks like he snuck a construction team in to help him without me noticing. Like the front, the back deck has a fresh coat of paint—an eggshell white that makes the wooden accents of the house pop. Updated Adirondack chairs circle a new steel firepit. Stunning ceramic planters hold the plants Nadine gifted me, giving everything a crisp, modern look. Ambrose has been kind enough not to mention the violas I killed by sticking them straight into the ground.

"Ambrose," I breathe.

"It's nowhere near finished, but it'll do for now. The plants you chose were perfect."

He's just being kind but my heart squeezes. We return to the front of the house and he helps me throw everything into contractor bags *with* gloves this time.

"I don't know what I'm going to do." I frown. "I didn't even order the materials for the new stairs yet. Who knows how long that's going to take to get here? Laura's going to have a field day with this one." I slap my forehead. "*Laura.* How else is she supposed to get into the house? I'll die if she hurts herself because of me."

"Just tell her to use the back entrance for now, she'll understand. Don't worry about the new stairs. I'll take care of it."

"How?"

"I know a couple of guys who have materials for projects like this just lying around. A few of them worked with your father back in the day."

"You don't have to do that, Ambrose. You've already helped enough, and I know you're not letting my dad pay you a dime."

His casual shrug confirms my suspicions. "Why *are* you doing all of this for free?"

"I owe Solomon."

That piques my interest. "For what?"

He glances at his watch before clearing his throat. "Let me know a good time to bring the materials over and I'll get started."

His dance around the subject only fuels my curiosity. "Well, if you're not going to let us pay you, then the least I can do is thank you with a drink. Beer at Bottlegrounds?"

I can see Ambrose's guard shoot right back up. I'm doing it again. Giving him mixed signals. But I can't help being pulled back to him, no matter the amount of guilt it causes me. I scratch my cheek. "I'm being confusing again, aren't I?"

"Yes," he confirms, breathing heavily. This heat must be hard on him with his asthma. Digging his inhaler out of his pocket, he brings it to his lips. His eyes hold mine as he pumps and I mentally slap myself for fixating on his mouth.

Again.

I cut the silence with a breathy laugh. "You're doing my dad a huge favor, the least I can do is treat you to a beer. One drink doesn't make us friends or anything if that's what you're worried about."

Ambrose's eyes trail down the length of me. Down the slope of my neck and over the curves and dips of my body. He takes his time and my jaw goes slack. When he narrows in on the wet patch of tank top clinging to my ribs, his jaw hardens.

"I don't want to be your friend." He drags his shirt over his sweaty face. "I'll be back in an hour, then we can go." With contractor bags slung over his shoulders, he leaves me standing there like a dummy.

Eyes closed, I lift my face toward the sky. The sun beats down on me and I exhale a ragged breath.

I've made a lot of bad decisions in my life.

None of those decisions have made my heart race as fast as Ambrose King.

Bottlegrounds is empty so we have no problem grabbing a seat at the bar.

Getting into a decent bar in New York means waiting upward of forty-five minutes or praying to the gods that a guy will find you attractive enough to offer his seat.

Ambrose picked me up in his Wrangler exactly one hour after I'd made a complete fool of myself. He left his scruff untouched but used a pomade to keep the hair out of his eyes.

"Want to sit at the bar?" he asks. He's effortlessly attractive in fitted black jeans and a heather gray crewneck. The cologne emanating from him smells like a forest after a rainstorm and I silently curse.

"Sure."

Everything I packed for this visit was either too professional or too casual, so the silky cowl neck top and distressed Levi's jeans I'm wearing tonight are definitely a choice.

As I settle onto the stool Ambrose pulled out for me, a hand slams down onto the counter a few feet away, making me jump.

"Well, I'll be *damned*. Is that Solomon Makinen's girl I see?"

Warmth courses through me at the sound of the thick Italian accent.

Lorenzo Rossi, the owner, approaches us with a broad smile, arms opened wide. "*Fragolina*."

Ambrose's brows scrunch. "*Fragolina*," he says. "What's that mean?"

"It means *little strawberry*." I laugh, leaning forward for double-cheek kisses. "It's good to see you, Lorenzo."

Lorenzo's been a friend of the family since I was born. He worked with my dad's construction company before it went under. Thankfully, he'd already opened Bottlegrounds a few years prior, which provided him with a financial safety net.

My dad also had enough savings for the fallout, but it helped that people in the surrounding towns contracted him for every little job. Most of the other men they worked with weren't so lucky.

"Ambrose, my man."

"Renz, good to see you."

"What can I get you two?"

"We'll start with two pale ales?" I look to Ambrose and he nods. I slide my card toward Lorenzo. "And you can keep the tab open."

Lorenzo *tsks*. "Put that away. Do you think I take money from Solomon Makinen's girl? Don't insult me."

I insist, but he won't hear it so I throw my hands up in defeat and thank him for his generosity.

Two and a half beers later, the tension starts to leave my shoulders and my conversation with Ambrose flows more easily. He stopped at one beer since he's the designated driver, so I drink for the both of us.

As more people filter into the bar, we move a tiny booth off to the side, away from prying eyes.

"Okay. Let's see, you saved the zoo." I list off on my fingers. "You're a member of the Big Brother program. You're fixing up my dad's house for free. What else have I missed?" I take a swig of my beer, my smile lazy from the buzz. "You still have all your organs, or did you give some away?"

He shakes his head, grinning. "You haven't missed much. When you left, I took some time off before going back to school to complete my undergrad. Did an accelerated program to get my MBA. I was working for an accounting firm when I got the call about the zoo."

I picture Ambrose in a suit at a corner desk and the image makes me snort. "An *accounting* firm?"

"I know." He laughs. "Not me at all. But at the time, I had my dad in my head. You know how much pressure he put on us about school."

"He was the worst," I grumble. "You're brilliant enough to do anything you want; I've always thought that."

Ambrose levels his gaze on me. "Thank you." My face heats as I twist a curl around my finger. "Anyway, it didn't take me long to realize the zoo was the right move. I'm just glad it's something where I can put my degree to use."

I down the rest of my beer, feeling brazen. "When did you meet Anya?"

"Two years ago, when Matty was four." He searches my face. "I hadn't been in a relationship with anyone until her."

Something deep within me cracks.

"I thought she was going to rip my head clean off my body."

Ambrose exhales and I wait for him to shut the conversation down, but he doesn't. "Anya's a good person. She loves Matty and feels a sense of protection over me. She probably didn't leave a good first impression when you met her, but she isn't always like that. She has her vices. We all do. She's just not as good at hiding them."

"Is she getting help for her addiction?" The question slips out of my mouth before I can stop myself and I shield my eyes in embarrassment. "I'm sorry, that just flew out of my face."

Ambrose rubs a finger across his bottom lip. "She is. And she's been doing well, considering. But there's a new guy she's seeing and he's a dick to Matty. She thinks we don't know but I've seen him sneak into their house with her a couple of times. I think he has her using again." His expression is pained. Ambrose doesn't just care about Matty, he cares about the people in Matty's life too.

"What will you do?"

"Nothing we can do. No matter how much you love someone, you can't save them from drowning. They have to love themselves enough to learn how to swim."

I mull that over. It feels like I've been drowning for the last seven years, but I don't know if I'm capable of swimming. Sometimes it feels easier to just let go and be dragged out to sea.

"Enough about me. What's it like being a fancy businesswoman in the Big Apple?"

"It has its pros and cons, like anywhere else. I love that there's always something new to experience and the feeling of getting lost in the crowd. But I'll never get used to the smell of piss in the subways or the prehistoric-size rats. Believe it or not, I miss living here. The grass isn't always greener on the other side and in New York, there's hardly any grass at all."

"You do web design, right?" When he sees the surprise on my face, he adds, "Laura may have mentioned it in passing."

A whisper of a smile pulls at my mouth. "Web design, branding strategy, and a few other things. Basically, I help a lot of companies look more professional in the online space. I never saw myself doing this kind of work but when I... when I missed high school graduation, I spent a lot of time distracting myself on my computer before the fall semester began."

A cloud of silence falls over us and all the things we leave unsaid. I drum my nails against the table while my face grows hotter by the second. "Slow Dancing in a Burning Room" starts playing on the jukebox and my eyes search the bar, desperate for a way out of my discomfort.

Ambrose slips out of the booth and holds out his hand. "Dance with me."

"I..."

He moves forward and weaves his fingers through mine. "Dance with me, Mara," he says gruffly.

I look over his shoulder at all the people who have yet to acknowledge our presence. People who would be sure to have an opinion on us even being here together.

"What if they see?" I ask, voice scratchy.

"Let them watch."

The look in his eyes is so firm, so resolute, that I can't help but give in.

I push my empty beer bottle aside and let him lead me out onto the tiny dance floor. I don't pay attention to anything or *anyone* around us, I just keep my eyes trained on Ambrose's chest. Warm fingers splay across the small of my back and he pulls me close until our faces are only inches apart.

Warmth spreads through me and I feel lightheaded. I don't know if it's the buzz of the alcohol or the man in front of me. My eyes drift closed as we sway to the music, not bothering to talk.

There's nothing to be said.

Ambrose pulls into my driveway at a quarter past ten and when he parks, he pulls the keys from the ignition. The overhead light clicks off and we sit, shrouded in darkness.

I clear my throat. "Thanks for the ride."

"Anytime."

My hand extends toward the door handle.

"Hey, Mar?"

"Yeah?" I whisper, turning back.

It's a struggle to make out Ambrose's expression as the sound of our shallow breathing fills the air. My logic center feels compromised in my inebriated state and suddenly, all I want is for him to kiss me.

Ambrose leans across the console, his breath a mix of malt and mint.

My heart rate accelerates as his hand sweeps past my head, behind me, and just when I expect his fingers to thread themselves through my hair... the door clicks.

"The lock gets jammed sometimes. It should work now."

He pulls back and I deflate like a popped balloon.

"Right," I mutter, getting out. "Thanks."

"Good night, Mara."

"Good night, Ambrose."

Once inside, I head straight for the guest bedroom and throw myself down onto the bed face-first. I slip my phone from my back pocket, immediately dialing my person.

"Well, if it isn't my long-lost best friend—"

"What the hell am I doing?"

She snorts. "Um. I know I'm your all-knowing, wiser half, but I'm gonna need more context than that."

"What am I doing spending time with the walking reminder of the worst night of my life?"

Tally goes quiet. She isn't used to me being so forthcoming. "Babe... I don't know much about your situation. I mean, the only time you give me any sort of insight into your past is when you're drunk off your ass. All I know is if something or *someone* can bring you some semblance of joy, don't throw that away."

My eyes sting. "I miss you."

"I miss you too. Now, I hate to leave you in your time of need, but I have like, thirty orders that I need to get packaged by tomorrow morning. Stunning work on the website, by the way. I feel like a real businesswoman."

"You *are* a real businesswoman. And that was just a first draft of sorts. I have more ideas up my sleeve."

"I love it when you talk dirty to me."

I snort. "Good night, Tally."

Her voice suddenly turns serious. "Mara?"

"Yeah?"

"Don't throw it away."

I clutch my pillow to my chest. "I'll try."

I really want to try.

THEN

AGE FOURTEEN

"Presentations will begin at the start of class, the first thing on Monday."

The entire class groans in unison.

"You all have four years left of this. I suggest you get used to it now."

A girl pipes up from the back of the classroom. "But Mr. Moinyhan, this weekend is the homecoming dance. All the other teachers are postponing assignments."

Mr. Moinyhan twirls the piece of yarn he always has wrapped around his index finger. It's a fascinating habit and one that always catches my attention. His bifocals fog up from his heavy breathing.

"Miss Lowe, I'm well aware. It's not homecoming without sweaty teenagers, questionable dancing, and young ladies crying in the bathrooms—trust me when I say that the smell of an impending school dance has permeated the air."

I laugh in my notebook.

"However," he continues, "we will push forth with the original purpose of this institution, which is to get an *education*. I look forward to hearing your thoughts on the riveting causes and aftermath of the Revolutionary War."

The groaning intensifies.

"Believe it or not, when I was your age, I preferred to excel in school, rather than be consumed with the trivial nature of school dances."

"Yeah, probably because no one would go with you," someone from the back mutters, eliciting a few snickers.

"Mr. Santos, since you're so eager to engage with the class, you and your partner can present first."

Luis Santos and the girl he's paired with make a sound of despair as the bell rings overhead, freeing us. Cat loops her arm through mine as we make our way to our lockers. When Cat originally found out her locker was assigned to another hallway, she bribed the girl next to mine to switch. She still won't tell me what the bribe was.

"I hate that class," she grumbles. "I mean, why even call it World History if we spend the majority of the time talking about the United States? No wonder the rest of the world hates us." I laugh even though I agree with her. "And I'm sorry, but that yarn finger thing he does is just weird."

"Cat, it's probably a nervous habit, be nice."

She sighs. "I'm just on edge because Maitland hasn't asked me to the dance yet."

"He'll ask, give him time."

"The dance is *tomorrow*."

"Maybe... maybe he's intimidated and doesn't know how to ask."

Cat swings open her locker and aggressively reapplies her lip gloss. "He'll probably ask Alexa Marx. Why wouldn't he want to ask a sophomore over fresh meat?"

"Why don't you ask him?" I suggest. "You don't need to wait around for some guy to make the first move."

She ponders my advice as I swap my history book for Spanish. "You know what? You're right. I will ask him." She straightens her spine. "I love this feminist energy you're giving off—it's very Susan B. Anthony of you. I still can't believe you won't come."

"The idea of attending an event with that many people makes me want to puke into a sock."

Her face screws into disgust. "You're a mysterious creature, Mara Makinen."

The warning bell music rings out, signaling the one minute we have to make it to our next class. I hoist my bag over my shoulder. "I can't be late for Spanish. Let me know what he says. I'll see you at lunch."

Cat smacks my butt as she speeds away. Her next class is four hallways over. "Au revoir!"

"That's French!" I call.

"Tomato, tomahto!"

I chuckle and haul ass to my next period. No matter how boring school is, she always finds a way to make it entertaining.

By the time lunch rolls around, I've mentally checked out for the day. It's pouring rain outside and rain makes me sleepy. I unwrap the sandwich I packed while Cat recounts how she asked Maitland to homecoming. Apparently, he *was* too intimidated to ask her.

She rambles on about the dress she wants while my eyes wander around the lunchroom. It's not long before they land on the table I'd usually avoid looking at by eating in the courtyard with Cat. The Lucky Four sit together, their belongings spaced out, monopolizing a table meant for ten.

Ambrose's chest shakes with laughter and for a moment I'm grateful to see it. He doesn't do it nearly enough these days. Sasha's hand remains locked with his as she whispers into Shayla's ear and when Ambrose lifts her chin for a kiss, I seriously consider chucking my carton of orange juice in their direction.

"Hello? Earth to Mara?" Cat sings, waving her fork in front of my face.

"Sorry, what did you say?"

"I said, why is Brandon Lang walking over here?"

I follow her eyes and sure enough, Brandon is making his way over to us, eyes homed in on me. He slides into the chair next to mine, his face lighting up with an easy smile. "Hey, Mara. Cat."

Cat taps away on her phone. "Brandon."

Brandon's my partner for our AP world history project and she's still bitter about it.

"Hey." I smile. "Did I forget to give you the rest of my printouts for the presentation? I could have sworn I did," I say, reaching for my bag.

"Nah, you're good. I got them. That's not why I came over." I tilt my head in confusion and Cat stops tapping. "I wanted to see if you were going to the dance."

Oh. That's not what I expected at all.

"Unless you're already going with someone," he adds.

Soft hazel eyes. I never really noticed Brandon's eyes before now. He's handsome in a boy-next-door sort of way. He's always been kind to me, he never makes me do more than my fair share of work and I like that I never feel jittery or confused around him.

Beneath the table, Cat crushes my ballet flat under her boot.

I really didn't want to go but it is nice to be asked. And who knows if I'll ever be invited to a school dance again? I could always call my dad to pick me up if it's a disaster and going as a group *would* make the dance more bearable...

"I'd love to go with you."

He claps his hands together. "*Awesome.* Okay, I need to stop by my locker before lunch ends, but we'll talk carpool details later." His smile turns flirtatious as he leans over me and pops one of my apple slices into his mouth. "It's gonna be a good time."

As soon as he's gone, Cat shrieks into my ear about stopping by the mall first thing after school. I love how happy this makes her. The bell rings and I collect my trash, casting one last glance across the room.

Everyone is gone except for Ambrose, who leans back in his chair, arms crossed.

He's watching me.

And his eyes are as clouded over as the storm raging outside.

"If Brandon doesn't kiss you, I will."

I glance down at my dress and grin. It was perfect in the store when I tried it on and it's just as perfect now in my bedroom. The sage-green tulle draws out the amber flecks in my brown eyes and it's fitted in a way that adds volume to my petite frame. The bust needs to be pulled in... a lot. But Mrs. King is a wizard with a thread and needle. I do one final twirl and Cat holds her fingers up like a pretend camera, clicking away as I pose. I've never felt so confident and the new emotion sits in my belly like warm honey.

The next morning, I head across the street so Alima can alter my dress. We're on a time crunch, but she's confident she can have it done before our pictures this afternoon. Cat's asleep upstairs and the house smells of fresh pumpkin bread, my favorite. I settle on the sofa in the den while Alima scours through drawers for her sewing kit.

"I could have sworn everything was in here, Mara, I'm sorry. I worked a double shift last night and my mind's all frazzled. I'm going to need a few minutes. Robby must have moved my stuff into the new office." I pretend not to notice the irritation in her voice. Robby and Alima King fight more often than not these days, but for some reason, they still haven't separated.

"No problem, Mrs. King."

"Mara," she warns.

"Sorry." I smile. "*Alima.*"

While I wait for her return, I decide to quickly run upstairs and grab the headphones I left in Cat's room the week before. Her bedroom is the furthest down the hall, connected to Ambrose's room by a Jack and Jill bathroom.

When I pass Ambrose's door, I slow down, noticing it's opened a crack. I tilt my head closer and listen for any signs of life.

Ambrose never leaves his door open when he's out.

Curiosity getting the best of me, I wiggle the tip of my shoe into the gap, pushing it open a few more inches before peeking inside.

Empty.

I extend my neck, listening for movement in the bathroom, but hear nothing. Quickly, I slip into the room and shut the door behind me as my heart pounds from the adrenaline. It's been two years since I've been in here.

I move toward the edge of Ambrose's bed, trailing my finger across the understated navy-blue quilt. It used to be an eagle bedspread because eagles were his favorite. Countless books and journals are strewn about, but it doesn't look messy. Just lived in. My hand extends toward a leather-bound journal and I immediately snatch it back.

Too far.

The room is sophisticated and simplistic, but if I'm being honest, it's boring. There's no life—no remnants of the intriguing boy I used to know as well as myself.

Something on the nightstand piques my interest so I head there next. The framed photo is heavy in my hands. I make a gagging noise as I look down at a photo of Ambrose with his arm thrown over Sasha's shoulders, the barely-there smirk I love so much playing on his lips. I'm so lost in my thoughts, I don't even hear the window close behind me.

"What are you doing in here?"

I jump back, ramming my ankle into the leg of the bed. Bloodshot eyes filled with contempt fix themselves on me.

Ambrose is disheveled in a crumpled white tee and a pair of faded sweat-pants—hardly a get-up one would run errands in. Noticing the photo in my hand, he crosses his arms over his chest.

I set the frame back down, internally cursing my trembling hand. "Sorry." My voice wavers. "The door was open. I thought—"

"You thought you could just barge in and snoop around?" he hisses.

"I wasn't snooping... I thought you'd be in here."

"Clearly I wasn't."

"Clearly." My teeth clench. "Why were you crawling in through the window anyway?"

At this point, I'm desperate to shift the attention elsewhere.

"You broke into my room and you're interrogating *me*?"

"Well, I-I, *you* were obviously sneaking back in."

"Are you always this observant?" He rips off his shirt and tosses it on the bed before pulling a clean one from his dresser. My eyes linger on the skin stretched tight over his hardened stomach.

Ambrose has *abs*.

That's new. And... interesting.

And now I've forgotten how to breathe.

"Eyes up here, Mouse."

"*Don't* call me that," I snap.

It's the first time I've ever raised my voice at him and his eyes widen slightly. His eyes roam my face as if seeing me for the first time. Blowing out a harsh breath, he leans against his desk and crosses his ankles. "I was with Sasha."

"Doing what?" I don't even want to know. I'm just a masochist.

His head tilts with genuine curiosity. "What do you think we were doing?"

Blood rushes through my ears.

Ambrose pushes off the desk slowly, stalking toward me until the tips of his shoes are pressed up against mine.

His tongue runs along the seam of his lips and his gaze drops to my mouth. "Have you ever been kissed, Mara?"

I consider lying. It's not like he'd know the difference. But I don't want to. I'm not afraid of him, which is why I lift my chin and lean in closer. "Not since I was eleven."

Something in his face softens.

He opens his mouth and when the bathroom shower turns on, we both flinch.

Ambrose moves away, his absence a punch to the gut. He pulls a hoodie over his head. "Go. Before she finds you in here."

No longer concerned about the headphones, I slip out his door and run back downstairs just as Alima enters, cradling a large sewing kit in her arms.

"I found it!" She grins.

I force a smile, not trusting myself to speak.

"Honey, are you okay? You look flushed."

"Yeah." I swallow. "Never better."

"You look stunning," Brandon whispers into my ear. He reaches for my wrist and wraps it in a corsage swallowed by white lilies and baby's breath.

My dad clears his throat. "Bible width apart, son."

"Dad, quit it," I grumble. He isn't even religious.

We pile into Maitland's dad's car and when I look out the window, I see a red Corvette parked in the King's driveway. The Lucky Four are already crammed inside, blaring music through the speakers.

Cat adjusts the straps on her crimson jeweled dress and squeezes my arm. "Tonight's going to be so much fun."

I squeeze her back. "You bet it is."

I'm not one for school dances, but even I can admit that the decorating committee blew it out of the water. The once understated gym has been transformed into a colorful, fantastical world resembling *Alice in Wonderland*. There's a literal red carpet that guides us to the entrance, leading us through the open mouth of the Cheshire cat. I wave at the familiar teachers volunteering at the check-in and food stations. Even Mr. Moinyhan is here, dressed up in a purple suit and multicolored top hat, which I'm sure wasn't by choice.

"Hi, Mara. Hi, Cat. You girls look lovely tonight." Mrs. Shannon, our algebra teacher, smiles, checking our names off her clipboard and collecting our tickets.

"Thank you, Mrs. Shannon," we reply in unison.

Cat loops her arm through mine. "Come on, I want to dance!"

I snatch a cup from the refreshments table and down it in one gulp. Hopefully, someone managed to sneak a splash of liquid courage into the punch bowl.

Thankfully, dancing in public isn't too bad when there are tons of people around you cloaked in semidarkness. The four of us form a tight circle and thrash our bodies around with no skill whatsoever. I enjoy the hell out of it.

We're doing our version of the wave when a voice amplifies over the speakers. Girls squeal left and right as we all shuffle to the outer rim of the gym.

Principal Sacks— an incredibly serious man—stands at the center in a Mad Hatter coat and orange wig holding a neon mic. "Settle down. Settle down."

The room quiets.

He reveals a black envelope from his coat and excited whispers buzz around us. "We'll start with the freshman." He squints, pulling the envelope closer to his face. "I can't see this; the font is too small," he grunts. "Janice? Where's Janice?" He cranes his neck, searching for his assistant in the crowd. "Janice, can you bring me my reading glasses?" That elicits a few snickers, and we wait in awkward silence as Janice's shoes squeak across the gym floor toward him. "Thank you, Janice." He clears his throat. "Right, then. Your freshman homecoming court representatives are... Catherine King and Maitland Brown."

The crowd goes *wild.*

Cat stares at me, wide-eyed, as I jump up and down, cheering. She has no idea how many people love her and that's exactly why she deserves to be on the homecoming court. Maitland grabs her hand and leads her to the center of the gym where volunteers place sashes around them, handing Cat a single red rose.

"Moving on. Your sophomore homecoming court representatives are... Sasha Baker and Ambrose King."

Screams resound throughout the gym as Sasha struts to the center, already reaching for her sash. Her baby-blue minidress and white stilettos make her look like the Alice our entire theme is centered around and Ambrose joins her side, thanking the kid who passes him his sash. His hair is clean-cut and styled to perfection—a far cry from the state it was in this morning. He's gorgeous in a maroon suit and somehow pulls off the most horrendous rainbow bow tie.

There's a sharp pinch in my chest. I can't watch Ambrose and Sasha be irritatingly perfect anymore.

I stand on my tiptoes to reach Brandon's ear, shouting over the cheers. "I think I'm going to run and grab some punch."

He glances back at the court, conflicted. "Do I have to come with you?"

Well, when you put it that way.

I shake my head. "I'll bring you back some."

Extracting myself from the crowd, I seek refuge in the quiet, empty hallway. A few teachers chat among themselves and I refill my cup while the rest of the court is announced inside. I take advantage of the low traffic flow and slip out one of the back doors into the courtyard.

The full moon gleams like a pearl against the dark sky.

Loosening the straps on my heels, I slip them off and stretch my ankles, which brings relief. I close my eyes. The silence is nice.

I knew I should have brought a purse tonight. I could have snuck a book in there.

The door behind me opens and I fly backward, cloaking myself in the shadow of a pillar. My heart stops when I see Ambrose walk forward, hands on his hips, pinching the bridge of his nose.

I watch his chest rise and fall, mesmerized. Wanting to get a better view of him, I step to the side, clipping my foot on a jagged rock.

"*Shit!*"

Ambrose whips his head in my direction. "Who's there?"

The only way out is through the door from which I came, leaving me no choice but to expose myself. I step out of the shadows with a sigh.

Ambrose narrows in on me. "Did you follow me out here?"

My face screws in disgust. He *would* think that. Like I don't have any-thing better to do. "There's only one door, so if anyone followed anyone out here, it was *you*." I shake my head, disappointed. "And to think you passed the ninth grade."

I plant my feet, fully expecting him to snap back. For the sharp words, the whirlwind of emotions we always fall into—hands clutched, irrevocably bound. But then, his chest starts shaking with silent laughter. Soon I'm laughing too.

"Nice tie."

"Nice dress." I suspect he's teasing me until I meet his eyes. He's utterly serious.

My body hums.

Ambrose jerks his chin toward my dress. "You look older."

"I am older." I roll my eyes, gesturing to his sash. "Shouldn't you be inside celebrating your win?"

I can see it now, Sasha scouring the halls in her stilettos, searching for her date. Ambrose nods, an unmistakable wave of sadness washing over him.

"What's wrong?" I ask.

"What makes you think something's wrong?"

"Because you're still out here, with me, when you could be in a room full of people who think the world of you."

"None of the right people."

I don't know what to say to that. Because I don't know who he wants the *right people* to be.

"Do you ever wish you could freeze time?" he asks. "Not forever, just... long enough for you to catch up. Figure out your shit." He hooks a finger under his bow tie, loosening it. "You ever feel that way?

I nod my head slowly. "All the time."

"Think it ever slows down?"

"What, life?" He nods. "I don't know," I admit. "But maybe one day we'll meet someone who makes it feel like it does."

We stand there, watching the dark clouds pass over the moon. Naturally, our bodies start drifting closer. Like we're opposite poles on two magnets. Like we don't have a choice.

Like we're inevitable.

Ambrose surprises me by hiking up his pant leg and kneeling to the ground, reaching for the heels in my hand. I bite the inside of my cheek as his palm curls around my calf, pulling each leg forward one by one to slip them on. He straightens, tucking both hands into his pockets. "Dances."

I grin. "Overrated."

"People."

"Dancing."

"Bodies."

I look at our bodies then—the little space between them—and a shiver runs down my spine. "Close," I whisper.

His gaze latches onto mine—a million conversations being had without words. Running a rough hand through his perfect hair, he releases a weary sigh. "You should get back inside."

I hold up a hand, thrown by the emotional whiplash. "Wait a minute." My laugh is hollow. "What the hell just happened?"

"Mara, please."

"If you would just—"

"Go back inside."

"—*talk* to me."

"I don't want to talk to you!"

The words are a slap to the face and I immediately stumble back.

Ambrose's shoulders fall. He looks defeated.

Exhausted.

"I don't want to talk to you," he repeats, barely a whisper this time.

With trembling hands, I smooth down the bunched-up tulle on my dress. "Well, then." My voice shakes. "Thank you for laying it out so clearly."

I push my way through the door and disappear into the crowded hallway. Spotting the girl's restroom ahead, I shove my way inside, claiming the first available stall. I hold out a full ten seconds before the sob claws its way out of my throat. Turns out Mr. Moinyhan was right.

It's not homecoming without a girl crying in a bathroom.

NOW

A week has passed since the night I thought Ambrose would kiss me. *The night I wanted him to kiss me.*

He sticks to his word and continues working on the house when he's not handling business at the zoo. I flew through the projects Helen set aside for me and now I've resorted to filling my time with crossword puzzles and Pinterest boards, which are strangely addicting.

When Ambrose showed up today, with sheets of wood in tow, I offered to install the porch stairs myself.

He laughed in my face.

Otso accompanies him outside, lounging near his feet. In his presence, the beast is a far cry from his usual temperament. He's relaxed and at ease. So much so, he could be considered a lapdog if not for his monstrous size. I have no idea how he came to be that comfortable around Ambrose. I still brace myself every morning when I leave my room in anticipation of being tackled by him.

Considering the fact Ambrose has been slaving away in the heat for hours on what was supposed to be my project, I figure the least I can do is bring out a pitcher of lemonade. I even add my secret ingredient, clover honey. I slip into a pair of cutoff shorts and an old band tee before heading outside.

"I come bearing gifts," I say, setting the pitcher and two glasses down on the railing.

Ambrose drags a tattered rag across his face and downs the entire glass in silence. Then another one. And another one.

"Wow. Either you're on the brink of dehydration or I make better lemonade than I thought."

Returning to the stairs, he grunts. "Both." His eyes flicker to the front door. "How is he?"

I know my dad can't hear me, but I lower my voice anyway. "As good as someone in hospice can be, I guess. I think talking makes him tired, so we mainly just sit in silence, watching movies and stuff." Clasping my hands behind my back, I remember the other reason I came out here. "Oh. Before I forget"—I pull out the magazine tucked into my back pocket—"my dad's still getting his *National Geographic* subscription even though I'm pretty sure he tried to cancel it years ago. You collect them, right?"

"I do." Mild surprise flickers through his eyes before he takes it and starts flipping through the pages. "Thanks."

I sip on my lemonade for a few seconds, unsure if I should go back inside. We haven't spoken much since that night at the bar. He's been at my house every day for the past week, yet he feels further than ever.

"The stairs are looking great," I offer.

"Thanks."

"Really. Better than I could have done. I bet your work on the house alone will be enough to get the realtor to raise the asking price."

He hums in agreement.

"You know, I'm sure—"

"I should get back to this if I'm going to finish by this afternoon."

Hearing his dismissal loud and clear, I duck my head. He's already shown me more kindness than he should—of course he's reached his limit.

Stupid, stupid, stupid girl.

He's here as a favor to my dad. Nothing more.

I collect the pitcher and glasses in my arms, faltering back a step when a scream rings out across the street.

Otso raises his head and barks, immediately alert.

Squinting my eyes, I follow the sounds coming from the house next door to Ambrose's. Anya and Matty's house. Anya's standing in the driveway, seething at a man who holds her forearms in a vice-like grip. I can't make out what he's saying to her but soon she yelps again, clearly in pain.

Ambrose drops his tools and starts speed walking toward the pair. I rush to tie Otso's leash around the railing and run to catch up to him.

"Anya!" he barks. "What the hell is going on?"

Anya whips her head around, still in the man's clutches, searching Ambrose's face for understanding.

I don't bother looking for Matty. He's spending the day with Laura at the park.

"Nothing, Ambrose. We're fine, we're just having a little discussion."

I move out from behind Ambrose. "Then why is he grabbing you like that? Doesn't he know how to use his words?"

Anya glares at me, but it fails to overshadow the fear she has of the man towering over her like a predator. His detached gaze lands on me and I stiffen. "I can use my words," he slurs. "I can do lots of things with my mouth. Wanna see?"

Ambrose growls through clenched teeth, "Don't you fucking talk to her. Don't even *look* at her."

His laugh raises the hair on my arms. "You were the one who came butting into our business, man. Let me talk to my girlfriend alone."

He tries to pull Anya away, but she looks at Ambrose, the plea clear in her eyes.

"You're not stepping a foot in that fucking house. Get the hell out of here or I will assist you myself."

He pauses and then laughs again, releasing Anya. His sinister smile is something out of a horror movie.

"No problem." He leans into Anya's ear, whispering something that makes her flinch before getting into his beat-up Toyota Corolla.

Anya doesn't waste time shifting her anger to me. "You just love inserting yourself into people's lives, don't you?"

I crumple at the accusation. "I wasn't trying to cross a line. I thought he was hurting you."

Ambrose lifts a hesitant hand toward Anya and she trembles like she's a frightened animal backed into a corner. "Anya, let's go inside."

"I'm not going anywhere with *her*," she shrieks, eyes bloodshot and wild.

I wait for Ambrose to come to my defense, but he just looks at me and jerks his chin in the direction of my house.

Feeling like I've been punched in the gut, I inhale a sharp breath. "I'll let you two be."

I walk back home with my tail between my legs, infuriated that I've let myself get involved.

What the hell am I doing?

I came here for one purpose. None of that includes getting mixed up with Ambrose again. I think back on what Laura said and mentally kick myself for not heeding her advice. Once inside, Otso plops on the floor, staring at me in earnest before licking my toes.

I make myself dinner—a sad recreation of Laura's pork fried rice—and curl up alone at the kitchenette. The only sound comes from the grandfather clock on the wall and its steady ticking puts me on edge. It's too quiet and soon the intrusive thoughts will bulldoze their way into the forefront of my mind. It's moments like these that make me want to drown everything out with music and raise the volume until my eardrums burst.

But I don't want that for me anymore.

I've never wanted that. I want to listen to the world and not be afraid of what I'll hear.

Teeth brushed and pajamas on, I crawl into bed. I thumb through my streaming app, searching for something with Julia Roberts in it. I'm halfway through *My Best Friend's Wedding* when I hear a *thump* at my window.

I disregard it.

A minute later, the *thump* rattles my window again, this time in a succession of three and I realize someone's throwing pebbles at my window. I jump out of bed, unlock the latch, and peer down.

"What are you doing here?" I hiss.

Ambrose looks completely relaxed with his hands buried in his pockets and it throws me off. Like we weren't just in an extremely awkward situation a few hours ago. "I need to show you something."

I don't know why, but that annoys me. "I'm going to bed. *Goodnight.*"

"Meet me in the backyard in five."

Hope flutters within me, and I stomp it down immediately, narrowing my eyes. "No."

He starts walking off, his voice floating away with him. "Meet me in five."

"Ambrose, I'm not coming down there," I whisper-yell. I no longer see his body. "Ambrose!"

I growl in frustration. *Jerk.*

I pull a ratty old sweatshirt over my tank top and change into a pair of leggings. I creep downstairs, careful not to make any noise.

The backyard is a sea of darkness and I stumble around, tripping on twigs and rocks. Speck Lake doesn't care much for streetlights. There's hardly a need when everyone knows everyone and cares for each other so well. They don't have to worry about monsters hiding in the shadows here.

After an extensive search, I spot Ambrose's silhouette in the corner of my eye. His body looms in the dark, still and stealthy. I know every inch of this backyard, but his presence makes me feel like the intruder. I close the gap between us.

"Is this where you kill me? Because if it is, I would have chosen a better outfit to be found in."

A sound that resembles a laugh escapes Ambrose, but without the ability to see his face, I can't be sure.

"What did you want to show me?"

A faint click and then the glow of a flashlight.

He steps to the side and only then do I realize we're standing next to Old Maple.

He tilts the flashlight, illuminating the small grin on his face before allowing it to disappear in the dark again. "Take a look."

I stare back at him, confused. I've been out here a million times. I know what Old Maple looks like better than anyone else. I raise my eyes to the old tree and the tree house that rests upon it. Air whooshes from my lungs, rendering me speechless.

Old Maple's tree house looks brand new. New in a way that highlights what it's always been, but more aesthetically pleasing. It looks *safer*.

The cracks in the roof and walls are filled and the stairs jutting out from the tree have been replaced. It looks like you can climb them now without fearing for your life.

The rot that's been taking over one of the windows has been taken care of and there's a little pulley system installed with a basket hanging on the end.

I can't look away.

"What did you do?" I whisper.

"When the real estate agent saw the tree house, she wanted me to tear it down. She said it was an 'eyesore.' I told her it was a part of the house and it needed to stay. She thought it would hurt the chances of getting a buyer if that was part of the stipulations, so I promised to fix it up—make it a bit more marketable. She conceded in the end."

I look at him then with utter disbelief. This man continues to surprise me. "But... why?"

His eyes soften, even in the dark. "You've lost enough."

Those three words rock me and I have to readjust my stance to keep from crumbling into dust on the ground. I don't speak, terrified that if I open my mouth, all the little broken pieces inside me will fall out.

Gentle fingers circle my risk. "Come up with me?"

We climb Old Maple together for the first time in a long time. Thanks to the new stairs, the climb only takes a few seconds and part of me wants to laugh at how much of a struggle getting up here used to be. Ambrose enters ahead of me and when I crawl my way inside, he has his body folded in on itself.

I notice my hands and knees don't ache like they used to when I'd climb inside. "Did you install *carpet* in here?"

The hearty laugh filling the air answers my question. I lay flat on my back next to him and we sit in comfortable silence for a few minutes.

"This tree house used to be our entire world," I whisper. "And now it feels like a tiny matchbox."

His shoulder grazes mine. "It served its purpose. Made us happy all those years." I can tell his head turns on his side to face me, but my eyes stay glued to the ceiling. "But we were never meant to stay this small."

I want to drown out his words.

Because I want to be small again. I want to hide away and disappear into the crevices of these walls. The world is too expansive—its mouth is always opened wide and ready to swallow us whole.

Something tickles my nose and I prop myself up on my elbows, sniffing the air. I lean closer to Ambrose where the scent gets stronger. Forgetting myself, I pat the front pocket of his shirt and thrust my fingers inside where I find the source of the delicious sweet scent. "Um. Why do you have sea salt caramels in your pocket?"

Ambrose looks at me like I've lost it, but then his chest rumbles.

"Answer me." I chuckle, smacking his arm. "You used to hate these!"

"What are you, some kind of bloodhound?" He laughs. "I carry them around for Matty. He's obsessed. I think it's starting to become a problem."

I pop one into my mouth and hum with pure delight. Pulling the rest of the caramels from his pocket, Ambrose drops them into my hand. "Here, have them all." He snorts. "I know they're your favorite."

I look at him sideways. "You remembered that?"

"I remember everything about you."

My mouth goes dry as I lick my salted lips.

I remember everything about you too. Everything about us.

I clear my throat. "You said you were helping my dad because you owed him. What do you owe him for?"

He sighs and turns away from me, taking all the heat with him.

I want it back more than I'm willing to admit.

"Summer after your graduation, I got into some trouble." He takes the wrapper from my hands and tucks it into his pocket before going on. "Last thing I wanted was to go back to school. I stayed in town for a few months and honestly, I turned into a shit person. Let my emotions get the best of me. Drank too much. And before I knew it, I was picking fights with people whose only offense was crossing my path. I was the worst version of myself."

He takes a deep breath.

"When your dad caught wind of what was going on, he got on my case. He had a way of talking to me that made me listen. You know my parents never mastered that. He bailed me out every time I was taken to the station for fighting. *Every* time. He started dragging me along for small builds around town. Nothing fancy, just things to do with my hands so they wouldn't find their way back to people's faces. If not for him, I'd probably be behind bars right now. He pushed me to go back to school. I owe him everything."

There are no words. Nothing I imagined comes close to what Ambrose just confessed. I don't waste time wondering why my dad didn't tell me about how badly he was struggling. When I left Speck Lake, I made it clear I was leaving its people behind too.

He smooths out the crease in my forehead with his thumb. "Hey, I understand why you left. I'd never hold it against you."

I nod. It's all I can do.

Ambrose repositions himself too many times for being confined to such a small space and I can tell he wants to ask me something.

"Just spit it out."

He turns onto his side and lifts his head, cradling it in his hand. "Why haven't you visited Cat since you've been back?"

The ringing in my ears is surprising considering I've been waiting for this question. But that's the funny thing about painful words. Anticipating them doesn't make them hurt any less. Sweat breaks out across my forehead as if the small matchbox we sit in is catching fire. My body knows to run before my mind does and I scramble up onto my knees, feeling around for the exit.

Ambrose grabs my arm. "Mouse, stop."

I yank it away too forcefully and it collides with the wall behind me. I curse under my breath, cradling my elbow in my hand. "Don't call me that."

"What are you so afraid of? You know she'd love it if you visited her."

"Oh, really? Did she tell you that?"

Ambrose flinches as if I've smacked him.

"I'm sorry," I breathe. "I'm sorry. I'm sorry."

We stare at each other in the dark.

Two broken people, trapped between four walls that look shiny and new.

"I'm not ready to see her, Ambrose," I whisper. "Not like that."

He wants to push me. He wants to push me and a small part of me *wants* to be pushed. But I'm self-aware enough to know that if he pushes me right now, I'll hit the road running. It's in my blood.

Instead, he reaches behind his head, flipping a switch I hadn't noticed. The inside of the tree house is flooded in warm amber from the firefly lights woven intricately across the ceiling.

He lifts his chin toward the entrance and there's not a trace of anger when he says, "So you can see where you're going."

"Why didn't you have those lights on the whole time?" I grumble, making my way out the way we came.

His warm breath curls around my ears. "Some things are easier to say in the dark."

THEN

AGE FIFTEEN

C hristmas reigns supreme.

It's the only time of year when everyone everywhere agrees that you should put your responsibilities on the back burner and partake in all things cozy, warm, and joyful. I'm convinced even the Grinch loved Christmas and what he truly disliked was annoying people, and can you blame him for that?

This year feels cozier, warmer, and more joyful now that I'm Brandon Lang's girlfriend.

When he asked me to be his girlfriend after homecoming a year ago, I said yes without hesitation. I thought that's just what you're supposed to *do*. Boy asks out girl. Girl feels lucky. Girl says yes. And so, I'm Brandon's girlfriend and I tell myself I'm happy. But more than being his girlfriend, I'm happy to belong to someone. I like that someone besides Cat waits for me by my locker and searches for me in the lunchroom. It's addictive—feeling seen. Feeling wanted.

On our first anniversary, I give Brandon a poster of his favorite comedian and he gives me a necklace with an infinity charm at its center. When I ask him what it means, he says, *"that we'll be together forever."* I don't feel that kind of commitment to him yet, but I nod and clasp the necklace around my neck anyway. I'm seen and I'm wanted.

Brandon dated other girls before me, but he's my first real relationship. He assures me that while I'm new to the world of dating, I'm the best girl he's ever been with and his favorite kisser. I never know how to respond when he says that.

I enjoy kissing Brandon, though I don't have much to compare it to. Every now and then when I lie in my bed and stare at the glowing green stars glued to my ceiling, I wonder why I don't replay Brandon's kisses at night like I do the kiss on the cheek I received years ago. But then I push the thought away before it riddles me with anxiety. *I'm seen and I'm wanted.*

Christmas break only began two days ago, but Speck Lake is in full holiday mode. Cat and Ambrose left for Florida to visit their extended family and I'm missing Cat more than ever. She spends every Christmas away, but this year feels different. We're fifteen and the throes of high school have ushered us into a weird phase of our friendship. Cat made varsity cheer and I spend most of my time writing reviews for the film club.

The downside is that we're busy all the time. When I don't have a deadline, Cat has a competition. When Cat doesn't have a game, I have films to catch up on. We continue to eat lunch together, but it's becoming apparent that our presence is highly sought out by our respective groups. Still, we cling to each other like white on rice.

With only three days left before Christmas, I invited Brandon to come over and build gingerbread houses with me. He's late and I've become impatient. I'm ready to attack the cookies and frosting with my mouth.

The doorbell rings and I jump up from the kitchen table. I pass my dad sitting in his armchair and he leans farther into it as if he had no intention of getting up anyway. I don't understand why he gives Brandon such a hard time.

I narrow my eyes, pointing a finger in warning. "*Be nice.*"

He rolls his eyes like a defiant two-year-old.

I open the door, ready to leap into my boyfriend's arm, but stop short when I see—

"Ambrose." My face falls. "Why are you here?"

His brow quirks. "Is that how you greet all your visitors?" His hands slip into his denim jacket as he waits for... well, I don't know what he's waiting for because I'm not inviting him in.

"How are you here right now? You're supposed to be in Clearwater with your family."

"But I'm not, am I? I'm here with you." He steps up to the threshold and dammit, I falter back a step. When he pushes past me, my mouth hangs open.

My dad's voice booms from the living room. "Close the door! You're letting all the warm air out."

"That's not how it works," I mutter.

I shut the door and stomp toward Ambrose as he hangs his jacket on a hook. "You can't be here," I hiss, keeping my voice low. "Brandon will be here any minute."

"What is *Blandon* up to these days?" he drawls, shaking the snow from his hair onto me.

I gasp. "You little mother—"

"Finally!" My dad laughs, scooping Ambrose into a bear hug. "I was waiting on you to get here. You want some coffee?"

"This isn't happening." I groan, pressing into my temples. "I'm a good person, so this isn't happening."

"Coffee would be great, Sol."

"*Sol*?"

Ignoring me, the two of them disappear into the kitchen, cracking jokes along the way like they're a part of some boys' club. I grab Ambrose's jacket off the hook and shove it into a nearby closet just as the bell rings again.

When I answer, Brandon's already smiling, looking more handsome than ever. He's bundled in a mustard peacoat, eyes glistening thanks to the high winds outside.

"Hi." He grins.

My heart doesn't flutter erratically, but it does flutter.

"Hi right back." I lean over the doorframe for a quick kiss. "Is your dad home?"

"Yes, I'm home!" my dad shouts.

"Kill me now," I mutter.

I take Brandon's hand and lead him straight into the kitchen, blocking his view of my dad and Ambrose. Deep down, we all know that's everyone's preference.

The old wooden table is covered in everything I bought this morning. I spent an hour organizing the bottles of icing, unwrapping the mini candied decorations and placing the gingerbread house pieces on each side of the table.

Brandon lays his coat over the chair, facing me, a tight smile marring his beautiful face. "You started without me?"

My smile falters. "I just took all the stuff out and organized it. I wanted it all to be ready for you, see?"

"Gotcha." His lips thin into straight lines. "Just thought it would have been nice to do it together. I didn't realize you wanted us to get through it so quickly."

I gasp, my eyes widening like saucers. "That's not it at all, I—"

"Hey." He chuckles, touching my arm gently. "It's okay. You didn't know. We all make mistakes."

Ambrose's heavy boots stomp across the floor and my dad's hand shoots out, clutching his shirt. "Why don't you come help me with something, son," he murmurs.

I force a smile, pulling out a chair. "Let's start."

We sit back, appreciating our work. Brandon reaches across the table for a high-five, and I laugh with pure satisfaction.

"Alright, babe. Dig in."

I whoop and break off the door of my gingerbread house, mercilessly shoving it into my mouth. He laughs and shakes his head, nibbling on the mini marshmallows from his roof. My dad saunters in and heads straight for the coffee maker. He refills his mug and places it in the microwave before coming over to observe our work.

Well, my work. He couldn't have given a rat's ass about Brandon's gingerbread house.

He scratches at the scruff along his jawline. "Yellow icing? Why didn't you go with blue?"

"Because yellow's her favorite color," Brandon interjects.

My dad frowns. "Her favorite color is blue," he says states matter-of-factly.

"I don't believe it is, sir."

Ambrose walks in. "How about Mara gets to decide what her favorite color is, hmm?"

Brandon looks at me then, waiting for me to settle the debate, and I writhe in discomfort. "My favorite color's yellow now."

I turn away as my dad frowns and Ambrose shakes his head.

An hour later when Brandon leaves through the front door, I announce that I'm going to take a nap and run upstairs, opening my window as he climbs up the trellis.

We splay ourselves across my bed, a jumbled mess of long limbs and warm hands exploring each other. I love moments like this with him. Everything's instinctual and I'm not required to take part in the mental Olympics of figuring out what I should or shouldn't say to him. I never disappoint him when it comes to my body.

Brandon kisses down the length of my neck and blows gently into the hollow of my collarbone, knowing it's one of my tickle spots and I giggle and squirm beneath him. His fingers linger at the waistband of my sweatpants, grazing the skin below centimeter by centimeter, testing his limits. When his thumb hooks the band of my underwear, I quickly roll out from underneath him, knocking the picture frame off the side table with my elbow.

"Shit."

I reach down to pick it up, but Brandon beats me to it. "Why do you still have this?" he asks. "You're all basically strangers now."

I snatch it from his hands and clutch it tightly to my chest. "Cat and I are still friends."

"Barely."

I sit up straighter. "What's that supposed to mean?"

He rolls his eyes, clearly annoyed. "Nothing. Please don't make this into something it isn't."

"Sorry."

"It's okay," he says, leaning over to kiss my cheek. Then, "I'm gonna head out. My dad comes back from his work trip today and I promised my mom I'd help make sure the house is spotless."

My heart softens. Brandon loves his mom immensely and doesn't care who knows it. I've only met his dad a few times, but it was enough to know that his idea of love is throwing money at people instead of developing an actual relationship. Whenever I ask questions about how they get along, Brandon brushes me off. I've stopped asking.

"Give Sheryl my love. And if you need any help with the cleaning, call me. I have nothing else planned for today."

Brandon shifts uncomfortably before giving me a quick nod. "Later."

I secure the latch on the window and settle back into bed, exhaustion seeping into my bones in a matter of seconds. Maybe I do need that nap. I stare at the framed photo—the last picture I have in my head before I go to bed each night. I allow the memories flowing through me to remind me of simpler times and soothe the unacknowledged ache in my chest. And as I drift to sleep, the comment I made only a few hours earlier wriggles in the recesses of my mind.

It's not my favorite, I realize.

The color yellow.

Christmas has only been officially over for seventy-two hours, but I already miss it. Dad and I spend the day curled up on our couch, rewatching classics like *It's a Wonderful Life* and *White Christmas*. My mom calls in the afternoon on her way to some swanky Christmas party thrown by vagabond artists. I can barely hear her above the backdrop of busy streets and pedestrians, but she assures me my gift is on its way.

"It's an Yves Saint Laurent lipstick set. All red. *Very* Parisian."

"Isn't that supposed to be a surprise?" I say, popping a marshmallow into my mouth.

"You're too old for surprises, *bebita*."

"Okay, Mom." I roll my eyes so hard, I'm surprised they don't get stuck in the back of my head. "I mailed you your gift too, but I'm not sure when it'll get to you. Customs confuses me."

"That's okay, baby. I have everything I need here."

Except me.

I'm not there, but that will never be a deal breaker for her. My dad glances over with pity in his eyes.

My voice hardens. "Well, since you don't care for surprises, it's a scarf. You probably already have scarves—*Parisian* scarves, so feel free to toss it to the back of your closet. Listen, we're in the middle of a movie so I'll talk to you later. Merry Christmas, bye." I slam my thumb on the *End* button before she can respond and toss my phone.

"Mara—"

"Look, it's my favorite part," I cut him off, hitting play.

He lets it go.

The Kings return home the next day. Cat and I haven't spoken for a week—a record for us—but when I text her asking if she's still up for hanging out, she responds with one word: *duh.*

We agree to meet at a small lake in the woods, a spot we've claimed as our own for years. Our hidden oasis. In the summer, the surrounding trees glint like emerald jewels and the winters transform it into something straight out of a Robert Frost poem.

I'm lacing up my winter boots when my phone dings.

Cat: Bring the sticks.

Me: Seriously?

Cat: Yeah. Hung out with the fam for too long and didn't have Ambrose there to balance out the torture. Need to get out some aggression.

Me: Um... Am I gonna get the brunt of this aggression?

Cat: You know it.

We haven't played ice hockey on the lake since Ambrose stopped hanging out with us. He was usually the referee and would talk Cat down when her competitiveness turned her into a mountain lion. I don't even care if we just pass the puck back and forth together, it'll be fun to reinstate the childhood tradition.

I trudge through the snow, finding my walk more enjoyable with the playlist I saved for winter. There's something about listening to Bon Iver when everything is cold and barren that just feels *right*. I inhale the cold air, letting his words carry me through the familiar trees, their hunched back branches marked by the passing of time.

A twig snaps behind me, and I whip my head around, yanking out an earbud. The woods are still and empty except for the muffled music humming in my clenched fist.

"Hello?"

Another snap sounds to my left and I jump in place.

"Boo!" a voice bellows, hands clamping down on my shoulders as I scream.

Cat stumbles back in laughter, clenching at the side of her navy coat.

"Cat!" I yell. "You're the absolute worst, I almost peed myself!"

She swipes a single tear from her cheek. "Oh Sally, you should have seen your face."

She imitates my reaction and I smack her playfully on the shoulder. I can never stay mad at her when she uses the nickname from our favorite movie.

"You two done?"

I scoff at the sight of Ambrose. "You again?"

"Again?" Cat asks, puzzled.

"What's he doing here?"

"I asked him to come. Practically made me beg. It'll be like old times!" She claps, elbowing Ambrose in his side.

He reaches for the hockey sticks under my arms as if his presence isn't an anomaly. "Couldn't leave you two out here to play alone. Knowing you ladies, only one of you would make it out of these woods."

"How chivalrous of you," I mumble under my breath.

Only Ambrose would make hanging out with us sound like he's volunteering his time at a charity event.

I swerve on my heels and head toward the lake. We break through the clearing and all my pent-up frustration dissipates. The ice on the lake is slick and untouched, proof that this place is still our best-kept secret. The trees reflect off the glass-like surface and I know exactly which colors my mom would use to recreate the scene. Sugilite blue and serpentine green.

"Ah, music to my ears." Cat throws her head back, smiling at the chirping birds above us, a curtain of golden waves spilling down her back.

Ambrose pipes up, a hint of excitement in his voice that even he can't hide. "I think they're robins."

We walk onto the ice without skates because we never use them. A long time ago, we realized that the risk of slipping and sliding on your shoes was a big part of the fun. My hair whips around my face and I use a silk scarf to tie it at the nape of my neck.

When my mom gave me this scarf, she went on and on about how it's designer and shouldn't be worn frivolously.

So naturally, I'm wearing it for outdoor horseplay.

"How should we decide who takes which side?" Cat asks.

The left side of the lake puts a player at a disadvantage due to a slope under the water. It makes the ice slightly uneven and you have to constantly be aware of your balance and coordination.

I hate the left side.

"What about Rock, Paper, Scissors?" I ask.

Ambrose smirks. "Aw, she's sentimental. How sweet is that?"

Cat jabs him in the rib and he grunts. "Don't be a dick."

"Who taught you to talk like that?"

She shrugs. "Maitland."

"And what else has *Maitland* taught you?"

Her grin is mischievous. "Oh, brother, I'm not sure you even want to know—"

Ambrose clamps his hand over her mouth, muffling her laughs as his face turns red. His eyes whip to me. "Mara. Pick something."

I unsuccessfully muffle my laugh behind my hand. "Okay. What about guessing a number one through ten?"

They both nod in agreement.

"Alright. I have it," Ambrose says. "What are your guesses?"

I choose four, my lucky number, while Cat picks seven.

"The number was six. Cat, you get the right side."

Cat hollers in excitement and I narrow my eyes at Ambrose. He probably gave me the left side on purpose but there's also no way for me to prove it.

"Stay on your toes, Mouse." He grins, making his way to the starting point.

I mutter an insult behind his back. Such a prick.

We position ourselves in the middle of the lake, bringing together the tips of our hockey sticks. Despite Ambrose's taunts, excitement hums through me. Out here, it's just the three of us like it used to be. A little older. A lot changed. But still just us three. Ambrose holds the puck above our heads, counting down from five. Before his mouth has the chance to form around *one*, a voice calls out from the edge of the woods.

"What do we have going on here?"

Brandon is already making his way onto the ice, the rest of us staring at him in shocked silence. My body stays frozen in place as he stops at my side, his warm lips meeting mine in greeting. They make me feel colder.

I find my voice. "What are you doing here?"

"I'm here to play."

"I mean, how did you *know* I was here?"

He shrugs nonchalantly. "I followed you."

I feel exposed and embarrassed, too embarrassed to turn toward Ambrose and Cat and see the judgment on their faces.

"We already have enough people," Ambrose responds through clenched teeth.

I steal a glance at Cat and her glare is identical to her brother's.

Brandon laughs, but it's condescending. "Well, now that I'm here, there's four of us. If my math's correct, that means we could easily do a two-on-two."

"Let's just go back to my house," I suggest, tugging on his sleeve.

He doesn't take his eyes off Ambrose. "Come on, man," he goads. "Look at you. Surely you can't be intimidated by someone like me."

To a stranger, it might sound like Brandon is being playful, but I recognized the challenge in his voice. Ambrose hears it too and takes the bait.

"Your funeral. Cat, you're with me."

Ambrose ushers Cat a few feet away to discuss their game plan while I stare at my boyfriend in horror. "Brandon. I told you I was hanging out with Cat today."

He smiles at me, but his words are ice. "I stopped by your house as you were leaving. You left your copy of *Wuthering Heights* at my place. I just wanted to see where it was you were sneaking off to in the middle of the woods. I wasn't even going to stay."

He moves closer to my ear, his whisper harsher than any scream could be. "But then I saw *him*. It's suspicious that my girlfriend doesn't want me to know that she's hanging around another guy, don't you think?"

My nose burns at the accusation. "I didn't even know he was coming! Cat invited him without telling me. I would never lie to you about that."

"Are you both ready or do you need a room?" Ambrose shouts, walking back our way.

Their approaching bodies are blurry and I quickly rub at my eyes. Ambrose looks from me to Brandon, his jaw locking while Cat's mouth turns downward.

I clap my mittens together and smile. "Let's do it! We're gonna crush you two."

Not even fifteen minutes pass before I realize that I spoke too soon. Brandon and I don't crush anything except our dignity.

The score is 10-2, much to Ambrose's satisfaction. What started as light banter has quickly turned into outright trash talk between the guys and Cat and I take turns rolling our eyes at their testosterone battle. Ambrose even refuses to use his inhaler when he clearly needs it.

Brandon snaps at me every few minutes, claiming I'm tripping over my feet too much or getting in his way, while Ambrose and Cat move fluidly around the ice, anticipating each other's moves.

When the score reaches fifteen for Cat and Ambrose, I throw my arms up in defeat, completely out of breath. I'll gladly give them the win if it means I can finally go home and defrost myself in a hot bath.

"I concede!" I yell. They're less than twenty feet away from us, but the winds have picked up, making it difficult to hear.

Brandon makes a disgruntled noise behind me and I turn as he slams the hockey stick onto the ice with shameless anger.

A soft *crack* escapes from where his stick makes contact, causing tiny fracture lines to stretch out toward my boots. In any other situation, the near-quiet breaking might have been a beautiful sight. Mesmerizing, even. But I'm aware of what it means here on this fragile spot of the lake.

"Hey! Don't do that. It's dangerous," Ambrose says, speeding over. His voice is serious and firm, losing all traces of the boy who pretends not to care.

"Do what? *This?*" Brandon slams the hockey stick on the ice again. The crack thunders through the air and the harsh sound reverberates in my ears. The hairline fractures become fissures and I yelp.

"Knock it off!" Cat yells.

Brandon's face morphs into an ugly mask of defiance, making him unrecognizable. He crashes his stick down again with a laugh, downplaying the gravity of the situation. The fissures turn into chunks of ice dislodging into the water at random spots around our feet. My limbs scream at me to run, but fear leaves me immobilized.

"Brandon, stop!" I cry.

"*Are you out of your mind?*" Ambrose bellows, veins bulging from his neck.

Brandon stops abruptly.

His body loosens and it's as if he's escorted the unhinged stranger who'd just taken control of his body back into the recesses of his mind.

"Relax." He laughs, tossing the stick across the ice at Ambrose's feet. "I was just playing around."

Cat glares at him before stomping away. Ambrose doesn't move an inch and for a moment I think he might punch Brandon in the face. I kind of want him to.

What happens next occurs too quickly for me to fully comprehend.

It takes less time than it does for someone to say "*One, Mississippi.*" Less time than it takes for me to realize that my last inhale of oxygen should have been a generous one because it was going to be my last.

I'm on the ice with Ambrose and Brandon, and then I'm not.

The freezing water is a knife stabbing every exposed inch of skin. My brain becomes sluggish like it's being dragged through the mud as it tries to catch up with what's happening. The first thing that comes to mind is how dark the bottom of the lake looks considering how bright it is outside. My throat constricts and my body thrashes about as it kicks into survival mode.

My hands stretch above my head, confusion and panic washing over me when they're met with solid resistance.

I'm floating away from the hole I fell through.

I flap my arms through the darkness and they propel me in different directions. I search for the hole, but my obstructed vision prevents me from finding my way out. Intrusive thoughts override my focus.

You're gonna die, they say. *You're gonna die, you're gonna die, you're gonna die.*

My legs go slack as I swallow more water. I don't feel so cold anymore and I welcome the warmth starting at my toes, and working its way upward. I cast my eyes above me once more. The sun has reached its peak in the sky, making the translucent ice above me glow with gold and I think *this must be what it's like to be trapped inside of a snow globe.*

The first thing I become aware of is warmth. Not warmth from being numb too long—true warmth. My feet are bundled in something plush and snug and the comfort makes me want to slip back into unconsciousness.

The next thing I become aware of is the mumbles. The voices fail at their attempts at whispering and float around my head, causing me to burrow farther into my cocoon. My muscles cry out as I move and I whimper in pain.

"Mara, honey? Are you awake?"

My dad's voice is close and I can smell the familiar scent of coffee on his breath. Words feeling too far away to grasp, I groan in response.

"I need you to sit up if you can. Show us you're alright."

Worry laces his voice, so I blink open my eyes and slowly heft my body into a sitting position. Focusing in on my surroundings, I see who the remaining voices belong to. Cat and Alima both sit on my bed, peering at me with identical expressions of relief. My dad exhales deeply, some of the tension disappearing from his shoulders.

"What happened?" I rub my eyes.

Cat scoots closer to me. "You fell through the ice. Drifted away from the hole... we couldn't find you."

Her eyes well up and I squeeze her hand. The hollows beneath her eyes are purple and I can feel her hand trembling in mine.

"I remember." I try to clear my scratchy voice but it's no use. "I tried finding my way back to it. I tried—"

"Shhh." Alima smooths back my hair. "No need to relive it. You're safe now."

"How did I get out?"

My dad scratches the back of his head. It must pain him having to talk about this. "You wouldn't have if that boy wasn't so *stupid* as to jump in after you," he says, but there's a hint of admiration in his voice.

Worry hits me straight in the chest. "Is Brandon okay? Where is he?"

"Brandon?"

"You said he jumped in to save me. Is he alright?"

My dad's jaw goes slack. "*Brandon* didn't save shit. That boy clammed up the moment you hit the water. Ambrose is the one who pulled you out of there."

I deadpan. "Ambrose?"

"Ambrose," he repeats.

I wait for the shoe to drop, for Brandon to jump out of my closet and tell me they're joking. Alima glides forward, cutting the tension. "What Brandon did was very irresponsible. We're just glad Ambrose was there and you're okay, Mara." Her voice is soft, but even I can make out the way her jaw tightens around Brandon's name.

My eyes survey the room. "Where is he?"

Cat and her mom look at each other, exchanging looks like they aren't entirely sure what to tell me and my heart thrashes around in my chest.

"*Where's Ambrose?*" I demand.

It's my dad who answers. "Stuck in bed, just like you. He's alright—just has a nasty ear infection."

I ignore the pain radiating through my body as I climb out of bed. Alima holds up both hands, running to block the door.

"Whoa, whoa, whoa. You're not going anywhere, little lady."

I yank a hoodie over my head.

"Mara Jimenez Makinen, you get back in that bed this instant," my dad orders. He never uses my full name and if I didn't hurt so badly, I'd laugh at how foreign it sounds on his tongue.

Cat sighs, inspecting her nails. "I don't know why you two even bother. You know she's not going to listen."

The truth behind her words must resonate with them because no one stops me as I leave the house and hobble over to 164 Winsome Lane. I refuse Robby's help, taking the stairs alone, biting the inside of my cheek to stop from passing out from the pain. I don't knock before barging into Ambrose's room.

"Why do you look like you're running from the cops?"

Ambrose sits upright against his headboard, a book perched on his knees. His contacts are out and black glasses frame his tired eyes. I allow myself an indulgent glance at his exposed chest.

I did almost *die* for crying out loud.

"I always knew you were dumb, but I didn't realize you had a death wish," I say, breathless as I lower myself onto the corner of his bed.

My near-death experience has made me feel rather bold. Plus, I'm afraid if I stand any longer, I might faint.

Ambrose's eyes flit to the bruised cut on my chin. "It's not like I could let my little sister's best friend die." He flips the page in his book with force. "What kind of brother would that make me?"

"You could have let Brandon save me. I'm *his* girlfriend."

His laugh is hollow. "If I'd left it to him, you wouldn't be sitting here right now."

The weight of that truth slams into me.

"Or maybe he would have saved you," he mutters. "I don't know. I didn't give him a chance—I jumped in right after you fell through."

I appreciate him trying to ease my embarrassment over the fact that my boyfriend left me for dead and it's a kind mercy I wouldn't have expected from him.

I chew at my nail—my worst habit. "You're kind of like the young George Bailey."

He scrunches his eyebrows.

"George Bailey. From *It's A Wonderful Life*. When he was a kid, his little brother falls through the ice while they were sledding. George jumps in after him, saves him, and gets an ear infection. You're George. I'm little Harry Bailey, the damsel in distress," I ramble. "I guess technically, he couldn't be a damsel in distress since he's a boy. The very fact that there isn't a male equivalent to a damsel in distress is *so* sexist and—"

"Why does he do it?" Ambrose whispers, almost to himself.

"What?"

"Why does George risk his life to save him?"

I trace the stitching on his quilt with my thumb. When I look up, I hold on to his gaze like he held on to me under that ice.

"Because he loves him."

NOW

The nightmares started last week and haven't let up since.

Sleep is hard to come by as it is but now the few hours I manage to get are being compromised as well. I've traded one nightmare for another.

I can still recall Laura's face when she told me that my dad's health had some new developments. It was code for *he's getting worse*.

But she didn't have to tell me. Because I can hear the way his body is giving out on him from all the way upstairs.

Feeling my way through the dark, I grab the glass of water on my nightstand. When I realize it's empty, I grunt in frustration.

Sliding out of bed, I step into my softest pair of slippers, the only ones quiet enough not to wake Otso. The rickety stairs are silent beneath the soles of my feet and I make my way to the fridge without the need for a light. I may not be the architect of this house, but I can find my way around with my eyes closed. This home of mine is embedded into the very fabric of my being.

I fill my glass to the brim and gently nudge the fridge door closed. It's when I pass my dad's door that I hear it.

Hear him.

Laura said the wheezing was normal, but it doesn't sound normal. It sounds unfair and unjust.

Help him, help him, help him.

My hand reaches for the doorknob but then hesitates. Maybe it's the nightmares, the fear, or even the lack of sleep, but a part of me feels like I'd do more harm than good. I don't have the words to soothe him.

It's an aching realization, realizing I'm not the kind of daughter he needs. I'm scared and small. A shell constantly on the brink of cracking. I can't offer the comfort he truly needs. How can I carry him when I can hardly carry myself?

Yanking my hand away, I quickly retreat upstairs and settle back into bed, the nightmare that woke me already fading into a distant memory.

I succumbed to my fears tonight.

But I will try again tomorrow.

Ambrose hasn't been by the house in a week and I pretend the only reason I know that is because the realtor called three times asking for an update on the house. Potential buyers are getting antsy and I want to tell them all to shove it.

Every day when my hands tackle a new project outside, I debate walking across the street to check in on him.

I could say something about needing his opinion on a paint primer or an outdoor light fixture but pride prevents me from doing so. Thanks to the internet, I've learned my fair share about home improvement and I won't play dumb to quench my curiosity. Not even for Ambrose.

So when I spot a skinny white envelope with *Ambrose* scrawled across the top resting on the kitchen table and Laura tells me it's a check, I jump on the opportunity and insist on delivering it myself.

"Are you sure?" Laura hesitates. "You might have to force him to take the money. That boy doesn't budge."

"I'm sure," I say. "Anyway, I'm already on my way out and I need to ask him something about fixing up the dock."

If Laura calls my bluff, she's kind enough not to verbalize it. I run upstairs for a quick shower. If I'm going to lie about needing to leave the house, I may as well run a few errands. I've been meaning to go back to The Plant Shack and buy more plants for my dad's room. Maybe if I surround him with other living things, he won't notice that my visitations have slowed down.

Envelope clutched in hand, I knock on Ambrose's door.

The last time I saw him was in the comfort of Old Maple. But now in the light of day, everything within me says to retreat, to disregard the secrets we divulged in the dark.

The door opens and my smile falters when I see that it's Anya. Sunlight flickers over her face, highlighting her puffy eyes and hollow cheeks. The only sign of life in her body is the disdain that burns through her as she looks at me.

"Yes?" she says coolly.

"Is Ambrose here?"

"Does he look like he's here?"

The smart-ass in me begs to rear its nasty head. *How would I know if you answered the door?* But it's a Tuesday morning. I can take the high road on a Tuesday morning.

"Well, when you see him, can you tell him to stop by the house? I have a check for him." I wave the envelope in my hand.

I wouldn't dare leave the money with Anya and she's smart enough not to suggest the idea herself. I turn to leave, but her voice follows close behind.

"Do you want to wait inside until he comes back? He should be here in a few." I meet her saccharine smile and it immediately makes me sweat.

A trap.

She's a siren beckoning me toward the dark, murky waters and alarms sound off in my mind, but I still reply, "Sure."

Like a dumbass.

Following close on her heels, she leads me into a den that bears no resemblance to the one I remembered. I create as much distance between us by settling onto the sofa—a deep, L-shaped monster that looks like it came from a modern design catalog.

I examine the rest of the room while she taps away on her phone.

The accent pieces scattered throughout the den are sleek and sophisticated. Sexy. The only thing I recognize here is the antique teak entertainment center. And the shelves are still packed with an absurd amount of VHS and DVD movies. My eyes travel to the corner of the bottom shelf where *Practical Magic* is.

"Promise me, Mar. Promise we'll always be sisters like Sally and Gilly."

"I promise."

"Where I go, you go, right?"

"Where you go, I go, Cat."

"So," Anya pierces the silence. "Ambrose tells me you've known each other since childhood." Her tone is bored, but her eyes are sharp. Predatory.

"Yes," is all I say.

"I've seen photos. Ambrose was all bean pole when he was Matty's age." At the mention of her son, her eyes gentle for a second before resuming their harsh state. A sly smirk plays on her face. "He's way more good-looking now, don't you think?"

She's dangling the bait right in front of me, urging me to take a bite.

"Where is Matty today?" I breathe.

She shifts her attention to a snagged piece of thread on the couch cushion. "At a friend's house."

My mind drifts to Laura and for a reason I can't pinpoint, the idea of Anya having a sibling fills me with unease. And the fact that it's someone so kind and selfless makes it even more bizarre. I fold the envelope in my hand.

"Maybe I should just give this back to Laura to pass on to Ambrose. She seems to know his schedule a lot better."

Anya's face sours. "*Laura* sent you? Why didn't she drop it off herself?"

I shrug. "I offered. She's been swamped lately."

"Sounds like Laura." She scoffs, flipping her hair back. "So good at playing martyr, she doesn't even have to ask people to do her bidding."

A sense of protectiveness for my new friend washes over me. "Laura's not like that."

"That's the impression she gives me."

"That's surprising."

"And why is that?"

"I'd have thought at least her little sister would think better of her."

Anya's eyes narrow in on me.

I've caught her off guard.

She didn't expect that we'd both know intimate information about the other. It's immature, but I revel in the small win.

Leaning forward, she props her elbows on her knees. "You know nobody wants you back here, right?" Her voice is barely a whisper. "It's because you're a coward."

There she is.

I've been waiting for the beast to come out. Why bother luring me into the den when she could've just ripped my head off at the door? Her words sting, but I can't say that I disagree with her. I am a coward. A coward who abandoned everyone I loved when I couldn't face the repercussions of my actions.

"I want to be gone just as much as you want me gone, Anya."

She freezes at my admission and I almost laugh.

Poor girl doesn't realize that I hate myself more than anyone else ever could.

The front door opens and her jaw goes tight. "He's made peace with what happened," she whispers. "Don't drag him back to that place—he blamed himself enough."

My throat seizes. "What did you just say?"

Ambrose rounds the corner, stopping short at the sight of me and Anya sitting across from each other.

My hands tremble and I slip them under my thighs, bearing down hard enough to focus on the pain instead of Anya's words.

Our silence is a tangible entity.

"Mara. What are you doing here?"

He doesn't move any farther into the room, but his scent is already settling into the space, making me heady. Anya doesn't say a word, more than happy to let me fend for myself.

"I was on my way out and thought I'd drop off this check to you. Laura's been busy." I clear my throat. "And you have to accept the money. Laura won't take no for an answer."

Not a complete lie.

I hold up the envelope as evidence, the tremor in my hand causing it to billow in the air like a kite. I lean forward, dropping it on the coffee table.

Ambrose's eyes jump from me to Anya, trying to assess the temperature of the room.

"I should get going." I fumble to grab my purse and keys from the floor.

When Ambrose says nothing, I duck my chin and make a beeline for the front door. Heavy boots trail behind me.

"Wait."

I turn around, wishing so badly that I hadn't. Will it always hurt to look at him?

Ambrose rubs the back of his neck. "I don't mean to be rude, it's just... I haven't seen you in this house since you were seventeen. Kind of caught me off-guard."

Oh.

I glance over his shoulder to the den as memories play out across my vision. Ambrose destroying me and Cat on the Wii. Alima setting down a platter of cookies and hot chocolate—even in the summer—while we watched *Practical Magic* for the millionth time. Ambrose ignoring my existence when we all started growing apart.

"I understand," I whisper.

Anya's words dance through my mind.

He blamed himself. I did that to him.

I mumble an excuse about being on a time crunch for the rest of the day before slipping out the door. And I realize that for the first time in a long time, it's a struggle to run away.

I don't know how long I've been posted up on this cold metal stool at Bottlegrounds, sipping away at my drink.

No matter how long you sit on metal stools, they always stay cold, biting into your skin, and keeping you from getting too comfortable. But it doesn't matter. I'm never comfortable.

I dig in my purse for coins to feed to the jukebox. The country music playing overhead isn't helping my mental state.

"Oh shit, look what the city rats dragged in."

A rambunctious laugh comes from the corner of the bar and my head shoots up. The man approaches me slowly and I take my time perusing the length of him. His features are hard to make out in the dim lighting, but it's no question he's tall and *very* good-looking. Doesn't vodka make everyone good-looking though?

He slides onto the stool next to me and rests his face in his hand, eyes briefly dropping to my drink. "Hi, Mara Makinen."

The way he says my name...

His lips twist into a smirk.

"Dean." I laugh, dropping my face into my hands. "Because of course it's you."

Only now do I see the same Dean Healey who charmed his way through school when we were kids. His boyish charm has been replaced with something more manly and assertive, but that *smirk*. That smirk confirms that Dean could still stare a girl into whatever whim he conjures up.

I offer him a small smile. "Hi."

"What brings you back to Speck?" He takes a swig of his beer, waving off the guys he was hanging with as they leave for the night.

"I have family affairs to see to." My teeth punch into my lemon wedge. "I'm not staying long."

The ever-present playful expression on Dean's face becomes subdued and it's an unusual sight. "Heard about that. I'm sorry."

"Thanks."

Sitting here with him feels weird. We aren't friends.

Dean shrugs off his jacket and asks the bartender for a round of shots.

I give him a questioning look.

"What?" He grins. "You know what they say: those who speak, do; those who can't, drink."

My head falls back with a laugh as I accept the shot in front of me and clink it with his. "*Salute*."

An unidentified number of shots later and I have to say, the brute with the easy smile can get you to toss spirits back like it's water. I'm officially at the point where the drunken giggles flow freely.

"So what are you up to these days?" I ask.

"I'm a pilot."

I gasp. "You are not."

"Four years now." He lifts an amused brow. "I don't know if I should be pleased or offended by the shock on your face."

"No, no, it's amazing!" I rush. "Sorry, I'm just surprised is all. I always thought you'd be like, a bull rider or something."

"Yeah, well, turns out the boy who couldn't keep his feet still on the ground belonged in the sky."

That makes me smile. "I'm happy for you, Dean."

He drags his finger along the rim of his glass, a contemplative look on his face. "You know, I used to have the biggest crush on you."

I cough out a laugh. "Excuse me?"

"Yep."

"No, you *didn't*. Get out of here with that." I chuck my balled-up napkin at his face and he easily deflects it with a grin. "You barely talked to me when I came around your little posse."

"Only because you were already spoken for."

"Bullshit." I snort. "Brandon and I didn't start dating until my freshman year."

"I wasn't talking about Brandon."

My mouth hangs open, but nothing comes out.

"Don't worry about it," he says, his tone playful again. "It never would have worked out between us anyway."

"And why is that?" The tension retreats again.

"I don't do good girls."

"Gross, did you just say *good girls*?"

I laugh so hard that some of my drink splashes onto him.

"Have you seen him yet?" Then he shakes his head with a laugh. "What am I saying? Of course you have. You two always find your way back to each other."

That soothes something in me.

"I don't know." I sigh. "My life is complicated. So is his."

"Ah, so you've met Anya."

A frown tugs at my mouth. "You know her?"

Dean shifts in his seat, diverting his gaze. "Sort of. How's she doing?"

"I wouldn't know," I say, narrowing my eyes with suspicion. There's something in his face that I've never seen before. A genuine sense of concern and if my eyes aren't deceiving me... affection.

He cares for her.

"Uh oh." I giggle, wagging a finger in his face.

"What?"

"You're in deep shit, my friend. You've got that look in your eye."

He points at his chest and mouths *me?* before laughing. "What look might that be?"

"Trouble, that's what it is." I wave down the bartender for another round and pat his arm. "Welcome to the circus."

For the next hour, we talk about a whole lot of nothing, and yet we're content. Being around Dean is easy and casual. Nothing like being around Ambrose.

As if thinking about him sends up a distress signal, my phone starts buzzing against my thigh.

Ambrose.

We swapped numbers a few weeks ago when we needed to coordinate a supplies drop-off for the house, but we haven't used the method of contact since. Until now.

Hey, I need to grab a toolbox I left in your dad's garage. Can I stop by?

Not wanting to appear like I have nothing better to do than keep my eyes glued to my phone all day, I let the message sit for a few minutes. I take my turn at the dart board before I type back:

I'm not home.

I'm sweating. *Why am I fucking sweating?*

Afraid of seeing how long it takes him to message back, I motion to Jackson to pass me another shot, to which he responds with an enthusiastic clap. My phone pings.

Where are you?

Ambrose's forwardness isn't unusual. He's not one to beat around the bush. If he wants to know something, he'll ask. I glance at the clock on the wall that says it's eleven thirty. Everything in town besides the bar is closed by this time and I can't risk getting caught in a lie, so I type:

At Bottlegrounds with an old friend.

His response is immediate.

You don't have friends.

I gasp and begin typing with a vengeance, unfazed by how careless I'm being with my spelling.

Firdst of alll, how would you know???

Dean hits the bullseye and I stomp in frustration as my phone pings once more.

I'd know.

I tell him he's being rude by sending him a gif of Stephanie Tanner and just when I think the conversation may be over, he shoots off another message.

How are you planning on getting home?

I slump against the wall.

His interrogation's chipping away at the fun I'm trying to convince myself I'm having.

I don't know how I'll get home. I'm drunk, but not irresponsible enough to attempt driving myself. I'd ask Dean, but he's just as drunk as I am and I wouldn't be surprised if he has a list of girls who'd come rescue him from himself and tuck him into bed tonight.

As if I don't already feel terrible about my life decisions, a dull pain begins spreading through my temples. I lazily surf the internet for a taxi service that might still be open at this time while Dean restarts our game of darts, singing off-key to the song playing overhead.

When the bar entrance jingles, I don't bother looking up.

I'm not sure I could if I wanted to. My head feels like a bowling ball weighed down in my arms.

Dean straightens on the stool beside me, waving to someone I can't see. I'm about to just give up and fall asleep when a warm hand presses up against my lower back. I shudder out a breath when I meet Ambrose's hard eyes.

"Let's go." He tugs me off the stool, his posture tight.

I look at Dean and frown, my vision drifting in and out. "You traitorous man. I thought we had something."

His laugh is soft as he signs for the large tab we've created. "I'm sorry you had to find out this way, beautiful. You got her, man?"

"Always."

Ambrose carries most of my weight as I walk on shaky legs to the door. His arms around me are firm, yet incredibly gentle. I keep the image of my bed at the forefront of my mind as motivation to keep my body from completely shutting down.

When we reach his car, I balk at the sight of Anya in the passenger seat. I stumble backward, gravel scattering beneath my boots.

"On second thought, I don't need a ride," I slur.

"Oh, really?" he grits. "And how will you get home?"

"My friend."

Ambrose crosses his arms. "What's your friend's name?"

"Car."

"Your friend's name is *Car*?"

I'm swaying now. "Cara. I meant, Cara."

Before I can escape, Ambrose draws closer, dwarfing my small frame. "Get in the damn car."

I puff out my chest and lower my voice as deep as it can go, imitating him. "*Get in the damn car.* Oh, look at me, I'm Ambrose and I can be bossy because I'm as tall as the Chrysler Building." I roll my eyes, scoffing. "You know, you can't tell me what—"

Ambrose lifts me over his shoulder like I weigh no more than a sack of flour and I shriek. He swings the door to the back seat open, chucking me inside. Reaching for the seat belt, he attempts to buckle me in, but I swat at his hand and he makes a sound of frustration.

"Brat."

"Caveman!" I snarl.

When he sticks his key into the ignition, I turn my head and let out an embarrassed groan at the sight of the fourth person in the car.

Matty.

He's half asleep, but my yelling must have roused him because he stares at me with rapt attention from his booster seat. I lean my head against the window, unable to face him in my pathetic state.

As we drive, I force my eyes shut and lean my head against the window. Ambrose and Anya's voices in the front are hushed, but I don't have the energy to eavesdrop.

Once I'm sure we're in my driveway, I immediately let myself out. I blindly stumble up the porch stairs and try multiple times to get my key into the keyhole, telling myself it's taking so long because it's pitch-black outside.

I don't fight Ambrose when he pulls the key from my hand, opening the door himself, and I don't fight him when he laces his fingers with mine, pulling me inside.

Silence engulfs us as we watch each other in the darkness of the entryway and I stand there awkwardly, waiting for him to leave so I can collapse right here on the floor and sleep.

He blows out a harsh breath and scoops me up into his arms. I'm too drunk to be embarrassed as I wrap my arms around him and bury my face into his neck.

When he sits me on the edge of my bed and my body flops backward like a dead weight, he pulls out his phone and starts typing. Slipping it back into his pocket, he pulls me into an upright position.

"Where are your pajamas, Mara?"

"Dirty," I mumble. My face falls forward, thumping against his stomach.

He sighs and gently lays me back down, moving away toward the dresser in the corner. I turn my head to its side. "You don't have to be here," I whisper, my eyes getting heavier and heavier. "I didn't ask for your help."

Soft hands on me and a silken voice curling around my ear. "You didn't have to."

I don't recall kicking off my shoes or tucking myself into bed or even wrapping my curls up in a silk scarf, but when I wake in the middle of the night with a large glass of water by my face in nothing but an oversized T-shirt and fuzzy socks, I can still smell the fresh linen scent lingering on my skin.

THEN

AGE FIFTEEN

A lot of girls my age would kill to spend their summers in Paris, but I'm not one of them.

In another life, I'd be enamored by the magic of the city. I'd appreciate the twinkling lights of the Eiffel Tower that look like fireflies when you squint your eyes.

I'd be glad to eat my body weight in the fresh baguettes wafting through the windows on early foggy mornings. I'd walk a little slower while passing the live musicians outside the hole-in-the-wall cafés who play as if they need the music more to survive than the money being tossed into their hats. I'd see Paris for all it has to offer.

But I have qualms with the City of Light.

Paris is not the bearer of my wanderlust, but my bitterness. Paris is the shiny thing that stole my mom away from our family, enticing her with its glitter and gold. No, Paris isn't a lover of mine and I vowed from the age of ten that it never would be.

So when I'm forced to visit the city every summer as per my parents' divorce agreement, I do so with as much pushback as I can muster and this summer is no different.

When I step off the plane, my mom's gaze immediately drops to my graphic tee, which reads: *Paris: The City You Smell Before You See*.

"Very funny," she mutters, pulling me in for a tight embrace.

She smells the same even though everything is different. Vanilla with a hint of rose. For a second, I abandon my stoicism and embrace her back, inhaling her scent as my eyes sting.

Every year she looks younger and more alive like she's aging in reverse. There's a lively bounce in her step and she manages to turn heads in every space she occupies. She's pure vibrancy and I understand why the city won't give her back to me. She doesn't belong in Speck Lake.

"How was your flight?" she asks.

I readjust the duffel on my shoulder and shrug. "It was fine. The plane food wasn't half bad this time."

She laughs and I notice a stranger in my peripheral vision smiling at her in return. "Well, if that's where your standards are, I haven't done a good job at exposing you to all the food Paris has to offer. Are you hungry? There's this little Moroccan place that just opened right next to my flat and the kefta mkaouara is *divine*. We can beat the dinner rush if we head straight there."

She's already thumbing through her phone, searching for an open reservation when I put my hand over hers. "Mom, I'm exhausted. I'm sorry. Is it okay if we rain check?"

Her shoulders stiffen, but she doesn't express any negative emotions. She never does.

Feel something. Anything. Show me that it's okay to do so.

She squeezes my hand with a smile. "Sure. Let's get you some rest."

The next morning I stir awake to the smell of fresh croissants. The sun slips through the drapes that hang in the guest room and a male's laughter mixes with my mom's in the kitchen. I brush my teeth before throwing on a clean pair of jeans and a T-shirt I got when I joined the film club at school. If the only thing standing between me and fresh croissants is a few minutes of small talk, I'll do it.

Small sacrifices.

"*Bonjour*, Mara!" Jean-Paul exclaims, pulling me in for a hug before I'm fully in the kitchen. My arms hang limply at my sides until he lets go.

"JP." I accept the mug of coffee my mom extends toward me.

Jean-Paul resembles a wind-up toy that can go and *go*. It's like someone wound him up and he malfunctioned, never knowing when to stop.

He's always happy—which makes me suspicious—and he always smells like praline. He's a baker, a prestigious one according to Parisian standards, which explains the croissants.

I don't have anything against Jean-Paul. In fact, under any other circumstance, I might enjoy being around him. But like Paris, Jean-Paul is relegated to the side of my list of *things I refuse to love on principle*.

"So, what are we to do today?" he says, clapping his hands in excitement. I've known him for two years now and every time he speaks, I picture the little French candle from *Beauty and the Beast*. If he weren't a baker, he could be a model. He's one of the most beautiful men I've ever seen. Rich ebony skin glows against deep-set eyes the color of clay. I can't help but wonder if my mom's not only obsessed with pretty things and pretty places but pretty people as well.

The silence becomes unbearable as we watch each other. My mom always makes me feel welcome during my visits, but we never actually spend much time together. She prioritizes her art and leaves me to my own devices while she drowns herself in her work. I've already made a list of the new bookstores and cafés I plan on exploring today.

She clears her throat. Her hand swoops down to grab a chignon pin from the counter and twists her unruly curls into a bun at the nape of her neck. People say I'm a mirror image of her and I can only hope it stops at our looks. "I need to get in some studio time. Julien has been pestering me about the second phase of my ceramic series and I'm more than behind. Mara, there's food in the fridge if you get hungry." With a thin shawl wrapped tightly around her shoulders, she smiles like her reasoning is sufficient.

Turning to Jean-Paul, I bring the warm mug to my lips. "I'm heading to a few bookstores to look for a biography on Joan of Arc. I need to write a summer report on her, but thank you for—"

"Wait a minute," he says, gawking at us. "Isabel, it's her summer vacation. We must spend the time together." I can't tell if his frown is on my behalf or not.

My mom tightens the shawl around herself, pinning me with a pleading look, practically begging me to get her out of spending time with me. It's almost comical.

I give him my most casual smile. "I'll be here for weeks, JP. We'll have enough time for everything."

Relief pours off my mom in waves and I brush it off before I can let it wound me. Jean-Paul looks unconvinced, but eventually, he concedes.

"Fine." He stares directly at my mother. "But the Paris International Film Festival is in two weeks. Mara, I know you enjoy films. We will all go. *Together.*"

There's heavy reproach in his voice and my mom quickly agrees to appease him, giving us each a peck on the cheek before zooming out the door. I don't know what impresses me more; the fact that he's pushed back with my mom or the fact that he remembered my love of film.

Using my mom's exit as a distraction for my own, I backtrack toward the guest room, reaching out to snag one of the croissants on the way. Before I can wrap my fingers around the delicious piece of heaven, Jean-Paul intercepts, lifting the entire plate into his arms. He smiles broadly, showcasing a mouth full of perfectly straight white teeth.

"Have breakfast with me."

My narrowed eyes say *well played* and his quirked brow says *I know.*

We squeeze into the tiny kitchen nook and I waste no time stuffing my face with the croissant. The filling is dark chocolate—warm and gooey with slivers of almonds in the center. These croissants alone make the trip worth it.

JP passes me an extra napkin while using his own to brush the crumbs off his shirt. "So. You have a boyfriend, yes?"

"Yes," I say, taking another bite.

He grins. "What is the name of this lucky gentleman?"

I garble around the chunks of pastry in my mouth. "Brandon."

Amusement flickers over Jean-Paul's face and he begins to laugh.

I bristle, sitting up straighter. "What's so funny?"

He laughs again, reaching for another croissant, this time one with assorted nuts over the top. "Usually when a lady speaks of the one she loves, she glows like the Seine River at night. I ask you about your love and you'd think I asked you about the weather."

I shift in my chair, which isn't a chair, but a repurposed stool. It's uncomfortable as hell.

Artists.

"Of course I love Brandon, he's my boyfriend."

"Ah. Because you cannot have one without the other?"

The question is more inquisitive than harsh and I take a moment to mull it over. Do I assume I love Brandon only because we're in a relationship?

Jean-Paul interrupts my thoughts by gently tapping my hand. "Don't let my curiosity alarm you. I'm nothing but a rambling old man. I've been letting the poetry get to my head."

I grimace, checking the time on my phone. "I should go get ready." I put my plate in the sink and snag another croissant for later.

"Mara," he calls, and I turn at the waist. "Keep me updated. On what you learn of Joan of Arc."

My smile is genuine then. I give him a quick nod and close the door behind me.

The bookstore is smaller than any I've seen—even in Speck Lake—which is saying something. But despite its modest size, the tiny nook houses more books than any other bookstore I've visited. Books of all genres are haphazardly strewn about, stacked on chairs and tables and even the floor. How a person can find what they're looking for is beyond me and eventually, I conclude that the purpose of this place may be for the book to find *you*.

I wander around the two aisles, careful not to knock over the stacks at my feet and before long I'm staring sideways at a tower of biographies, not one indicating Joan of Arc as its subject. I refrain from sighing in frustration at the place's lack of organization, afraid the sound will echo. There's another bookstore I found on my map that's only a few blocks down. Maybe I'll have more luck there.

"Can I help you find something?" The woman's voice is unnervingly close and I jump back in surprise, bumping into the nearest book tower, causing a few to fall onto the floor.

Apologizing profusely, I bend over to retrieve them. Hopefully, they aren't damaged. I only have thirty euros to my name right now.

"Leave them."

I peek at her from my crouched position, confused. Leave them? Leave the precious new books on the floor like dirty old shoes? The horror in my expression causes the corner of her mouth to twitch. Not quite a smile, but more of a suggestion of one.

THE TWO OF US

"If a person cares only for the words inside when the outside is pristine, the person doesn't care very much at all to begin with." And with that, she turns on her heels, heading back to the front counter.

"Wait!" I stumble after her.

She pulls books out of a big brown box and begins organizing them into piles in front of her. Only her raised eyebrow indicates to me that she's listening.

"Do you have anything on Joan of Arc?"

She stamps the books as she nods. "The nineteen-year-old peasant girl who heard voices from God. I have two. The first is a shorter read covering more of her life before the war. The second is an all-encompassing history. That's the one you'll need if you *truly* want to understand the warrior. Though, I can't see why a young *chérie* like you would spend all her time reading instead of taking part in the many mistakes Paris has to offer."

I scrunch my nose. "Why would I want to make mistakes?"

For the first time, she smiles and it lights up the cramped, dingy bookstore. "Sometimes mistakes are fun." She winks.

She's older than my mom, but I can't pinpoint her age. Not that it matters. Like most of the women I've seen in Paris, she's effortlessly beautiful. She's not attempted to cover the crow's feet hugging her eyes or filling the lines around her mouth. Her face says she's well-lived and isn't a stranger to laughter—so much so, the remnants have permanently etched themselves onto her face.

I pull the coin purse from my messenger bag. "I'd like the full history, please."

She nods like she's proud of me. "Great choice."

While she sets off to a corner of the store that looks like it's been ransacked by a group of bandits, I move toward the woven baskets off to the side. According to the sign, handmade trinkets created by local artisans lie inside, each unique and one of a kind. I pull a few out to inspect, admiring their magical quality. The same sort of magic that only exists in a city like Paris.

I gently move each piece aside and a glimmer catches my eye. It's a suncatcher in the shape of a small cat curled in on itself. It's a tiny little thing, taking up little space in the palm of my hand and I lift it to the morning light pouring in from the window. I twist the cat side to side and fractured light breaks off in a million directions, drowning books and surfaces and my skin in rainbow streaks. I hold the entire color spectrum in my hand.

"That one is the last of its kind. The artist who makes them, Céline, has advanced Rheumatoid Arthritis and can no longer work with her hands. Her son brought over the last of her pieces and they sold out in a day. Must have gotten lost at the bottom."

When I look up, her expression is grim and I wonder if she knows Céline personally. If she feels the pain in her own hands whenever she talks about her.

I twirl it in the light once more. "I'll take it."

I place the suncatcher on the counter alongside the biography she retrieved from the back. As she searches for tissue paper to wrap my purchases in, something else from the basket catches my eye. I only need to examine it for a few seconds to know it was created for him. We don't speak anymore and I'll probably never give it to him, but I have to buy it if only to hold on to it for safekeeping. I set the piece on the counter for the woman to include in my purchase.

"Fifty euros," she says and I blanch in embarrassment.

I should have asked how much each item costs before allowing her to wrap them up so nicely.

"I'm so sorry." I spread my money out on the counter before digging through the spare pockets in my bag for spare change. "I'm a bit short." I assess the items one by one, weighing the importance of each. "Can you take out the book?"

Nodding, she carries the brown bag toward the register behind her and retrieves my receipt. When I take the bag from her, confusion fills me. It's weighty. I peek inside, seeing all three items.

"Excuse me, I think you made a mistake. I didn't give you enough money for all this."

"Like I said, *chérie*, sometimes mistakes are fun."

The next two weeks pass in a blur as I spend every spare moment I have reading about Joan of Arc. I jump in and out of bookstores, binge French films, and devour every baked piece of heaven Jean-Paul brings home each morning. He tries not to hover and I show my gratitude by offering him a fact about Joan of Arc each time we cross paths. My mom remains entranced in her work and the only times I see her are before bed when she comes in to say good night, buried under layers of dried clay and linseed oil.

I've all but forgotten about the film festival until Jean-Paul comes home one evening and stands in my open doorway, hands on his hips.

"Um, *bonjour*?" I say.

"I know *casual* is the American way of life, but to wear sweatpants to the Paris International Film Festival? Mara. This hurts me."

My eyes widen and shoot to the calendar hung up on the wall.

"You forgot." Jean-Paul sounds relieved. "If you get ready quickly, we will still have good seats on the grass. We leave in twenty minutes, yes?"

"Yes!" I dive for the towel on my desk and start rummaging through my suitcase for something presentable to wear. "What about Mom?"

"She will meet us there."

Forty-five minutes later we pull into the parking lot of the festival. I grab the tote at my feet before stepping out of the car, triple-checking that I remembered to bring a small blanket and light sweater. When Jean-Paul pops open his trunk, I hold in my laugh.

Packed side by side is two tote bags and a picnic basket overflowing with items he's packed for the night. An assortment of quilts and mini pillows and a basket that makes a clinking noise of glass-on-glass when he picks it up. It doesn't take a genius to guess the contents. I'm pretty sure wine runs through his veins.

Surprisingly, we made good time and we end up snatching the spot closest to the jumbo screen. Families and friends scatter about on their blankets and mats and I wonder if we all look like a quilted blanket from an aerial view. The mini stage erected beneath the screen with has a handful of chairs and microphones resting on them.

"After each film, the director and some of the cast will give us insight and answer questions from the audience." Jean-Paul points.

I nod, keeping my eyes locked on the stage, feeling excitement bubble beneath my skin. I've never had the opportunity to witness something so close to the entertainment industry. In Speck Lake, I can watch all the movies I want, but here I get a sneak peek behind the veil.

A tall, lanky guy who looks like an intern steps onto the stage, letting everyone know that the first film of the night, a black-and-white indie called *La Lune est à Nous*, begins in ten minutes.

I tap Jean-Paul's shoulder as he organizes his makeshift charcuterie board. "Is she close?"

He glances down at his phone, shoulders tense. "She should be here any second now."

The chatter around us dies down as everyone begins settling in. The opening credits dance across the screen and Jean-Paul leans in, whispering something about my mom running a little late due to an issue with the master kiln at her studio. I push back at the hurt begging for entrance in my chest and focus on the film. I'm not shocked, but that fact does little to lessen the blow.

About a third of the way through the film, Jean-Paul whispers through gritted teeth that my mom is only going to be able to make it for the second film and I lift a shoulder in indifference, consumed by the conflict taking place on the screen. The heroine, Colette, is contemplating how to tell her lover, Françoise, that she's responsible for his brother's death.

Halfway through the second showing of the night, a film noir called *Une Vie D'ombres*, I turn my attention to Jean-Paul. He single-handedly crushed a bottle of wine by himself, disappointment weighing down his hunched shoulders.

"These films are great, JP. Never would have heard about them without you bringing me here, so thank you."

Weary eyes meet mine. "I'm sorry, Mara." A slight shake of the head. "I don't see how she could do this."

I don't have the heart to tell him that this isn't out of the ordinary. That my mother flaking out on me feels like a natural aspect of our relationship.

"It's really okay." I pat his arm with a smile, trying to lighten the mood. "She's been like this since I was a kid."

He flinches at that before taking a swig from the new bottle of wine he's just opened. "She's an enigma, your mother," he rasps.

I grow still.

"When I married her, I thought: there it is, there is the light I've been searching for. She was a blazing torch, an ember in the flames, and if you were lucky enough to be in her presence, she shone on you. Danced around you with that... with that *glow* of hers." He twists the silver band on his finger. "But she is selfish. I don't think she means to be. She simply... can't see the people or things beyond her own light."

I slip my hands under my blanket to hide their trembling.

"And I love her," he whispers like it's a curse and a blessing. "I would choose to disappear in her light any day. But I am sorry for you, Mara. I am sorry that you did not get to choose."

I keep my eyes glued to the screen, holding my breath to keep the tremor in my throat at bay.

JP affords me a small mercy and returns to his cheeses and wines, not pushing the conversation any further. And when the film ends, I join the crowd as we stand to our feet for a standing ovation. We're all strangers and yet, I feel less alone.

We trek back to the parking lot and load up the car. Settling into the front seat, I pull my book on Joan of Arc into my lap. He drives in silence as I read and when we return to the flat, it's dark and empty, my mother nowhere to be found. I chuck my shoes off by the door, muttering a halfhearted good night.

"You'll have to let me know your thoughts when you read about Joan of Arc surrendering to Lyonnel de Wandomme."

I stop short, turning around slowly. "What did you just say?"

When Jean-Paul realizes what he's just done, he grunts and face-palms with an embarrassed laugh. "Forgive me. I've had too much wine and look, now I have gone and spoiled the surprise."

"You... you already know the history of Joan of Arc?"

He blinks once. Then again. "Yes."

"How?"

He examines his fingernail before lifting a shoulder an inch. "I took a class on the life of Joan of Arc when I worked toward my license, er—I believe it is called an *undergraduate degree* in the states."

He yawns behind his hand and neatly tucks his shoes in the corner before pouring himself a tall glass of water. He's completely nonchalant as if he hasn't just told me that he's practically an expert on the *one* topic I've been rambling about for the past two weeks.

Baffled, I ask, "Why?"

He doesn't miss a beat. "Why what?"

"Why let me go on and on every day about her life? Why sit there through it all? You probably know more than I do—why listen to me?"

He tips his glass back, chugging the rest of his water. Shrugs off his jacket and throws it on the coat rack in the entryway and when he returns, his eyes are solid.

"Because you have things to say. And people should listen."

NOW

I'm watching *Casablanca* on my phone and answering work emails when Laura calls out for me.

I drag my feet downstairs and find her hunkered down in a chair, rubbing an alcohol swab over the top of my dad's hand.

"Can you grab my medical bag from the living room? I think I left it on the sofa."

I nod and when I return with the bag, I sit beside my dad's sleeping body. I run my finger along the purple veins in his free hand, hopeful that he'll sense my touch in some way. Laura gives him something I assume helps with the pain and I watch intently. She rubs her eyes, tension pulling at her shoulders.

The longer I stand here, the more anxious I become.

"Is there anything else I can get you, Laura?"

She shakes her head, avoiding my eyes.

"Okay." I start to leave but then take a step closer to her instead. "Are you sure everything's alright?"

"Yes, honey," she says, pinching the bridge of her nose. "I'm sorry, I don't mean to be so detached. Your father needed some extra attention last night and I didn't head home until three. Now my sister has gone MIA and my nephew is staying with me." She sighs. "I shouldn't be throwing my problems onto you."

"Anya's missing?"

"Haven't heard from her in two days. It's not unusual for her to dump Matty on me or Ambrose, but she usually at least calls."

Overwhelming concern seeps off Laura. I'm by no means friendly with Anya, but I don't wish any ill will upon her.

"I'll keep an eye out for her, okay?"

She nods, but there's no relief in her eyes. She resembles a woman who's lived a thousand lives and in every single one of them, she's her sister's keeper. I can relate to that because it's how it used to be between Cat and me.

I let thoughts of her in then. Not for very long, maybe a second or two. A brief allowance. I speculate where she is right now and if she's happy. In the days of protruding collarbones and knobby knees, I was her keeper and she was mine. Who kept her now?

I could go see her. I owe her that much. But that would require courage and that word has never been synonymous with Mara Makinen.

Leaning over the bed, I kiss my dad's cheek and I feel the tug of the wave. The wave of emotions that would wash me away and obliterate my existence if I let it. But I can't. Because if I do, I'm not sure I'll ever recover.

"Slow down or we're going back."

I give Otso my best authoritative stare but he continues to pull me along like I don't need my arm to remain attached to my body.

He leads me back toward the front yard and I pretend to be impressed when he drops a stick at my feet like a peasant offering a gift to the royal court. I'm *oohing* and *aahing* over one particularly impressive branch when someone calls my name.

Matty bounds across the street, running for no good reason, the way little kids always do. With flushed cheeks as bright as his hair, he reminds me of a little fox chasing a rabbit with haste.

"Hey, little man." I smile, widening my stance so Otso doesn't run off and drag me along like a rag doll.

Matty stops by almost every day now and I've gotten used to seeing his face around my yard. At this point, I think I even look forward to it. Go figure.

"Can you show me my surprise now?" he says, cutting to the chase.

I snort. "You waste no time, I see. Come on, it's in the back."

We end up in the backyard, just a few feet in front of Old Maple. I jerk my chin toward the small box resting against the bottom of the trunk.

"No *way*," he whispers, peeking inside. "How did you find it?"

I position Otso behind me before leaning over the baby squirrel curled up into a ball. Its eyes are closed but one tiny leg twitches every few seconds, letting me know it's still alive. Hopefully, the warm rice sock I placed next to it will help until its mom comes back.

"Must have fallen out of the tree," I say.

"Will it be okay?"

"I think so. Everything I read online said mother squirrels usually come back for their babies. But if she doesn't come back by tonight, there's a wildlife rehab place in Bangor I can call."

Matty bends down and whispers, "Keep fighting."

My heart nearly explodes.

I guide us away from the tree, not wanting to spook the mother squirrel just in case she comes back sooner rather than later.

"Mara?"

"Yeah?"

"You're pretty cool."

I stop walking as my mouth hangs wide open. Sweet, gooey warmth fills my chest. That is *not* what I expected.

Getting a compliment from a kid is one of the most satisfying things in the entire world because they can be brutally honest. One time a third grader I babysat told me my green sweater looked like vomit and I got rid of it the next day. "You really think so?"

He nods. "I think that's why Ambrose likes you so much. You just *got it.*"

I throw my head back, laughing at that. "Oh yeah? And what's '*it*'?"

"I dunno." He shrugs. "The thing that he needs."

My heart stalls in my chest and I'm no sap, but my eyes immediately water.

I don't think Matty understands how meaningful his words are. One thing I've learned since meeting him is that people don't give kids enough credit. They're inquisitive and thoughtful. Smarter than we think and often underestimated. They could probably teach us a lot if the world wasn't so hellbent on convincing them they don't know what they're talking about.

"I have it too, you know," he adds confidently and that gets me laughing even harder this time. I wipe the tear escaping my left eye as I try to catch my breath. "I can see that."

"Because I'm kind, and good at soccer, and I help people get up when they fall."

"That's nice—"

"I'll show you. Fall."

"What? I—"

"Fall!"

"Okay!"

I throw myself down onto the ground, biting back my laughter as Matty struggles with all his might to try and pull me up. He tugs and tugs, his face turning beet red, but my slack body doesn't budge. Otso jumps around in excitement, licking my face as I squeal.

"How come no one invited me to the party?"

I whip my head around as Ambrose stares down at us, a ghost of a smile pulling at his lips.

"Ambrose," I breathe, scrambling to stand. "Hi."

He reaches forward, pulling a leaf from my hair and my face burns. "Hi."

"What are you up to—h-how are you?"

"Ambrose is taking me on an expedition!"

I want to squeeze Matty and give him a lifetime supply of ice cream for butting in. "Expedition?"

Ambrose purses his lips and my gaze shamelessly latches on to his mouth. "Matty here doesn't believe that the Mourning Dove is the most wide-spread backyard bird in North America. Says he has to 'see it to believe it.'"

I give Otso's ear a scratch. "I don't know, I might be with Matty on this one. I've never seen a Moring Dove either."

"*Mourning* Dove," Ambrose corrects with a frown. "And just because you haven't seen it doesn't mean it's not there."

Matty and I smirk at each other, secretly reveling in the fact that we both know how to get under Ambrose's skin. When Otso pulls on the leash, sniffing in the direction of a squirrel, Matty asks if he can walk him for a minute. I nod and Ambrose says, "Stay close."

Once he's out of earshot, Ambrose speaks first.

"How are you feeling?"

I know the real question behind the question. How am I feeling after getting pathetically hammered and attempting to fall asleep on the cold, hard *floor*?

"Better. Sorry I put you in that situation." I rub the back of my neck. "I'm embarrassed."

"Don't be. It happens."

I snort. "I doubt you've gotten so drunk someone's had to carry you to bed."

His mouth twitches as he shrugs. "I've gotten close."

We watch Matty as he runs around the bushes with Otso.

"So listen, I'm going to stop by tomorrow night. I finally found a sliding door that will fit in the back of the house, and I want to leave the parts in the garage."

I nod. "Sure. I'll text you the garage code."

"I already have it."

Of course. Because we used to be close. Because he and Cat used to spend just as much time in my house as a kid as I did.

"Right," I whisper.

Matty skips back to us, Otso galloping in tow like the happiest dog in Speck Lake. His hair is drenched in sweat, but he doesn't seem bothered by it.

"We're going to the lake tomorrow for a party," Matty says. "Will you come?"

I take the leash from him and readjust Otso's collar. Matty inviting me to the lake instead of Ambrose feels a lot like your friend asking their parents if you can spend the night when you're right in front of them. Inexplicably awkward.

"Um… I don't know, I have a lot of things to get done around the house."

"You should come," Ambrose says.

Something flutters in the pit of my stomach and if I'm not mistaken, it feels a bit like hope. He doesn't give off the impression that this is a pity invite and I'm surprised he wants me there. As if sensing my next thought, he says, "Anya can't come. She has a few job interviews."

Matty again nods in confirmation with a smile the size of Maine. That smile is enough to secure a yes from me.

"Alright. But I must warn you"—I bend down to tickle his side—"I show no mercy when it comes to chicken fights."

Matty's laughter fills the streets and Ambrose stares down at him with adoration in his eyes.

"Okay, bud. If we hurry, we can scour the park for that wolf you swore you saw and then go get burgers for dinner, what do you say?"

"Yeah!"

Ambrose dips his chin in my direction. "We'll head out at noon tomorrow."

"See you then." I wave them off.

As they drive away, I contemplate whether I've made the right decision. It's one thing, doing this back-and-forth dance with Ambrose, but I don't want to bring Matty into the middle of it. What he needs in his life right now is stability and people who will remain constant. People who will help mold him into the person he's supposed to become.

But maybe I don't have to be temporary. Maybe permanence is something even the lowest of low deserve.

Rounding the front of the house, I notice a blue Toyota Corolla screeching its way up Anya's driveway. The door pops open and out falls Anya's now ex-boyfriend—the scraggly asshole I had the displeasure of meeting weeks ago. His feet drag to the front door and I feel a smug sort of satisfaction knowing no one's going to answer.

The fists that come down heavy on the door echo throughout the street and I flinch. Then he starts yelling Anya's name. I'm so distracted by the rage in his voice, I almost miss the fact that he's trying to pry open a nearby window. When it doesn't budge, he eyes the trellis leading up to the second-story balcony—the balcony that opens into Matty's bedroom, which I know because I've seen him throwing paper airplanes from the ledge.

My eyes flit around the cul-de-sac, hoping I'm not the only one witnessing this. I should just go inside or call Ambrose, but he would just rush back here to handle it himself and I don't want Matty seeing this guy.

My feet move on their own and the moment I reach the driveway, Otso releases a low growl. "She's not home," I say, intentional about keeping my distance.

I'm met with a smile that makes me feel violated in a million different ways.

"Hey, beautiful. Was wondering when we'd cross paths again."

"Can't say the feeling's mutual."

He laughs, faking a blow to the chest and when Otso's growl kicks up a notch, his smile thins into a straight line, dropping all pretenses. "There's something of mine in this house. I need it."

"Well, I'm sure when Anya gets back, she can help you find it. Until then, I think you should leave."

"The thing is... that's not gonna work for me."

Otso tugs against the leash and only then do I realize that the sun has fully set. The street is cast in deeper shades of purple and grey as dusk approaches. Without any streetlights, we'll be covered in complete darkness soon enough. There's no time to waste.

"How much?" I blurt out. "How much does she owe you?"

His eyes go round, clearly not expecting that. He watches me for a moment before he smiles and says, "Thr—seven hundred."

My hands itch to smack the smug look off his face.

I bit down hard on my tongue, drawing blood.

Am I seriously going to pay this deadbeat off? I shouldn't but if it were to make him stay away from Anya and Matty for good, isn't it worth any sum of money?

Ambrose would kill me if he found out. Then, he would find this guy and kill him. All around, there would just be a lot of killing going down. That's why I'll need to make sure he never finds out.

"Okay," I agree and his brows shoot up, almost reaching his hairline.

He probably would have settled for a hundred bucks.

"I'll leave it in a white envelope in my mailbox at five a. m. tomorrow morning. Take the money and get the hell out of Speck Lake. If anyone sees you, you're on your own." I make my voice as hard as steel. "And if I so much as catch a *whiff* of your existence around here again, I will make your life a living hell. Because make no mistake, I have the means to do so."

Adding to the distance between us, I walk backward toward the end of the driveway. "You have ten minutes to leave before I call the sheriff."

I don't wait for a response as I speed walk back to my house, the adrenaline pounding against my eardrums. I'm already overcome with the guilt I feel knowing I'm going to keep this from Ambrose. But if it means Anya has one less thing holding her back from getting better, it's worth it.

I did the right thing. I know I did.

I forgot how much I missed our lakes.

September is almost over and even though the changing season has officially sent our temperatures into a decline, we swim for hours. The chill in the air kisses my wet skin and it feels like a resurfaced memory I never intended to forget. Laughter reverberates through the air and I smile to myself.

When we got here, my steps were slow and unsure and I pretty much used Ambrose as a human shield. But I wasn't met with disdain or judgment as I'd expected. I was hugged and loved on and for the first time in a long time, I allowed it.

Matty skips rocks with his friends and I dig my toes deeper into the sand. Ambrose plops down beside me with a carton of loaded nachos in his hands. He holds them out to me.

My eyes widen, mouth already salivating, as I pluck a few and shove them into my mouth. "Mmm. If there's one thing the city can't replicate, it's Annie McLaine's loaded nachos." I reach for another. "Damn, you hit the jackpot too. There's not a bare nacho in here."

"I scooped up the top," he says.

"What?"

"The top of the nacho platter," he clarifies. "I only took the ones that were loaded with the good stuff."

"You stood there and carefully extracted the only nachos that had adequate toppings? You don't even like nachos."

"No. But you do."

"Ambrose King, are you flirting with me right now?" I shove another nacho into my mouth because honestly, I don't know what else to do with my hands.

A light chuckle escapes him. "Trust me, Mara. When I flirt with you"—he brushes a crumb from my mouth—"you'll know."

When. Not if.

I want to ask him to clarify that, but a bucket of water drops over my head, drenching me from head to toe. Matty runs away laughing with his friends close on his heels.

"Matty! Not cool!" Ambrose yells, removing the sodden nachos from my hands. "Sorry about that, Mouse."

I can't help but laugh as I pull my soaked shirt over my head, leaving me in nothing but the old black bikini top I scrounged from a storage box. "It's fine. He's just being a kid."

"Here, put this on." His crewneck lands softly in my lap.

"All good. I'm not cold."

He blows out a harsh breath, eyes briefly grazing across my chest. "Just put it on." He turns his attention to the nachos he doesn't like and I pull the sweatshirt over my head, biting back a small grin.

Standing up, he holds his hand out. "We'll dry off faster if we sit on the dock."

Voices from the party fade to a distant whisper as we walk hand in hand to the dock's edge.

Boaters wave as they pass and I smile at a little girl being pulled across the water on a tube, bopping up and down like a popcorn kernel on high heat. Her giggles and shrieks ring out, punching through the air with unfiltered joy.

I lay back on the warm wood, releasing a sigh. "Remember that summer when we came here like, every weekend and you would tease me for knocking out in this exact spot because the sun made me sleepy?"

"Everything makes you sleepy. You could fall asleep standing up if you wanted."

Not anymore. Now sleeps feels like a distant memory, a forgotten skill, but I don't tell him that.

"That was also the summer you forced me to learn the handshake from *The Parent Trap*," he adds.

"I didn't force you!" I gasp, shooting straight up. I will not stand for this revisionist history. I aim a jab at his ribs, but he blocks me, his chest shaking with laughter.

"Okay, okay, you didn't *force* me. More like, persistently suggested. But I couldn't say no to you. Well, no, that's not entirely true. I could, I just never wanted to." His mouth twists into a grin and I match it with one of my own. Then he laughs abruptly. "You were so cute too—you'd never ask for anything outright. If you wanted an ice cream cone, you'd say, 'Ice cream would sure be nice on a hot day like this' or if you wanted to play scrabble, you'd say, 'Hey, any new words you could teach me?' His voice takes on a somber quality. "And on that day, you said, 'Ambrose, I bet you a million bucks you could never learn this handshake.'"

"Oh, gosh." I shield my face with my hands. "I did do that, didn't I? That must have been so annoying."

"Nah." He shakes his head. "It was sweet. You were always so considerate of everyone else. You just didn't realize that it was okay to want things. That it's *still* okay to want things."

Our eyes lock and it's like he's trying to etch those words into my heart now. Because he knows that I still suffer from the very same affliction.

Of course I want things. I'm human, after all. But I've always been under the impression that getting what you want correlates to getting what you deserve. And if that's the case, then I should keep the *wanting* to a minimum.

"I still remember it," he says with a smile.

"Remember what?"

"The handshake." He jumps to his feet and brushes his hands clean on his thighs before extending them out to me. "Do it with me."

I choke out a laugh. "Right *now*?"

"Yes, right now, come on."

Realizing he isn't joking, I slowly stand to my feet, unable to hide my stupid grin. He takes my hand like we do this all the time and counts down from three before humming the familiar tune.

Our muscle memory springs to life and we keep our movements in sync, twisting and turning and laughing the entire way through. When we finish, we're out of breath—smiling at each other like two kids with a secret.

"Hey!" Matty yells, stomping our way. "That's our handshake!" He pins Ambrose with wounded eyes and my heart squeezes.

"Oh, buddy." Ambrose cups the back of his head, pulling him in for a hug. "It is our handshake, but I borrowed it from Mara when we were kids. She's the one who taught me and because of that, I was able to teach you. Think we can share?"

Up until now, Matty has been enamored with me but I think he might be re-evaluating.

"I don't know…"

Ambrose leans down to his ear, whispering something that I won't forget for a very long time. "Don't worry. All good things come in threes."

The moment we pull into Ambrose's driveway with sun-kissed skin and sand between our toes, it starts to rain. First a gentle mist, then a downpour smacking violently against the pavement.

A light from the den flickers on and the front door opens. Anya runs out with an umbrella, looking casual but pretty in a mauve tracksuit. Ducking inside, she quickly unbuckles a sleeping Matty from his booster seat and envelops him in her arms.

The kiss she lays on his forehead is gentle and something strikes me then.

This is a woman who loves her child wholly and completely. No matter her vices.

"Did he have fun?" Her eyes bypass me in the passenger seat.

Ambrose's smile is pleased. "Yeah, the Carlson twins were there so he was excited to see them. Got a raging belly ache from all the food he stuffed his face with, but I think he'd do it again if he had the chance."

Anya chuckles, making her look years younger. More alive underneath the purple bags and deep lines tattooed on her face. "Glad you all had a good time."

You *all*? Does that include me? I try my best not to look bug-eyed.

I shift my body to respond but Anya closes the door, dampening the booming thunderclaps outside. She jogs in the direction of her house, disappearing from our view.

What in the world was *that*? I turn to Ambrose, but he looks just as confused as I am.

"Thanks for today," I say. "The swimming, the food, the ride—everything. I needed it." My teeth bite down against a yawn as I grab my purse from the floor.

He starts to put the keys back into the ignition. "Wait, let me drive you back over to your place."

"It's just across the street." I laugh. "A little rain won't kill me."

"Then I'll walk you to your door."

I consider objecting but who am I kidding? Ambrose gives me a run for my money when it comes to stubbornness.

"Only if you're sure."

"I'm sure." He places a hand on the door handle. "Ready?"

"Ready." I smile.

Cursing ourselves for not checking the weather for the *entire* day, we count to three and make a run for it. Rain pelts down on us, soaking the clothes we managed to get dry in the sun not too long ago.

We both trip a handful of times and my foot sinks into a muddy puddle that causes me to audibly gag, but somewhere along the way, we start laughing.

Ambrose's grip on my hand is warm and steady as he carefully leads me up the stairs of the front deck.

He doesn't stop until we're backed up against the wall, out of the water's reach. Our labored breaths are muffled by the storm, but I watch Ambrose's chest rise and fall all the same—the sharp angles of his face lit by the glow of lightning dancing across the night sky.

Then he turns to me, his expression darkened.

With each flash of light, he takes a slow step closer, not stopping until we're face to face.

Except now, he's not staring at my face.

His eyes are latched onto my mouth and a shudder works its way through me.

Time slows as my body becomes more aware of his. The way his fingers wrap around my hip, and his breath goes shallow. His soaked T-shirt stretched thin across his chest. Everything about him looks better wet. His dark hair, his full lips—everything.

His palm coasts down the side of my face until it cups around my chin, using the pad of his thumb to brush a rain droplet from my bottom lip.

"You're a little wet," he rasps.

There's a hunger in his eyes I've never seen before.

My heart beats erratically as I wait for him to close the gap between us, but he doesn't move.

"What are you thinking?" I whisper.

"I'm thinking I want to kiss you."

That's all I need to hear for my fingertips to circle the nape of his neck and lift onto my toes.

Soft lips lightly brush against mine and—

The front door swings wide open.

Ambrose doesn't move an inch, but I jump back, my foot slipping from under me.

Laura does a double take when she sees Ambrose shoot out a hand to keep me from falling on my ass.

"Oh. I'm sorry." She blushes. "I didn't mean to interrupt..."

"You weren't interrupting," I say breathlessly. "Everything okay?"

Her eyes linger on Ambrose before bouncing back to me.

"Yes and no." Her mouth twists into a frown. "Before you start to worry, your father is fine, but I think I might be coming down with something." Now that I'm looking at her, she does look a little pale. "I can't risk getting him sick. He wouldn't..." She forces a swallow. "I need you to take care of him tonight, Mara. I called his other nurse, Charlene, but she's with another patient for the night."

"*Me?*"

I've watched over my dad plenty of times during the day but never overnight.

She reaches for my hand but then pulls back, most likely not wanting to contaminate me.

"I can give you everything you'll need," she assures me. "And I am only a phone call away—I will be available to you *all* night."

My eyes go wide. "I-I can't, you can't."

"You can and you will because you *have to*." Her tone is resolute. "You have to do this, honey."

"I'll stay with her."

We both turn toward Ambrose, completely forgetting he was there.

There's a steadiness in the way he holds himself. Deep-set determination in his eyes as he watches us.

"I remember everything you taught me," he tells Laura. "I'll stay."

Laura nods and quickly rattles off a to-do list. I listen, mentally packing away all the critical information.

When she backs out of the driveway, I stand there watching the empty street, unmoving.

Large fingers swallow mine and lead me into the house.

Stopping at the foot of my bed, Ambrose kicks off his shoes and lifts his shirt over his head. When he lies down on the left side, I almost choke.

A wave of nerves falls over me. Going from whatever that was outside to *this* is jarring.

He pats the space next to him. "Come to bed." When I don't move, he lets out a soft sigh. "We're just sleeping, Mouse."

"Don't call me that," I mumble.

After a quick trip to the bathroom, I flip the light switch off and crawl in next to him.

We both face away from each other, his back gliding against mine as he breathes.

I shift my body, trying to get comfortable, but with everything running through my mind it feels near impossible.

Ambrose clutches my bouncing leg. "Stop wiggling."

"I'm trying."

"What's wrong?"

"I'm scared."

The bed creaks under Ambrose's weight as he turns to face my back. Large fingers meet the back of my head and he starts smoothing the hair away from my face. The gesture is so kind, so *tender*, that I want to cry.

"I know," he says gruffly. "Me too. But we'll get through it together. Okay?"

"Okay," I whisper. "Thank you."

"Mara, look at me."

I twist my body, seeking his eyes in the dark.

"I don't want you to thank me for showing up for you. I want you to expect it from me. Because I'm confident enough to know that I'll follow through every single time. In whatever way you need me, I'll follow through." Then he says, "Rest. I've got you."

The moment he says it, I know it's the truth. Every part of me wants to take care of him in the same way, but how can I do that when I'm pouring from an empty cup?

One step at a time.

Tilting my head back, I take the step that should have happened the second I saw him in Hensens. "Hey, Ambrose?"

"Hmm?"

"I'm sorry I left you when you needed me."

His body stills as he looks down at me. When he doesn't say anything for a few heartbeats, I wonder if I've made a mistake, but then he slips his hand under the sheets and laces his fingers through mine.

"I forgive you."

My eyes trace the cupid's bow above his lip and I find myself leaning forward, the smell of him making my head swirl.

"Sleep, baby," he whispers, kissing the corner of my mouth. I know at that moment he sees the past fall like a veil over my eyes because he starts running his fingers through my hair again. "Nothing bad is going to happen. I promise."

The breath trapped in my chest releases and for the first time in my life, I do exactly what Ambrose King tells me to do. The thing I haven't been able to do without the help of a drink or music or an exorbitantly long film in a long time.

I sleep.

THEN

AGE SIXTEEN

My finger punches the doorbell for the third time while I bounce my foot impatiently.

All three cars are parked in the driveway, which means everyone's home.

So why aren't they answering the door?

Fanning my face, I groan against the heat.

I give it one last go and rap my fist against the door three times. Finally, I see a shadow getting closer through the glazing.

"Took you long enough." I scoff. "Jeez, Cat. It's hot as bal—"

Ambrose opens the door, a smirk playing on his face. "Hot as what?"

I roll my eyes. "Where's Cat? She still asleep?" I nudge my way inside, already walking toward the stairs. I glance around for Alima and Robby, but they're nowhere to be found.

"She's not here," he says, following me.

Stopping on the second stair, I turn around with a frown.

"What do you mean she's not here?"

"I thought it was pretty self-explanatory."

I breathe forcefully through my nose, pulling my phone from my pocket.

When Cat answers, I can hear multiple girls giggling on her end. "Hello?"

"Hey, where are you? I'm at your house."

"Sally, my love! I'm at a festival in Bangor. A few girls from the team invited me last minute." My heart drops.

She forgot.

Ambrose folds his arms and I angle my body away so he doesn't see the disappointment on my face.

"Did you forget what today was?" I ask, voice low.

"*No*," she insists before lowering her own to a whisper. "But can you remind me just in case?"

"My driver's test, Cat," I grit. "You were supposed to help me practice today. I can't believe you forgot!"

She gasps. "Wait, wait, wait. No, I distinctly remember we planned to do that next weekend."

"We said that *last* weekend, Cat. The test is tomorrow."

She must have stepped away from whatever crowd she was in because her voice becomes clearer. "Mara, I am *so* sorry." She groans. "I messed up."

This isn't the first time Cat's done something like this. It's not like she does it maliciously, but sometimes her desire to socialize and never miss out on anything makes her flighty and unreliable. I love the girl, but she gets some friendship points docked today.

I rub my eyes, suddenly tired. "Don't worry about it. I'll figure something out."

"Let me ask someone to bring me back—"

"It's fine." I walk back down the stairs. "By the time you get here, it'll be time for our dress appointment. Wait—you did remember our dress appointment *right*?"

"Yes," she rushes. "I'll be there. I swear."

Prom is next weekend and we have our last dress fitting today. The thought of going to prom with Brandon should fill me with butterflies and excitement, but all I feel is an overwhelming sense of obligation. It doesn't help that I had to shell out half a paycheck to afford my dress.

Cat spends the next few minutes apologizing profusely and we eventually say goodbye.

I don't know what I'm going to do. If I don't pass that test tomorrow, there's no way my dad's going to get me the car I've been eyeing in front of Lorenzo Rossi's house. He's a good friend to my dad and all, but he'll sell that car to the first person who comes knocking. He needs the money.

I've been working my butt off, putting in shifts at The Plant Shack after school and my dad was kind enough to write me a check when I told him I was only five hundred dollars short. The only condition he had was that I pass my driver's test first. I'd have him practice with me, but he's a nightmare in the passenger seat.

Blinking back tears, I keep my head down as I go to leave. Ambrose blocks the door, watching me with a pair of keys in hand. He tosses them to me and I barely catch them.

"What's this for?"

He twists his baseball cap around so it sits backward on his head. My heart trips up at how good he looks and it stokes the embers of my frustration.

"I'm gonna teach you how to drive." I don't move an inch and he lets out an exasperated breath. "You coming? I don't have all day."

I chuck the keys back at him with a glare. "Don't do me any favors."

That's when I hear the yelling upstairs.

Sharp words fly back and forth, punching their way through the walls. If I didn't have my eyes glued to Ambrose, I would have missed him flinching.

You'd be doing him the favor if you got him out of here.

"Fine," I mutter, opening the door and shielding my eyes from the sun. "But I pick the music."

"Just take your foot off the break."

"Don't rush me."

"We've been sitting here for ten minutes."

Shifting my torso, I glare at Ambrose. "Well, I thought you were going to teach me how to drive a car, not a *transformer*." I wave a hand around the massive truck.

There's no way I can drive this thing.

"I offered you the booster seat from the garage," he points out. "You said no."

I bang my head against the headrest and groan. "You are so annoying."

"Look," he says, sliding closer to me on the bench seat. "All you have to do is lift your foot off the brake and ease it onto the gas. Cars are sensitive machines, so be gentle with them. Go slow. Not too much pressure—"

"I want to drive the car, not go to second base with it."

He snorts, but I see a patch of red blooming on his neck. "What do you know about second base, Mouse?"

"*Mouse?*" I shake my head. "I'm not a child anymore, Ambrose."

Piercing green eyes flicker to my face and linger there. "I know you're not a child anymore." His voice lowers. "Trust me."

All I can do is stare at him.

He clears his throat.

"Right," I say. "Okay. So, gentle pressure. Go slow with it." My face burns at how that sounds. "Got it."

"Alright, let's see it then."

I take a deep breath and reposition my hands on the wheel. Taking my foot off the break, I move it to the gas and press down gently, just as he instructed. The car starts to roll forward on the abandoned lot and I smile.

Feeling a little more confident, I add some pressure and soon enough, I'm looping around the lot at a normal speed limit.

I break out into a laugh, feeling giddy. "I'm driving, Ambrose. I'm actually driving!"

My eyes swing to him and he has the biggest smile on his face. The kind of smile that would always be on display if it were up to me.

"Eyes on the road." He laughs, tipping his head toward the windshield.

Ambrose surprised me today.

He could have been a million other places and he chose to spend it with me and my questionable driving skills.

It means more than I'd like to admit.

After another two hours or so, Ambrose says I can stop whenever I want; convinced I'm going to pass my test tomorrow with flying colors.

We swap seats and he settles in behind the wheel while I check my phone.

"Do you need to get home?" he asks.

"Not really." I lean back with a shrug. "I don't have to be at the dress shop for another three hours."

He nods, a thoughtful look on his face. I wait for him to start the car back up and race us home so he can finally be rid of me but he stays put. Like he's engaging in some sort of internal battle. That's when it hits me.

He doesn't want to go back home.

Can't say I blame him. Who would want to go back to the one place that should represent peace and safety, only to be a spectator to endless screaming matches?

Ambrose came through for me today and we may not be friends, but I can still be friendly.

"Would you mind if we just drove for a little while?" I ask, tucking a curl behind my ear. "We don't have to talk or anything. I just don't think I'm ready to go home yet."

I wait for him to say no, to shut me down, and ice me out like he always does.

Instead, something close to relief settles over his features and his body sags into the seat.

He twists the key in the ignition and pulls out of the abandoned lot. We set off on an empty back road, one that's known for providing an unobstructed view of the lakes in the distance.

"Yeah, Mara," he says, voice rough. Leaning forward, he turns the radio up a bit higher. "We can do that."

"So," I say as Cat and I exit the dress shop. "Should we get Cinnabon like old times? I'm still full from lunch but I think I can fit one in. Or three. I believe in myself."

"You pick. Anything you want is on me after I royally screwed up today." She sighs. "Who did you end up practicing with, anyway?"

I shrug. "My dad."

Cat unfolds and refolds the receipt in her hands, discomfort written all over her face.

"You okay?" I ask.

"Actually, there's something I wanted to talk to you about."

The tone of her voice stops me in my tracks and I narrow my eyes. The last time she sounded like this, she ruined my favorite sweater. "What?"

Her eyes land everywhere except on me. She hates conflict and always has. "My brother."

"Yes?"

"Ambrose."

"I'm aware that's his name, go on."

"Well..." She swallows. "I may have told him to reserve the remaining seats at our dinner table for prom."

"May have?"

"No, I definitely did."

"You *what?* Cat, you know he and Brandon can't stand each other. They won't last five minutes sitting at the same table!"

"It's his senior year and he wants to experience prom together. How could I refuse? It was like a freaking *miracle*. I miss the relationship I used to have with him."

She has a point there. The fact that Ambrose suggested the idea is kind of a big deal.

Maybe I can figure out a way to keep them out of each other's orbit. I sigh, rubbing my temples. "It'll just be him?"

"And... the rest of them."

She doesn't have to spell out who *they* refer to. Call me difficult, but I don't feel like spending my prom night dodging insults from Sasha Baker. And despite feeling like Ambrose and I connected earlier, I don't expect him to keep it up when we're in public.

"*I can't believe this,*" I hiss.

"I couldn't tell him no, Mara, he's my brother."

"A sad excuse for one, if you ask me!"

Her face falls and I'm instantly ashamed that I've said something so grotesque. Something I don't even mean. How is it that we can do that so easily?

"Why would you say that?" Her voice cracks and my heart along with it.

"I don't know," I whisper, blinking back tears. "I don't even mean it, I just think... I think I wanted to hurt you."

"Well, congratulations. You've succeeded. How does it feel?"

"Terrible." My face crumples. "So terrible, I think I could vomit right here, right now."

"Maybe don't do that." She sniffs, folding her arms. "I don't have the energy to hold back your hair."

"Cat, I'm so sorry. I didn't mean it."

She links her arm with mine, and I start to breathe again. "I don't like you very much right now."

I hang my head. "I know."

"But I still love you."

"I know."

I'm still wallowing in guilt when Brandon comes over that night. I think about Cat the entire time we make out, and sensing something is amiss, he asks, "Are you thinking about someone else right now?"

"Cat."

He rolls over onto his back. "Usually that would be an extreme turn-on, but unfortunately, I don't think I stand a chance against her."

I smack his arm. "Shut up."

He laughs, sitting up. "I have something for you."

I scoot to the headboard of my bed and cross my legs as he pulls something small from his pocket. The little square box is a rich green velvet with a red silk ribbon tied around it in a perfect bow.

"What is it?"

He pulls the small gold band from the inner cushion. "It's called a promise ring."

Setting my hand in his lap, he slips it onto my ring finger. I look closer and the band looks as if it's made of intricately woven branches. A small garnet stone lies at its center.

Picking up on my confusion, Brandon says, "It's my birthstone."

"Yeah, I know. How... sweet."

"I just figure with how serious things are getting, it's nice for you to have something to represent that. To show people that you belong to me."

"We need a ring to say all that?"

"It's supposed to be romantic, Mara. If you don't like it, I can return it."

"No, no," I rush. "I love it. I swear. It's just... what exactly are you promising?"

"That it's me and you forever. That no one will ever love you as much as I do."

I can't decide if that's romantic or not.

It's unsettling—the idea that no one will ever love me as much as Brandon. I think it sounds like the most depressing thing in the world, yet I twist the ring around my finger and lean into him.

"I love it. I love you. Thank you," I whisper, kissing him deeply.

We settle back onto my pillows and begin discussing which movie to watch.

"Hey." I nudge his side. "Why didn't you use my birthstone?"

He laughs like it's a stupid question. "Because I don't know it."

And I laugh along with him, ignoring the little voice in my head telling me that there's nothing even remotely funny about that.

By the time Saturday rolls around, I'm already looking forward to prom being over.

Brandon's next to me while we wait to enter the ballroom, a pocket mirror up to his face, examining himself for any last-minute flaws.

His reaction to my dress was exactly what I'd hoped for and he barely kept his hands to himself the entire ride over.

The low-cut, slinky black dress is so far removed from what I'd usually choose for myself that I decided to make the rest of my appearance match. The hair that drapes over my shoulder is pin straight, coal liner rims my eyes and my lips are a deadly shade of red. The bottom of the lipstick tube literally said "Dead Red."

Besides sitting together at lunch, Cat and I haven't spoken much since the store incident and anxiety chews away at my stomach.

She told me she was getting a ride with Ambrose and while I want to search for her and apologize again, I don't want to put a damper on her prom experience.

We reach the front of the line where teachers are cross-checking tickets.

"Name?" Mr. Moinyhan asks.

"Mara Makinen."

He does a double take. "Miss Makinen. I hardly recognized you."

I grimace. "Thank you?"

He hands me a wristband and crosses my name off the list. Brandon returns to my side, draping his arm over my shoulder. "Ready, milady?"

"Yep."

As if he knows my history with school dances, Mr. Moinyhan gives me a sympathetic look, twirling a familiar string on his finger. "Good luck in there."

Brandon squeezes my hand and leads us to a small table inside to find our dining seat assignments.

"Mara Makinen and Brandon Lang."

A young girl with glasses scans the roster. "Table twelve."

We glance at the linen-lined table that's already occupied. Cat's shoulders shake with laughter at something Maitland's saying in her ear and the growing crowd forces us to move in their direction.

We slip into our assigned seats, pulling the attention of everyone else present.

Shayla Marks leans into Dean Healey's ear, whispering something that makes him bite his lip and I cringe. Directly to their left, Ambrose studies me with a frown. Sasha's glare bounces between me and Brandon, venom infused in her eyes, and Cat sits quietly while Maitland and I exchange polite 'hellos.'

I'm pretty sure I had a nightmare once that went exactly like this.

I tap Cat's hand with my finger with a smile. "You look amazing."

She smiles back but it doesn't reach her eyes. "Thanks, Mar. You do too."

She's forgiven me but I can tell she still feels the effects of my words. Cat has a habit of forgiving people before she's ready and while it comes from a good place, it can make her a little passive-aggressive.

She cares more about making sure you feel forgiven instead of taking the time to process and move on from the pain. What she doesn't realize is that this feels worse than if she were to be angry at me outright.

I clear my throat. "Cat, can we talk in private?"

"Mait, grab a bite with me?" She clutches Maitland's hand and escapes to the buffet table.

I slump in my chair and fiddle with the napkin in my lap.

If this is how the rest of prom is going to go, it's going to be a long night.

When Cat returns ten minutes later, I throw myself into the line of fire again. "Hey, Cat?"

"Maitland, do you want to dance?" Maitland looks at me with pure pity in his eyes before nodding to Cat and they leave the table without looking back.

Brandon returns to the table, dropping a bread roll onto my plate.

"Oh, I asked for two," I say.

He spears his fork into his salad. "You already ate two. Trust me, I'm doing you a favor."

Sasha laughs from across the table and my face burns with humiliation.

Something slams down hard on the table and we all jump.

"Apologize to her."

The sound of Ambrose's voice, the unfiltered anger in it, makes all of us look up.

His glare is firmly locked on my boyfriend.

Brandon tries to play it off with a laugh and Ambrose leans forward, jaw hard as steel. "You see this suit I'm wearing?" he says in a deadly tone. "It's nice. *Very* nice. My mom worked a double shift to get me this suit." His eyes flicker to me briefly. "You couldn't have come here tonight with a more beautiful girl if you fucking tried. Now, you apologize to her or I'm going to have to hit you in front of all these people. It'll ruin my suit and trust me when I say, that will piss me off even more. So tell me, Brandon"—his head tips toward me—"am I going to mess up my suit tonight?"

I can't see the shock on my face, but I'm sure it looks similar to the kind Sasha wears across from me.

Brandon turns to me, his face blotched red, and clears his throat. "Sorry, Mara."

Ambrose pushes his chair back then and holds a hand out to Sasha. "Let's go dance."

He hooks his arm around her waist and ushers her in front of him. As his body brushes against my chair, he drops an untouched bread roll onto my plate without anyone noticing.

Brandon sits in silence for a few more minutes before he turns to me and says, "Meet me in the lobby in five minutes."

He disappears and I'm thankful to be alone.

No part of me wants to go find him, but it's not like I have many options at my disposal here. Cat looks conflicted every time she looks at me and it's not like I can just strike up a conversation with someone I don't know.

I mean, I could, but I'd rather eat glass.

Dropping my head onto the tablecloth, I let out a groan. I should have just gone with the film club to the Indie Film Fest.

Grabbing my phone and clutch, I set out to find Brandon. May as well get this over with now.

Spotting him by the elevators, I'm taken aback to find him smiling from ear to ear.

"That guy's an ass," he chuckles. "But I'm not going to let it ruin our night. Look what I have."

I squint at the white thing he's swinging back and forth in front of my face. "What is that?"

"Our room key. I booked us a room here so we could dip out early and have some alone time."

Oh.

Bile burns my throat and it surprises me how quickly my body says no to something my mind said yes to for weeks. "Right now?"

"Yes, right now."

I glance over my shoulder. "But there's so much dance left."

"Dance?" He laughs. "Forget about the dance, you hate dances."

"No, I don't."

"Don't what?"

"Hate dances. I don't like them, but I don't *hate* them."

"Okay," he says, growing irritated. "You don't like dances, but you don't hate them. Whatever. Let's go." He reaches for my hand, but I pull away.

"I don't... maybe we should rain check." My eyes naively scan the room for Cat.

Brandon laughs it off until he realizes that I'm not joking. Then his voice hardens to stone. "You're kidding me. Mara, you promised me."

I jerk my head back. "Excuse me? I didn't *promise* anything."

"You did, you promised!"

"When exactly did I *promise* to have sex with you, Brandon?"

"*This,*" he growls, shaking my hand with the ring he gifted me. "This is your promise."

"*What?*" I sputter. "You said—you said this ring meant—"

"Forget what I said! Come on, you're not stupid. No guy spends that much money on a girl and doesn't expect anything in return."

My jaw drops and he dares to look like I'm the one who's blindsided *him*. Suddenly, it all hits me at once.

All the times he pushed me in ways I didn't want to be pushed or criticized me for being human. All the times I gave him my attention and energy only for him to make it seem like it was his right as opposed to his privilege.

Because that's what being with me is. That's what being with *any* girl who treats you with love is. A fucking *privilege*.

"I can't believe I wasted two years of my life with a little *boy*." I shake my head in disbelief, clasping my hands tightly to keep from wringing his neck. "And let's get one thing straight, Brandon," I seethe, taking a step toward him. "Even if I did make a promise like that, I am allowed to revoke it any time I want. You could have had my ass in the palm of your hands and I could have still said no. Better you learn that now." When I pat the side of his face, his nostrils flare with anger.

It's amazing how quickly things can change.

One moment I'm a girl named Mara Makinen who loves a boy named Brandon Lang and the next moment I'm not. One moment, I look at him with love and adoration, and the next, he's the ugliest thing I've ever seen.

I don't feel sad or heartbroken or even a little bit mad. A part of me feels slightly bitter that I've given him a chunk of my life but what I mostly feel is an overwhelming sense of relief.

I think this is what people call an epiphany.

Twisting the ring off my finger, I slip it into his hand as he gapes at me.

"Thank you, Brandon." I laugh, an enormous weight sliding off my shoulders. "*Thank you.*"

I leave him standing there like a scowling statue while I set out to look for Cat. I'm squeezing through couples grinding on each other when my phone *pings* with a text from her.

SOS. Meet me at Ambrose's car.

The last time I received an SOS text from Cat was in the sixth grade when she started her period for the first time at school. We don't take the distress signal lightly, which is why I slip off my heels and run barefoot into the parking lot.

I stop at the trunk of Ambrose's beat-up station wagon, looking in every direction for her. When I hear footsteps running up behind me, I turn to find Ambrose bent at the waist, trying to catch his breath.

"Where is she?" he asks.

"I don't know. She texted you too?"

"Yeah," he huffs. "Did she say what's going on?" I can see him struggling to catch his breath in the dark and my hand instinctively reaches for my clutch where I keep a spare inhaler for him. The one I ask Alima for every time the old one expires just in case of an emergency. Just in case he forgets his. She's never once told another soul about it.

"Hey, take a deep breath." I keep my voice calm. "She told us to be here, so she'll show up—"

"I'm right here." Cat shoots her hand up, coming out from behind a minivan.

My level-headed exterior crumbles as I rush to her side. "Cat, what's wrong? Are you okay?"

"*I'm* fine." She holds her hand up, stopping me before I can scan her for injuries. "But *we*," she says, pointing between the three of us. "We are not fine."

"What are you talking about, Cat?" Ambrose asks.

She crosses her arms. "We sat not a foot away from each other in that ballroom and yet you'd think we were separated by *oceans*. It's bullshit. This has gone on long enough." She points a finger at Ambrose. "You're going off to college and we only have one more year before we're thrown into the real world too. We need each other. I don't know when this friendship between the three of us got so complicated, but that ends *right now*."

"You've got to be kidding me, you used SOS for *this*?"

"*Shut up*, Ambrose," Cat snaps and he does. "You're both coming with me." Her delicate fingers dangle a set of keys in front of us.

His eyes bulge, patting his pockets. "How the hell did you—"

"And if you *don't*," she cuts him off. "I will never forgive the two of you."

"Wait," I say. "What about Maitland?"

"He was more than happy to go home early." She sighs, rolling her eyes. "He's still not over that cold and you know how guys get when they're sick. It might as well be the end of life as we know it." Her hands smack down on the hood. "Now get in the car."

She disappears into the driver's seat and slams the door shut, waiting patiently for us to join her. She's not leaving us much of a choice. We either do what she says or prepare ourselves for the longest grudge she'll ever have.

Ambrose paces in a circle while Cat flips through the radio stations. "You think she's bluffing?"

"Um, have you met your sister?"

He laces his fingers on top of his head and blows out a frustrated breath.

"What? You worried about what Sasha will say if you skip out early?"

"No, I'm not worried about that, we aren't even—" He shakes his head. "Never mind, it doesn't matter. Let's just get in and get this over with." He pulls out his phone and starts texting.

Biting our tongues, we slip into the car and Cat pulls out of the parking lot, driving in the direction of an undisclosed location. If she wasn't my best friend, I'd think this is a murder plot.

We don't speak the entire ride and when the car slows over the crunch of gravel twenty minutes later, Ambrose pipes up. "I can't believe you parent-trapped us," he grumbles.

I snort. "I can."

"Quiet, both of you. Mara, Ambrose keeps an obscene number of T-shirts in the back. Grab two."

"What? Why?"

She slips out of the car only to duck her head back in. "We're going swimming."

I have to say, treading water in Lake Bonnie wearing nothing but one of Ambrose's oversized T-shirts is the last thing I thought I'd be doing on my prom night. But here I am. Here *we* are.

"So, what now?" I ask, splashing Cat.

I can tell she wants to laugh but she keeps her face stoic for show. "We need to backtrack our history. Figure out where it all went wrong."

"I don't think I can tread water that long," Ambrose says.

Cat splashes him and when he chokes on the water we all laugh.

"Cat." I soften my voice. "People grow apart. It's just life."

She shakes her head. "No. See, I don't accept that. Because I love Maitland, but us three? We're soul mates."

I dip my head back in the water, releasing a pent-up sigh. "What would you have us do?"

"A restart."

"A restart?" Ambrose raises a brow and she nods.

"Forget everything that we did or didn't do right before this very moment and move the hell on. We're going to be in each other's life forever. I've never been so sure about something in my entire life." She fails at hiding her smile. "Shouldn't we at least make it a good time?"

I give her a weak smile. "You know you don't have to convince me, but this one?" I point at Ambrose. "You'll never get him—"

"I'm down," Ambrose says.

Cat and I say, "What?" at the same time.

"You want a restart." He runs a hand through his wet hair. "I could use one of those. Leave all the old shit behind. Let's do it."

I narrow my eyes, studying him. "This isn't a joke, Ambrose. How do we know you're not going to wake up on the wrong side of the bed tomorrow and change your mind? You've made it very clear once before that you don't have a problem with leaving friends behind. Don't sign up for something you can't handle."

Ambrose's pale green eyes watch me with a level gaze. "Guess you're just gonna have to trust me."

"Trust *you*?"

"That's right."

They both stare at me in silence as I consider his words. A large part of me doesn't believe him. I mean, his track record speaks for itself.

But isn't that the whole point of starting over? To wipe the track record clean and not hold it against someone? Maybe a big part of someone changing for the better is having faith that they're *capable* of such a change.

I roll my eyes, giving in to the spark of hope tugging on my heartstrings. "*Fine.*"

Cat thrashes in excitement and we block our faces against the spray of water.

"Let's shake on it," she says. Ambrose and I take hold of her hand and she rolls her eyes. "Grab each other's hand, you two."

I mentally prepare myself for whatever excuse Ambrose is about to spout but his warm hand interlocks with mine in the water.

He holds my gaze and my throat constricts. "Restart." He nods.

I take it with a grain of salt but allow myself to give him a small smile. "Restart."

Cat sighs in satisfaction. "Wow, you guys. That was a really beautiful moment—I have goosebumps." She lifts the arm of the hand I'm holding and I drop my head back, laughing. "Now that that's settled, Ambrose, stop tickling my foot," she chides.

"I'm not tickling your foot, genius. Both of you are holding my hands."

Cat and I stare at each other, our eyes becoming saucers on our faces. Cat screams at the top of her lungs and soon Ambrose and I join her. We kick our way back to shore, laughing and screaming, and for the first time in a long time, our laughter is a chorus that binds us together in the quiet night.

NOW

Something has shifted between Ambrose and me. It isn't cataclysmic or in your face. It's steady and subtle—a mixture bubbling in a beaker on low heat. When I wake up the morning after Laura went home sick, Ambrose is long gone.

I strip the sheets that now smell of him and a folded piece of scrap paper floats to the floor.

> Had to leave early to drop Matty off at school. Text me if you need anything.
>
> Did you know you snore?

"I don't *snore*."

At the sound of my voice, my cracked door swings open, and Otso barrels straight for my midsection. Tackling me onto the bed, I let him shower me—thanks to the excess saliva—with kisses. The way this dog has grown on me is incredible and a little frightening. I never thought I'd feel this way, but I'm pretty sure I can no longer live without him.

"Hi, boy," I coo, nuzzling my nose into his fur. He licks the whole of my face and I let him. Who have I become?

Laura knocks lightly on the door even though it's wide open.

"Hi, Hon. I came in through the back door, hope that's okay. I'll keep my distance, I just wanted to check on you."

It's sweet of her to make sure I'm still mentally and emotionally intact after last night. And the only reason I am is because my dad's condition stayed pretty much the same. Not better and not worse. Just constant. At some point in the middle of the night, I crept downstairs to check on him and ended up falling asleep and curled into his side. Ambrose must have carried me back to my bed when the other nurse, Charlene, got in.

I present Laura with my best smile. "I'm as okay as can be."

"I owe you a huge apology. I feel terrible for throwing you into the pit like that." Her throat is scratchy and I hate that she's wasting her energy feeling bad about something that doesn't warrant an apology.

"Laura, in no universe should you apologize for leaving last night. You did what was best for you, but more importantly, what was best for my dad. We're lucky to have you."

She wrings her hands together. "It's not like me to get sick. I take all the necessary precautions—"

"*Stop.* Seriously." I laugh, helping Otso up onto my bed. "You did nothing wrong."

When Laura sees the determination on my face, she nods in defeat. She doesn't move from my door and I take a moment to mull over her appearance. Laura's always had a sort of effortless grace about her, but right now she looks bone tired. Red-rimmed eyes and deeper face lines.

"Is there something else bothering you?"

She looks up at my ceiling, contemplating. The breath she releases is weary. "It's Matty. His birthday is tomorrow." I nudge Otso away from my face so I can give her my full attention. "Anya told me she was reserving the Blade Arcade in Ellsworth, but when I called them today to confirm, they said a reservation had never been set. Matty's already invited all his friends from the Big Brother and Big Sister program. I don't know what I'm going to tell him and Anya's not answering my calls."

My face falls. "Have you told sheriff Lang?"

She shakes her head quickly. "I don't want him out looking for Anya. If he finds her, I'm not sure what state she'll be in and that'll cause a whole other mountain of issues. Best if we just keep this between us and Ambrose."

"I won't say anything," I say, racking my brain for other options. It's not like we have skating rinks and bowling alleys in Speck—those are things we'd have to drive out of town for. The only thing I can think of that excites Matty to no end is Old Maple...

I shoot to my feet. "What if we have the party here?"

"Here as in... your home?"

"Yes! The backyard is massive, and Ambrose installed a new grill to impress that swanky real estate agent. We have a tree house. We can come up with some games. I'm not the best cook, but I'm pretty sure seven-year-olds live off pizza and cake."

"I couldn't possibly ask that of you."

"You didn't ask. I offered." She looks skeptical. "Besides, this house could do with some giggling kids running around. A bit more *life*." I smile wide, hoping to convince her.

She practically chews off her nail beds but eventually relents. "What the hell, let's do it." She claps her hands. "Thank you, thank you, thank you! I'll run out and get the decorations today.

She calls Otso out of the room, thanking me three more times before closing my door. I brush my teeth and shower, surprisingly invigorated for the new day. As I go downstairs, I stop in front of my dad's door. Taking a deep breath, I let myself in and kick off my shoes, sliding into the open space on his bed.

"Hey, Dad," I whisper. "I thought we could have a little father-daughter date. Hope I didn't catch you at a bad time." I laugh to myself. If he was conscious, he'd find my joke funny. I prop my phone on my knee, swiping through the list of movies. As *Princess Bride* begins to play, I lean back into the free space on his pillow and he shifts his body slightly. I can't prove it, but I think he knows I'm here. And I think he's happy about it. I blink rapidly against the wetness in my eyes.

"This is a special book," I say, reciting the lines from the opening scene. "It was the book my father used to read to me when I was sick and I used to read it to your father. And today, I'm gonna read it to you."

My dad's eyes stay glued shut, but his expression is soft. Peaceful. The remaining patches of golden hair on his scalp have thinned out significantly, becoming dull and brittle, but he's still the best-looking dad in Speck Lake. I lean down close to his ear. "Don't worry, Dad," I whisper. "You still give Wesley a run for his money."

When Laura said she was going to decorate for the party herself, I expected a few balloons here and there. Maybe a handcrafted banner if she was feeling wild. But the house I come back to this afternoon after picking up food and drinks is *not* the same house I left.

The backyard is decked out with streamers hanging from the trees, barrels filled to the brim to bob for apples, and multiple piñatas hanging from Old Maple. The theme... well I can't tell what the theme is. It looks like Party City threw up in my backyard.

"I know what you're thinking." Laura takes the chips from my hands and dumps them into serving bowls. "I didn't know what he'd like best so I just went with a little bit of everything." She adjusts the mask around her ears. She's already feeling a bit better but she still insists on keeping her distance today, not wanting to risk passing anything on to my dad.

Ambrose comes up beside me. "Are you kidding? It turned out great. I wish you were my aunt."

He always manages to look good in that not-trying-to-be-hot, hot kind of way and today is no different. His dark hair is wet and tousled like he just got out of the shower, and he's wearing an olive sweater that compliments his eyes. I try and fail to avoid staring at the jeans that perfectly hug his ass.

You're at a seven-year-old's birthday party, stop mentally undressing the guests.

I exhale my sexual frustrations. "I agree. It's amazing. Matty's going to freak out."

And Matty does freak out. Turns out, having a party with multiple, unrelated themes is perfect for children who have the attention span of a goldfish. I can't help but smile every time a kid tells Matty that it's the best birthday party they've ever been to.

Ambrose makes his rounds with the parents and program volunteers, and I struggle to not think about the kiss last night. Can it even be considered a kiss? Yes. I'm telling myself yes.

We haven't talked about it and I'm not sure Ambrose even wants to. I'm glad things aren't awkward between us, but a small part of me wonders if that means last night doesn't mean as much to him as it does to me.

"Why so serious?" Ambrose hands me a cup of punch. "You do know you're at a party, right?"

I make a face. "Hilarious."

"How are you doing? Last night was a lot to handle."

"I think it was a lot for *me* to handle. You, on the other hand, know how to keep a level head."

"That's not true." He shakes his head. "I get upset. I lose my cool. I break just like every other human, Mara."

It hits me then that I've never asked Ambrose how he's handling my dad being in hospice. They have a deeper relationship than I could have ever imagined, and I've been too selfish to realize that I'm not the only one navigating these uncharted waters. There's an entire town that loves Solomon Makinen.

"And are you?" It's almost painful to swallow. "Breaking?"

His smile is genuine. "Not right now."

Matty runs at full speed toward us and Ambrose catches him in his arms, swinging him over his shoulder. Matty screams for mercy as I run forward and tickle him between his ribs.

When Ambrose sets him back down, I ruffle his hair. "Happy birthday, kid. Didn't know what you wanted so I have fifty bucks in my purse with your name on it."

His jaw drops open and I chuckle. He probably thinks he's rich now. He thanks me and tugs on Ambrose's shirt. "Is my mom here yet?"

He scratches the back of his neck. "Not yet, bud. I'll come to find you when she is."

Matty doesn't seem satisfied with that answer, but he runs off and returns to his friends anyway.

No one has seen or heard from Anya and we're all feeling on edge about it. Laura spent the entire morning leaving voicemails, begging her to at least let us know she was alright.

What if she ran into her ex on his way out of town? What if by getting involved, I made everything worse and now she's in trouble?

Fear clutches me by the throat.

I need to tell Ambrose what I've done.

"Ambrose, can we—"

"Hold that thought." I follow his eyes to the group of people eating by the grill. "The sandwiches are running low on that table and if I don't keep the flow of food steady, Laura will have me by the neck." He chuckles, speeding away into the house.

I force my feet to move, desperate to walk off the tightly coiled knots in my stomach.

The sounds of children's laughter hug the space around my house as the afternoon carries on and I hope that the joy and love around us find their way to my dad's little corner of the house. I hope it makes an appearance in his dreams, comforting him.

Ambrose doesn't come back for the better part of an hour, and I assume it's because he's being a good host.

When I see him organizing napkins all alone in a corner, I take advantage of the opportunity.

"Ambrose?"

He's laser-focused, folding the napkins into lotuses. Where did he even learn how to do that? "What's up?"

"I was just wondering if I could talk to you for a second when you have a moment."

I lick at my chapped lips and when Ambrose faces me, his brows furrow with concern. "We can talk now."

"I-I can wait until you have more time."

"I always have time for you, Mara." His warm voice is steady. "And if I don't have time, I'll make time. Sit," he says, pointing to a folding chair. I plop myself right down.

Squeezing my eyes shut, I take a deep breath. "It's about Anya, I—"

A deafening crash cuts me off and I flinch at the sound, whipping my head around to see where it came from.

Anya hovers near a group of parents lounging in Adirondack chairs, multiple cases of beer bottles scattered around her feet. Ambrose and I immediately rush to her side.

I grab an empty trash bag from nearby. "Anya, are you okay? Don't move, I'll grab a broom for the glass."

She looks up at me like a deer caught in headlights and I can't stop the gasp that escapes my mouth. Her eyes are so bloodshot, the whites of them are almost nonexistent. Scraggly hair hangs over her shoulders and her gaunt body folds in on itself like she no longer possesses the strength to hold herself up.

She sways toward me, flip-flops crunching over the broken glass. "You wiggle your way back into Ambrose's life and now you think you can have my *boy*?" she slurs. Even her flush of anger seems to exhaust her.

"Anya," Ambrose warns.

The parents surrounding us watch in silence, not daring to move.

"Anya, let's go inside and get you cleaned up. We can talk there," I say gently, moving closer.

She stomps her foot and thick shards of glass pierce her shoe. I wince as blood starts gushing over her sandal. She doesn't even notice. "I'm not going anywhere with you, bitch. You've taken everything from me." Her voice cracks in half. "*Everyone*."

Before I can ask what she's referring to, she says, "Jason loved me. We had issues and our relationship was far from perfect, but he loved me and now he's gone because of *you*. Because you couldn't mind your own damn business."

"What's she talking about, Mara?" Ambrose is looking at me now.

Shit.

"Didn't your girlfriend tell you?" Her laugh is pained. "She ran him out of town. Wrote him a check and paid him off."

I avoid Ambrose's disappointment by keeping my eyes trained on Anya. "You deserve better than him."

"And Ambrose deserves better than you. All you do is ruin things. You're the reason she's not here anymore, you do know that, right?"

Ambrose's back stiffens. "That's enough."

The floor seems to sway under my feet.

She turns to the shell-shocked parents around her as if she's only now noticing their presence. "Did any of you know Catherine King? Do you know what happened to her?" Her bony finger points in my direction. "Mara can tell you."

"I said that's *enough*!" Ambrose growls.

The smell hits me.

A pungent aroma of ammonia wafts around my nose and I look down. A spot on Anya's white jeans grows larger by the second.

She's urinating herself.

"Mommy?" Matty stares at his mom with a mixture of fear and confusion.

My chest constricts. "Anya," I whisper, rushing forward to cover her front side with the trash bag.

What happens next is a blur.

I can only assume from the burn in my eyes that Anya's thrown alcohol in my face. Blinded, I stumble backward and everyone around us unfreezes from their positions, their voices erupting in a frenzy. Arms carry me away and Anya's screams of protest get quieter as I'm led to the kitchen sink. I flush my eyes out with cold water and when my vision clears, I thank Mrs. Sanchez, who I only met this afternoon, for helping me.

"*Está loco como una cabra*," she mutters.

"Don't say that." I frown, patting my eyes with a paper towel. "Thank you for your help, but please don't say that." She throws her hands up and shrugs.

Anya's not crazy. She's *sick*.

When I finally return outside, everyone has cleared out except Laura and Mrs. Sanchez's son. I thank her again and apologize for how the party ended and she tells me not to worry about it, leading her son to their car.

"Where's Anya?" I ask.

Laura's face is blotchy and tear-streaked. "Ambrose took her and Matty home. She slammed the door in his face and refused to let either of us in." She sniffs. "Ambrose went out looking for her dealer. Thinks she may be on something new."

Exhaustion hits me with full force and I rub my eyes.

"I'm so sorry, Mara. So sorry."

I don't bypass the part I played in all this. "Me too."

Sleep evades me that night.

I toss and turn in bed, jumping out toward the window every time headlights pass by. Ambrose still isn't home yet and anxiety chews away at my nerves. How long does it take to talk to a drug dealer? I don't even want to think about Ambrose having to confront someone like that.

I'm staring at the blue house, willing his car to appear in the driveway when I see a faint trail of smoke emanating from the house next door.

Anya's house.

I press my fingers into my eyes, clearing my vision. It's exhaustion and fear, that's all.

But then I squint, pushing my face against the window, and it becomes clear that this is no hallucination. The full moon shines on the house just enough to make it noticeable.

Puffs of smoke spill out of the downstairs window. My eyes dart to each window of the house and when I don't see any lights turn on, I dress quickly, tripping over my sneakers midrun on my way out the door. Otso's barks echo throughout the house as I leave him behind.

Sprinting across the street, I'm baffled by how quiet Winsome Lane is.

I reach for the door but stop myself before touching the doorknob. I lightly tap the back of my hand against the handle, reeling back at its heat. I survey my surroundings.

There's a door I could try at the back of the house, but I'd have to jump their fence and I don't want to waste precious time.

Think, Mara. Think.

I run to the ivy-covered trellis.

It goes all the way up the house, ending at the balcony of Matty's room. Without a second thought, I begin to climb.

I thank my Pilates classes for the strength in my thighs as they carry me upward. I haven't climbed a trellis since I was a teenager and even then I'd only climbed my own. When I haul my body over the balcony, I peer through the window, shocked at the lack of movement inside.

Is anyone even home?

Not willing to risk it, I tug off my hoodie and wrap it securely around my elbow. Inhaling a deep breath, I brace myself before punching it through the glass. Bits of glass spray into the air and I shift my face away from the debris. My hand unlocks the door from the inside and I hiss at the sting of shards cutting into my skin. Once I stumble into the room, my eyes blink rapidly to adjust.

Matty and Anya are curled up together in his bed, fast asleep.

Leaping forward, my hands clutch onto Anya's shoulder. "Anya, wake up. There's a fire."

"Mmm." She groans, pulling the sheets higher over her face.

Now is not the time to be gentle.

"Wake up!" I grab the neck of her shirt with more force. She comes to, paranoia clouding over her eyes. Considering she owed someone money up until yesterday, I'm sure being shaken awake in the middle of the night is the last thing she wants.

"There's a *fire* in your house, Anya," I grit.

"Fire?" she mumbles. Understanding floods her eyes and sits up. "I left the teakettle on."

"Come on. Hurry." I scoop Matty into my arms and guide us to the balcony.

Anya sways on her feet, not completely sobered up yet and I say, "I'm going to carry him down." She nods, grabbing the edge of a dresser to steady herself.

Matty doesn't stir as I wrap his legs firmly around my waist. I use my hoodie to tie his body to mine and my arms scream out in agony as I carry us down the trellis. My leg muscles are monsters, but my upper body strength resembles that of a newborn calf.

I exhale in relief as I gently lay Matty in the grass, every muscle in my body now throbbing. He begins to wake and confusion clouds his eyes. "Don't move, Matty," I whisper. "I'll be right back."

I attempt to pull myself back up the trellis, but my arms shake with fatigue. "Anya!" I shout. "Anya, can you climb down?"

No response.

I peer above me but can't see her from my vantage point.

My jaw clenches. "Fuck."

Biting the inside of my cheek, I climb, a metallic taste filling my mouth. By the time I reach the balcony, my limbs are numb and Anya's nowhere to be found.

"Anya!" I step through the shattered door. In just a matter of minutes, the entire room has filled with smoke. Anya must have tried to get out by going through the house because the door is wide open. Having learned enough about fires to know open doors make the situation worse, I run forward and kick it shut. I catch sight of a small body digging through a chest from underneath Matty's bed.

"What the hell are you doing?" I cry.

"I can't leave his baby photos. They're all I have; I can't leave them!"

I grip her shoulders as she stuffs the photos into her bra. Smoke billows around us and I hack into my arm, my throat burning like a furnace. Grabbing a shirt from Matty's dresser, I bring it to Anya's face. I'm worried about how the smoke will affect her with all the drugs currently in her system.

"Go. I'll grab the rest of the photos."

She hesitates, but I shove her toward the balcony. "Go now!" I push. "Climb down the trellis. Matty's down there and he needs you."

At the mention of Matty, she nods and runs out. I return to the drawer, seizing the remaining photos.

Matty on a merry-go-round. Matty at the beach. Matty and Anya looking happier than ever before.

I cough so hard, I gag. My eyes feel like someone's taken a hot poker to them.

Once I've snagged the last four-by-six photo, I stumble outside, gasping for fresh oxygen between coughs. I can hear sirens approaching in the distance.

Through squinted eyes, I begin my descent.

I pause every moment the world starts to spin, and then I keep moving. My foot snags on a handful of branches and I plummet the remaining five feet to the ground. I exhale with relief when I see firemen running up the driveway toward us.

From what the EMTs told us, we made it out just in time. Had we been inside ten minutes longer, our situation would be a lot grimmer. Luckily, the smoke inhalation is minimal, but we still go to the hospital to make sure we're in the clear. Laura meets us there, tight-lipped and stoic.

When I get home, I jump straight into the shower, scrubbing the grime and soot off my skin. My movements are slow and mechanical, and I figure it's because I'm still in a state of shock.

Pulling on my pajamas, I hear a pounding at the front door. I dash down the stairs before Otso has a chance to wake my dad again and swing the door open to find an out-of-breath Ambrose.

"Are you out of your *fucking mind?*"

I sigh. "Not any more than usual. Ambrose, what was I supposed to—"

"You have to be the dumbest, stupidest, most—"

"I'm not going to just stand here while you *insult* me. I had to—"

"*Stop talking, Mara!*"

I clamp my mouth shut.

Ambrose grabs my shoulders and shakes me, his eyes wild. Terrified. "What is *with* you and fires, huh? Do you know what I would've done if something happened to you?"

My heart splits in two. "Ambrose," I whisper.

"If I lost you? If I fucking lost *you*, Mara?" His voice cracks. "I wouldn't survive it. I just got you back."

I wrap my hands firmly around his wrists. "I know. I'm okay." I rub my hands up and down his arms. "I'm *okay*."

Ambrose scans my features, and when he reaches my neck, his eyes darken. He steps closer to me, backing me up until I'm pressed firmly against the wall and the door closes with a soft *click*. His chest presses into me and my stomach hollows.

Lowering his head until our lips are only inches apart, his rough fingers curl around the base of my neck. His thumb presses against my throat and my head falls back on its own.

When he lifts the gold chain out from my shirt, I stop breathing.

Twisting the locket in his hand, he runs a finger over the grooves of its engraving.

My hummingbird.

The one he gave me. The one I've worn every day since I turned eighteen except for the moments I've been around him.

My voice is breathy. "I know you're upset. I didn't...I know this isn't what you expected after today but I just—" I inject an ounce of control into my voice. "I don't know what to say."

"Then stop talking," Ambrose growls, crashing his lips down on mine.

My body reacts on its own accord and I press into the kiss, savoring the feel of his soft lips.

He grinds his hips into mine and I gasp at the delicious pressure. The desperation. Our movements are frantic and impatient as our bodies react to each other in the dark.

We're the perfect fit and it's a satisfying realization.

Ambrose pulls me closer as if I'm not already close enough. Lifting my arms over my head, he cages me in place. His tongue opens the seam of my mouth and I finally let go, a small moan escaping my throat.

"That's my girl."

Heat pools at my core as he wraps my legs around his waist and hoists me up with ease. Our jerky movements knock a picture frame off the wall and it crashes on the floor, but we ignore it. Ambrose grunts as I pull his hair, nipping at the skin exposed under his collarbone.

It's not until his hands graze under my shirt, causing my skin to pebble, that I'm pulled to my senses.

"Wait," I breathe. "We can't."

"We can." His mouth consumes mine again and my back arches into him instinctively. Like my body was created for the sole purpose of binding itself to Ambrose King. He sucks on my bottom lip and I know if I don't stop now, I never will.

I shove him away before he kisses me again. "We shouldn't do this, Ambrose."

He stops then, rearing his head back a bit to search my eyes. "Do you want this?"

I don't respond.

"Tell me what you *want*, Mara."

I can't answer him. Because it's not about what I want. It doesn't matter what I want. Not anymore. I no longer allow myself the privilege of wanting anything.

Ambrose shakes his head, disheveled hair falling into his eyes. "You can't do this anymore. You can't keep punishing yourself."

I look away and he closes in on me again. I back up against the wall, wishing I could disappear into it. His eyes are drowning with rage and passion. Each emotion fighting to be front and center. I envy his ability to let himself feel so deeply.

His breath tickles my skin. "I want you, Mara. God, you have no idea how much I want you. How much I've wanted you. But I won't touch you again until you ask me to. When you're ready to admit what it is that *you* want, you come find me."

The door slams behind him and I wince, already feeling the effects of his absence.

I remain glued to the wall long after he leaves.

For the first time in a long time, tears start streaking down my face and I bend down, retrieving the picture that fell to the floor. I can't remember the last time I let myself cry and that terrifies me. I'm unraveling.

He's unraveling me.

I drag my thumb across the dust-covered surface and the clear streak reveals its subjects.

With a watery smile, I take in the picture of Ambrose, Cat, and me. We're huddled together under a large towel at the lake, floaties at our feet, smiling wide for the camera. It's from the summer we learned how to do backflips at Lake Bonnie and watched our first *R*-rated movie. We were safe. We were together. I clasp my hand over my mouth to muffle the sound of my broken sobs.

We were happy.

THEN

AGE SEVENTEEN

My dad slides the bowl of scalding chicken noodle soup in front of me.

I roll my eyes. "You know I'm not sick."

It's senior skip day and my dad's pretending like I'm sick so he can assuage his parental shame of letting me skip school.

"You are sick. Look at you, *princesa*. Your hair is dull and your eyes look tired."

"That's just how I look, Dad."

He pushes a glass of OJ and a bottle of cough medicine across the table. "I'm going to leave this here. And then I'm going out for the day to run errands. I'll probably go straight to sleep when I get home tonight, unable to check on you. Whatever you do, do *not* leave this house." He winks. "And don't even *think* about sneaking out with your friends, especially to visit the zoo after hours where certain people tend to go on this day every year." He's full-on smiling now.

"You're scaring me."

What I don't tell him is that I plan on spending the entire day in bed. My senior year looks vastly different than my junior year. Brandon and I have been broken up for an entire year. I never spoke to him after what happened at prom and he made no attempts at apologizing. We became strangers just as quickly as we fell in love. Or at least, what I thought was love at the time.

Even though Cat and I are busier than ever, we took that night at Lake Bonnie seriously. And surprisingly, so did Ambrose. I haven't seen him much since he started college, but when I do see him, it's like all the years we've spent on what feels like different sides of the planet cease to exist.

We don't look back anymore. There's only now and what comes after and I'm okay with that.

I shuffle through the college brochures Cat dropped off yesterday and a buzz of excitement runs through me. We're still committed to moving to the city together after graduation. When Cat texted me this morning asking if I'd changed my mind about tagging along with her and her cheer mates today, I told her I was more than happy to take the day to chill alone.

Also, the idea of taking part in mischief and rule-breaking makes me ill.

My dad leaves the house, the giddy smile still plastered to his face and I curl up on my bed.

Clicking on the TV, I push play on *Ferris Bueller's Day Off*. I thought it was fitting.

Halfway through the movie, my eyelids grow heavy and I drift off to sleep while Cheddar licks the crumbs of Doritos from my hand.

I jerk awake to the sound of tapping on my window. A glance at the clock on my nightstand says it's eleven thirty at night.

So much for a wild senior skip day.

Tap, Tap, Tap.

The pebbles bounce off the glass and I rub my eyes. Cheddar stares back at me, completely aloof.

I toss a pillow at his face. "You're no help."

Sliding into my slippers, I unlatch my window. Below is a dark silhouette I can't quite make out and it's only when the person pulls down their hood that the curtain of glowing blonde hair gives them away.

"What are you doing here?" I whisper-yell.

Cat does not attempt to be quiet. "I'm rescuing your ass."

I glance over my shoulder at my comfortable bed and bowl full of snacks. "Am I in distress?"

"You're the only person sitting in their pajamas on senior skip day, so I'd say yes."

Is this a pity invite? I told Cat it was fine for us to have other friends, but maybe she didn't believe me. Suspicion keeps me rooted in place.

Cat huffs in exasperation. "They want to meet you. Seriously. Now hurry up, I'm getting cold."

I refuse to look a gift horse in the mouth. "Be right down."

When I stride up to Cat, she eyes my clothes and snorts like a pig. "What are you *wearing*?"

I do a twirl in the all-black ensemble I picked out for the night. "What's wrong with it?"

"Nothing... I just didn't realize a member from *Men in Black* would be joining us tonight."

"I just figured I should be incognito if we're to be taking part in questionable activities tonight."

Cat laughs and I smile. It sounds like church bells on a Sunday morning.

She points to the car parked in the street where music pulsates through the windows.

"Wait," I say, grabbing her sleeve. "What if... what if they don't like me?"

She shrugs like the answer's simple. "Then they don't like *us*."

She extends her hand and I grab on tight, the identical scars on our palms melding together.

"Ready, Sally?"

"Ready, Gilly."

The parking lot of the zoo has a handful of cars parked when we arrive, which means seniors have already snuck their way in.

It's close to midnight as we jump out of the car, doing last-minute checks on our outfits. Cat looks stunning as usual and her two friends, Ruby and Grace look just as great.

Suddenly, I feel self-conscious.

"Cat, I can't go in there like this. I look stupid."

Her brows pinch. "You don't look stupid. You look like a hitman, but you don't look stupid."

"*Cat*," I groan.

"Okay, okay. Rubes," She turns to Ruby Niven who's leaning up against the car with a cigarette between her lips. "Do you have something Mara can wear?"

Ruby hops off the trunk and opens it. "Let me check."

Her head disappears as she rummages around, pulling out clothes from various nooks and crannies like her trunk is a Mary Poppins purse. The mess would usually stress me out, but right now I'm grateful.

"Put this on," she says, tossing me something silky with a smile.

I jump into the backseat and when I come back out, I keep my arms crossed tightly over my chest.

When Cat sees me, she shrieks, and then her friends do the same thing.

"Really?" I ask, hesitating. The shimmering gold camisole cascades around my small chest in a delicate, yet confident way. I've never worn anything like it and I'm not even sure I can pull it off.

Cat exchanges a look with her friends and then they all laugh.

"What?" I bristle.

She shakes her head, looping her arm with mine. "Just the fact that you could have almost spent Senior Night in the outfit you came in instead of *this*." She lowers her voice. "It's a scary thought."

I burst out laughing and so do the rest of the girls as we make our way inside.

Thanks to Marco Riley, who works at the zoo, we're able to sneak in through a shortcut for only five dollars. We walk into the atrium and there's already music pumping through speakers and beer pong tables set up. Our entire senior class is here, laughing and having a good time. I can't believe I almost skipped out on this.

We're on our second round of flip cup when Ambrose walks in with a few of his friends and my heart flutters in my chest.

I lean into Cat's ear. "What's your brother doing here?"

She shrugs, biting the rim of her Solo cup. "Maybe he came to pregame. Tomorrow's his birthday, remember?"

Ambrose is only a year older than us, but somehow college has already aged him. The once raging storm in his eyes has dwindled to a gentle crash against the rocks.

Being away from home has inserted a calmness into his step, something I never thought was possible. I still haven't gotten a clear picture of when exactly he and Sasha broke up last year but there's no chance I'll ask him or Cat about it.

And I didn't forget that Ambrose turns nineteen tomorrow. I'd never forget it. But what I don't understand is why he'd rather spend it back in Speck Lake than with his new college friends.

Fingers snap in front of my face. "Need a napkin? You're drooling on me."

I flick Cat's forehead and she cackles. "Am not."

Hearing his sister's laugh, Ambrose saunters over, leaving his group behind. My shoelaces become my new fixation as I chew the skin around my thumb.

"Hey, Mouse."

I twist at the waist. "Oh, hi!" Cat frowns at my abnormally high pitch. "Didn't see you there."

Glancing around at all twenty people in attendance, his mouth curves into a smirk. "Yeah, definitely hard to spot someone in this crowd." He winks.

My throat goes dry. Did he just...?

"What am I?" Cat interjects. "Chopped liver?"

Ambrose slings an arm over her shoulder and plops a loud kiss on her head before pulling her in for a noogie.

"Cut it out!" She scolds, biting back a laugh. She shoves his chest, wiggling a ping-pong ball in his face. "Wanna play?"

"And embarrass you in front of your friends? I'm good."

Cat throws up double middle fingers before joining Ruby and Grace at the beer pong table.

Ambrose watches me unabashedly as I sip my drink.

"I like that," he says, jerking his chin toward my top.

I point at my chest. "This? Oh, it's not mine. Ruby lent it to me. It doesn't really fit right." I laugh, pulling the chain strap back over my shoulder. There's no way to adjust the tightness so it keeps slipping off every few minutes.

"Well, considering every guy in here can't take their eyes off you, I'd say it fits you just fine."

"*What*? I—No."

He bites down on his smile. "Come on, Mara. You know you're gorgeous."

I balk at him, trying to make sense of his words.

"How's school?" I ask, changing the subject. "You're a..." I struggle to remember his school mascot. "Black Bear? Did I get that right?"

Amusement dances across his face. "You've been doing your homework on me. I'm honored."

I roll my eyes. "Don't let it get to your head."

I'm trying my best to play it cool but being playful with Ambrose like this... it's affecting me on a physical level.

Laughter rumbles through his chest. "School's good though," he says. "It's been a bit of a transition, but I think I've finally got the hang of things for next year. It'll be nice to come back home for the summer. I've missed you guys."

My hand trembles ferociously and beer sloshes out the sides of my cup, wetting my shoe. Ambrose gently tugs the drink away from me, downing what was left and I swallow at the sight of his full lips around my cup.

"Happy early birthday, by the way," I murmur, my cheeks aflame.

"Thanks." A flash of a smile. "Are you gonna be at the party tomorrow?"

"Do you want me to be?"

He pretends to think about it and I swat his arm, making him laugh. "Yeah, I do."

"Okay." I grin. "Then I'll be there."

"Good." He takes one small step closer to me. "Hey, you should drive up to campus after graduation next week. We could check out a couple of bookstores—see a movie." He makes his voice low and sultry. "They have more than *one screen*."

I bark out a laugh, quickly muffling it with my hand. "Sure, that sounds fun. I could ask Cat—"

"Not Cat. Just you."

Ambrose's friends start shouting his name obnoxiously, announcing they're ready to leave and his long fingers curl around my shoulder, slipping the stubborn strap of my top back on. Dropping his hand, his thumb sweeps gently across my knuckles. The thought of Cat seeing us mortifies me, but I don't dare move. I couldn't even if I wanted to.

"See you tomorrow, Mouse."

The nickname doesn't sound so harsh then. This time it makes my pulse quicken in anticipation.

Ambrose pushes his way through a group of seniors, laughing alongside his friends on their way out.

I drag my feet back over to the beer pong table, unsure of what just happened. When Grace offers me a mini bottle of water, I gladly accept. I tuck myself into Cat's side and she bumps her hip with mine.

"Go for it," she whispers, handing me the little white ball. Her smile is light, but her eyes are serious—overflowing with deeper meaning—and a part of me thinks she may not be referring to the game.

Ambrose has more friends at his party than I've had in my entire life.

Cars are parked bumper to bumper, overflowing from the driveway onto the street and a handful of them are parked on the grass in the front yard—wheels sunken deep into the ground.

Alima will *not* be happy about that. But I guess you only turn nineteen once.

Seeing how everyone showed out with their outfits as they step out of their cars, I'm immediately glad I put a little more effort into getting ready. I smooth my hands down my velvet minidress and rake my curls away from my face. Pulling out a compact mirror from my cross-body purse, I do one last check on my make-up.

Exhilaration sparks to life within me.

The small gift box hangs at my side as I squeeze through the throng of people loitering near the door. Music blares from the speakers and couples grind against each other in the den. I set out on a search for Cat but when I can't find her, I head into the kitchen for a drink.

Bypassing the sodas on the counter, I drop to the cooler on the floor and snatch a bottle of water.

My eyes scan the area for Ambrose, but it's hard to see anyone clearly through the crowd.

This is just a *tad* bit overwhelming.

Drink in hand, I escape up the stairs with the sole intention of seeking asylum in Cat's room.

When I reach her door, I jiggle the handle, but it's locked. I knock two times. "Cat?"

"We're busy!" Maitland shouts and I can swear I hear Cat's giggles somewhere in there.

I snort, backing away to give them some privacy.

My eyes drift to Ambrose's door. It's cracked open, but the lights are off inside.

I'll just hide out for a few minutes.

Slipping inside, I engage the lock behind me. I don't bother turning on the lights before lying down on the bed. I massage my temples in a circular motion, my eyes instantly growing heavy.

I don't realize I've dozed off until I wake to the sound of someone clearing their throat.

My gaze locks on the shadowed figure leaning back in the rolling chair and I shriek, grabbing the nearest object and throwing it.

"*Ow!*"

The desk lamp flips on.

"Ambrose?" I breathe.

"You know," he says, voice muffled, "this is the second time you've been shocked to find me in my room."

He clutches his nose, leaning his head back a bit.

I gasp. "You're bleeding."

"You're good," he says, laughing under his breath.

"Don't move." I scramble off his bed and run into the bathroom. Gathering a huge first aid kit in my arms, I rush back to his side.

I pull out a bundle of gauze and gently press it against his nose. He covers my hand with his, applying more pressure.

"I'm sorry," I whisper with an apologetic smile.

His shoulders shake. I can't believe he's laughing about this. "It's okay. I hear when a girl picks on a boy, it means she likes him."

Rolling my eyes, I remain focused on his nose. My fingers brush the scruff on his chin and my breathing becomes uneven. "Of course I like you."

His warm fingers squeeze mine, causing me to lower my eyes to his. "I like you too."

My heart skips a beat and I drop my hand, turning away.

"Mara—"

"What are you doing, Ambrose?"

Hearing his footsteps behind me, I spin on my heels before he gets too close and I lose all sense of logic. "You keep... flirting with me and while it's fun and feels good at the moment, it's *confusing*. We didn't reestablish a friendship just for me to become one of your little playthings."

"Okay let me stop you right there." His voice hardens. "You are not and never will be a *plaything* to me."

"Then what am I?"

"Everything. You're everything to me."

A shiver runs through my body.

His words bring on a wave of joy but also fear. And that fear? It prepares for battle by morphing into anger.

"I'm not doing this right now, Ambrose. Not on your birthday."

"Don't do that," he demands softly. "Don't shut me out."

I scoff. "Oh, that's *rich* coming from you. You practically wrote the handbook on shutting people out." A thought hits me then. "This is why you and Sasha broke up, isn't it?"

He runs a hand over his face.

"Answer me!"

"What do you want me to say?" he grits. "That the moment I found out you broke up with Brandon, I couldn't pretend for one more second that it wasn't you I wanted the entire time?" A breath shudders out of me. "That I *hated* myself for wanting you the way that I want you after treating you less than you deserved?"

"You keep me at a distance for years, Ambrose. For *no* reason." I blow out a frustrated breath. "Things are just getting back to normal between us."

"You don't understand," he says, distressed.

"Don't tell me what I don't understand." I hold up a finger. "I understand that you used to be one of my best friends in the entire world and then one day that meant nothing to you. I understand that you never even told me *why* you pushed me away. You still haven't. And now I'm supposed to believe that you cared about me the entire time? That you wanted to *be* with me?" My voice goes raw from the yelling. "You owned every part of me and you threw me away like trash."

He moves closer, reaching for my hand but I pull away before he makes contact. "I know, Mara. Trust me, I know. I hate myself for it and I'll accept you hating me too if you just *let* me explain."

"*No.*" My voice cracks as I back away, hands searching for the door knob. "It's too late, Ambrose. It's too late."

NOW

L aura's house looks like something out of *Lake Living*.

Any excitement I feel about seeing her place for the first time is quickly overshadowed by the purpose of my visit.

When Laura asked me for a week off because Anya and Matty were moving in with her, I told her to take two. Anya's house was salvaged from the fire, but the damage was extensive. Despite Ambrose going over there to repair things every day, it'll take a least a year to restore.

I step out of my car and take in the small cottage sitting on the quieter side of the lake, nestled between rows and rows of cherry blossom trees. I distinctly remember Laura saying her parents planted them before her mom passed and I wonder if she ever got to see them bloom.

I knock on the door and it opens almost immediately. Matty's in a pair of dinosaur pajamas, his hair an absolute disaster.

"Hey, cutie. Just wake up?"

His eyes shift to the ground. "No. All my clothes are at home. Auntie Laura says she needs to buy me new ones because they got burned."

Dammit. Why didn't I think about that before I opened my big stupid mouth?

"Well, clothes are overrated." I ruffle his hair. "I'd rather be in my pajamas like you." He doesn't return my smile or laugh like he usually does and it's a knife to the heart.

"Are you here to see Auntie Laura?"

"Yes."

"I'll get her." He walks away, shoulders slumped.

Laura steps through the door moments later, pulling me in for a bone-crushing hug.

"Thank you," she breathes, reaching for the medical bag she asked me to bring over. "Who's with your dad?"

"Nurse Charlene. She's been a huge help these last two weeks and she was more than happy to post up with him for the rest of the day. Plus, I made her double fudge brownies." I snort.

"How's he doing?"

"Great, I think. Considering the circumstances." I let out a dry laugh. "Otso hasn't left his bed in days."

"*Days?*"

"Yeah." I shrug. "But that's normal, right? I mean, he loves his owner. Man's best friend and all that."

"Hmm," is all she says.

I drag my nails across the back of my neck as the question I've been wanting to ask for days rears its ugly head. I just blurt it out. "Will you teach me?"

Laura's brows pinch with confusion and the words start spilling out of me.

"I want to do more for my dad." My eyes blink rapidly. "I want to take care of him the way you take care of him. I want—I want him to know that I showed up for him. That I became the daughter he deserved, even if it wasn't until the very end. I'd like to help you bathe him." My lip quivers. "And change him," I whisper. "And if you could teach me, I'd really—"

Laura yanks me into her arms and doesn't let go. I shut my eyes against the tears as her gentle hands stroke the back of my hair. "Yes, sweetheart." Her voice breaks. "Yes, of course I will."

We stand there for a few minutes, finding comfort in each other's embrace until I tell her I should head back. I don't have anywhere to be, but I'm afraid of what staying here will do to my emotions.

We say our goodbyes and as Laura closes the door, a hand shoots out to catch it.

Anya opens the door wider and steps into view. Even though she looks like she's lived a million lifetimes, she still looks better than she did at Matty's party. I take a measured step back, unsure of what she'll do next.

Laura eyes her sister. "Anya..."

"Can I talk to you?"

"I don't think that's a good idea," Laura says and Anya faces her.

"I'm not going to throw another beer on her," she grumbles. "All you have in your fridge is water."

Anya's eyes swing to me as she leans against the threshold, waiting.

I exhale a ragged breath. "Sure."

We walk to the end of the dock and I peer over my shoulder, hoping Laura's supervising us through the window just in case Anya decides to push me off.

Okay, I don't think she'd do that.

Okay, maybe I think her hand would accidentally slip and do the opposite of pulling me in for a hug.

She sits, her legs dangling over the edge and I follow suit.

We stare out at the water and I avoid looking at her just in case she attempts to kill me with her eyes.

"I owe you an apology."

My head whips around so fast I'm surprised I don't break my neck.

Her laugh is dry. "I know, right? Me apologizing. I promise I'm sober. Today at least."

She's making a joke. Do I laugh?

No. Too soon.

I study her, confused and if I'm being honest, a little suspicious. "Why?"

"Because you saved my kid's life. Simple as that. Now we're even."

I want to point out that I've never done anything to her, but I have a strong feeling she's keeping score of my past and settling a debt on behalf of those affected by it. And for that, I can't blame her.

I nod, my eyes following a robin across the sky. "We're even."

We don't try to fill the silence as a crisp breeze dances through the trees. A white flag may have been raised, but that doesn't mean the conversation will flow easily.

I fiddle with my keychain, curiosity getting the best of me. "Can I ask you a question?" Guarded eyes meet mine but she doesn't say no. "Why Jason?"

She snaps the twig in her hand and blows out a harsh breath. "Matty had colic as a baby."

My brows shoot straight up.

"I know." She smiles in a way I've never seen. "You'd never guess it by the way he is now." She swallows. "But he would just cry and cry for *hours*. Like he was put on this very earth for the sole purpose of crying. Like he already knew a little something about the cruel world he'd been brought into and he was mad as hell about it." She tosses the crumpled bits of wood into the water. "It scared me because I thought that meant he'd be like me. That he'd feel too much, way too often."

I offer her an encouraging nod.

"The world... the world has always felt a bit too heavy for me. I see things or hear things and I can't forget about them the way other people can. I think I recognized that same thing in you the first time I saw you. It was in your eyes."

"What was?"

Her smile is sad. "Everything."

My throat tightens and something soft covers my knuckles.

Anya's holding my hand. And I'm letting her.

"Anyway, when our mom died... the world got heavier. Suffocating. It weighed on me. But when I had Matty, everything changed. I got clean. I saw the good along with the bad. The joy along with the suffering. It stayed like that for a while but then I started to feel it again. The heaviness. It was so *loud*. And when I met Jason, he said he could help me find the quiet. It lived at the bottom of a glass pipe, but yeah... it was quiet."

I squeeze her hand.

"I'm an addict, Mara. I know that. I just got a little lost in the quiet I craved so desperately. But the night of the fire..." She shivers. "It was quiet and death was screaming all around us. I need to listen to the noise again. I need to feel the heavy. For Matty. I can't run from it anymore."

I blow out a breath. "I get it."

"I know you do."

We chat a little longer and before I leave, Anya tells me that she's entering a rehab program in a few days. I offer to drive Matty to her visitations when Ambrose and Laura can't for as long as I'm in Speck Lake.

We aren't friends. Not even close. But there's a unique connection that forms when you love the same people.

For Matty's sake, I hope Anya gets better.

I've been standing in front of Ambrose's door for five whole minutes contemplating whether to knock or not. Anya's words bounce around my mind. *I can't run anymore.*

It feels like someone's sucker punched me in the gut. Anya and I share a common thread. We run. We're runners. Because we're afraid of how heavy the weight of our emotions can be. How all-consuming. I let my mom convince me that those emotions were too much. That something was wrong with me–that I just needed to "toughen up."

But for the first time in my life, I don't want to toughen up. I want to fall apart and I want to do that in the arms of the person I feel safest with.

Ambrose.

It's this realization that has me pounding on his door three times.

The door swings open and Ambrose stands in front of me wearing nothing but a pair of sweatpants riding low on his hips. Blood rushes through my ears and I remind myself why I'm here. Beads of sweat line his forehead and my eyes drop to his bandage-wrapped knuckles. *I knew* I heard the rattling of a punching bag when I walked past the garage.

I take a small step. "Can I come in?"

He hesitates before moving just enough to create a small opening for me to slip through. Heated eyes stare down at me and I can't help my audible intake of breath as my chest grazes his.

When you're ready to admit what it is you want, you come find me.

I stalk past the den, making a beeline toward the kitchen. I prop my hip against the marble counter and Ambrose saunters in slowly, staring at me like I'm not wearing a ratty old Tommy Bahama T-shirt with a coffee stain on it. Something about him is different. Predatory. Like he no longer cares to hide the fact that he wants me.

The planes of his chest are defined under the harsh kitchen lights, and I drink him in, committing him to memory. There isn't a single part of me that has inherited my mom's artistic skills, but at this moment I'd kill to paint the man in front of me.

Ambrose lifts his arms and clenches the doorframe above his head. "Know what you want yet?"

There's an edge to his voice and it's just like when we were younger. Except this time, I want to cut myself on his edge instead of run away from it.

"I... I just—"

"Go home, Mara." He turns away.

"Don't be an asshole, *give* me a minute!"

His head turns back slowly, eyes lit with amusement. "You've had seven years."

My fingers squeeze the bridge of my nose.

I shouldn't have come. I've been in his house for five minutes and we're already baring our teeth.

"This was a mistake. I should go."

"Go ahead, Mouse. Run away." He scoffs, grabbing a beer from the fridge. "You should have a fucking endorsement deal from Nike."

"Don't *call* me..."

My eyes catch on something to the left of his head. It's easy to miss, but it's there. Glued to the corner of the fridge door.

I stare in awe, shocked that it's still in pristine condition after all these years.

"Where did you get that?" I whisper.

Ambrose looks confused at first, but then he follows my gaze and releases a small sigh. I move forward, reaching my fingers out to touch the stained glass on the magnet.

He positions himself between me and the magnet like I'm going to take it back or break it into a million little pieces. "After you left that night on my birthday, I saw it sitting on the counter. When I opened it, I knew who it was from."

It's no bigger than a sand dollar. And it's just a magnet but the stained glass makes it look like a relic. I bought it for Ambrose during a trip to Paris. To anyone else, it might seem like a random gift, but it makes sense to us.

The little mouse stares back at me, its eyes crafted from ruby and azure-colored glass. We were just getting back on good terms again and I wanted him to have someone to remember me by while at school. Even if no one else understood it. Even if it came in the shape of a silly little magnet on a fridge.

"You kept it all this time?"

A vein ticks in his jaw. "It was all I had left of you."

This time, I move first.

I hurl myself toward Ambrose, knocking the breath out of me as our teeth clash.

Beer still in hand, he wraps his free arm around my waist and hoists me up onto the counter. He makes a sound I've never heard before and my ankles clasp firmly behind his back, erasing what little space was between us.

We cling to each other, our panting breaths mingling in the air. I grind against him, the pulsing sensation coiling tight at my center. My tongue darts toward his but he rears his head back, gripping my chin in his hand.

"What do you *want*?" he breathes. Every part of him is tensed—a bow-string pulled tautly.

I drag his bottom lip between my teeth and tug. "You."

The sound of relief that comes from him strikes me like lightning. Our lips meet and all his reservations melt away. I dig my fingers into his hips, wanting more. Needing more. He fists the back of my hair and pulls, dropping hot kisses along my exposed neck.

"Did you miss me?" His nose grazes the dip in my throat and a needy whimper escapes me. "Because I missed you. I missed you every fucking day. I miss you right now and you're right in front of me." He says it so firmly that I know it's how he truly feels—that he's not just gracing me with niceties.

Our movements become jerky and less controlled. The beer bottle slips from his hands, shattering across the floor. "Hold onto me, baby," he whispers, scooping me into his arms. He moves us toward the stairs, my nails clawing desperately at his back.

When he lowers me onto his bed, I'm surprised by how quickly he got us here with his eyes half-closed.

I reach for the band of his sweatpants, but his hands fly to the hem of my shirt. "Arms up," he demands.

I oblige.

My heart beats erratically as my clothes fall to the floor, leaving me in nothing except my underwear. I scoot backward toward the headboard and Ambrose wraps his arm around the small of my back, carrying me the rest of the way.

His mouth crashes down on mine like he's trying to brand me with his lips. He pulls away abruptly and when he sits back, devouring the sight of me, I huff with impatience. He chuckles.

"My gorgeous girl," he whispers, dropping a soft kiss on the inside of my wrist. "This is the last gentle touch you'll be getting from me."

Electric currents run through me as he lowers his body flush against mine. His fingers pause at the elastic band on my hips, the question clear in his eyes and I nod uncontrollably.

Ambrose explores the length of me, touching and tasting—pushing me to the edge. He drags his teeth over my rib cage, nipping the skin there, and my back arches off the bed.

"Ambrose, *please*. Are you gonna make me beg?"

"I don't know." He smirks. "Would you?"

I dig my nails into his back and he grunts. His arm juts out, knocking the alarm clock off his nightstand as he fumbles for the drawer. I stop him, pulling him back into my arms. "I'm on the pill."

Weaving one hand through mine, he slides it above my head and presses it firmly into the mattress. My breathing goes ragged.

With one smooth thrust, he pushes into me and a moan falls from my lips. His shaky hand pushes the hair from my face. "*Fuck.*"

I trail feverish kisses along the curve of his neck like we're running out of time.

His name falls from my lips over and over again like a whispered prayer.

We rock against each other, perfectly in sync, and slowly, our movements become more demanding.

Feeling the need for release creeping in, I bring the back of my hand to my mouth.

Ambrose pries it away, dragging it above my head to join the other.

"Don't," he rasps, biting my lip. "I want to hear you."

He picks up his pace and my stomach clenches, the pressure between my thighs cresting until I can't go any higher.

When the part of me that's been wound tight for the last seven years finally explodes, I cry out and Ambrose devours the sound in his mouth. My body trembles from the high and Ambrose supports my weight, pumping in and out of me until his shoulders go rigid. Before my legs give out for good, I grind my hips against him in a circular motion and his grunts of release follow closely behind.

We fall against the mattress, a tangled mess of limbs as we catch our breath.

The soft blues of dusk dance through the cracks in the curtains as Ambrose pulls the covers back and we slip inside, facing each other.

I draw shapes on his chest while he plays with my hair and I think that if this is what the rest of my life looks like, they'll call me one of the lucky ones. My fingers inch along the side of his bicep and a tattoo I've never noticed peeks through. I angle his arm to get a better look and my heart stops.

Con amor para siempre.

With love forever.

Frozen still, I reread it repeatedly, waiting for it to disappear like a mirage.

"You lied to me that day."

My eyes fly up to his face.

Solid green eyes look down on me. He doesn't look hurt or upset, just curious. I clutch the gold chain around my neck and give him a slight nod.

"Why?"

I chew on my lip. "I think... I was afraid if you knew what it meant, you wouldn't want me to have it anymore."

Ambrose pulls me closer, tucks me into him, and cradles the side of my face. "I still would've wanted you to have it."

Suddenly I feel like a lovestruck eleven-year-old again and I burrow down deeper into the covers. Ambrose yanks them away and I laugh despite my embarrassment. I feel my cheeks warm as he beams at me.

"Why are you looking at me like that?"

"How could I not?"

My heart swells beyond my chest cavity and I lean forward, brushing my lips against his. I'm swimming in warmth and contentment.

"You should *only* wear this," I say, my hands returning to his body.

"I'm naked."

"Exactly."

In one swift movement, he rolls me onto my back and kisses me deeply. He hooks my thigh over his hip, every part of him hardening against me.

"Greedy," I murmur, a little breathless.

"Only for this. Only for you."

I pull him into me once again and this time it's unrushed.

This time, we make love.

It's only an hour later when I wake to the sound of a phone buzzing on Ambrose's nightstand.

I jump out of bed and grab it before it wakes him. He's been at Anya's house, working on repairs day in and day out all while managing operations at the zoo. He needs the rest.

I move my thumb to silence the call but before I do, my eyes trip up on the name.

Mom.

A sickening wave of bile burns at my throat knowing I'm only one swipe away from Alima's voice. From the woman who treated me like her own daughter. The woman whose life I've tragically altered forever.

Does she somehow know I'm with Ambrose right now? I've heard stories about a mother's intuition. Mothers who know when there's something wrong with their children. Mothers who know when you're lying. Mothers who know when their kids have sex for the first time. Mothers who just *know*.

My breathing becomes choppy at the idea that Alima knows I'm in bed with her son, and I quickly ignore the call, hoping it severs her omniscient connection to him.

I creep to the foot of the bed, moving like a burglar in the night, and snatch my discarded clothes. I dress in record time and as I'm backing out of Ambrose's room, I cast one last glance at him. My body and my heart tell me to get back in bed. Back in the place I feel whole. But the image of Alima kicking and screaming forces me to close the door behind me without a word.

And the quiet wraps its familiar arms around me.

Someone's poking my butt.

I pull my head out from under my pillow and glance over my shoulder with bleary eyes.

I must be hallucinating.

A stupid grin stretches across her face as she stares down at me.

My brain takes its sweet time registering what's happening but when it does, I sit up at full speed.

"Tally, what the hell are you doing here?" I croak.

She climbs into bed next to me and leans back on my pillow as if it's completely normal that she's in my bed. In my childhood home. In *Maine*. "I missed my best friend."

I gawk at her through the heavy strands of hair shrouding my face. "How did you know where I lived?"

She interlocks her fingers, a mischievous smile tugging at her mouth. It reminds me of Cat.

"I called your dad's nurse, Laura. You left her number on a sticky note on your fridge. Told her who I was and she was *very* accommodating when I said I wanted to surprise my best friend in the entire world."

"When I gave you a spare key to water my plants and feed Cheddar, I didn't think you'd resort to snooping."

A snort accompanies her smile. "Do you even know me?"

"Wait... who's watching Cheddar?"

Her smile is strained.

"Tally, I swear, if Jeremy force-feeds my cat asparagus, I'll kill him."

She tips over with laughter.

It just doesn't make any sense. Tally hates flying. She once told me she'd rather sit through a root canal than be on an airplane, which is how I know her visit isn't as casual as she's making it out to be. "Why are you *really* here?"

All pretenses slide off her face and empathy fills its place. "You've been gone a while, babe. Figured you could use a friend."

Understanding hits me like a ton of bricks. She thinks I need a friend because she knows my dad doesn't have much time left. No one's in hospice forever.

Tally's stomach rumbles and her cheeks flush pink. "Sorry. I didn't eat before my flight and the lady next to me stole my peanuts while I slept. Mind if I whip up something to eat?

I give a slight shake of my head before escaping to the bathroom to shower.

As the water beats down on my back, I lean my face against the cool shower tile and my mind drifts to the man across the street.

Ambrose.

Last night was a dream I should've known I'd be forced to wake from. I just thought we'd have a little more time.

Trudging downstairs, I find Tally making blueberry pancakes from scratch, bouncing around the kitchen like she's been here a million times.

Plopping down at the table, I curl my knees up to my chest. "Are you sure you're here for me, or did you just need to go somewhere far enough to eat whatever you want?"

She rolls her eyes as she whisks. "I'll have you know that I finally stood up to Jeremy."

"Do tell."

"I told him I'm my own person with my own food preferences," she licks the batter off her forefinger, "and I won't hide them anymore. Juice?" She holds out a glass of orange juice that I happily accept.

"Thank you." I take a generous sip. "Okay, so wait. Tell me what he said."

Tally sets a plate of fresh pancakes in front of me and I almost drool on the spot. She folds her arms and I snort. Where did she find that apron? "He said the only reason he kept making me eat that shit was because I pretended to like it." Her head shakes. "I gotta say, communication does wonders."

"You don't say."

"You should try it sometime."

I choke out a laugh. "Damn. Gut me, why don't you."

"I'm just *saying*. You tend to avoid conflict." The doorbell rings and before I can speak around the food in my mouth, Tally jumps up. "I'll get it!"

I glance around, frantically searching for an escape route. I could run up to my room, and pretend I'm not here, but I'd have to pass the front door, which defeats the purpose.

"Look who's stopped by," Tally says, walking back into the kitchen. Ambrose trails behind her, looking fresh and... well I can't read the expression on his face.

He jerks his chin to the pancakes in front of me. "Morning."

"Morning," I garble around a bite of pancakes.

Tally throws me a look of disgust before facing Ambrose. "Who are you?"

Ambrose drags his eyes away from where I sit and leans in for a handshake with a friendly smile. "I'm Ambrose."

Recognition fills Tally's eyes and I want to drag her away before she says something that will make me sink farther into my chair. I widen my eyes at her and to my relief, she makes her face unreadable. "Ambrose. Hmm. I've never heard of you."

Ambrose laughs. "And who are *you*?"

"Her best friend," she says, jutting a thumb at me.

My gaze swings to Ambrose, readying myself for the disappointment in his eyes but there's nothing but a genuine smile on his face as he watches me.

"Tally, can I have a minute with Mara?"

I shake my head quickly behind Ambrose's back.

Don't leave me. Don't leave me.

"Sure. I was just about to hop in the shower. I still smell like the belly of an airplane." She laughs, wiggling her brows as she backs out of the kitchen.

Best friend, my ass.

Ambrose sits down and grips the seat of my chair, pulling me closer to him. He takes the fork out of my hand, eating the chunk of pancake on it. "You left last night."

I swallow. "Yes." I don't realize my knee is bobbing under the table until his cool hands bring it to a halt.

"Are we good?"

"Yes," I repeat.

"Good." He uses his thumb to wipe away the syrup on my lip and puts it in his mouth. "So, listen," he says. "I'm going out of town on Saturday and I want you to come with me."

Despite my internal battle, curiosity gets the best of me. "Where?"

One heartbeat. Then another.

"My mom's house. To visit Cat."

I try to stop it. I do. But everything in me short circuits. My posture becomes rigid and my vision shifts in and out. I shake my head. "No."

"What do you mean, *no*?"

"The word pretty much speaks for itself."

He leans back in his chair. "Are you kidding me right now?"

I don't answer.

Ambrose pinches the bridge of his nose. "I should have seen this coming." He stands up, the chair screeching against the hardwood. "Nothing's changed for you, has it? You're never going to face what happened. Even if it means destroying what we have." He stomps forward, lifting my chin. His eyes are a swirling storm of anger, but his touch is gentle as ever. My throat tightens.

"I waited for you," he rasps. "I'm *still* waiting for you. But you gotta meet me halfway." He searches my face with a look of desperation as his thumb brushes the side of my jaw. "Can you meet me halfway, baby?"

When my silence prevails, his hand drops down to his side.

"You're a coward," he whispers, voice gravelly. "And I won't erase her from my life just because it hurts." He starts to leave but stops at the kitchen's entrance, his face grim. "She wouldn't have wanted this for us, Mara. Do you remember the night of prom at Lake Bonnie? Do you remember what she said?"

I remember everything.

"She said the three of us were soul mates. And it's the truth. It's always been the truth."

He leaves me to mull over his words, the door softly closing behind him more painful to hear than if it were slammed shut. I stare at the plate in front of me, amazed at how one of my favorite foods in the world suddenly tastes like dust in my mouth.

THEN

AGE SEVENTEEN

"Dear graduates. I don't know what to say. High school was a bitch and I'm pretty sure the real world won't be any different…"

I can't help but laugh.

"Thank god you aren't valedictorian."

Cat slurps down the rest of her smoothie. "I could have been. If I cared enough."

And she's right. She's without a doubt the smartest person in our class, but she prefers to put her efforts elsewhere.

"You only want to be valedictorian so you can do the speech. Trust me, you'll have plenty of stage time on Broadway," I say, doing a little shimmy in excitement.

Cat got into the theater program at NYU, and I received my acceptance into their film school last week. Everything is falling into place. Now, all we need is an apartment that won't require us to sell vital organs on the dark web.

"What about this one?" She slides her phone across the table and I look at the listing she pulled up.

"Mmm, that one's not gonna work. It's out of our price range. You're looking at the net rent, not the gross rent. See, look," I say, pointing out the fine print.

She growls and I understand her frustration because I feel it too. Finding an apartment has been harder than we expected. Every place we've found so far has asked that tenants make forty times the rent. Cat's convinced it's a cover-up for money laundering. We're trying to schmooze her parents into being our guarantors but it's not a sure thing yet.

"Don't worry," I assure her. "We'll find something."

"Do you think we should get a dog?"

"With the kind of rent we'll be paying, we won't be able to afford a dog."

"A cat?"

I consider that. "I could bring Cheddar," I offer.

"Uh. Never mind..." she says, averting her eyes to the bottom of her empty cup.

I choke on a laugh. "What's wrong with Cheddar?"

"Nothing's *wrong* with him, Sally. He's just... old. He's more like a fifty-year-aged cheddar now. I think the city might scare a few lives out of him."

I mean, she's not wrong. Cheddar groans the way a senior citizen does every time their back gives out and as much as I'd love for him to join us in the move, it just isn't feasible.

Changing subjects, Cat reaches for my smoothie, helping herself. "So the thing is..."

I attempt to reclaim it and she snatches it away with contempt in her eyes. Like I should be ashamed for not wanting to share. My brow lifts. "There's a thing?"

"You and Ambrose."

If my drink was still in my possession, I'd have choked on it.

There's no me and Ambrose. There's no Ambrose and me. No sentence should ever incorporate the two of us so closely together. I express as much to Cat.

"Listen," she says. "All I'm saying is, the last couple of times you two have been around each other, there's been a certain... tension in the air." She wriggles her fingers in front of her.

"I have no idea what you're talking about."

"Yeah, I'm not too sure about that. And if you want to know what I think—" Maitland, bless his soul, suddenly appears behind Cat and throws his hands over her eyes.

"Guess who?" he sings.

Cat inhales deeply. "I don't know, but whoever you are, you smell hot. Like Sandalwood and bad decisions. Don't tell my boyfriend."

Maitland growls playfully and showers Cat with kisses, tickling her until she screeches like a hyena.

"Are you girls coming out with us tonight?"

He's referring to the bonfire. A tradition all the seniors take part in the night before graduation. They hike through the woods for about an hour to Penny Lake and make a five-foot bonfire. It used to be taller, but there was an incident in the 90s where the fire got out of hand, so these days, seniors play it safe.

There's music and dancing and alcohol, but the best part of the tradition is the wish-burning. Every senior writes down a wish they have for the start of their post–high school life and throws it in the fire. It's the only aspect of the night that intrigues me.

"I don't know, are you going to carry me?" Cat asks. She rejects anything physical unless it's cheerleading or exercising her arms by reaching to the bottom of a bag of chips. I'm no better.

"I'll always carry you, babe."

They start making out and when I clear my throat, Maitland must think it's because I'm inquiring about who will carry me because he says, "Jensen

Martinelli is coming too. I'm sure he wouldn't mind having you over his shoulder, Mar."

Cat bursts into laughter and my face grows hot. I take my near-empty smoothie cup from her, sipping at the remnants. Maitland lets us know he'll pick us up tonight before he rushes off to pick up his pressed cap and gown before the dry cleaners close.

Not willing to let Cat resume our previous conversation, I gather our trash and remind her that we're supposed to help her mom set up the house for our graduation party. Alima insisted our parties be thrown together and a deep part of me loves her for it.

"Ready?" Cats asks, jingling her keys.

I smile. "Let's do it."

It's a quarter past seven when we finally put the finishing touches on the house.

I avoid making eye contact with Ambrose the entire time and whenever he gets too close, I find an excuse to escape to another part of the house.

Cat watches us with suspicious eyes and I make a conscientious effort to avoid her too, escaping her presence any chance I get.

Alima ambles past me with yet another bin she's pulled down from the attic and I bite back a laugh.

With the number of decorations strewn about, you'd think she's hosting a banquet with a hundred mouths to feed instead of a graduation party.

"I hate that you're planning this entire party by yourself," I tell her. "When was Mr. King supposed to get in from his work trip today?"

"He was supposed to be home before noon, but it seems as though he's forgotten his watch." Her voice is clipped as she wipes the sweat from her brow.

"I didn't even know accountants had work trips."

"Neither did I."

I frown. "Well, everything looks great. Seriously, it looks like you hired professionals."

"You think so?" She sighs, dropping a kiss on the top of my head. "Thank you for saying that. I just want it to be perfect for you two."

"It will be." I take another bite. "You didn't go this big for Ambrose, did you? I can't remember."

Alima bumps her hip with mine and chuckles. "We weren't even sure he'd graduate."

"Always my biggest cheerleader, Mother," Ambrose drawls, entering the room with a bundle of graduation balloons in his arms. He ties them to the leg of a chair before giving me a pointed look.

When a timer sounds off in the kitchen, Alima excuses herself.

Ambrose walks toward me, hands buried in his pockets. I turn back to my little workstation, folding the last of the dinner napkins into a swan.

Closer now, my body instinctively reacts to his presence. "Talk to me."

"No."

"Yes."

"*No.*" I spin around. "This," I whisper-hiss, pointing between us, "is not a thing. *We* are not a thing."

"Bullshit."

I scoff. "I can barely stand you half the time."

He takes a step toward me, eyes blazing, and drops his voice to a whisper. "Is that so?"

"It is," I say, but my voice holds no conviction. I'm grasping for straws at this point. "Not to mention, it would break Cat's heart. I'm *her* best friend."

He deadpans. "She'd be the first person on board and you know it." I did know that. "Besides, this isn't some stupid game of dibs. If it were, Cat would be shit out of luck."

My breath hitched in my throat. "How do you figure?"

Tipping my chin up with his free hand, he forces me to look at him. "I saw you first."

"Mara?" Cat calls out from upstairs. Her footsteps grow louder as she makes her way down and I gasp, stumbling back a few steps. Ambrose crosses his arms, never once taking his eyes off me.

I frantically circle the den, looking for something to busy my trembling hands with.

Ambrose rolls his eyes. "Get a grip, woman."

"You." I point at him. "Shut it."

By the time Cat walks into the den, I'm holding a cookie platter out in front of me like an offering.

Glancing from me to Ambrose, she grabs a cookie with a look of confusion. "Um... thank you?"

Kill me now, my eye is twitching.

"Okay, moving on from whatever is going on in here." She looks at me. "If I have to touch another hot glue gun tonight, I'm going to respectfully ask you to push me off the roof. We need to leave *now* or else we'll be here all night. Let's go get changed."

Without sparing another look toward Ambrose, I allow Cat to drag me upstairs to get ready for tonight.

Maitland rolls into the driveway half an hour later with Jensen Martinelli in the passenger seat and I overhear Ambrose ask Cat who he is. I'll never admit it out loud, but a small part of me secretly hopes that Ambrose is watching as Jensen joins me in the back seat, giving Cat shotgun.

I'm fucking hot.

It isn't because of the red body-hugging halter top Cat lent me for the night and it isn't because of the jeans I outgrew sophomore year, which I spent fifteen minutes squeezing into because Cat said they make my ass look great. It's because we're standing in front of the tallest bonfire I've ever seen in my life.

When we first arrived, the fire was at a reasonable height and it stayed that way until I learned that Jensen Martinelli is somewhat of a pyromaniac. He thought it'd make the night more "memorable" if he added fuel to the flames.

Literally.

Maitland had to confiscate the jug of fuel from his hands when people started to complain.

Cat and I rest on an abandoned tree stump, sipping from the flask she swiped from her dad's office. We're both struggling to write our wishes down on scrap pieces of paper.

"Only one wish?" Cat groans, biting the cap of her pen. "That's too much pressure."

"I know. I'm afraid I'll wish for the wrong thing."

My leg taps nervously on the pile of branches at my feet and my gaze drifts to the woods around us for inspiration. What do I wish?

The problem isn't thinking of a wish. The problem is thinking of a wish that I'd choose above all others. Because I wish for many things. I wish that things between Ambrose and me weren't so complicated. I wish my relationship with my mom was better. I wish my dad would find someone who would take care of him after I leave for college. I wish for many, *many* things.

As I fold my paper into a tiny square, I look over at Cat. Firelight dances across her round face. She's hunched down with her brows pinched in concentration, scribbling down her wish with her lucky purple pen. I walk as close as I can to the fire without feeling like my face is going to melt off and throw the square in. As the flames crackle around me, I let my eyes fall shut.

Tomorrow, everything will be different.

Everyone loosens up as the night progresses. Where students once lectured Jensen on his fire-throwing ways, they soon goad him on, encouraging him to make the fire bigger. I blame the alcohol.

The flames rise higher and so does the tension in my neck.

"Are we sure this is safe?" I ask.

"Sure." Maitland takes a sip of his water. "As long as it doesn't spread."

"We're in a *forest*," Cat slurs. She passed drunk an hour ago and when I tried to take the drink from her hands, she tried to bite me like a piranha. She won't be happy with herself when she's forced to endure graduation horns with a hangover tomorrow.

"Okay, but don't we think that maybe it shouldn't be so *big*—"

"Fire."

"Yes, thank you, Maitland. I know it's a fire. What I'm saying is—"

"No," Maitland croaks, his voice growing frantic. "Fire!" He points behind us and when I turn, I can't believe what I see.

In a matter of seconds, the fire sparks onto a tree twenty feet from us, engulfing its body in flames. It spreads quickly, catching onto the trees like they're candle wicks and everyone watches, frozen in horror. It's not until someone yells, "Run!" That we all disperse like ants on a crushed anthill.

Maitland pulls Cat into a run as I swoop down to pick up our bags. I push my feet to move faster, to keep my focus ahead of me, but I continue to glance back over my shoulder at the horrific sight. Smoke closes in on us, mixing with the shadows of the night.

I stop for a second, digging in my bag for the flashlight I brought, but come up short. It must have fallen out.

Black plumes shroud the woods and I begin to choke. I don't realize I've been separated from Cat and Maitland until all I see are unfamiliar faces whizzing past me.

"Cat!" I yell. "Maitland!" I run deeper into the woods, away from the worst of the smoke, suddenly grateful I've only had a few sips from Cat's flask.

My shoelaces snag on an exposed tree root and I go down, face-first. Gasping at the pain, I roll over onto my back and lift my hand to the burning sensation above my eye. When I pull it away, it's covered in blood.

"Hey! I've got you." Some random guy I'm pretty sure doesn't even go to our school bends down and throws my arm over his shoulder, lifting me off the ground. He carries the majority of my weight as we continue to run.

By the time we make it to the clearing where people are congregating, it feels like days have passed.

My eyes scan the area, searching for my friends, and when I see a small group of students huddled together, whispering and covering their mouths, the ground sways beneath me.

I hear Maitland shouting and suddenly I'm running, shoving my way through the bystanders who observe but make no move to help.

Is everyone here drunk?

At the sight of Maitland's ashen face, I fall to my knees in front of him as he cradles Cat's limp body in his arms. His shirt is off and he's holding it to her head where a steady flow of blood drips from her hair.

"What happened?" I cry. I look to Jensen for an answer, but he's stunned into silence.

"W-We were running and she tripped." His eyes are dazed. "She hit her head."

I bring my hand to Cat's face. "Cat? Cat, can you hear me? It's Mara. Open your eyes for me."

Cat groans in pain and I almost cry with relief. Pain is bad, but if she's still alert that means it's probably not life-threatening.

"Let's get her to the car," I say.

Maitland's eyes widen. "Mara, you're bleeding."

"I'm fine, I promise. Focus on Cat."

We lift Cat into our arms and continue our trek toward the access point. When we finally arrive back at the parking lot, firefighters are already making their way in and questioning students on the sidelines. I ask if we should stay to give a statement, but Maitland points out that Cat and I have been drinking so we decide it's smarter to head straight home. Jensen helps us into the back while Maitland turns on the car and then we're peeling out of the parking lot.

When Cat comes to, she groans, rubbing her eyes.

"What is it, Cat? Are you in pain?" My hands tremble as I keep her head steady in my lap.

"I forgot to throw my wish into the fire." She pouts. "I'm such a nincompoop."

I laugh and so does Maitland from the front seat.

She's okay.

"You're not a nincompoop." I brush away a tear running down my nose. "We can save your wish for another time."

"Okay." Her eyes flutter shut. "Because it's a really good one, Sally. Really good."

"I don't doubt it, Gilly."

"Mara?"

"Hmm?"

"Why are you always taking such good care of me?"

I smile. "Because we're sisters."

She sighs a happy sigh. "That's nice. I love Ambrose but I've always wanted a sister."

"Well, you got one," I whisper. She starts to speak again but I stop her. "Shh," I say, brushing the hair from her face. "Sleep."

We pull into the King's driveway and reality hits me like a bullet train.

There's no way I can bring her into the house and have her face Alima like this.

I pinch the bridge of my nose and shoot a text to Ambrose. He doesn't respond, but five minutes later I see his black figure slip out the front door. He ignores me as he scoops Cat up from the back seat, throwing both Maitland and Jensen death glares. I follow closely at his heels in silence.

Ambrose gets Cat into bed and I take the time to hide out in their shared bathroom. I'm brushing my teeth for what must be ten minutes when he walks in.

"How is she?" I swallow.

He leans against the doorframe and crosses his ankles. "Fine. She's out like a light. The bleeding on her head stopped—it was just a small cut. It's the huge lump that'll be a pain in the ass in the morning."

When I face the mirror again and spit out my mouthwash, Ambrose wraps his cool fingers around my wrist. I prepare for him to ream into me for not keeping a better eye on his baby sister. His blame won't hold a candle to the blame I'm already putting on myself.

His thumb lifts to my cheek, smearing a streak of soot that's gathered there. Angling my chin toward him, he examines the cut above my brow.

Crouching down, he grabs the first aid kit out from under the sink, rips open a disinfectant wipe with his teeth, and begins cleaning the cut.

"*Ouch!*" I cry out against the sting.

There's no sympathy in his eyes as he leans forward and lightly blows over the cut, his minty breath falling over my face. He applies a butterfly closure over top and gathers the trash in his hands.

"Take a shower. Then meet me on the roof." He stalks away without another word.

I hide in the shower until the water runs cold. And even then, I force myself to bear the ice-cold temperature as punishment for what's happened. It's not until I'm standing naked in the bathroom that I realize I forgot to grab a change of clothes. Not wanting to disturb Cat, I peek into Ambrose's room to make sure he isn't there.

Dashing to his dresser, I steal a warm T-shirt and a pair of sweatpants before climbing out onto the roof. Ambrose waits for me, knees bent to his chin. He doesn't acknowledge my presence until I'm sitting right next to him.

"What you both did tonight was stupid."

"I know."

Ambrose traps me with his stare. "You could've gotten hurt."

I shiver, thinking about how much worse tonight could have been. "I know."

He rakes his hands through his hair and I don't know what else to say, so I settle on saying nothing.

"Is there something going on between you and that Jensen guy?"

My laugh is clipped. "Why? Are you jealous?"

"Yes." Ambrose faces me head-on, his expression serious. "Yes, I am."

With a deep sigh, he tilts his head back and looks up at the night sky. "My dad's having an affair." The shock renders me speechless. "It started when I was a freshman in high school. Some lady from Bar Harbor. Her name's Sharon." He shakes his head. "Saw them together one day when I was picking up eggs for my mom at the grocery store and they were standing together in the baking aisle, reading the ingredients on the back of some cake mix." His laugh is pained. "I walked right up to him and he didn't even have the courtesy to look ashamed. He fucking *introduced* her to me, Mar." I slip my hand into his and he holds on to it like it's a lifeline.

"When I got home that night, he called me into his office. Gave me this fucking speech about the power of a 'man's word.' He wanted my word that I'd keep quiet about what I'd seen." Ambrose blows out a breath and the cold air fogs up around his face.

"And did you?" I ask but I already know the answer because I know the kind of person Ambrose is.

"I told my mom that night." His eyes are sad. "She already knew."

My chest is weighed down by the new secret. I'm thinking about how much of an asshole Robby is when Ambrose says, "My dad's affair changed me, Mara. I became so *angry*. I knew that if I kept spending all my time around you and Cat, one of you would notice something was off. My money was on you noticing first. You've always watched people so closely. I just figured staying far away from you was better than dragging you into the shit I needed to work through."

His explanation rocks me to my core. "Did Cat ever find out?"

Ambrose shakes his head slowly. "My mom begged me not to tell her. She said she wanted to do it herself once she got her affairs in order to file for the divorce."

Confusion fills my eyes. That was four years ago and Mr. King is still living at home.

Reading my thoughts, Ambrose says, "I know. She's put it off all this time. Whenever I bring it up, she either finds a way to change the topic or Cat enters the room. I think she's afraid of being alone."

All this information is too much to bear. The veins in my temples begin to throb. How am I supposed to keep something like this from Cat? I can't. *I won't.*

"It's okay if you feel like you have to tell her," Ambrose says. "My mom's had enough time."

All I do is nod.

"I'm so sorry Mara. I'm sorry I made you think that I was ever anything less than crazy about you. I hate that I had to pretend that our friendship meant nothing to me, but I'm tired of pretending. I'm tired of pretending that you're not one of the most important people in my life.

"You hurt me," I whisper. "You left me when you swore you wouldn't."

"I know." He nods, expression pained. "And I'm incredibly sorry."

I lace my fingers through his. "I forgive you." His eyes widen slightly at that. "But I'm also going to make you work for it," I tack on for good measure.

His eyes are so serious when he says, "You better."

Blowing out a weary breath, I lean into him. "I think we might love each other."

He pulls me into his chest and chuckles softly, planting a kiss on my forehead. "I think you might be right."

"I thought you hated me."

Ambrose inches closer to me and I've never seen eyes look so apologetic. "I could never hate you, Mouse." He licks his lips as his gaze falls to my mouth. "There were a lot of things I wanted to do to you over the years and none of them included making you feel hated."

"Like what?"

Ambrose leans forward and brushes his supple lips across mine. My pulse quickens.

Something buzzes through my body and the invisible tether between us tightens, pulling me firmly against his chest.

I open my mouth and he lets himself in. He gently pushes on my shoulder, laying me flat on the roof. Long fingers work their way through my hair as he traps my body under his. Heat spreads low in my stomach and all the things that felt wrong with Brandon feel right now that it's with Ambrose.

He tears his mouth away from mine, his voice tight with restraint. "That's what I wanted to do."

"What else?"

His laughter sings through the night and I smile. He sits up and grasps my hand, tilting his head toward the window. "Come on. I'll show you."

The moon glows brightly in the room as Ambrose and I reintroduce ourselves to each other on his bed.

We kiss and touch and whisper truths that we used to keep buried deep. We talk about the things we've missed over the years and the things we saw when we thought the other wasn't looking. When I mention Cat, Ambrose assures me that we'll tell her about us in the morning. *Together.* And when I try to extract myself from his arms to go to bed, he pulls me back into his pillows. All five times.

"Stay with me a while," he says. "I'll make sure you're back in Cat's bed before morning."

I kiss him deeply, chuckling into his ear. "You better." He scratches my head and traces shapes onto my back until we fall asleep.

But it's not Ambrose who wakes me the next morning.

I'm not there when Cat dies that night.

I don't know what time it happens. I don't know if it hurts. I don't know if she cries out for me or if the last thing she feels in this world is my absence. I don't know if it's long and drawn out or as quick as falling asleep. I don't know any of that because I'm with Ambrose.

I'm with Ambrose when the morning light filters through his room and I'm with him when Alima's bloodcurdling screams pierce through the air when she realizes why we've overslept on graduation day. I'm with Ambrose when the paramedics pump Cat's chest for longer than the usual twenty minutes because *she's only eighteen*. I'm with Ambrose when the doctors at the hospital tie the words "fall" and "brain bleed" together like two ropes in a bend knot and I'm with him when we all sink onto the cold hard floor like dominos, weeping enough to cause the eyes of the strangers around us to water. I'm with Ambrose when Alima clutches my shoulders in agony, screaming, "Where *were* you?"

Where was I?

Where was I?

Where. Was. I.

I was with Ambrose. And it's because I was with Ambrose that I can never be with Ambrose ever again.

NOW

When Tally reveals herself from her hiding spot, I'm still sitting in front of my pancakes, frozen like a statue at the MoMa. She heard everything.

Tally's the angriest I've ever seen her as she stomps toward me. "What the hell is wrong with you?"

"Don't start." I chuck my plate into the sink.

"That man is crazy about you, and you just sent him on his way like he was a vacuum salesman!"

"What's your point, Tally?"

"My point? My *point*? My point is, I'm tired of watching you get in your own way. You've tried so hard to block the pain out of your life that you've blocked out love too. You're my best friend in the entire world and I can list on two hands the personal details I know about you."

My heart drops. "Tally..."

She shakes her head in disappointment, but she looks sad. "You can't give people crumbs forever. We deserve more. *You* deserve more."

She retreats to my room and I sink back into my chair, my legs shaking so hard they thump the underside of the table. Ambrose says I'm a coward but I'm worse. I'm the reason Cat's dead. I knew she had a bad fall on her head and I told her to go to sleep. I told her to fucking *go to sleep*. I knew better. I *know* better. It's Head Injury 101. And then I left her side to fulfill my selfish desires. It's a decision that's haunted me for years.

I don't deserve to see where Cat ended up. After I skipped graduation and left town, I didn't want to know about the funeral proceedings. Shame prevented me from asking my dad where the Kings buried her. I'd only realized she'd been cremated when Ambrose told me his parents moved out of town. Alima wouldn't leave Speck Lake without Cat.

Thinking about her feels like bleeding out. My best friend. My sister. *My Gilly.*

How do I talk about her in the past tense when I feel her presence around me still? There's something that happens to a person on a molecular level when they lose their other half. It renders them utterly useless. For the past seven years, everything I've been able to accomplish has felt hollow. As if it doesn't matter in the end. Because my life ceased to matter to me the morning of graduation.

Graduation.

That's what hurts most of all. Cat talked about graduating high school ever since we were twelve. She was the kind of person who lived her life looking ahead. Not in the way that stopped her from enjoying the present, but in a way that inspired you to dream for the future with her. I can't forgive myself for robbing her of that milestone. It wasn't even a question for me that I'd skip graduation. You couldn't have paid me to walk across that stage.

What did people think when they saw Cat's name on the program but didn't see her walk up to receive her diploma? Did they think she skipped graduation? That she was late? I hated the possibility that anyone could be judging Cat that day. So, I skipped it. Because if they were going to judge Cat, I wanted them to judge me too.

When I got home from the hospital, I didn't waste time burning my cap and gown. It wasn't enough to throw them away, I wanted them to cease to exist—right down to the last thread. I almost felt guilty when my dad watched in horror as I threw the silky fabric and tassels into our fireplace. Only when the garments were reduced to ashes beneath the logs did I let the tears flow.

It was the last time I cried.

I flew to New York three days later with every penny I'd saved in high school. And when Ambrose frantically banged on the front door beforehand, I told my dad to tell him I'd already left.

"You can't leave without telling him, Mara," he pleaded.

"Tell him I'm already gone, or I swear you'll never hear from me again." That's when I learned how cold my voice could be. How easy it is to bulldoze past people when you have nothing left. When you feel nothing but complete emptiness inside. Hurt people can be dangerous people.

So, Ambrose was right when he called me a coward.

If I'd just stayed with her, things could have ended up differently. I've played it out a million times in my head since that night.

Ambrose would ask me to stay a while and I'd refuse because I know how deep of a sleeper he is. I *know* he'd forget to wake me up. I'd kiss him on the cheek and make my way back to Cat's room to sleep and when I'd hear her thrashing in pain, I'd stir awake and ask if she was okay.

When she wouldn't respond, I'd call out for Alima and tell her to call 911 because I remember the fall from the woods. The paramedics would arrive in record time because there's rarely ever traffic that late at night. They'd get to her in time and when she reached the hospital, she'd be stable. They'd have to perform surgery, but the surgeon would call it a miracle. *Good catch*, he'd say to me. *She's so lucky to have a friend like you.* We'd still miss graduation the next day, but it'd be okay because we'd be curled up in Cat's hospital bed with chocolate pudding cups, making fun of the valedictorian's speech on my laptop.

But that's not what happened.

I avoided Ambrose for all these years because I was convinced he'd hate me as much as Alima did once the dust settled. We held each other in the hospital, but we were at the height of our emotions. I didn't want to hang around for the moment he realized I could have prevented Cat's death by staying with her that night. And no matter how much I wanted to punish myself, I couldn't bear the idea of Ambrose looking at me and seeing the reason why she was no longer on this earth.

The day I ran into him in the grocery store, I was ready for it. The screams. The anger. But it never came. My confusion deepened every time he showed up at the house, willing to breathe the same air as me. And when I realized he still wanted to *be* with me, my heart soared and plummeted at the same time. A collision of my deepest wish and widest fear.

Because if Ambrose still wants to be with me, I'm sure I can't stay away from him. No matter how much I feel like I don't deserve it.

Instead of joining Tally upstairs, I walk on numb legs to my dad's room. I've found myself seeking solace with his sleeping body almost every day at this point, which is why I don't immediately realize his eyes are open. I'm stroking the leaves of a snake plant near the window when I hear his voice.

"*Princesa.*"

I whip around, afraid that the voice is from his ghost and I've missed the moment he left this world, just like Cat. His head is still, elevated on a stack of pillows like it always is, but his expression is alert. The most alert it's been since I've returned. I haven't seen his irises in their entirety until now and I almost fall to the floor in a puddle of tears.

I run toward him. "Dad." I lift a hand to his cheek. "Hi."

"Hi." He smiles.

"How are you feeling? Can I get you anything? Do you want me to call Laura?"

His voice is groggy but still carries a degree of the strength I've always loved him for. "No. I just want to look at you. I'm glad you're here now, Mara."

The tears are flowing freely down my face. He doesn't remember that I've *been* here. For months. That we've already spoken and laughed and made some of my most treasured memories together. That reveals more about his current condition than anything else and I squeeze his hand tightly as if the gesture is the only thing necessary to keep him tethered to this world.

"I'm glad I'm here too, Daddy. I'm sorry it took me so long to come back home."

"Better late than never. For everything."

My hands shake.

"I think I've messed it all up," I whisper. "Again."

The sigh he releases reminds me of when I was a little girl and it sparks a new wave of tears. Now that they have started, they won't stop. "Why won't you let him love you?"

I shake my head forcefully. "There's too much pain and I... I don't want to feel it all. The last time I did, it broke me."

My dad's voice is scratchy as he tries to respond, so I grab the cup of water on his bedside and slip the straw into his mouth. After a few sips, he gathers his energy to continue. "It didn't break you, Mara. It changed you. There's a difference. You've always felt things so deeply, ever since you were a little girl. It's one of my favorite things about you. I know your mom tried to teach you to hold it all in. It's how she was raised. But we need to stop that cycle here. With you."

I'm soaking his pillow with the tears I've kept hostage inside for years.

"Mara," he whispers, laying his fragile hand on mine. "Be grateful. Love is the *best* thing that can come from pain like that."

I shudder out a long breath and it's like someone's taken a match to the ice that was frozen around my heart. The innermost parts of me thaw and the warmth that claws its way out reminds me of the summers Ambrose, Cat, and I used to spend together.

"I'm sorry." My eyes squeeze shut. "I'm sorry I couldn't give you more of myself before now. Before you got sick."

"You've given me the best thing a father could ask for."

I lean back, searching his face. "What?"

"You gave me a daughter who loved me."

Sobs rack my body and his voice is gentle when he says, "Can I ask something of you?"

"Anything, Dad." I sniff. I would do anything for him at this moment, I realize.

But his request is simple.

"Watch a movie with me."

I smile so wide my jaw feels stretched. Salty tears fall into my mouth as I reach for my laptop. "What should we watch?"

"*Princess Bride*. It's one of my favorites."

My smile is watery. "Since when?"

"Since it became one of your favorites."

My chest cracks open and I can swear people hear the sound from miles away. I lift his comforter and join him underneath. Otso doesn't hesitate to snuggle between us and I grab hold of one of his paws for comfort. More for mine than his. Leaning forward, I kiss the top of my dad's brow.

"As you wish."

My dad dies on a Wednesday. He dies at peace, free of pain, and asleep in my arms. He dies loved, surrounded by people who thought the world of him.

I never gave too much thought to the exact day he'd leave this world. I stopped thinking so intricately about loss when Cat died. But when it happens, I know I'll look at Wednesdays a little differently for the rest of my life.

I firmly believe that wherever my dad ends up, Cat's there waiting for him. She'll greet him with her arms open wide and insist on giving him the grand tour. They're each other's keepers now.

Take care of him, Gilly.

Take care of her, Dad.

The funeral is beautiful. There are more kinds of flowers than I knew existed and I thank Nadine profusely for donating so many from her shop. Her eyes overflow with tears when she says she'd bring an entire garden to my dad's funeral if she could. Comments like that happen a lot. I learn just how many lives my dad touched. He showed up for people. Made them feel supported by his actions. I have a lot to learn from him.

I'm thanking people for coming and inviting them to stop by the reception at the house for food when I spot Ambrose watching me from afar. He leans against a large sycamore tree wearing pressed dress pants and a dress shirt with the sleeves rolled up to his elbows. Dad would've loved that. He hated fuss.

I embrace Laura and Tally, letting them know that I'll meet them back at the house, and walk over to him. Despite the way we left things the last time we saw each other, Ambrose grabs me and envelops me in his arms. I breathe him in, holding on tight like my life depends on it. I think it does.

"I'm sorry for your loss," he whispers into my hair.

I search his eyes. "I'm sorry for your loss too."

Even if I wasn't there to witness their relationship over the years, I know my dad's passing weighs heavy on him.

We hold each other's gaze for what feels like hours before I force myself to speak. "There are things... I need to work through, Ambrose. And I can't give myself to you until I take the time to work through them."

He's quiet for a minute before nodding. "I'm a patient man."

Blood rushes through my ears and I drop my forehead to his chest. "Why?"

"Because I love you, Mara." My eyes fly to his and his smile is sad and hopeful all at once. "Don't look so surprised."

"Still?"

"Always." He pushes the hair from my face. "I've loved you since the day you knocked on my front door with that godforsaken cat in your arms." I choke out a warbled laugh and his voice becomes rough with emotion. "I've loved you since that kiss outside of Old Maple and I've loved you since we both lost the person we loved the most. I loved you then and I love you now. And if you'll have me... I'll love you until my last breath." My tears fall freely now. "You're the love of my life, Mara, but you're my best friend too. I like you as much as I love you. I could have a million lifetimes with you and it still wouldn't be enough. So, take your time."

"I—"

"Don't say it."

My face falls. "What? Why not?"

"Because when you say those three words," he says, dragging his thumb across my bottom lip, "I want to see our future in your eyes. Not our past."

I nod even though it feels like my heart is breaking.

"I'm going to come back," I whisper. "I swear, Ambrose. I don't know how long it will take but I will come back to you."

His lips brush across mine and it's as soft as the cold breeze around us. "I know you will," he says. "And then we'll get our happy ending."

A single tear glides down my chin. "It's that simple?"

"It can be."

He plants one last kiss on my knuckles and turns on his heels, leaving me alone beside the sycamore.

As cars find their way out of the parking lot, I walk back to my dad. The cemetery workers use an intricate pulley system to lower him into the cutout piece of earth and the flowers people placed on top of his casket follow him into the ground. I make a silent wish that they'll grow around him and keep him safe.

I dig through my purse and pull out my phone before I change my mind.

It rings twice before the voice on the other end picks up and I sigh in relief.

"Mom? It's Mara. I'm sorry to call so late but... I need you."

I didn't realize how much I'd missed Paris. The moment I let go of all the resentment I hold toward my mom, I let go of all the resentment I hold toward the places and things connected to her.

When she picks me up at the airport, I don't fight her embrace. I want to grill her on why she didn't come to the funeral, but I don't. The shield around her emotions is ironclad. And as much as I want her to crumble alongside me, I realize that sometimes you have to love people more than you want to change them. She's on her journey and I'm on mine.

She gives me my space over the following days. I walk through the cobblestone streets and pretend like everywhere I go, I take Cat with me. So far,

I've taken Cat to experience the Louvre, the Eiffel Tower, and overpriced crepes.

Maybe that's how we are supposed to honor those who are no longer with us. Maybe we're supposed to keep living *for* them. And if that's the case, I'll do it for Cat and my dad.

On the night before I leave, I'm lying in the dark, almost asleep, when there's a soft knock on my door.

"Come in."

I shift my head and see the small silhouette of my mom walking toward me.

"Can I... can I sleep with you tonight?" she asks.

The darkness hides my surprise and I scoot back toward the wall, making room for her on the small twin-sized bed.

I study her in silence as she lies flat on her back, staring aimlessly at the ceiling.

"Did I ever tell you how your *abuelita* died?"

That catches me off guard. She rarely talks about her mom. I start to shake my head, but then remember she can't see me. "I don't think so."

She rubs her hand across her chest like she's soothing something there. An ache invisible to the naked eye.

"She died of a broken heart." Her voice is barely above a whisper. "My parents were forced into an arranged marriage when my mother was only seventeen. My father was head over heels in love with her. Thought she hung the moon." That brings a smile to my face because that's something I already knew. He looked at my grandma the way... the way Ambrose looks at me.

"The problem was," she continues with a soft voice, "my mother had already given her heart away to someone else. A farm boy from the next town over."

I've always known that my grandparents had an arranged marriage, but I just assumed it was something they both consented to. It never crossed my mind that they could have loved anyone else.

She turns onto her side to face me and even in the dark, I can make out the deep lines of her frown.

"My mother was a good woman, Mara. She took care of me and my father and despite her situation, she was easygoing. Funny, even. But when she heard the news that her first love had died?" She blows out a harsh breath, shaking her head. "It altered her. Cracked something in her spirit that could never be repaired. She became... hardened. Severed all ties to her emotions. Come to think of it," she muses. "I don't think I ever saw her cry."

And there it was. Where the cycle began.

"I believed that made her strong—her refusal to verbalize the pain. And I made it my mission to be strong in that way too. I promised myself that if I needed to complain or cry or feel, *truly* feel, I would express it on a canvas, not in my personal life. I promised myself I would never let love close enough if I thought it could shatter me upon losing it."

I swallow around the lump rising in my throat.

"I succeeded in my goal of never loving anyone that deeply, Mara. Until I had you."

My eyes close against the tears.

"I know I've run away from you because of it, *mi cielo*." Her voice shakes. "And at this point, I'm not sure I can be any other way. All I know how to do is be afraid." Then she adds, almost inaudibly, "But I want to try."

The truth behind her words—the new sense of understanding it gives me—is a lot to take in. It doesn't fix everything between us. Not even close.

But it's a start.

I grab her trembling hands and pull her in closer.

A sharp, broken sound escapes her and just like that... she's gasping.

Wrapping my arm around her, I tuck her head under my chin the way my dad would have. Because it's at this moment that I realize I want to be *exactly* like him.

"I'm here." I tremble. "I'm with you."

We fall asleep in each other's arms.

The next morning, I let my mom sleep in and JP drives me to the airport.

"You look different. Lighter," he says. "I've never seen you look at Paris through such eyes." His warm smile glows in the morning light. I'm lucky to know someone like him and I'm glad he's able to love my mom in a way I'm not able to just yet.

He folds me into his arms and I squeeze him tightly before grabbing my duffel bag from the trunk. "I have a feeling I need to take another look at a lot of things."

NOW

T he first thing I do when I get back to New York is start therapy.

It's easy to fall back into my old routine, but I'm determined to keep my promise to Ambrose and take the time to work on myself.

When I have my first session with Mitsu, she tells me she does things a little differently and I don't know what that means but I know I need different.

She's kind and patient and she gets me to talk about Cat in a way that feels like I'm celebrating her and mourning her at the same time. I really like that. I like that I don't have to choose between the two. Because I'll always mourn Cat.

"Healing isn't linear, Mara," Mitsu says. "Some days it's five steps forward and other days it's seven steps back. There's no finish line. The goal is just to keep *stepping*."

So I do just that. And there are days when thinking about Cat makes me laugh until my belly hurts and days when it makes me cry so hard I'm afraid I'll drown.

But I'm thinking about her.

On the day that marks two months since our first session, I walk into the room and Mitsu greets me with a smile.

"Sorry I'm late," I say. "Someone threw up on the 6-train and then there was a delay."

"Not a problem. I'm just glad you're here."

I settle into my favorite comfy chair, folding my hands in my lap. "So what's on the schedule for today? I liked those negative thinking trap worksheets you gave me last week—do you have more?" When a smile blooms across her face, I frown. "What?"

"Nothing," she says. "You've just been making a lot of progress, Mara. It's nice to see."

"Don't get all sappy on me, M." I point. "You promised you'd stop making me cry so much. I can't keep leaving here with raccoon eyes."

She waves me off. "Here, I have something for you." Reaching behind her chair, she grabs a box with a green bow.

"Are you supposed to give clients presents?" I grin, setting my bag down. "Doesn't that cross some sort of line?"

She rolls her eyes and I laugh. I like that she doesn't treat me like porcelain about to break. "It's not a present. It's *homework*."

"Ah, right, right," I tease. Opening the box, I take a look inside and my brows scrunch in confusion. I hold up the broken pieces of a ceramic bowl, careful not to drop them. "Thank you?"

She chuckles, taking a sip of her coffee. "It's called kintsugi."

I repeat the word back to her and she nods.

"It's the art of putting broken pottery pieces back together with gold," she says. "The idea behind it is that even when something's broken, we can always put it back together. And when we put it back together and embrace those cracks of imperfection, it's even stronger and more beautiful than before."

The corner of my lip twitches. "Deep. I like it."

"I thought you might."

Searching inside the rest of the box, I come up short. "Does this thing come with a manual?"

"I'm confident you'll make do without."

My chest shakes with a laugh as I slip everything into my bag and zip it closed.

"Have you thought about when you might go back?" she asks.

"I didn't realize that was an option."

Her head tilts in a way I've become accustomed to. "What do you mean?"

Leaning back in my chair, I release a heavy sigh. "I don't know. I mean, don't I have to wait until I graduate from therapy or something?"

"No." She laughs. "You don't have to graduate therapy before you permit yourself to accept love into your life. You can be with Ambrose *and* continue to work on yourself. Those two things can co-exist and do for many people."

I know that should make me ecstatic, but all I feel is fear.

Mitsu leans forward. "It's okay to be afraid. Just don't let it keep you from moving forward with your life. Because there *is* life after this, Mara. And it can be a beautiful one."

"What if I ruin it?"

Her gaze is steady. "Then you'll fix it."

I drop my head back against the chair. "I hate it when you're right."

She goes back to sipping her coffee, an easy smile poking through. "Most people do."

That night when I get home and lay the broken pieces on the floor of my tiny New York apartment, I think of everything Mitsu said. I imagine Ambrose, Cat, and I as the shards in my hands finally coming back together, held firmly in place by the gold. A material known for being malleable; open to change, but one that never tarnishes.

By the time I slide into the booth at Cross Tavern, Tally's already sipping away at her fruity cocktail.

"Hey," I say, catching my breath.

"Oh my gosh, you're actually wearing it! Turn around, let me see, let me see."

Rolling my eyes with a laugh, I shift my body so she can see the back of the embroidered t-shirt she made.

It's just a plain white tee, but there's an embroidered heart with the words *therapy is hot* in the middle.

Mitsu had quite a laugh when I showed her.

"How was the session?" she asks, passing me the bread basket.

"It was good." I take hearty a bite. "Same old, same old."

Her brows raise. "And?"

"And she thinks I'm ready to see Ambrose again. If I want."

"Do you want?"

Thanking the waiter for our water, I laugh under my breath. "Is that supposed to be a trick question?"

"Then what are you still doing here, you big dummy?"

"I *live* here, Tally. I can't just up and move."

She shocks me by tossing her head back with a laugh.

"You *hate* New York. I mean, I know you loved living here in college but that was years ago. You're always saying how desperate you are to go back to a slower life."

For the first time in our entire friendship, I hate how well she knows me.

Because if I'm truly being honest with myself, I've wanted to leave the city for a while now. And while I can appreciate everything it's given me, everything it has to offer, my heart still calls another place home.

Speck Lake.

I've battled that truth for a long time. People are always dying to leave their small towns, clutching to the idea that big dreams can only exist in big cities. But my dreams are no less important just because I want to go back to a town with a population of two thousand.

They are my people, through and through.

I want nothing more than to go back and help get the town back on its feet in whatever way I can.

Still, another excuse surfaces. "I can't just quit therapy because I'm in love," I point out. "That wouldn't serve anyone."

With an exasperated sigh, Tally snatches my phone, holds it up, and straightens her back like she's giving a presentation.

"This is a phone." She points. "Many people use this device to look up their symptoms on *WebMD*, but it can also be used for video calls. Virtual therapy, my friend. It's revolutionary."

I attempt to grab the phone back, but she deftly moves out of reach.

"What are you so afraid of?"

Shoulders slumped, I bite down harder on my straw. "It's been two months. What if things have changed for him?"

"You're making excuses. That man is absolutely *gone* for you. Like, climb-up-a-fire-escape-to-profess-his-love gone for you. It would be sickening if it weren't so romantic. You know, what?" she says, sounding fed up. "No. Let me handle this."

I almost don't realize she angled the phone toward my face to unlock it until I see her freshly manicured nails typing away with fervor.

"Tally, what are you doing?" I whisper-yell. "Don't you dare!"

Despite how fast I slide around the booth, she manages to fight me off one-handed.

By the time she passes it back to me, beads of sweat line my forehead.

I pull up the text thread I have with Ambrose and search for any new messages laced with sexual innuendos.

"I didn't text him, calm down."

"Then what *did* you do?" I grit.

A notification banner pops up on my home screen then, alerting me of a new email.

Hesitantly, I swipe to open it. I blink three times to make sure I'm seeing it correctly.

It's a digital receipt for a flight to Bangor, Maine.

Something that feels close to hope works its way through my chest and a sigh of relief escapes me. "Oh," I whisper.

I glance up at Tally with watery eyes, only to find that hers have a similar sheen to them.

"And it's one-way." Her voice shakes.

Closing the gap between us, I fall into her side. We hug each other so tight, it's hard to breathe.

Many people go through life without having a friendship as life-changing and sacred as the one I had with Cat. But even fewer people get to experience a friendship like that *twice*. To say I'm one of the lucky ones is a severe understatement.

My arms squeeze around my best friend even tighter.

"I'll make sure to come and visit soon," she says. "But it's time for you to go home."

THEN

AGE THIRTEEN

"This doesn't feel like a good idea. Or at least, a sanitary one."

Cat and I sit cross-legged on the floor of her bathroom, a razor blade in the middle of us. She snuck into her dad's closet and stole one from an old-school barber kit he was gifted at his bachelor party years ago. It's dull and kind of weird looking. She keeps reaching for my hand, but nerves make me pull it away.

"It's sanitary, I just put it under hot water. Don't be such a baby."

I scoff. "If I'm the baby, why don't *you* go first?"

"Because if I go first, I won't be able to do yours and we both know you won't do it."

She has a point. Blood makes me queasy.

We just finished watching *Practical Magic* and Cat can't get over the scene where Sally and Gillian cut their hands to make a blood oath. It's an act that binds two people together forever. A promise of sorts.

So here we are on Cat's floor, palms exposed like we're about to play a game of hot hands. Except we'll be slicing each other's hands instead of slapping them. I think I prefer the latter.

"All I'm saying is, is this really necessary?"

Cat blows out a dramatic sigh and leans her head against the toilet. "We're thirteen, Mar. We just started high school and whether we like it or not, things are gonna change."

Unease fills my stomach. Cat's rarely ever worried about the future.

"I just want us to promise to always be there for each other. A promise so big, it goes beyond words."

I understand where her head's at, I do. Even the discussions we've already had about our hopes for high school are different from each others. Cat's thinking of trying out for the cheerleading squad and I'm planning on joining the film club. We're becoming two people who have more differences than similarities, but that doesn't mean we want our bond to be severed.

"Two sides of the same coin," I whisper.

Cat sits up. "Hmm?"

"We're like two sides of the same coin. Different... but the same. High school *will* change things. But you're always gonna be my best friend, Cat. You're always gonna be my sister."

I push the sleeve of my shirt up even higher and thrust my palm forward. "Do your damage."

Cat's grin transforms the atmosphere around us and suddenly, I'm excited about what we are about to do. She brings my hand close to her face, her jaw set with laser focus.

Five minutes later and we're clasping each other's hands, a steady stream of blood leaking onto the floor.

"Um... we should get some Band-Aids and clean all this up." I start to get up but Cat yanks me back down. "Wait!" Her expression is serious. "Promise me something."

"What?"

"Promise me..." She scrunches her nose in thought. "Promise me that no matter what, it'll always be the two of us."

I grin, squeezing our clasped hands. "The two of us. I promise."

When we finish cleaning the bathroom and wrap our hands in first aid gauze, we return downstairs to finish the movie. We ignore Ambrose's suspicious glances as we each hide a hand behind our backs.

"What are you doing?" I say as Cat pushes the rewind button on the remote.

"I want to watch it again."

I grab the bowl of popcorn and we throw our heads down, sharing the large pillow between us.

Sally: *I feel like I'm never gonna see you again.*

Gilly: *Of course, you're gonna see me again, we're gonna grow old together! It's gonna be you and me. Living in a big house, these two old biddies with all*

these cats. I mean, I bet we even die on the same day!

Sally: *You swear?*

Gilly: *Here. My blood. Your blood. Our blood.*

Sally: *I love you, Gilly-bean.*

Gilly: *Yeah. I love you too.*

NOW

As I wait for the door in front of me to open, a breeze dances through the trees, lifting the hair off my shoulders.

"Hey Cat," I whisper to the sky. "Stay close to me for this one."

As if she's whispering in response, the wind picks up and swirls the leaves at my feet into tiny wind eddies.

The door opens and Alima stands before me, a baking apron tied securely around her waist and a speck of flour on her cheek. She looks older, but the same as I remembered. Her warm-brown eyes are still warm even though they hold a shade of somberness, a permanent addition, I'm sure. For all of us. Neither of us speaks for a handful of seconds. Seconds always feel fast until you need them to be and right now, seconds feel like the slowest unit of time in existence.

Alima pulls the door open wider, motioning for me to come in. My heart beats so fast, I can hear it thrumming in my ear and I become afraid of not being able to hear anything she'll say.

She leads me to a small living room area and gestures toward the matching love seats. When I sit down, I begin fiddling with my keys, trying to remember the first part of the speech I've prepared. It's Alima who saves me from my loss of words.

"I've waited for this day for seven years," she says, sitting down next to me.

Her voice is neutral and I'm unable to gauge the level of anger I know she feels toward me. I'm uncomfortable with how close she's sitting next to me.

Would she slap me? Oh no, would Alima *slap* me?

I would if I were her. I try to put a little distance between us and start scooting away when she reaches forward and takes hold of me.

Alima's hug is the saddest expression of affection I've ever experienced. Neither one of us moves as our sobs of brokenness fill the air. The notes of our pain sing out together into the space around us and it's a devastating melody.

"I'm so sorry," I cry into her sweater. I'm soaking it, but she doesn't seem to mind.

Alima pulls back to look me in the eyes. "No, Mara. If anyone should be apologizing, it's me. I let my emotions take me someplace ugly that day. I needed someone to blame and you were a nearby casualty."

I sob harder as she strokes the curls away from my face. "When the fog cleared enough for me to realize how I must have made you feel, you were already gone. Your dad wouldn't tell me how to get ahold of you."

"I thought you blamed me," I whisper. "*I* blamed me."

Alima shakes her head, her expression solemn. "I could never blame you, Mara. I could never blame someone Cat loved so much. You were like a daughter to me. You still are."

I can't believe the words coming from Alima's mouth. My brain hurts at the idea that she doesn't hate me. It's difficult to accept that the truth of the situation is different from the story I've been telling myself in my head. But that's the thing about truth. Sometimes we mistake our emotions for the truth. Sometimes *our* truth isn't the truth at all.

Alima and I huddle close on the loveseat as she asks about my life and everything she's missed. She seems happy that Ambrose and I have crossed paths again and I want to ask her if she's become aware of any omniscient abilities lately.

She divorced Robby after Cat passed away. Said she didn't want to waste her life taking important people for granted and giving too much of herself to those who didn't deserve it. When she said she started a baking business after receiving too many horrible baked goods after Cat died, I couldn't help but laugh. Alima's baking skills always put *everyone* to shame.

I'm not surprised in the least when she explains how her new business focuses on providing quality baked goods to those who've experienced loss. It's the first time I realize there can be good things that are birthed out of such horrible situations.

"I did always love your chocolate chip cookies," I say. "I'm pretty sure they're to thank for giving me any semblance of curves in high school."

She laughs and it sounds so much like Cat, I want to make her laugh again and again.

"Come with me," she says. "I want to show you something."

She leads me into the kitchen just as the timer above the oven goes off. I laugh when she pulls two sheets of chocolate chip cookies out. We help ourselves to the cookies and chat some more.

"Do you mind if I ask you something?" I clasp my hands in my lap to stop them from shaking.

"Anything."

"Can you tell me what happened to her?"

Alima nods and pulls her cardigan tighter around herself, her eyes shifting to the window beside us. "They called it an intracranial hemorrhage. Said it was most likely due to the fall, which she probably couldn't feel the full impact of at first because of the alcohol."

I flinch and she locks eyes with me.

"They made it clear that she wouldn't have made it that night, whether she was alone or not. There wasn't anything you could have done, sweetheart. If you leave here today learning one thing, it needs to be that."

I press my hands into my eyes and steady my breathing. "Thank you."

I didn't realize how long I'd been here until I see the golden glow of the sun setting outside.

"I don't want to keep you." I smile. "It's getting late. I should go."

Before I finish buttoning up my coat, Alima motions for me to follow her to the back of the house. The patio opens out into a huge wheat field, the land going on as far as my eyes can see. I was confused when I drove up to the house—it's in such a remote location—but now it all makes sense. A secluded residence like this has the advantage of providing an ample amount of land.

"It's beautiful."

She hums in agreement, looking at the field with similar adoration. As if she's seeing it for the first time too. She points to a lone tree in the middle of the field, about fifty feet away. A maple tree with large branches and foliage serves as a shaded oasis. You'd think the tree felt lonely, standing there all by itself, but it looks right. Like it's there for people to take refuge under it.

"That's where Cat's ashes are," Alima whispers, tilting her head toward the tree.

I want to be buried under a huge tree. The biggest tree. So everyone can come and rest under me.

What comes out of me is a mixture of joy and sorrow. I'm crying, but I can't stop the laughs escaping from my throat. "It's her tree."

Alima grins. "She made sure I knew how she wanted to be buried too. I think she told everyone."

My laugh deepens. "That sounds like her."

"Go," Alima says, placing a palm on my back, and giving me a gentle push. "Rest under her for a little while."

As I stand under the maple tree, the sunset becomes an explosion of gold around me. I sink to my knees and graze my fingers over the flat headstone.

Catherine Marie King

Jan. 13, 1995 - May 13, 2013

Our beloved daughter, sister, and best friend

May we always look forward to tomorrow like you.

I trace the indentation of the words *best friend* repeatedly. It's a small gift, one I'm not even sure Alima realizes she gave me.

"I'm sorry it took me so long to get here, Gilly," I whisper.

When I stopped by the store before driving to Alima's house, I didn't think I'd be able to have this moment in front of Cat. I stand up and pull the Snickers bar from my jacket pocket. I peel back the wrapper and take a huge bite, choking out a laugh.

"A Snickers bar in your honor. Are you happy?" I laugh harder when I remember the other part of the request Cat made when we were thirteen. I don't allow myself to ruminate on the fact that Alima could be watching as I start swaying my hips with abandon. I move my arms to the invisible beat, dancing to the song playing in my head.

"Well, I heard about the fellow you've been dancin' with all over the neighborhood..." I start.

I only get to the third line before I bend over at the waist, clutching my side from the laughter.

"Okay, yeah, no," I gasp between laughs. "We're not doing that."

I can picture it. Cat smiling down or up or around at me from wherever she is.

"I love you, Gilly." I wipe my eyes. "I'll come back again real soon."

It's a promise I don't intend on breaking. I turn to head back to the house when a myriad of colorful fractals dance over my body. I glance above me and gasp. Hanging from a low branch is the suncatcher I got for Cat when I was in Paris. It sways in the wind, painting the ground in Technicolor, and my heart soars. It's the best place my gift could have ended up. I grin and tap the cat-shaped suncatcher with my finger, watching it sway in the light.

"Bye, Kitty Cat."

"Are you sure this is going to work?"

"Of course it is. You think I'd steer you wrong?"

I make a face at Anya. "I mean..."

She snorts, her mouth curling into a smile. "Fair enough."

It's the first time I'm seeing her since that day we held up our white flags on Laura's dock. I know she'd be the first one to say that her work with her addiction isn't over yet, but I'm still proud of her. There's a calmness that rests on her features now and it suits her. She hands me the copied key to Ambrose's house and I slip it into my back pocket.

Matty calls out to Anya and she glances over her shoulder from where she stays in the doorway. "What is it, buddy?"

"Who is *Dean*?"

My eyes widen and Anya's shoulders go rigid. "Matty, I'm gonna need my phone back."

"Anya—"

"Good luck," she says, closing the door while I protest to tell me what that was all about. "You're gonna do great!"

The door slams in my face and I stand there for a second in utter shock. When my feet finally remember how to work, I return to the car.

One thing at a time, Mara. One thing at a time.

Twenty minutes later, I'm anxiously pacing around Ambrose's den, waiting for him to get home.

When Anya suggested I surprise him, it sounded like a good idea at the time. But now that I'm here, my nerves are getting the best of me.

I should have called first.

The front door's handle jiggles and I stop walking, immediately smoothing out the creases in my sweater.

Ambrose is typing something on his phone when he walks into the den, so he doesn't see me at first. I clear my throat and he jumps back, startled.

"Oh, fuck! *Fuck*. Mara, you scared the shit out of me."

I grimace because that wasn't part of the plan. "Sorry."

His breathing evens as he slowly makes his way toward me. Those green eyes that I love so much scan my face, then the rest of my body. His tone is rougher when he says, "What are you doing here?"

I start pacing again, trying to garner courage from the carpet to my feet like static electricity.

If he keeps looking at me like that, I won't be able to do this and I *need* to do this.

"I have some things I need to say to you." I point at his chest. "So, you just... you stand right there and don't talk."

Ambrose's eyebrows lift in surprise, but the corner of his mouth twitches. "Okay."

I face him head-on.

"I'm not perfectly healed," I say and damn does it feel good to finally be able to admit that. "I'm not sure that I ever will be. What happened to me, what happened to *us*, was life-changing. We're changed forever, whether we like it or not. But what I've learned is that... that's okay." My laugh hitches in my throat. "Because the changed version of me still loves the changed version of you. I'm *in* love with you, Ambrose." I take a step closer, my voice shaking. "I've loved you since the moment I knocked on your door with that godforsaken cat in my arms." My eyes water as I repeat his words. "I loved you then and I love you now."

Ambrose's eyes are glassy, but he doesn't speak and I begin to sweat. His eyes drop to the vase on the coffee table. "What's that?"

I grab the vase and lift it a little. "It's kintsugi," I say. "It's the imperfect parts broken...." I squint my eyes, trying to remember the eloquent words Mitsu used but my nerves cause me to fumble. "The broken parts are our imperfect pieces, coming together." Then I add with a small laugh, "I think."

Ambrose smiles and it's all I need to see before my feet start moving toward him.

"Even amid the imperfection, it's still beautiful."

He's within reach now, his eyes darting over my face.

"We're still beautiful, Ambrose," I whisper, taking one step closer.

"Hold on," he says, his voice rough from unshed tears. "If you take another step...that's it. You're stuck with me. So you better be sure because I can't let you go again. I won't."

"You promise?"

"I swear."

A sound of relief escapes me as I fly forward and our mouths collide.

His hands are on my face, in my hair, on every inch of my body.

Ambrose and I cling together and it feels both like drowning and coming up for air.

There's nothing like it, being in the arms of the one you're meant for. It's like a gentle caress from the universe. A pause in the fabric of time and space as two people who are and will always be, throw their hands up and stop fighting the inevitable. Because that's what Ambrose and I are.

We're inevitable.

We have the kind of love people write about.

My hands find their way under his shirt and he pulls away abruptly, smiling down at me. "Will you come somewhere with me?"

I fold his hand into mine.

"Anywhere."

"It's only been open for a month but it's already a hit."

Ambrose flips a switch and the once-dark theater is thrown into a sea of blue.

I gaze upward at the dome-shaped projection above us and my hand flies to my mouth.

It's *stunning*.

Every living creature of the ocean is projected onto the ceiling, swimming and exploring, and living. The quality is so crisp and clear, it's hard to believe we're not underwater.

Ambrose comes to my side before looking up with a grin.

"They usually reserve these types of theaters for planetariums, but I was able to do something similar for the zoo. Thought it would be nice to offer people a more interactive experience." He bumps his hip into mine. "Like it?"

"Like it?" I whisper. "Ambrose, it's incredible."

He smiles like a cute little nerd who's just won the science fair.

"That's not what I wanted to show you though. Come over here."

"There's more?" I laugh, following him. He leads me off to the side of the theater where framed photos line the wall. There are close-up shots of famous *National Geographic* photos, but there are also not-so-good kids' drawings of what I think are supposed to be zoo animals.

Ambrose stops in front of a tall metal drop box about four feet tall and pulls a set of keys from his pocket.

I step closer to get a better look.

He unlocks the little latch and opens it, motioning for me to come closer and take a look.

That's when I see the little mound of folded notes inside.

Gathering a few in his hand, he holds them out to me. "Read them," he says, chuckling at my confused face.

I unfold the first note, a pink little square with bubbly handwriting.

My wish is that my mom and dad to get back together.

Frowning, I reach for another, a note neatly folded in on itself.

Liliana Martinez kissed me yesterday and I wish it could happen again.

A laugh escapes me and I turn to Ambrose. "What is all this?"

I watch his eyes trail back to the ceiling, back to the ocean above us.

"Did you know that the ocean has an area of about 139.5 million square miles?" he whispers. There's awe in his voice. Reverence.

"It's this vast place that holds so many things we're only just beginning to learn about. People are always saying that if you have something that needs to be released, take it to the ocean. It'll tuck them away for safekeeping."

His gaze flickers down to me.

"I wanted to make a place where wishes could live forever. A place where they could be tucked away for safekeeping."

My throat constricts.

He reaches into his pocket again and pulls out another key—this one tiny. I watch with curiosity as he reaches for a miniature box resting in the corner of the huge container.

"Now this one." His voice softens. "This one's my favorite."

He places a yellowed scrap of paper in my hand and time slows.

I'm convinced I've stopped breathing.

"My mom found it in her things," he says. "It's from the night of the wish burning. She gave it to me last week."

I nod, unable to form the words.

With shaky hands, I slowly unfold the note.

And in the arms of the man I love the most, I read my best friend's last wish.

> A wish is something that cannot or probably will not happen. I just looked it up. Which sucks if you think about it. So if I have to make a wish, I wish for wishes to become more probable. Especially Mara's.

Tears stream down my face but I'm happy.

I think I've never been happier. Ambrose presses a kiss against my temple. "I love you."

Curling into his embrace, I smile. "I love you, too."

He tucks everything back into the box for safekeeping and laces his hand with mine, leading me out of the theater. When we reach his car, there's a look of anticipation in his eyes. I know I'm wearing the same look.

"So?" he asks. "Where do you want to go next?"

My fingers tighten around his.

"Let's go home."

EPILOGUE

FIVE YEARS LATER

The clouds dance overhead—clear and vibrant strokes against the unmarred pallet of the sky. We lie under Cat's maple tree on a handful of beach towels because Ambrose forgot to put the picnic blanket in the laundry after Sol spilled fruit punch on it. Again.

I glance over at the little boy to my left. *Our* little boy. He's turning four in a few weeks, but some days it feels like he's turning forty. He has an old soul.

"Do you think clouds get lonely?" he asks, pointing to a big clump of white drifting away from the others. Ambrose looks at me and smiles. Sol has a habit of personifying inanimate things. He can't fathom the idea that not everything has feelings. He's intuitive. Gentle and kind. Like his grandfather, whose name he bears.

"I don't think so," Ambrose says, scratching his head. "But even if they do, all clouds come back together eventually, so it won't be lonely for too long."

Sol nuzzles into Ambrose's side, satisfied with his answer. Ambrose always knows how to answer his questions in a way that encourages his curiosity rather than stifles it. I wink at Ambrose, letting him know he did well.

"Cat! Cat!" The little girl in my arms wriggles out of my grasp, jumping and pointing at the sky.

I tilt my head, looking for the animal she sees. As if he understands the word and its meaning, Otso stirs from his slumber, the warning growl from his mouth making Sol giggle.

Otso's getting old, but he still has a lot of spunk left in him. Enough to keep the kids entertained. We let him join us outside since Cheddar lays claim to the guest room. Every day that cat is still alive shocks us all.

I squint up at the sky. "You see a cat? Where, baby?"

She jumps faster, impatience filling her body. "Der! Der!"

We all laugh.

She's only two, but she can't for the life of her figure out how to correctly say the word *there*.

"I think I see it," Ambrose says.

I snort, assuming he's just trying to appease her, but then he points to his left. And right there, clear as day, is a cloud in the shape of a cat's head—pointy ears and all.

"Do you think it's Aunty Cat?" Sol asks. We told him recently about who Cat is and how she's no longer with us, but that she would've loved being his aunt. Ever since then, he'll ask if different things are Cat. The breeze through the trees. The butterfly on the windshield. The cloud in the sky. His imagination reminds me of her and it makes me love him even more for it.

"It could be," I say.

Alima waves her arms from the sliding door to let us know that the cookies are ready. Sol doesn't waste time running toward the house and Ambrose follows close on his heels, challenging him to a race.

We make it a point to visit Alima's house as often as we can. Family takes precedence over everything for Ambrose and me. And when he asked me what I wanted as a wedding present the year after my dad died, I said, "To go back home for good."

So, we packed up the tiny New York apartment we shared and moved back to Speck Lake, making 164 Winsome Lane the place we started our new chapter.

I was able to take the new position at my job fully remote, focusing on designing websites for authors and filmmakers, and Ambrose was happy being able to run operations for the zoo in person again.

And when a little girl knocked on our door saying she'd just moved into the house across the street, the one that looked like a lemon drop, I stood to the side, watching history repeat itself as Sol accepted her invitation to play in a familiar tree house. Winsome Lane has witnessed a lot of things fall apart, but it's witnessed a lot of things come together too.

"Mom, hurry! Matty, Laura, and Anya just got here!" Sol calls, poking his head out the sliding door. I grin to myself, knowing how excited he is. He's Matty's little shadow.

I bend down to pick up my daughter with curls the same color as the wheat field before me. The same color as her aunt's.

"You ready for some cookies?" I ask, tickling her sides.

Her giggles ring out into the sky and the birds chirp as if they're singing back to her.

"Cookies! Cookies!" she chants. "I love you, Mommy."

She's generous with her *I love yous* when food is involved, and I can't help but laugh.

"I love you too, Gilly."

THE END.

Thank you for reading!
If you enjoyed *The Two of Us*, I'd be so grateful if you left a review on your preferred platforms. Your time and feedback are invaluable gifts.

ACKNOWLEDGMENTS

Writing a book feels very reminiscent of Meredith Grey standing in front of Derek Shepherd saying *pick me, choose me, love me*. This being my debut novel, I never in a million years thought I would get to this page—the page where I get to thank people. I am incredibly thankful.

To my editor, Ellie. Thank you for taking a first-time author's words and making them shine.

Thank you to Victoria, Ben, and Anastasia. You are three of the most creative and inspiring people I know. When I stared at the words of my manuscript into the wee hours of the night, wanting to tear my hair out and run away with the circus, it was your energy and discipline I channeled.

Thank you to my ARC readers and all the support you have given me. You all are amazing!

Thank you to the bookstagram community who has championed me and this book from the beginning. I am constantly amazed by how you all show up for authors. A special thanks to Candice, Monica, Mary, and Mariana. You, ladies, have been the best cheerleaders anyone could have.

And lastly, thank you to the reader! Thank you for taking the time to read this story. I know there are so many things you could be doing with your free time, so this means the world.

To my sweet daughter. You are still too young to read these words, but you inspire me to channel my brave. I know you won't be little forever, but I hope you'll always let me cuddle with you and tell you stories.

And to my husband, Luke. I love you endlessly. Thank you for believing in me and this book when my confidence faltered. Thank you for stepping up with our little girl every time I needed time to write and doing it with the biggest smile on your face. Even when she would puke on you. You are the best partner, the best teammate—the best everything. I may have an obscene number of book boyfriends, but you're the only husband for me.

ABOUT THE AUTHOR

Taylor Torres is a twenty-something-year-old living in New York City with her incredible husband and vivacious daughter. When she's not hiding behind a book, she's daydreaming about sweeping romances and heartrending one-liners. That's usually when the writing comes in. She loves seeking inspiration from the people around her and the stories they live to tell.

Subscribe to her newsletter at:
www.authortaylortorres.com/newsletter.

Made in the USA
Middletown, DE
18 October 2024

62883226R00209